John Tr[...] bestselling first nov[...] bsequently made into a successful TV film under the title *Codename Kyril*. Since then he has had a string of acclaimed novels, including *The Mahjong Spies*, *Krysalis*, *Acts of Betrayal*, *Blood Rules*, *The Tiger of Desire* and *A Means to Evil*. *Against All Reason* is his twelfth novel.

From the reviews of his previous novels:

A MEANS TO EVIL

'On the evidence of this outstanding psychological thriller, John Trenhaile's reputation as an author of real talent is well-founded. What starts off as a seemingly straight-forward murder story develops with increasing and chilling fascination into one of the best novels I have read this year. It reaches a surprising climax, one of stunning intensity that jolts like an electric shock. A wonderful read.'

New York Daily News

THE TIGER OF DESIRE

'A powerful novel . . . takes the reader through every twist and turn, yet manages to conceal the shattering truth right to the very end.'

Sunday Mail

ACTS OF BETRAYAL

'Shocking . . . the suspense, woven by a British writer hailed as the heir apparent to le Carré, is killing.'

Today

A VIEW FROM THE SQUARE

'Trenhaile's excellent novel leads the reader on a tortured path of bluff and double bluff, suspense and its release. You couldn't ask for more.'

Sunday Times

THE MAN CALLED KYRIL

'A wonderfully tough and fascinating story that kept me guessing to the very end.'

New York Newsday

WORKS BY JOHN TRENHAILE

The Man Called Kyril
A View From the Square
Nocturne for the General
The Mahjong Spies
The Gates of Exquisite View
The Scroll of Benevolence
Krysalis
Acts of Betrayal
Blood Rules
The Tiger of Desire
A Means to Evil
Against All Reason

JOHN TRENHAILE

AGAINST ALL REASON

HarperCollins*Publishers*

HarperCollins*Publishers*
77–85 Fulham Palace Road,
Hammersmith, London W6 8JB

This paperback edition 1996
1 3 5 7 9 8 6 4 2

First published in Great Britain by
HarperCollins*Publishers* 1994

ISBN 0 00 649686 5

Set in Meridien

Printed and bound in Great Britain by
Caledonian International Book Manufacturing Ltd, Glasgow

For Gerry Lactam.

Who taught me how to laugh, along with Richo
With love
'Tom'

SOCRATES: *Tell me this, however: is excessive pleasure compatible with moderation?*

GLAUCON: *How can it be, since it drives one mad just as much as pain does?*

SOCRATES: *Can you think of a greater or keener pleasure than sexual pleasure?*

GLAUCON: *I can't – or a madder one either.*

Plato's Republic
Trans. GMA Griere
Revised by DCD Reeve

PART ONE

DR/THELMA VESTREY turned into Main Street with one purpose in mind, and that was killing.

Like any pro, she'd taken care not to stand out from the crowd. Pushing thirty, clad in jeans and a sweatshirt, tote bag slung casually over one shoulder. Just another young woman eyeballing the shop-windows of a small town in southern California, with an occasional glance at an attractive male face or curvaceous butt.

She paused for a second and looked into a window, casing the street through the corner of one eye.

She began to walk down Main.

There weren't many people about. A couple of teens, one leaning against his motorbike. Few singles of both sexes.

Married couple, elderly . . . it wouldn't be them.

Mother with baby-cart. *Watch that cart!*

This was a pedestrian-only mall. No cars to give her cover. Or to cover anyone else . . .

As she came level with Marty's Bar its door opened and four men came rushing out. Thelma swivelled smoothly towards them . . . but they ran past.

Not this time.

Where are you, my friend? Come play with me . . .

She stopped outside James's Gems. Lovely shop, lovely name. There was a necklace in the window, on a cushion: diamonds, emeralds . . . Thelma's mouth watered.

Don't hesitate, never drop your guard, walk on.

Another thirty feet, and she had him.

Cool dude, black jeans, white shirt, mirrored shades. *Oh my boy, my sweet one, come to Mommy . . .*

He was crossing Main on the diagonal, coming towards her. He'd registered Thelma. She was a target.

11

Robbery, Rape, Rip-Off – the three 'R's. *Which?*

Come on, come on, come on. Ten feet, closing to five, three . . .

He walked by without a backward glance. Thelma's heart was beating too fast for comfort. She looked over her shoulder. The dude kept walking.

As her head started its return journey, movement.

Twenty-five feet away, nine o'clock, doorway of bank . . . while her brain computed, Thelma's right hand was already half into the waistband of her jeans.

Her body swung through one hundred eighty degrees.

The .38 police-issue was where it should be, grip warm and dry.

Out, safety catch off.

Point . . .

People were scattering in all directions. Everyone hit the deck, no exceptions, no heroes on Main this day.

. . . and . . .

Thelma launched herself to one side in a flying dive.

Shoot!

One slug, two, three, *roll*!

She came to a halt against the plate-glass wall of a supermarket just as it cracked into a thousand crystals that showered down around her. Thelma clenched her hands over her head for protection. Hostile return fire. *She'd missed, shit!*

Roll, roll, roll . . .

She was up again, she was running, the target hadn't moved.

Doorway. In. Back against the wall, slither out, left hand over right wrist, breathe in, out, *one shot*, into the doorway again, out other side, low this time, left hand over right wrist, breathe in, out, *two shot* . . .

The blood was coursing through her ears so fast she scarcely heard the three long blasts of a whistle, followed by one short.

People were getting up, dusting themselves down. Thelma found herself leaning against the nearest wall, panting. The baby-buggy, released by its mother when the shooting started, had rolled to a stop beside her. She looked down. The baby sported a Hitler moustache. A doll.

'Thelma.'

Jack Madden was walking down the street towards her, clip-board in hand, ear-muffs slung around his neck. He beckoned. Thelma heaved herself off the wall. Her adrenalin was boiling off now, evaporating along with her courage.

Jack came to a halt next to the cardboard cut-out that had materialized in the doorway of the Wells Fargo Bank. Human-sized and roughly human-shaped, it didn't have a face, just black and yellow zones, and it was to one of these that Jack now accusingly pointed.

'Thelma,' he said, 'I've told you before. I've *told* you. Aim for the vital organs.'

His finger was resting on the cut-out's crotch, where three messy holes had been drilled in a yellow section, two over-lapping.

'Thelma, did you hear what I told you? Did you *listen*?'

Thelma treated him to a Vestrey Special: one of those zany smiles that, when fired off by a honey-blonde, no man can resist.

'Jack,' she breathed, 'I'm a psychologist. I heard what you said. But I knew what you wanted *really*.'

Jack Madden was the Paradise Bay police department's chief armourer and senior weapons-training officer. Twenty years of teaching men and women how to shoot straight hadn't altogether deprived him of nice-guy qualities. His lips twitched. Then he was laughing. Everyone was laughing.

'Thelma,' he said, once he'd recovered. 'If I sign you off, will you swear to take your ass out of my range and never bring it back?'

'Deal.'

'Then welcome to the real world of the Paradise Bay Special Force Unit. As of now, you're licensed to bear arms on, and be assigned to, hostile-environment activities by night or day.'

'*Whoopeee!*'

*   *   *

An hour later, Thelma blew into her house like a tornado taking the mid-western states by storm: 'Who's in the shower? . . . Kirsty, did you borrow that red shirt of mine, you plate of Puppy Chow? . . . Mom, can dinner be ready two minutes ago?'

Her mother was waiting at the top of the stairs. 'There were three calls for you,' she said. 'Thelma . . . Thelma, *did you hear me*?'

'Three calls, yeah, whoopee!' came from the bathroom. Then the door opened, and a blue shirt, grey skirt, bra and panties floated through to land on the floor by Rachel Vestrey's feet. Rachel sighed and bent to pick them up. At twenty-eight, she reminded herself, you'd already borne two kids, were holding down a full-time job and running a house, and if you dropped clothes on the floor they eventually became part of the rug.

'Did you have a good day?' she hollered.

'Great!' The shower obscured the message somewhat, but Rachel caught the tone. 'Who called, who wants me, who's going to kill himself if I don't deliver?'

'Well. Your father, I guess.'

The shower stopped. 'How is he?' echoed a voice so small that Rachel had trouble associating it with what had gone before.

'Oh, he's fine. Not that he'd tell *me* anything.'

In the bathroom, Thelma turned on the shower again.

'Don't you want to hear about your other calls?'

'Later,' came a muffled voice.

Thelma normally sang as she soaped away the cares of the day, but suddenly she didn't feel like singing. Roy Vestrey, a film editor employed by one of the majors and professional big-time shit, had left home three years before to live with a continuity girl in Westwood. He'd also left Thelma's sis Kirsty, grieving; Roy Junior, a grown-up but bitter son; a gutted wife; and a screaming-mad, rattlesnake-angry, spitting and mauling ball of fire called Thelma. Three years can, under certain circumstances, seem like no time at all. Thelma loved Roy. Loved him almost as much as she hated the very sound of his name.

By the time she'd cleaned herself up, however, Thelma was more or less back to her sunny self. As she rolled on roll-on before the mirror she counted her assets, found there were two as per normal, and grinned at her reflection. She was attractive, in a streamlined way, though her gamine face could never be

14

described as beautiful, and much she cared! She applied moisturiser, saving a dab for each compact breast, and turned first left then right in an effort to suss out her profile.

'You,' she announced, 'are one fit young lady . . . as the avuncular doctor murmured, sliding his hand around her . . . ummmmmm . . . shapely shoulders. Whee!'

She danced along the corridor, butt-naked, into her kid sister's room. Kirsty was dividing her time between biology homework and the latest Cure album, but not dividing in the classical sense of half-and-half.

'Hey!' she said, as Thelma snatched up a red-and-white striped cotton shirt, 'I was wearing that!'

'Was, will, but not am, sweetheart. Jeez, I wish someone would teach that Robert Smith to sing!'

'Bitch.'

'Slut. And if I find my Opium's dipped below the pencil mark I'll drown you in what's left.'

Ten minutes later she was sliding down the banister, swinging her suede draw-loop bag around in a circle, like a propeller. You could always tell how happy Thelma was by the rpm's of her bag. This evening she was somewhere around a seven.

'Mom,' she said, rocketing into the kitchen, 'gimme food, gimme water. Gimme a big fat slobbery kiss.' She pecked Rachel on the cheek. 'Mm, looks yummy.'

'Take your finger out of my potato salad.'

But Thelma was already helping herself to a pile of it. 'Who else called?' she asked, though the words didn't come quite as clearly as that.

'Andrew Mitchel, to know if you were free to go sailing tomorrow, and that guy from CSR Aviation again.'

Thelma dropped her spoon. 'The helicopter guy?'

'Yes, wanting to know what you thought of the trial lesson and should he book your name in.'

'No money,' she wailed. 'No cash. Mom. Mom-my dear-est . . . '

'No way am I paying for you to fly helicopters.'

'But Mom . . . '

'Thelma, for goodness' sake! You're nearly thirty, you have a regular job; why in hell should I pay out to have you risk your life? Go risk it on your own income.'

Thelma pouted. Dad was so mean, he'd scrimped and saved as a substitute for living, so that when he'd walked out on his family the pot the court had ordered him to hand over to Rachel had been humungous. And now, despite that, Rachel was just as bad: saving for old age when she was only fifty-one. Thelma licked her spoon. Made a helluva potato salad, though.

'I'm nearly twenty-nine,' she said. 'Call me thirty again and I'll sue. Besides, guess what happened today?'

'Who needs to guess, when your face looks like Las Vegas on a holiday weekend? Those stupid guys up at police academy graduated you to Special Force.'

'Yup. And they're not stupid.'

'They don't have to do the body-count. Thelly . . . '

'Aaarrghhhh!'

'Thelma, you're a clinician.'

'Who does a lot of police work. Who is retained by the Paradise Bay police department to go on the streets and counsel, advise – '

'Oh, spare me!'

' – officers who risk their lives. Hostage-takes. Hold-ups. Mother, as of today I'm a *player*!'

Rachel sighed. 'If you say so.' She poured two glasses of iced tea. 'You going out tonight?'

'I sure as hell am.'

'With . . . ?'

'The guys.'

'Policemen, I suppose?'

'Policemen are sexy. It's the uniform.'

'Well, don't stay out late.'

'Thought I was nearly thirty.'

'Thought you were going to sue me if I said so.'

'You'll be renting out my room next.'

'I wish. Oh, how I wish.'

Which was a lie, because when Roy had walked off to join his twenty-year-old continuity girl in congenial sin Thelma had moved out of the apartment she shared with a nurse from St

Joseph's Hospital and gone home to watch over mother; and, to their mutual astonishment, this was an arrangement they loved. (And boy! was it cheap, if you were caught up in the state of California's Year Of Living Meanly.)

'Must go,' she cried.

Rachel was putting the finishing touches to a salmon pie: she slid it into the oven and switched on the TV. 'I thought you wanted dinner?' she protested.

'No *time*!'

Thelma was already out the door and halfway down the drive to where her '88 Bronco was parked.

'Thelly!' Rachel hollered from the porch. 'You take care, now!'

But her words were lost in a squeal of tyres.

*   *   *

Daniel Krozgrow turned out to be as mean a cribbage player as he was handsome.

'Thirty-one for two. Your count.'

'Fifteen two, fifteen four, and the rest don't score.' Thelma threw down her cards in disgust.

Daniel Krozgrow and Thelma Vestrey were the last guests in the dining-room of the Paradise Highway Motor Lodge, which had started life as a barn and still retained certain barn-like qualities: high, cavernous, a mite dusty. They were sitting at a window table, with cards, paper and an empty bottle of Scotch between them. The boys from the Paradise Bay police department had stopped by, as they usually did when Daniel was in town for the FBI, and Thelma had appointed herself an honorary boy for the occasion. This wasn't difficult, because she was junior consultant psychologist to the department, and she'd just made Special Force, and everybody loved her.

Becoming an honorary boy also meant she could sit next to Daniel, one of life's greater goals.

'Ah-*ha*!' Daniel smirked. 'You missed a run of three and one for his nob, so I get to score your hand.'

'Wait a minute, wait a minute – you never told me that rule.'

'Listen, it was *you* who asked *me* to teach you cribbage – '

'Honest cribbage!'

' – When me and the guys were happy to play poker all night, and why do you think they left, huh? Because *you* – '

Thelma picked up a pencil and crossed through his scores, writing I WON, I WON! at the bottom of the paper.

'Now I know why you're a *child* psychologist,' Daniel said, reading her scribble upside down. He signalled the proprietor. 'PJ, champagne for the real victor here, and charge it to Dr Vestrey's account.'

'Coming right up.'

PJ Robertson was sixty, running a little to fat, bald and cheerful: most people's idea of Mine Host. He and Daniel had become good friends over the two years since Krozgrow had adopted the Lodge on his frequent trips north of LA. The FBI would have paid for Howard Johnson or Travelodge, but there was an FBI network of Places To Stay (Classified; Password-Users Only) and PJ was on it with a star against his name.

'Don't you dare bring champagne!' Thelma flared. 'I'll have a club soda next time, and the FBI can pay for it. I'm a taxpayer, I pay enough for *them*. Anyway, I've got to get some sleep.'

PJ went off, chuckling.

'What are you doing this weekend?' Thelma asked Daniel. *Why don't you invite me to the beach?*

'Thought I'd go up to Pittsburgh. There's a drag-race derby. Might take Mikey.'

'How is he?'

'Little brother is fine.' Daniel drained a glass that was already empty. 'For someone living in a squat, panhandling, shooting up, he's fine. How about you?'

'Mm? Oh, the weekend . . . work.'

'Bad for the heart.'

'As if you cared. Walk me to the car,' Thelma said, standing up. 'If you please. Kind sir.'

It was a cool night; she was glad of the fresh air after so long spent in the smoke-laden company of 'the guys'. She'd drunk too much, of course, in celebration of her sign-off to carry a gun. A

18

clinical psychologist pushing thirty should know better, she thought as they approached her Bronco, the last vehicle left in the lot. *You have a stack of work this high, your skin and eyes need sleep, you'll have a hangover in the morning, and for what?*

For him. This man beside her; yes, you, buster: the guy who doesn't know I'm born. What is wrong with you, Daniel? There's someone else, that I know: a woman you never mention, making you sad.

Okay, okay, here's what'll happen. You, Daniel, will say (any minute now), 'Thelma, mind if I tell you something?' To which the answer is: *Anything!*

Or you'll smile, in that diffident, appealing way of yours, and say, 'Thelma, how long have we known each other now?' And I'll answer, *Too long to waste more time, strip!*

Or: 'Come to my room?' Answer: *Why exhaust ourselves walking inside?*

What Daniel actually said was, 'See you, then. Have a good weekend.'

To which the (unspoken) answer was: *Oh, shit!*

'You too,' she said, swinging her long legs into the Bronco. 'Get some rest.'

She arrived home to find the house in darkness and everyone in bed. She went to the kitchen for iced water. On the table was a brown envelope, legal-paper-sized, with a FedEx badge in the top left corner, addressed to Dr Thelma Vestrey. Thelma picked it up and saw from the slip that her mother had signed for it at nine thirty. She frowned. What kind of time was that to deliver packages? Marked 'Urgent' . . .

She opened the envelope. It contained several sheets of pale green notepaper, covered in bold handwriting.

'*Madame,*' Thelma read, '*tomorrow morning, we have a meeting, you and I. I am Aurelia Delacroix, Richo's mother . . .*'

'Oh, *God*.'

That, Thelma thought bitterly as she hauled her ass upstairs, was the last thing she needed before going to bed: to be reminded of the odious creep who was her least favourite patient. Ricardo Delacroix. Richo. She'd read it in the morning; too tired now.

But then at least there is this consolation (she continued, throwing her exhausted body onto the bed): the day is over now, and things can't get any worse . . .

She was wrong.

* * *

A couple of hours after Thelma had tottered home to bed that Friday evening, there were still more people crammed into every nook and cranny of Mamaluke's four bars than you'd see on Newport Beach at noon. The atmosphere, a nauseating compound of noise and heat and smoke, pulsed to the beat of Dougie and His Elasticated Howsers. The liquor licence was good until dawn and the young crowd partied with the manic enthusiasm of a species headed for extinction.

But the downstairs bar, Auntie Mary's, was different. There, silence ruled.

A man and a woman were seated opposite each other at a round table. They were hemmed in on every side by a crowd of curious people whose eyes never deviated from that table-top. Cards were scattered upon it, along with Coke bottles, a pendulum and a toy gyroscope.

The two people sitting opposite each other made a contrasting couple. The woman, in her late teens or maybe early twenties, had a thin, pale face framed by gleaming hazel hair that closely coated her skull, making her look somehow fragile. She was wearing a mauve silk shirt and blue jeans, plus a pair of rope-soled sandals.

The man was black, fully ten years older, bearded and broad of shoulder. He'd come wearing a brown suit, though now he'd taken off the jacket, which was slung over his chair-back, to reveal red suspenders over a wide-striped shirt. He was holding a knife.

This knife . . . it was the kind of thing you might buy at a hardware store to slice meat into steaks. About twelve inches long. Blade tapering from one-and-a-half inches by the hilt, down to a wicked point. Black plastic handle. Gleaming in the dim light. Sharp-looking, like its handler.

The black man spoke. 'Ready, Sam?'

The girl nodded. She stretched out her forearm so that it lay on the table, extended towards the man. He clasped both hands around the knife's handle and raised it. For a moment the blade floated against the revolving strobe-ball, stars dancing off it. Then he stabbed down with all his might, driving the knife through the girl's palm, into the table.

The crowd gasped. One or two spectators turned away, or covered their eyes. But within seconds all attention was once again focused on that table-top, where the girl's hand lay skewered to the wood.

Blood oozed up around the blade. Sam's face was hard to decipher. She seemed to be concentrating on an intellectually demanding puzzle: her eyes were shut, her brow furrowed, but she didn't cry out. There were over one hundred people in Auntie Mary's at two fifteen (that was the police estimate, anyway) and all of them were later unanimous: the blade had gone right through Sam's hand into the table, and there was a lot of blood.

The black man had released the knife the moment he'd driven it home. Now he produced a bandanna and threw it over the mess on the table. He gripped the knife handle through the cloth and pulled. For a few seconds he held the knife, now wrapped in silk, suspended so that the folds of the handkerchief still concealed Sam's hand; then he lifted the knife away.

Sam's hand lay on the table, white, unmarked, whole. Of the blood upwards of one hundred people had just seen there was no sign.

For a second there was silence. Then the room erupted in a roar. People stood on chairs to clap and cheer. Aproned waiters who'd been keeping to the sidelines during the show now darted here and there, bearing trays of foaming bottles high above the heads of the crowd. People were talking: 'How'd he *do* that?' 'Did you see the blood?' 'They do it by controlling their minds, I read about it in Hyderapore.' Sam and her black associate rose, smiling, to give each other five. Sam swept the paraphernalia of her magician's craft into a Louis Vuitton tote bag and hitched it over her shoulder.

'You want a beer?' the black man asked.

'No, thanks, John, I'm for home.'

'Sure?'

'I'm sure.' She smiled and patted his sleeve. For a moment they stood close, talking quietly – several witnesses remembered that, and some of them commented that it looked like she was holding him at bay.

After that the picture fragmented.

Mamaluke's main entrance was on the waterfront opposite Paradise Bay's marina. Samantha Brenton (Sam to those who knew her) came out alone, crossed the road and spent a few moments leaning over the rail by the sea, maybe just enjoying the fresh air. Then she struck off east, going down 'A' Street, and that would eventually have brought her to Fountainside, Paradise Bay's trendiest quarter. Which had a certain logic to it, because Sam's magician's shop, the one she owned in partnership with the black guy, John Xeres (pronounced Cerise, as NBC and the rest would never tire of telling a nation soon to be weary of him) was on Twelfth, at the heart of Fountainside. Maybe she'd been planning to put that night's earnings in the safe, because people had been generous: Randy Stevens, Mamaluke's general manager, would later recall how Sam's plastic bucket on the bar had been overflowing with bills.

One other person had something to contribute. A name: Arthur.

Matthew McManus was the last person to see Samantha alive, whilst walking to his Mercedes, parked down a side-alley off 'A' Street. He learned of the murder from TV and came to see the police voluntarily, which surprised them, since he had a reputation as a small-time shady operator with a host of dubious import-export scams to his name.

He'd been dining at Il Giorno's, and he'd drunk a lot, although liquor didn't have much of an effect on Matthew McManus. As he approached his car he passed a doorway where two people were talking in low voices. He later identified one of them as Sam Brenton; the other stood far enough inside the doorway to lack a face.

'The other' . . . a sexless description. Matthew told the police that this second person had one of those voices certain singers have: could be male, could be female, hard to say. As Matthew passed the doorway, Sam turned to walk off in the opposite direction and the voice called: 'So what should I tell Arthur?' She replied: 'Go to hell.' That was all. By the time Matthew had gotten into his car and turned the key, there was nobody to be seen.

The killer's note described it like this:

*

I follow the bich from club and it all go to plan like we knew. She take 'A', me too. I call her soft into the alley. I tell her I like her act, we have friends in common she say Who? I tell her. She don't like. I tell her who sent me, she say Go to hell. Strong spirit. I follow her, talking soft. She say: I don't want to hear about the past. It's over. Dead.

Now she is dead too.

*

Back in Mamaluke's, John Xeres, pronounced Cerise, had another couple of Coors in the downstairs bar. A few people tried to make conversation; he brushed them off. Once or twice he was observed resting his head on his hands like a man with problems.

At some point – a matter of contention, this – he left. John claimed that was at approximately two thirty. He said he'd decided to go in search of Sam. They'd been living together and had split up three months ago, after a row involving another woman, but they'd managed to keep their professional act on the road and he wanted to get their personal show back on the road, too. Unfortunately, he didn't know where she was living: he'd asked her, but she wouldn't trust him with the address.

John decided he'd walk to The Spelling Game, which was their shop, because he knew that Sam sometimes went there after a show, to put her earnings in the safe. He arrived around three to find it locked and dark. He started walking west, back towards the sea.

Some rowdies were obstructing the sidewalk and he crossed the road to avoid them. He saw they were oriental, and that one of them was throwing up. Orientals had just begun to appear in Paradise Bay, having colonized certain parts of LA and even Santa

Barbara. John was afraid these might be Cambodians, whom he regarded as dangerous.

On the other side of the street, just a few yards down from where he'd crossed, was a hole between two buildings. A demolition gang had been at work, tearing down a shop-cum-apartment conversion and leaving steel girders wedging up the walls on either side.

John walked into the dark gap where the building had been, and the police could not understand why he did that. Look at it from our point of view, they told him. You're cruising along a street, you get scared, you cross the roadway and then what do you do? You turn down a dark alley, putting yourself in *more* danger. So explain why you did that, please? And all poor John Xeres could say was that his instincts had ordered it. That the place had a bad smell, a very bad smell, and suddenly he knew he had to find out what had gone so horribly wrong here. Knew it involved Sam, too.

He picked his way around piles of bricks and fallen plaster and the remains of windows and suchlike, and all the while this smell was growing stronger. Not a real smell, just a way of saying that his instincts knew the worst. When he'd retreated about twenty yards from the street, he stumbled over something soft. He lit a match and knelt down. At first he didn't see anything. Then he noticed a thumb. It was lying on the concrete and it had been severed cleanly. At which point John began to laugh.

He claimed later that this was the laughter that comes from relief. He knew, he said, that Sam had been working on this wonderful new routine which involved cutting off her own thumb and its being found some place, say in the bar where she was working that night, and then she would miraculously reunite the thumb with the rest of her. But the trick was proving more difficult to develop than she'd anticipated. In that first second, John thought, 'She's done it!' and so he laughed.

Now those orientals he'd seen earlier were not, in fact, Cambodians, they were Chinese students from the UCPB medical campus at Bel Cove, and although they'd been overdoing a birthday celebration they were responsible citizens. When they saw this character deliberately cross the street and go onto a vacant lot and light a match, they got curious. They went to find out what was going down. They arrived in time to hear John laugh, and then the match went out. One student had a key-ring with a miniature flashlight on the end. Seconds later, everybody could see everything.

Someone had murdered Samantha Brenton. He'd used a knife. She lay on the ground with her hands folded over her breasts. Both her thumbs had been severed – one lay on the ground beside her, one couldn't be found – and so had the forefinger of her right hand, and her kidneys had been removed, along with her womb. Whoever did it showed a fine grasp of surgery, as the city Medical Examiner was quick to point out. But what really gave this murder class, as far as the media were concerned, was the calling-card.

Clasped between the remains of Sam's neatly folded hands was a slip of white cardboard. It measured ninety-one by fifty-nine millimetres and on it was printed, in curly italic black letters, *'P.B. Butcher'*. Whoever's card it was evidently cared naught for expense: the edges were deckled in gold.

*   *   *

The Paradise Highway Motor Lodge – 'Best Rooms Best Rates Best in The West' – was Daniel Krozgrow's second home. Almost his first: he didn't care to spend a lot of time at his bachelor apartment in Santa Monica, convenient though that was for an FBI Field Profile Co-Ordinator based in Los Angeles, and any chance he got to travel north, he took.

He was in Paradise Bay at the end of a week-long series of meetings. He'd driven up the previous Monday with a Toshiba laptop, its one hundred and twenty megabyte hard disk stuffed full of data; nineteen cardboard folders; and the hope of somehow forgetting Diane Cheung by haunting the places where he'd known and fallen in love with her. Which, as he was first to acknowledge, was actually pretty stupid.

He was thirty-five, not getting any younger, and hung up on a beautiful Chinese woman. Two years previously, Paradise Bay had endured its moment of infamy when a serial killer called

Tobes Gascoign had dispatched a number of young white males, only to perish in a fire before he could be brought to justice. Dan and Diane Cheung had worked on that case as colleagues, fallen in love (he'd thought) after they'd wrapped it up . . . and parted within months. Now she was gone; she'd moved away without even telling him her new address. But she filled his dreams at five o'clock that Saturday morning, making him toss and turn and throw himself this way and that across the king-size bed.

When the phone rang it almost came as a relief.

'Dan . . . PJ.'

'Uhhhh . . . ' Daniel struggled up in bed and reached for his specs. 'What time is it?'

'Little after five. Sorry to disturb you. Guy name of ter Haar's called; wants to speak with you.'

Andy ter Haar was a Paradise Bay detective, among the brightest and the best. Daniel made a crash exit from the headache-hinterland between wakefulness and sleep. 'Put him on. Any chance of coffee?'

'Right up.'

There was a click; and Daniel heard the background noise of a squad room that never slept. 'Andy? What gives?'

'We have a body. Another one. Another card.'

'Butcher?'

'I'll spare you the grislies, but it looks like our pal, yeah.'

'Where and when should I show?'

'Got an incident briefing here at seven.'

'I'll be there.'

Daniel scrambled out of bed and into the bathroom. He shaved quickly, then took a shower almost too cold to be borne, before struggling into the comfortable, crumpled chinos and sports jacket that were his uniform. Staring into the mirror, he combed the strands of his sandy moustache into tight order, completely ignoring his long, tousled hair, and while he did that his mind was running over a well-furrowed track – what was it about Paradise Bay that attracted serial killers?

Of course, he told himself as he sipped PJ's Colombian brew, of course it was too early to be sure about that. Three months ago, back in February, he'd worked briefly on the murder of a young woman called Yolanda Kastin, who'd had both her thumbs removed and been eviscerated. Now ter Haar was telling him that hadn't been a one-off.

This was a law-abiding community, a backwater of clean living and civic awareness. Two years ago, its residents had found it well-nigh inconceivable that a monster might stalk their town.

Now they had another one.

*　　*　　*

Thelma Vestrey didn't sleep much. Those damn birds, how dare they sing so early in the morning! *And why was she alone in this lovely bed where no loving ever got done? Grrrr!*

Enough (she said to herself at six ten), enough is enough. Outside, the sun was up. She scampered downstairs, quietly, so as not to waken Rachel or Kirsty, and poured herself a half-pint of juice which she took back up to bed.

The brown package that FedEx had delivered the night before lay on her bedside-table. Thelma opened it with a sigh and began to read.

Madame, tomorrow morning, we have a meeting, you and I.
I am Aurelia Delacroix, Richo's mother. There are things I want to confide in you. Things you must know.

I was born in a village near Boghar, south of Algiers, the product of a liaison between my mother and a French soldier, from whom I inherited my European looks. My mother was sent to relatives in the countryside, and to conceal her shame the family put it about that she was a widow. I had a sister, Nada; we were twins. We had a little brother, after a time, but he died young. I remember the flies eating his eyes, while he cried. Our relatives were too poor . . . When the baby fell sick, it was a death-sentence.

My uncle never smiled until the baby died. Then he smiled for the first time I can recall, and he said, 'The child is blessed indeed.' My mother sobbed all night.

Nada and I received no schooling. In the day we ran wild, as we pleased, in the street. At night we would gather round the story-tellers in the square and listen, frog-eyed, to their romances, and we would giggle and be told to shush by the grown-ups.

My uncle gathered dung, my mother and my aunt travelled into Boghar every day, seven days a week, to clean house for a wealthy unbeliever who traded in precious stones. By the time Nada and I were ten, it had been decided that we must become servants too. My mother had high hopes of us finding work in Alger (the town you know as Algiers). One day, her employer came to call. His name was Abdel Haydar, may his spirit rot in agony for all time! He brought with him a grinning devil called Dr Kobrussi. Dr Kobrussi said, Yes! Yes! he could find work for us in the city. My uncle smiled for the second time. He bartered us away in the street, being too ashamed of our hovel to invite his guests inside.

We drove away in a dusty old jeep, as we were, without a bag or a toy between us. Nada and I cried when we kissed our family goodbye, but we both felt (we were like all twins, we knew each other's thoughts) that we were bound for paradise. Our tears dried as swiftly as the desert after rain. Even when Dr Kobrussi took my hand and put it on his crotch, while with my other hand I waved goodbye, I still thought I was going to heaven.

He took us to his house on the bay by El Harrach and for the first time we saw what a home could be like. A maid cleaned us up. She swore terribly; we'd never heard a woman use such words before, but I suppose we must have been messy. She threw clean clothes at us – pretty floral dresses, with bows and even straw hats. Nada and I ran around this wonderful house, shrieking with laughter, stuffing our hands into our mouths.

That night, we stuffed something else into our mouths: more food than we would see in a month at home, and of a quality we'd never seen. Nada was sick. I held it down, but only after a struggle. Then we were given a strange drink of tea that made us sleep.

As if in a dream, I remember men coming into our bedroom. I couldn't move, but I could hear what they were saying without understanding the language. It was French, of course. One of the men, tall, with a beard, wore a white uniform. A ship's officer. There was much haggling. After a while the officer beckoned one of the other men. He leaned over Nada, sleeping on the same bed with me, he spread her legs and shone a torch between them. Then he probed her with a long, thin, flexible wire. Afterwards he did the same to me. We'd been marketed as virgins, he needed to be sure.

They left. I fell asleep. I awoke to find us in bunks, Nada on top, me below. Her vomit woke me. (We were at sea, in a storm.) Her vomit trickled over the edge of her bunk, onto my face.

The next two days were torture. We had no water, you see. Only towards the end of the second day did they think to bring us each a cup of water that tasted of tin. Then they tied us hand and foot, and gagged us, and I was terribly afraid, for what if we were sick and the gag choked us? I was only ten, but I understood about such things. I have an instinctive understanding of so much, Dr Vestrey, and it all dates back to my childhood.

They loaded us into a tiny boat. We landed somewhere on the French coast, I don't know where. The rest of the journey was by lorry. We were given a dry bread roll and some more water. A man travelled in the back of the lorry with us. Every time we came near people, a town, he threw a tarpaulin over us. He would sit there, his back to the cab, looking us over. He was only about twenty, I think, and he had a bad eye: worse than a squint, some-thing wrong with it. After a while he started to come under the tarpaulin. He cuddled and fondled us, but he didn't dare do too much; we could smell his fear. He kissed Nada's mouth, and mine too, but that was his limit.

At last we got to Paris. I'll tell you about that when I can bring myself to face it.

Thelma stared at the paper. The account stopped, just like that! She turned over each sheet in turn, looking for the rest, but there was nothing.

'Wow!' she said to the wallpaper. 'Wow!'

What an *incredible* childhood! Gee whiz!

Thelma showered and swallowed a croissant before bidding goodbye to Erasmus the cat, and Rufus her American cocker, and hitting the road.

A mischievous impulse inspired her to dial Daniel Krozgrow on her car-phone. What would he say, being woken from his motel bed so early? Why, he'd be *thrilled*! To be called to share the dawn, a moment of sensuality and joy, what luxury! And she had the perfect excuse of a wake-up call: he was going to visit his brother in Pittsburgh . . .

Thelma stood slightly in awe of Daniel and his relationship with his brother: the way you do when you're at school and there's this one dude (only ever one) who's so cool and laid-back about stuff that would cause you to curl up and die if it happened in your own family.

Daniel's brother Mikey should have become a police pilot, that's what their father thought, but Mikey wanted to paint and sculpt. He got into drugs, had to beat a rap in Miami, ended up in Pittsburgh, living rough. Daniel had not only declared his brother's history to the FBI, he'd carried it like a badge of pride. Colleagues admired him for not trying to hide family baggage which, according to folk legend, was bound to hinder promotion. Thelma knew Daniel did not believe that particular folk legend. She wondered what he'd do if someday he started to believe it.

Anyway, her handsome hero would need to make an early start, she'd give him a wake-up call, nothing more. *Nothing more! Got that?*

So she was smiling broadly when the click came, followed by PJ's voice; but as she heard what he had to say her smile faded.

Thelma retracted the aerial with a snap. What could be important enough to drag Dan from his bed so early?

A mile down the road she joined Route 1, north of Lompoc. She turned on the car-radio: Caltrans assured her there were no traffic problems between her and St Joseph's Hospital at Bel Cove, five miles away. Buck up, Thelma, she admonished herself sharply: you are twenty-eight, and one hot-shot child psychologist. You have had your failures, but do not lack success, and no man can take that away from you, even if he's gorgeous, as unobtainable as the President's personal number, and out working at seven on a Saturday morning. (She liked dedicated men, always had. They reminded her of everything her father was not.)

Oh yes, and you finally quit smoking and it's been seven months and two days since you dragged on a Camel.

She thrust a tape into the deck and began to listen to her voice-recorded case-notes. 'Ricardo Rashid Delacroix, known as Richo. Inherited by me from Diane Cheung when she left. Seventeen years old, son of Aurelia and Naim. Only child, no siblings of either sex. Mother and father absent. Child presents as suffering from anti-social behavioural syndrome that takes a variety of forms. Now studying at Sacré Coeur Academy near his home, which is a ranch in the Greenhorn Mountains. Sacré Coeur is a small, exclusive school specializing in teenagers with behavioural and learning difficulties. Impression I have of mother, who I've not met, is: domineering, assertive, query manipulative. She's determined the boy should go on to take a Master's, the usual things, but he needs sorting out. The boy presents himself as assured, charming, but sly. He's had a variety of analysts and knows how to play us: see D. Cheung's notes, in particular heading Month Two.

'Session two. See notes on file. Impressions: his multiphasic graphs show a worrying knowledge of clinical techniques. I am conscious that he views me as a sex object; if right, this won't work.

'Session three. See notes on file, plus CA form 37A. Richo is *very* charming and a little bit sad. Knows he's a mess, can't get a handle on what's wrong, the usual things. Normal sex life. Have had to warn him about come-ons. When I explained that I'd have to take this up with his parents, he became abusive. Before that, many of his replies had been tangential or simply irrelevant.

'Session four. . . . '

But Thelma jabbed her finger on the Eject button, unwilling to be disturbed in traffic by red-hot anger.

There had been an incident in session four. The Delacroix family tree contained a lot of mixed blood – according to Richo, his mother was part French, part Arab, his father Filipino – and in the boy that added up to a gloriously attractive appearance. An athlete's body, a darkly brooding air . . . When he'd tried to kiss Thelma, it hadn't been exactly painful, *but* . . . it was enough to indicate that Richo's therapy had to end. This morning Thelma would have to break the news to Aurelia Delacroix: not a prospect she relished.

She parked the Bronco in her reserved space. There was a viewpoint to one side of the lot, complete with telescope and etched-steel map. She walked over to it and drew down half a dozen deep breaths. To her right lay the cool, clear expanse of blue ocean. On her left was the conurbation known as Paradise Bay.

St Joseph's Hospital stood on a cliff overlooking Paradise Bay to the south. The town was Santa Barbara in minor key, and, because it lacked its own mission, tourists beating El Camino Real tended to pass it by. This was a quiet little spot with its own sleepy charm and zoning control that was enforced with a severity the Iraqi secret police might have envied. Spread out below Thelma was a broad expanse of greenery, flecked with palms and red-tile roofs, white walls and Spanish grille-work and avenues extending as far south as she could see, where the coast wove east and Washington Avenue, Paradise Bay's main drag, joined Highway 1. Many miles to her left, she could make out the San Rafael mountains.

She hurried inside, feeling refreshed. She made her way along the corridor to the office that had once been occupied by Diane Cheung, possibly America's foremost clinician specializing in teenage psychological disorders, and which was now hers, Thelma Vestrey's. Well, almost all hers, because Diane's departure had left a hole too big to be filled by one person. Geoff Diamond shared the roomy office with Thelma, and they were both supervised by Professor Alan T. Gomez, who had written *the* book on senescence and was known around these parts, strictly behind his back, as Alzheimer. But today Thelma had the office all to herself, which was as well, because the last thing she wanted was to be interrupted during a session with Richo's mother.

The nurse on duty phoned to say that Aurelia Delacroix was already waiting in reception. Thelma, fired with curiosity to meet the writer of that extraordinary letter, went out to discover a woman in a striking green dress, chic and tight-fitting, and a tall, slim man with extremely short grey-and-white hair who stood by her side in the stiff posture that comes of military training. His tanned, rather grim face, with dimpled chin and moody eyes, underlined that impression, as did the clothes he was wearing: fawn slacks, supported by a broad red leather belt, and an open-neck shirt that matched the slacks exactly.

Thelma greeted Aurelia and asked, in her usual impulsive style, 'Wow, where did you get that fabulous dress? I *covet* it.'

'What, this old rag? Pouf! It's one of Paco's rejects, that's all. I always pop into Rabane when I'm in Paris and he's sweet on me. You know how it is?'

Rather than waste time wistfully wondering how indeed it was, Thelma glanced at the man and asked, 'Is this Richo's father?'

'I'm Shimon Waldman,' the man said, sticking out his hand to be shaken. 'Naim's associate.'

He had a dry, firm handshake and good eye-contact; but before Thelma could find out more about him she became aware that Aurelia was fighting back tears, so she quickly ushered the two of them to her office. Shimon took Aurelia's arm and guided her to the nearest chair, lowering her into it as if she were cherished.

'So little time,' Aurelia murmured dejectedly. 'Oh, God . . . You read my letter, Madame?'

'Yes, I read it.'

'And what did you think?'

'I thought . . . that it posed more questions than it answered.'

Aurelia seemed distressed, yes; but suddenly Thelma found herself transfixed on the sharp, probing points of the woman's eyes. They were remarkable eyes by any standards: cyan-blue, with gold flecks and high, arched brows that had been plucked into a line no thicker than a pencil-lead. Eyes imbued with the power to dazzle, even terrify: looking into them, Thelma knew a moment of unease.

'Mrs Delacroix,' she said gently, 'we can talk about your letter in a minute, but first . . . I hate to be the bearer of bad news, but I'm afraid there's nothing more I can do for Richo. He needs psychiatric help.'

They were both gazing at her now, with rapt attention.

'You mean, he's suffering from mental illness?' It was Waldman who spoke.

'He may be. I stress: I'm not qualified to diagnose that. But he sees conspiracies everywhere and he defends them with every appearance of rationality. To break through that requires skills I don't have.'

'So he'd have to go into hospital?' Aurelia croaked.

'It could mean that, yes.'

Aurelia broke down sobbing. There was something false about those sobs, however; so much so that Thelma was left with the strange feeling that the prospect of sending her son to hospital made Aurelia almost *glad*. She dabbed her eyes dry and wriggled upright in her chair. 'It's a terrible thing,' she said, 'to have a family history like mine. If only you knew the half . . . '

'But I don't, and that's been such a handicap. If you'd come to see me before, trusted me, perhaps I could have helped more? Look . . . is it too late now? I don't think so. You've already started to tell me your story. Come.'

Thelma indicated a chair for Shimon and he sat down, continuing to watch Aurelia as if he were her bodyguard.

'Madame Vestrey.' Aurelia Delacroix, in complete contrast to her earlier apparent weakness, spoke with the authority of a teacher imposing order on a troublesome class. 'I'm proposing to take a great risk. To put myself in danger. I wouldn't consider doing this, except that my son likes you. No, he adores you. I've started to write everything down. You've seen part of it. I've managed to write more. Shimon, please . . . '

Shimon Waldman had placed a leather attaché case beside his chair. Now he opened it and took out an envelope, together with a passport; these he handed across the desk. Thelma examined the passport first. It was a brown booklet with gold letters on it: 'Pilipinas Pasaporte'.

'Page seven,' Aurelia Delacroix commanded.

Thelma opened the passport. Page seven contained leave to remain in the United States, valid until June 15 this year. She calculated. Approximately four weeks away. 'Your passport?' she inquired.

'Mine, yes. My husband and son have similar visas. In a few weeks from now, we are all out, gone. For ever.'

'And that's a bad thing?'

'It's the end of my son's life, Madame.' Aurelia's tone had turned calm and reflective. 'A month from now, either we shall both be dead, or it'll amount to the same thing.' She glanced at Shimon. 'He'll confirm that I'm not mad, I haven't been drinking,

34

I don't approve of drugs. He knows the story, you see. He's been there from the beginning.'

Shimon nodded. 'She's not exaggerating.'

'But . . . excuse me, but do you have to go with your husband? I mean, presumably you have funds. Why not just stay here, apply for new visas?'

'It's . . . complicated. If we did that, we'd still be in danger. Physical danger. Besides, Richo is still a minor, his father can take him wherever he wants.'

Thelma unsealed the envelope Shimon had given her and examined its contents: a dozen or more pages of handwriting. 'I can't read all of this now,' she said.

'Of course. All I ask is that you read it soon. Then you'll understand why my son needs treatment, here, in the States, and why we must find a means of staying.'

Thelma gathered all her courage and said, 'I'm sorry, Mrs Delacroix, but I really can't go on with Ricardo as my patient.'

'Madame.' Aurelia reached across Thelma's desk and took her right hand between both her own. 'I implore you. I *beg* you: read what is in that envelope.'

Thelma knew she should refuse. But, looking into those scorching, cyan-coloured eyes, she lacked the will. To have lived through a childhood like that, and survived . . . surely Aurelia deserved a little more? One last attempt at healing her son, was that so much to ask?

'I'll . . . I will read this, then we'll talk again.'

Aurelia squeezed Thelma's hand. 'Thank you,' she whispered. 'Thanks be to God.'

She rose, Shimon likewise, as if he were her shadow. 'Madame,' she said, 'I want you to know one thing you will *not* find in that account.'

Aurelia stalked towards the door, which her companion was already opening; there she turned and delivered her devastating exit line in throwaway fashion. 'My husband intends to have Shimon murdered.'

The door closed behind them. Thelma stared at it for several seconds, not quite convinced she was alone, that the melodrama had played itself out. Aurelia left behind a mild redolence of heavy perfume, combined with a hint of perspiration, of *meat*. Thelma rose and went over to the window. She threw it open and inhaled deeply. It took a few moments for the inner turmoil to settle into memories of a consultation, rather than an uneasy dream.

She put away Richo's file after adding a page of handwritten notes. As she flipped open the filing-cabinet a sheet of paper fell out of his cardboard folder, and she knelt to retrieve it. Diane Cheung's note to her, as successor-therapist. *Beware, baby, beware.* Just that.

Thelma frowned. Diane had been so thorough when handing over her case-histories, yet on this one file she'd left but a single note. What had happened between her and Richo before they parted, what could have prompted such atypical mystery?

Thelma had a couple more patients to see before lunch, one a seven-year-old boy who'd been traumatized by witnessing his mother's death at the hands of an intruder, the other a fourteen-year-old with a record of breaking into liquor stores who'd been referred to her by the Juvenile Court. Thelma made little headway with either, that bright Saturday morning; her mind was on the Delacroix clan.

She couldn't quite dispel her regret at not having ditched Richo. Perhaps she should have told Aurelia about how, during session four, he'd kissed Thelma, and been slapped for his pains.

As she was saying goodbye to her last patient the phone rang. She was tempted to let it go, almost did; then she picked up and knew a moment's elation, for it was Daniel Krozgrow, inviting her to lunch.

*   *   *

Daniel replaced his mobile phone in its wallet. Oh, come on, he told himself: it's not so bad. You're not really *using* Thelma by taking her to lunch: she's an okay, head-together woman, a friend, she'll have Diane's phone number, and her professional instincts will make her see that contacting Diane is *right*. You don't want to romance Diane any more, it's only professional: we have another serial killer, she dealt with the last one, what could be more natural than calling her to discuss this new development? Now concentrate on the job in hand, will you?

He aligned the sheets on his clipboard and considered the topics at the head of page three: 'II. Crime Scene. How many? Environment, time, place? How many offenders? Organized, disorganized? . . . '

He was standing in the middle of the empty space where John Xeres had discovered Sam Brenton's body a few hours before. It was a hot day and Daniel had stripped down to his shirt-sleeves, while around him the Paradise Bay police department came and went and photographed and recorded and noted and sketched. The body parts were long gone, down to the morgue, where a full post-mortem dissection and examination would by now be under way. Daniel glanced at his watch, calculating the earliest he could expect a report from Forensic.

He'd been here for five hours, on and off, and already he knew a great deal about the man – he knew it *was* a man, for example – who'd carved Sam Brenton. Some things came easy. Experts like Daniel had the FBI's comprehensive databases at Quantico HQ to draw on when they were preparing their profiles of a killer, but experience was worth more than any computer-program. Certain types of people committed certain kinds of crime, and they almost invariably went about it in a certain way: behind all the mumbo-jumbo, that was the whole secret.

So, Daniel already felt confident about quite a number of things. For example, the perp had set out that night, deliberately, with a view to committing what the FBI categorizes as 'organized sexual homicide'. According to the profile, compiled from hundreds of different case-histories amassed over the past decade, he was a risk-taker, a high-roller, and he almost certainly knew Sam Brenton before the fatal act. Assuming he ran true to type – and killers usually did – he was personable, neatly dressed and articulate. Judging from those same case histories he could well be black. There was a high probability that he stood amongst the bystanders beyond the yellow-and-black tape strung across the entrance to the abandoned lot, savouring his moment of glory.

Daniel surveyed the street. Perhaps fifty people stood there, gawping, amidst the forest of microphones and aerials. Which of you did it? Daniel wanted to shout; Come over here and show me how . . .

Which one of you is 'Arthur'?

There was a triangle here: Sam, her killer, and 'Arthur'. Matthew McManus might not be the world's best witness, but he was adamant about the killer's final word: a man's name. Who was Arthur? Where was he? Was he standing behind the tape now, perhaps?

Daniel became aware that his eyes were no longer focused on the crowd, they were snagged by a far-from-enticing vista. His future.

For the past two years he'd worked his butt off, every hour God made, and achieved nothing. Zilch. Next month he was due in Quantico for biennial assessment and review. What was there to review? Daniel tried to think of a single career-boosting scoop, and failed.

So. He was going to find this killer. Find him, and put him behind bars for ever and a day. That, or send him to the electric chair. Somebody was going to fry in this town, P.B. Butcher or Daniel Krozgrow, and he was damned if it was going to be him.

He heard a commotion further down the street, and saw that a car carrying Peter Symes, Paradise Bay's police chief, was about to pull into an area closed off from the rest of the lot by streamers. Reporters clustered around, but blues held them off while Peter disembarked, so they had to be content with shots of his charcoal grey suit, Pierre Cardin tie and Church's lace-ups. When he donned sunglasses and looked around, a full head above his nearest rivals, the resemblance to a Family Don was remarkable.

Daniel sauntered over and shook hands. Peter, being Peter, put a fatherly arm around Daniel's shoulders, beamed a mouth full of perfect teeth, led him behind the car where the media couldn't overhear and yelped, 'What the hell is going on here?'

'We have another serial, Chief.'

'Don't say that.' Peter became aware that his head was half-turned towards the sleepless cameras and rearranged his gleaming white teeth into an even bigger smile. 'Don't tell me we have a serial killer in Paradise Bay again, 'cause I don't . . . want . . . to hear.'

'Serial killers are like problems, they always come in threes. Wait and see what they've got lined up for you next year.'

The press, becoming impatient, cut off Peter's response. 'Hey, Chief, give us a statement!' 'Camera's over here, Chief, lookin' good, man . . . ' But one voice carried over the rest. Angela Souvrain, of CBS, shouted, 'Chief Symes, is it true we're faced with another set of serial killings?'

'Well, *shit*,' Peter snarled, and then he gave Daniel the biggest smile yet while patting his shoulder as if he were a favourite dog.

The two men went over to the barrier. Peter insinuated himself next to Angela Souvrain in such a way as to present his right profile to lens.

'Sam Brenton was murdered here,' he said, 'just behind where I'm standing, in the small hours of this morning. I can't tell you more until I've had the forensic report, but it was apparent to the officers who were first on the scene that she'd suffered mutilations, and those mutilations were not dissimilar to those suffered by Yolanda Kastin last February. That's all.'

Amid the hubbub, Angela Souvrain's voice rose out like a clarion. 'Mr Krozgrow, as FBI field profiler you took credit for solving Paradise Bay's last serial killing two years ago; can we assume your presence here today means you're closing in on another killer, or does it cast doubt on your earlier findings?'

Daniel became aware of clutching his clipboard to his chest like a shield. There were so many things wrong with that question, so many false assumptions, and innuendoes, and even one downright lie (he had never taken or been awarded credit for solving the previous crimes) that he didn't know where to start.

Daniel swallowed. Here goes . . .

'Well, ah . . . well, the first thing I would say is that I'm not convinced we're dealing with a series of deaths here. As you know, it doesn't become a series until three or more related deaths have occurred. Secondly, and categorically, this has nothing to do with the Gascoign case of two years ago. For which, incidentally, I claim no credit. Gascoign tortured and murdered a number of single white males before kidnapping a boy and being surrounded by police and perishing in the subsequent fire. After that, the killings stopped.'

There was a moment of quiet. Daniel saw Peter, who had been nodding throughout his speech, wink approval, and the tightness in his chest slackened a notch.

'Unless,' Angela Souvrain said, 'Gascoign had nothing to do with the earlier killings but the real perpetrator had enough sense to hang the blame on him when opportunity presented itself. Or we have a copycat killer. Is it true, Mr Krozgrow, that this killer leaves calling-cards? Like Gascoign?'

Daniel gazed at her, hating her, wondering how the hell she'd found out. 'Yes,' he said. 'It's true.'

'Both times? Kastin and Brenton?'

Through gritted teeth Daniel said, 'Both times.'

'Thank you.'

*   *   *

Thelma was, naturally, early for her lunch date. She grabbed an ocean-side table at the Pierrot, named for the rickety pier on which it was built, and ordered a glass of Laurent-Perrier pink champagne.

Thelma had a thing about this particular *marque*. It went back to the time she'd gone for interview at St Joseph's, newly- but under-qualified, sassy, thinking what the hell, *somebody* has to get the job. She'd been interviewed by Alzheimer, AKA Professor Gomez, and Diane Cheung: a beautiful but somehow ineffably sad woman who'd smiled at her gauche attempts to impress, and concluded the interview by asking, 'You love life, don't you?' And Thelma had done this truly stupid thing: knowing she'd blown it, she'd spread her arms wide and crowed, 'Yep! Whoopee!'

And so she'd landed the job.

Diane had briefed her on the more important files, then gone away. No one knew why she wanted to leave, or what was haunting her, but Thelma quickly got the feeling that people were glad to see the back of her. She had become a depressive influence on the psychological services department that she'd headed for so long.

Diane left Thelma a present: a bottle of Laurent-Perrier pink champagne, standing atop the stack of patients' files. The attached note read: 'For when you don't love life quite so much. Be happy.' But Thelma had opened it anyway, nine o'clock in the morning though it was, and loving life though she did, because that was her style, and she'd shared the fizz with everyone.

'Be happy,' Diane had written; Thelma could never recall those words without thinking that what she'd really meant was, 'Be happier than I ever could be.'

Funny: with one exception, the stack of files supporting that marvellous bottle of champagne had been compiled in alphabetical order, but Diane had left Richo Delacroix's file, with its cryptic note, on top. Now why should Thelma suddenly remember that . . . ?

While she waited for Daniel she slipped the papers out of Aurelia's envelope and settled down to read this second instalment of her life story. At first she kept half an eye on the entrance, where Daniel would appear any moment, but it wasn't long before Thelma forgot all about the one-and-only.

We came into Paris on a wet, blustery evening and were taken to an apartment in rue Burq. Our room was on the fifth floor, overlooking roofs. Years later, I can still remember the gutters overflowing with rain from a heavy sky, and pigeons awakening us with the beat of their wings. The ceiling of our room was low and angled. We shared a bed. There was scarcely space for us and that bed. We had to learn to use a toilet, bidet and shower. Our nice clothes were stripped off: for weeks we lived wrapped in sheets and towels.

An Algerian woman called Basma looked after us. She could speak French and for an hour each day she taught us. Nada picked it up faster than I did, repeating things over and over until she had them by heart. Unlike Basma, she never lost patience.

The pimps tried to separate us, once. We shrieked and yelled, until in the end our owners brought us together again. But we didn't get to eat for a week.

We'd been in Paris three months, never seeing the street outside, when the buyers of flesh began to generate an income from us.

Basma made sure we were especially clean that first night. She was in a strange mood: stern, as usual, but jollying us along, too. She seemed preoccupied. She told us that an important person was going to spend time with us and we must do whatever he asked. She dressed us identically, in fresh white clothes: long dresses, Arabian in style.

We were taken to a grand house in the 16th, not far from the Trocadéro. The car drove into a courtyard, the street-gates were shut behind it. A woman met us at the door and took us up to a bedroom. It was the most opulent room we'd ever seen; to this day it stands comparison with my adult memories of the Ritz in Madrid, the Pierre in New York or the Manila Hotel.

The bed was huge, white, virginal as we. Nada and I sat on it, silent, holding hands. Another door opened and a man entered. Probably not above thirty. Pale skin. His French didn't sound much better than ours. He went over to a refrigerator and brought out a jug of orange juice, along with two glasses. He poured juice for us. We accepted with shy smiles. This was nice.

The orange juice contained a drug, of course. We quickly descended into a state of passive acceptance, watching all that went on as if from outside ourselves. He disrobed us carefully, making sad tutting noises when a button popped off Nada's dress. He laid us on the bed before taking off his clothes and coming to lie between us. First he lay on top of me, moving up and down with his eyes closed. I felt ashamed and a bit afraid, but mostly bored.

He knelt between my legs and pushed them wide apart. Then he lifted my feet so that the soles were resting on his chest and licked his forefinger before inserting it into me. He encountered resistance and that brought a smile onto his face. He wriggled forward on his knees. That was the moment when I grasped what he meant to do, and screamed. His smile widened. He placed a hand over my mouth and thrust his hips forward.

What happened next took only a few minutes, I later supposed; but it felt like the whole of her lifetime to a kid who had celebrated her eleventh birthday the week before by scrounging a second biscuit from Basma.

Afterwards, he lay down between us and rested. I could feel wetness beneath me and associated this with the iron tongs that were ripping my insides apart in sweeping waves. I put my hand down there; it came back scarlet. But by then he was already at work on Nada. He took longer over her, because I'd drained his stamina, but she seemed to please him more.

He got up, dressed without even bothering to shower and left, putting one hundred francs on the dresser, as a pourboire. I didn't know, then or later, how much he'd paid for the two of us, but I hoped it had bankrupted him. I came to hope that he went to prison and was raped there, because that would be even more painful than what he'd done to Nada and me. In the months that followed, I became a connoisseur of sexual pain.

So that was the first time. Nada and I were in a state of shock. We lay on the bed for God knows how long. We held each other. We cried not at all, though our eyes were hot. After a while the door opened and Basma came in. For the first time, we were pleased to see her. But she wasn't sympathetic. She shoved us into the shower, bundled us into bath-robes and took us away.

We didn't sleep that night, we planned our escape. But then we remembered that our uncle had sold us into slavery. We had nowhere to run.

The pimps treated us better, after that. We had more to eat, the food was good. Every so often the car would come and Basma would take us for a walk in a deserted stretch of the Bois de Boulogne, hovering close with the driver, terrified lest we bolt. They weren't to know we'd given up any idea of that. We were realists, even then.

What can be told about such lives? What good would it do to compose a faithful record of each act of sodomy and sin? We became used to it and didn't keep count. We learned fast how to please all kinds and conditions of men – and women too. How we dreaded those evil women! What drove them to torture little girls sexually? Were they failed, or frustrated, mothers? No, they were wicked. Nada and I saw much wickedness in rue Burq.

There were lighter moments also. Just occasionally a younger man would rent us and we were almost happy. Nada even had a beau for a time: a film-actor who loved her for her brown skin. He took her on his yacht in the south of France. Poor Nada: she came back with dreams of marriage coming out of her mouth, but if I exercised my privilege as blood-twin and looked inside Nada's head, I could see that she knew it for a dream. The actor never showed up again. But the week on the yacht had been lovely: champagne every day, and the gentleness of a father . . .

For years, my sole consolation was the knowledge that at least Nada had enjoyed this encounter before she died.

We acquired cynicism. We learned how to wheedle more of those precious pourboires and conceal them from the pimps. We passed through the hands of a succession of owner-managers. The house on rue Burq was a brothel, but whenever it changed ownership the stock-in-trade passed over too, as with a grocer's. Always we were squirrelling away money, against the day when we could run for it. We'd lie in bed until mid-afternoon, doing the calculations over and over again: so much to eat, so much for bribes, so much for a room, education, the means to travel far, far away from Paris.

There were other whores in the house, of course; many of them with backgrounds similar to our own. A few stood out in our minds: 'aunties', we called them. This one would teach us grammar, that one how to choose a perfume. Their names soon faded, but if I shut my eyes I can still see their faces, their morning faces: tired, lined, dead. Their evening faces were not like that, but then nor were they real.

*   *   *

A squad car dropped Daniel off at the entrance to the Pierrot, a charming picture of gaiety in the afternoon sun: flags flying, streamers, balloons, and those wonderful hallmark barber-pole pillars with ribbons of red, white and blue spiralling from ceiling to floor. He ambled down the deck to the restaurant, to find it almost empty. A glance at his watch showed him he was late – as usual. Damn . . . Then the waiter pointed out Thelma, sitting at a favoured table in the section cantilevered over the ocean, and for a moment Daniel just stood there, admiring the view.

She was pretty, although part of him recognized that hers was no conventional beauty. Thelma's skin was tanned and without flaw, and she had dove-grey eyes like pools of liquid peace and the kind of boyish, perfect figure that causes some men's hearts to lurch. She'd gone through many hairstyles since their first meeting, but today her short blonde tresses framed her face in a neat bob. In different circumstances, he might have wanted to be close to this girl. As it was . . .

'Hi,' Dan said, sliding into the seat opposite. 'Sorry I'm so late.'

'No problem.' She bathed him in a Vestrey Super-Special smile. 'I had something to read. Here – ' she pushed a pile of papers across the table – 'order us a drink and take a look.'

By the time Daniel had finished reading both parts of Aurelia Delacroix's account Thelma was well into her second glass of Laurent-Perrier. Daniel allowed the last sheet of paper to fall onto the tabletop and for a while neither of them spoke.

'I shouldn't have shown you that,' Thelma muttered. 'Breach of confidence. Anyway, what do you think?'

Daniel stared at the ceiling, he examined the ocean view through the window. 'So much of it reads like a novel,' he said slowly. 'Is any of it true?'

'Who knows? The boy's certainly weird enough.' Thelma filled him in on her experiences with Richo, not forgetting the kiss in session four.

'But you don't know *why* she's in danger?' Dan said when she'd finished.

'No, just that she is. She makes out her husband is, like, some kind of gangster. But she's obviously not poor, she could take off someplace else, just disappear, leaving Naim to whistle. Except that would mean leaving him with custody of Richo, which she doesn't want.'

'Hmm . . . Be careful with that,' Dan said, gesturing at Aurelia's letter. 'It stinks.'

'How odd you should say that: she *does* smell. Gamey. Like a buck that's been hung too long. As if she washes, but never quite enough.'

'What are you going to do?'

'I'd like to help them. But . . . ' Thelma sighed and shrugged. 'If I'm going on with the case, I guess I have to make contact with the father as a priority. Oh, let's not talk about it any more.'

Thelma called the waiter over and said, 'Can I just have some Greek salad? Dan?'

'Sounds fine to me.'

'Tell me about your day,' she said to Daniel, as the waiter scuttled away. 'Where were you at seven thirty this morning? Whose bed have *you* been sleeping in, growled Mummy Bear?'

'Well, how nice that you care.' He sighed. 'I think Paradise Bay may have a new serial killer.'

'No! Not that thing I heard on the radio, the Brenton girl?'

'Yes. The press are saying it's a copycat of the Gascoign case.'

'Why?'

'More name-cards. Cards printed with the name of a certain P.B. Butcher.'

Tobes Gascoign, who two years previously had qualified as Paradise Bay's first-ever serial killer, had developed a nasty habit of leaving one of Diane Cheung's name-cards beside his handiwork.

'Can I help?' Thelma asked.

'Well . . . actually, yes.' Daniel was twisting his glass this way and that, an embarrassed expression on his face. 'I suppose you don't happen to have a number for Diane Cheung, by any chance?'

Thelma deflated. 'I'm afraid not,' she said.

'But when she handed over her files to you she must have left a contact number, an address?'

'Don't *you* have it?'

'I tried the number I had, but she doesn't answer.'

'I know. It's so annoying. Once I needed to consult with her over a patient I'd inherited. I rang her house, got the answering-machine, so in the end I went up there . . . and she's in Europe. Plans to be away two years. No forwarding address.'

Daniel stared at her. 'Who told you that?'

'Neighbour. Sorry.'

She shot him a dimply smile, but he wouldn't rise. 'So tell me,' she said, 'what gives on the investigation? Got a suspect?'

Daniel made an effort to pull himself together. 'Oh . . . yes and no. Her boyfriend, guy called Xeres, is in the frame, but I know he didn't do it. No trace of blood, which there would have had to have been, and his demeanour's all wrong for a butcher-style killer. So no suspect, not really.'

'Leads, then?'

'Too early. Forensic tests on the cards are a must. We've had what *may* be a note from the killer. Handwritten. Boastful. The state of the body may tell us something. Profile, of course: top priority.' Dan frowned. 'Blood tests from every United States male called Arthur . . . funny, not.'

'Man or woman?'

'The killer? Man, no question. Probably black, right-handed and tall.'

'Age?'

'Prime of life. Someone with surgical knowledge and great physical strength.'

Their salads came and they started to eat. After a while, however, Daniel sighed and laid down his fork. 'The fact is, I need a break,' he said. 'If I'm ever going to make it anywhere in the FBI, I've got to get out of the LA office and head for Washington, soon. But I don't have enough brownie points. Nailing Butcher would swing it. That's why I was hoping Diane might . . .'

'Anything I can do? Apart from Diane's phone number, I mean.'

'You're very sweet.'

'That I am. Pass the salt. And remember: I'm with Special Force now, and I'm a hands-on kind of girl.' Unlike (she nearly added) Diane Cheung, whose reputed touch-me-not relationship with the Paradise Bay police flew in the face of all Thelma's ideals. 'Seriously, Daniel, it's quite likely they'll bring me in on it anyway, so don't hesitate to ask.'

They'll bring me in, she thought. *I'll see to that!*

*   *   *

Richo Delacroix joined downwind at seven hundred feet above the ground and there, to his right, lay the strip: two hundred feet wide by four thousand three hundred feet long, bearing 291 degrees magnetic. *Pinos Altos.* Home.

He selected ten degrees of flap, reducing the Cessna 152's airspeed to seventy knots, and judged the wind. The orange sock, clearly visible to one side of the runway, was half inflated and gusting gently. He'd perform a slip to landing, then, with a long final leg. No problem.

He re-set the altimeter and cast a sideways glance at his mother in the co-pilot's seat. As usual, she was sitting forward, tense and interested, with the tip of her tongue protruding between her lips. They'd scarcely spoken since he'd picked her up at Bakersfield's Kern County Airport, but these two spoke little anyway.

Suddenly Richo laughed. He had an awful laugh, a bit like a rook cawing: humourless and shrill. *Ha! Ha! Ha! Ha! Ha!*

'Now quiet, darling, quiet,' he exclaimed, 'we're going in. Shit, darling, no we're not, I need some spin practice. Whoosh!'

He flicked in the flaps, applied full power and began a climb. Heat and humidity put a ceiling on the plane's performance, but before very long they'd reached four thousand feet, and Richo was throwing the plane about in his slapdash version of a clearing turn, to make sure the sky was empty of other aircraft.

'Oh, Richo . . .'

'Ssh, darling, ssh. Reduce power, carb heat . . . I'm thinking, darling . . . up we go, up, up, up . . .'

He hauled back on the yoke. The plane climbed momentarily, but at the low power setting he'd selected it was soon verging on a stall. The horn sounded urgently. Richo ignored it. Back he pulled, back and further back, until suddenly the little Cessna lurched down and he kicked in left rudder.

'WheeeeEEEEEE!'

He adored spins. He let this one continue for three full turns. They were pointing straight down and falling like a stone. It seemed as though the plane hung stationary about a point, while the earth spun beneath it and his stomach hovered up by the roof. Richo stole a glance at his mother. She'd bared her teeth, her eyes were closed, but he knew she was enjoying it.

He should end the spin now. If he let it go on they'd lose another thousand feet and maybe never recover. You didn't always, not from a fully developed spin. Let it go around one more time. Here, on the edge, was where life got lived.

He wanted to take Thelma Vestrey up in a plane and scare her

48

to death. He wanted that *power*. Yes. Let her scream and scream, where nobody could hear . . .

Almost with disappointment, Richo stood on the right rudder pedal. As it reached the stop he jerked the yoke forward brutally enough to break the spin, and held his control inputs until the earth stopped revolving beneath him. He pulled back. It took a lot of strength. For one glorious, heart-stopping moment he thought he'd overdone it and they were going to crash, but then the elevators came in and the earth no longer filled his windscreen, there was sky above, a giant hand pressed him back in his seat and the blood was draining away . . .

Straight and level flight, he thought grumpily; such a bore. His eyes flickered across the instruments. Eight hundred feet above mean sea level – *shit!* 'Well, darling,' he said to Aurelia, 'that was close.'

She was half crying, half laughing. She managed to slap his shoulder. 'You idiot!' she said, 'you'll murder us both one day.'

'Ha! Ha! Ha! Ha! Ha!'

Richo stabbed in the carb heat control and set about preparing the Cessna for landing. Flaps ten. Fuel on. Mixture rich. That was everything. Oh, carb heat, he thought; how stupid, when I've just switched it off.

His hand strayed back to the carb heat switch . . . and paused. The cloud was broken stratus with a ceiling of two thousand feet, his temperature gauge told him that outside it was a pleasant sixty degrees. At Bakersfield they'd said something about high relative humidity, but Richo never paid much attention to weather briefings. He was an exceptionally skilful pilot for a seventeen-year-old, everyone said so. Weather was for wimps.

The strip was looming up rapidly now. He put the Cessna into a coordinated turn and quickly took her through base leg, on to final. He concentrated on his adjustments until the runway centreline was to the right of his windshield and holding constant position relative to flight-path, with due allowance made for wind.

He'd been trained to apply carb heat on final approach, just as he'd been trained to radio his presence and intentions on the Common Traffic Advisory Frequency, but who was going to be around here at this time of the afternoon, on a private landing-strip surrounded by two thousand acres of forest and meadow?

High revs, low speed: classic conditions for carb icing. But if ice did suffocate the Cessna's carburettor, engine rpm would drop and show the need for a five-second burst of heat, and that would solve that. Not much of a risk, and yet it was. Delicious!

Richo pushed the stick forward and trimmed away the control pressure for descent.

The approach route took him across a ridge of Jeffrey pine, necessitating a subsequent sudden reduction in height if he were to make the runway threshold. The centreline was beckoning him on and down, easy now, easy . . . passing five hundred, keep her above the pines . . . short-field landing, give her extra flap . . .

He was three hundred feet above the ground and a little low. Add more power – lots of it!

Without warning, his engine stopped. The blur in front of his eyes became a lazily windmilling propeller. For a second Richo froze. Then his finger jabbed down on the carb heat switch before racing to the starter: right magneto, left magneto, both . . . no spark.

Out of the windshield he could see the pine ridge streaking towards him. Before his hands could wrestle with the control yoke, his landing-gear had clipped half a dozen tree tops, tipping the plane dangerously forward. Richo hauled the nose up, over-compensating, and for a second the light aircraft wobbled between heaven and earth, almost stalled.

The ground rushed up at them, the runway centreline no longer dead ahead but skewed. Richo pointed the nose down in an effort to maintain enough airspeed to carry them those vital few feet to the threshold. He was giggling as well as sweating, and his heart beat with the kind of excitement that goes with getting laid.

One hundred feet, read the altimeter. The engine still refused to fire. Richo found time for one last glance at his mother. She sat upright and calm, her lips moist, eyes narrowed. She was enjoying this!

Thelma would hate it, when it came to be her turn. She'd

scream till her voice gave out. Maybe she'd faint. We'll see, he thought to himself; soon we'll see . . .

Richo giggled again. Then the nosewheel hit the ground at speed, dragging the plane through ninety degrees and they were going to die, this was it, the Awfully Big Adventure. *'Don't flip, motherfucker, don't flip you motherfucking son of a bitch, you bitch! Ha! Ha! Ha! Ha! Ha!'* Richo screamed and laughed and pounded on the yoke and then his body was catapulted against the harness, shutting him up at last.

The Cessna bumped along for a hundred yards: enough to turn it around completely before tipping over sideways. The starboard wing buckled and snapped with an ugly ripping sound. Richo remembered to turn off the fuel before he staggered out. As an afterthought, when he was already walking away from the wreckage, giggling uncontrollably, he remembered his mother and turned back. Once he felt sure there wasn't going to be a fire he approached the plane again and saw that she was still sitting upright, still smiling.

It was the devil to get her out, because she was on the starboard side, nearest the ground, and Richo had to go in via the port door, which was way up high, and Aurelia was heavy. In the end he managed to pull her free just as the Jeep and the fire tender came wailing up. She had a bruised cheek, and her pantyhose were split, but she stared down the fire-crew with disdain before hobbling over to the Jeep and climbing into it without help from anyone.

'What did you do?' Aurelia enquired as the driver headed off back to the ranch house; and Richo giggled again. He explained about the dangers of the carburettor icing up and how he'd decided to chance it. Aurelia considered it for a moment. Then she said, 'You're a very dangerous boy,' and kissed her son full on the lips.

*   *   *

'Oh Jacqui, they're so *cute*!'

'Shh. You'll frighten them.'

The two girls crouched before the hutch, peering inside. The stable was dark but Jacqui had a flashlight and she shone it so that they could see into the nest, where five tiny rabbits, eyes closed, stretched and crawled and wriggled around in the straw.

The girls were fourteen, but Annette looked older. Willowy and tall, she had a tendency to hunch her shoulders, as if ashamed of her five feet eleven inches. She'd just come in from a hack through the forest: her jodhpurs and riding-boots were stained with mud, her white shirt, open at the neck, was streaked with sweat and oil from the reins. Although pale, she nevertheless had the air of a zestful, open-air adolescent with few hangups, whereas inside lived a girl with aspirations to streetwise cred, total veganism and sex at an early age.

The other child, Jacqui, was wide-eyed, innocent and serious. Like her sister she had green eyes, but there the resemblance ended. She was well tanned, from an outdoor, healthy life, and dark skinned from heredity. Shorter by a couple of inches than Annette, she lolloped contentedly through life without feeling a need to change most anything about herself; and in this lay the girls' greatest contrast.

'Good golly!' she said. 'Look at the black one.'

Annette pushed her aside impatiently and knelt down. 'Which?' she demanded to know. 'They're all black.'

'That one, there, on the left – he's moving like the starlight express.'

For a few moments longer the girls watched the rabbits crawl blindly around their hutch, while outside shadows lengthened over *Pinos Altos* as the sun went down behind Chieftain Dome, and night began to steal across the lake.

A darker, taller shadow than the rest stood out slightly from the gloom beside the stable-door, stood out enough to be perceived as human if the girls had noticed, but they did not.

'Come on,' Jacqui said, standing up. 'I don't want Flopsy to eat them.' (Flopsy was the rabbits' mother.)

'Would she do that?' Annette sounded interested, rather than aghast.

'She might. We have to leave them alone for a week or two more.' Jacqui looked at her sister. 'You won't tell *him*, will you?'

'About the bunnies? God, no. Are you crazy, or something?'

For a moment the only sound in the stable was of munching from one of the stalls, or the clop of a hoof as a horse moved around restlessly. Then Annette said, 'Richo tried again last night. He pounced when I was going back after chow. I'd left my Mace in the bedside drawer.'

The sisters eyed each other without speaking, while from the doorway the shadow that was human watched, and listened, and made its plan.

*   *   *

It was almost dark as Aurelia limped along the path that led upwards, through clumps of pine and fir, to Richo's cottage. Ahead of her she could see lights gleaming through shadows cast by the trees, and knew he was in.

She was carrying a plastic carrier-bag that wriggled. A present for her son. Something to cheer him up, after their accident in the plane.

The sandy path wound through the groves in a series of S-shaped bends. You couldn't see the main ranch house from 'Hansel', which was the name Richo had given his *casita*. (Hansel and Gretel: how he'd loved that story as a child!) It was the biggest of the guest-houses dotted through the grounds, but also the plainest. Its green and white board frontage heightened its resemblance to a barn. Only when you went inside and saw how opulent the furnishings were, only if you explored the gym and pool in the basement, the gun-room, only if you went upstairs and listened to the Bang & Olufsen sound system or watched one of the three TVs, did you realize that this was no ordinary weekend cottage.

Aurelia was panting slightly as she pounded the wrought-iron knocker. The recent plane-crash had left her more shaken than she cared to show. Bruises, she reflected, hurt in proportion to the age of the sufferer; what went unnoticed at thirteen could render you helpless at thirty-nine. She was glad when Richo opened the door quickly. Often he kept her waiting. Some days he wouldn't let her in at all.

'Hi, darling,' he said, standing aside. He was holding a tumbler but his breath smelled sweet when he kissed her and she could detect no sign of drunkenness. Scotch didn't affect him unless he finished off a half-bottle at a sitting, which made him violent.

'Do you want a drink?' he asked, as she walked through into the kitchen.

'A small one.'

The kitchen had the look of a TV studio set: everything freshly unwrapped. Indeed, to Aurelia's knowledge Richo had never used this room for its intended purpose, and why should he? If he wanted a cup of coffee he could go across to the main house and have someone make it. She sat down at the pine table and took a sip from the glass he gave her. Richo always poured liquor too strong, but this evening she felt like a drink.

'Naim says the plane was insured,' she said. '*Oh, la!* What a fuss! He wants to know if you're all right.'

She laid the plastic bag on the table. It stirred fitfully. Richo eyed it as he sat down opposite his mother, but made no comment, although his eyes had shrunk to two tiny blips of gunmetal.

'Tell him I want a Beech Starship as a replacement,' he said.

'I suppose that costs a million dollars, does it?'

'And the rest!' Richo wagged his forefinger at Aurelia and giggled. Even his mother disliked that loud falsetto giggle: *Ha! Ha! Ha! Ha! Ha!* 'Six million plus.'

'Forget it.'

'A Mooney Porsche, then.' Richo had turned sulky. 'I can't be expected to live without a plane, not out here in the boondocks.' He pronounced it 'bondocks', with an accent that was slightly but unmistakably 'foreign'.

'He'll buy you another Cessna. If you're lucky.'

Richo jumped up and began to pace the room. 'He's such a cheap bastard!' he shouted.

'He feeds us. After a fashion.'

My sweet, Aurelia thought, but you are lovely! Slim, athletic, muscular, with such wonderful *fesses*: no wonder the girls all die for you. And so handsome, with your Filipino blood and French genes . . . to be seventeen again, ah . . .

'He feeds us, yes, and I'm fed up. Ma . . . ' His voice turned wheedling; he came to snuggle up to Aurelia in the chair beside her. 'Ma, be good to me, take care of me, darling.' He nuzzled his mouth against her breast, and all the breath left Aurelia's throat in a sigh.

'Look,' she whispered, 'I've brought you a present.'

The plastic bag had been making eerie rustling noises. Now Aurelia picked it up and showed Richo what was inside.

'A rabbit,' he breathed. 'One of Jacqui's?'

'Yes.'

'Does she know?'

Aurelia merely laughed.

Richo delved into the bag and took out the rabbit. The creature was only a few days old: four inches long, black all over, and hairless. Its eyes were closed and it snuffled fitfully in the boy's hand. When he stroked the animal it jumped and uttered a tiny cry before settling back to sleep again.

'How long would it take to drown?' Richo asked.

'Three minutes. Fifty dollars say three minutes.'

'Two minutes. I'll see you and raise you another fifty.'

'All right. But no cheating.'

'Darling, would I ever cheat you?' Richo pursed his lips into a sexy moue and Aurelia kissed them.

They stood up and moved to the sink. Richo ran cold water into the plastic bag and watched it fill, while Aurelia set her watch. When the bag was bulging, Richo turned off the tap.

The rabbit lay at the bottom of the bag doing a tired crawl with all four legs. Its mouth wrinkled, as if it were about to sneeze. A small bubble of air came out of its mouth, another from its anus. It stopped moving for a while. Then it recommenced its weary struggle for life. Strange, Aurelia thought, how something so young, so ignorant of the agony of earthly existence, could nevertheless yearn to survive. It floated up to the surface and stayed there for a few seconds before sinking, helpless, although still it did not give up. More air bubbles escaped from its nose. Now its limbs were scarcely twitching. It rolled over and floated on its back, its little face twisted into a rictus of pain.

'One minute fifty,' Richo crowed. 'I win.'

The rabbit twitched. Its front legs swept sideways, it turned over and sank. Aurelia and Richo watched it anxiously, but the animal did not move again.

'You win, darling,' she murmured. 'As always. Here.' She took a hundred-dollar bill out of her purse. As she handed it to Richo he said, 'You let me win,' and for a horrid moment she thought there were going to be sulks. Her back ached, she was bruised and blistered, she could not face sulks tonight. But then Richo's face cleared; he threw his arms around Aurelia and pecked her cheek.

'Thanks for the rabbit,' he said. 'Will you tell Jacqui?'

Aurelia pretended to think. 'You should be the one to tell her,' she said. 'You can console her; that's what brothers are for.'

*   *   *

The following Friday turned out to be one of the few days in the year when Thelma could leave work early. She arrived home fired up with the intention of making over her entire wardrobe.

There was a problem about that. Kirsty, her sister, had a habit of filching Thelma's clothes – which fitted her, dammit – without prior authorization.

'Those white jeans are *mine*!' Kirsty screeched.

'Are not!'

'Are so!'

'Oh, give them here!' Thelma tugged vigorously on the right leg, while Kirsty hauled on the left. 'Do I have to sew a name-tag in everything I buy now?'

Kirsty released the jeans with a scowl. 'You'll be claiming that shirt, next.'

'I wouldn't be seen dead in that shirt.' Thelma held up the garment with a suspicious frown. 'You pig! This *is* my shirt. You dyed it *yellow*!'

'Did not!'

Thelma flung the shirt onto the floor of Kirsty's bedroom, close to tears. Was nothing sacred any more? She was about to rip into Kirsty when her sister said, 'Dad's coming around tonight. Wants to talk with Rachel.'

Thelma stared at her. 'Are you sure?'

Kirsty nodded. Thelma gnawed her lower lip. 'You going to be here?'

'I guess.'

Suddenly they were sitting together on the bed, their arms around each other.

'Staying in tonight?' Kirsty asked – not just a question, more of a request.

'Well . . . I don't think so.'

'Oh, Thelly . . . '

'Aarrgh.'

'Thelma.'

'That's better.' She hesitated. 'I'm not sure what I'll be doing tonight.'

They loved Roy as only daughters love their fathers, but there was a lot of not-very-luggable emotional baggage around and they still kept tripping over it.

'Hey,' Thelma said gently, 'time for the news. Let's go get some nachos, yeah?'

Kirsty nodded. They went downstairs together. Rachel was in the kitchen, preparing to boil lasagna-sheets. While Kirsty fixed the nachos, Thelma turned on the TV.

'Oh, my God!' she shrieked. 'It's my hero! My Brucie Willis on stilts!' She crossed both hands over her breasts and closed her eyes.

'It's who?' Rachel asked, puzzled.

'Daniel Krozgrow.'

'Crazy name, zany guy,' Kirsty observed.

'Ssh!' Thelma stuffed a hand over her sister's mouth. *'Listen!'*

The reporter was standing in front of a police van, Daniel by his side. Now the camera panned to take in a large crowd being kept at bay by blues. Waterfront, somewhere. Down on the beach, in the angle between a breakwater pier and the sand, it was just possible to see people bending over an object, and a man taking photographs with a huge camera on a tripod. Crime scene; Thelma knew a murder when she saw one.

'Oh, Jesus,' she breathed. 'Not again . . . '

'Nineteen-year-old Patty Ann King,' the reporter was saying, 'had no chance against a ruthless and calculating slayer who, police think, may have been tailing her for days as she worked the streets. Daniel Krozgrow, field profiler for the FBI, has more details. Daniel . . .'

'Normally we don't like to go public too early,' Daniel said, 'but the person who found Patty has already talked with TV and newspapers, and we think there's most to be gained by being open. She was killed with a knife, probably a butcher's knife, not much before dawn today. She'd been opened up, mutilated, by somebody with knowledge of surgery. Her kidneys and womb had been removed, and also her thumbs had been cut off. Beside the body was a sheet of paper with some writing; it's illiterate and we still have work to do deciphering it, but it seems pretty clear that this is the killer's signature – his calling-card, if you like.'

He went on to talk about similarities with the murders of Sam Brenton and Yolanda Kastin, but Thelma was no longer listening.

'Gotta go,' she announced, grabbing her purse. 'See you all later.'

'Oh, *Thelma*!' Kirsty wailed. 'You *promised*.'

'I never did. Give my . . . remember me to Dad.' On the step she paused. 'Sorry, kid,' she muttered to Kirsty. 'Make it up to you, but this is work. 'Bye.'

Because she felt guilty at abandoning them she slammed the porch door with quite unnecessary force.

*   *   *

'Put it on the table,' Daniel called, hearing someone knock on his door. 'Right there . . .'

Only when the expected cup of coffee failed to materialize did he glance up to find that Thelma had silently entered the office they'd temporarily assigned to him and was standing almost close enough to touch.

'Hi,' he said.

'Just thought I'd see if you needed anything.' His expression was puzzled, so Thelma blundered on, 'I saw you on TV earlier tonight. You were great. The way you handled those questions, boy! Whew!'

She'd had a lot of time to think, on the drive over; enough to realize that this was a dumb, dumb move for a smart woman to make. Too late now, though.

'Thanks. What I hope you did *not* see, or hear, is the statement made by the person who found the corpse. She was out at six a.m., exercising her spaniels called, and you're going to love this, Sprocket and Ball. Sprocket, normally an obedient hound, wouldn't come when she called. Seemed to be eating something. Guess what?'

'Oh, my God.'

'Nice juicy kidney. Left one, if you're interested. Owner of the dog could only fret about whether it might get sick.' Daniel shook his head. 'Some people . . . '

He pushed back from his computer and stood up with a yawn. 'I'm bushed. So tell me, what brings you here, really?'

'Um . . . going bowling with some of the boys in Robbery.'

Daniel took a vial of eye-drops from his pocket and refreshed his vision. 'Got time to walk to my car?'

'So how about the note?' Thelma asked as they went downstairs. 'The one you mentioned on the news?'

'Oh, that. Well, it was a sheet of Legal-sized paper and once, a long time ago, it had been stapled to something else by a pin that left traces of rust.'

'What did it say?'

'We haven't got every word yet, but broadly something like this: "I have got you jumping, I will see you do more, you will catch me if you rise from your bed early in the morning and go in search of the sign of P.B. Butcher esquire of Fountainside." Plus some stuff to suggest very strongly that there was another person involved, perhaps this Arthur character. Written in black ink, probably felt-tip, by a right-handed person keen to disguise his writing. That's as far as the Paradise Bay lab could take it. The paper's gone to Virginia, for full analysis.'

'Fountainside . . . what to make of that?'

'Well, it's given me an idea.'

'Yes?'

'But I don't want to talk about it just yet.'

They passed through the door to the parking-lot into a warm, moist evening, and walked towards Daniel's Carina. He got in and wound down the window. 'Oh, one other thing. Do you dye your hair?'

Thelma gazed at him, speechless. This was the loveliest, funniest, most lust-provoking law enforcement officer she'd ever met, but she couldn't always follow the way his mind worked.

'Reason I ask is that, according to the lab director, the card we found beside Sam Brenton had been in contact with high-concentration hydrogen peroxide.'

'Oh . . . bleaching. Hair-dye.'

'Right. So, are we looking for a hairdresser here? One called Arthur, perhaps? The problem is that every second household medicine chest contains hydrogen peroxide in some shape or form. The lab director said, and I quote: "Apart from being in common use as an antiseptic, it's also employed in the ageing of wine, dyes, electroplating, fat-refining, and how much more of this would you like to hear?"' Daniel laughed. 'Narrows it down, doesn't it? 'Night, Thelma.'

He reversed out of his slot and swung the Carina around, driving off with a wave. Thelma heaved a sigh and tried spinning her bag a revolution or three. Its engine didn't fire. Her fault. She should have said, Let's go to a motel and play a round of Who-can-get-undressed-fastest?

For a supposedly hot-shot psychologist, she was pretty damned insecure.

*   *   *

The file in front of Thelma was entitled 'State of Calif. -v- Richard Roe (Minor)', and it was a real bitch. She'd been brought in by the defence to testify, the trial had been set for the following week and she was nowhere near ready.

'Richard Roe': the pseudonym protected a thirteen-year-old boy who'd allegedly raped his classmate of twelve and then tried to strangle her. The defence was severe mental retardation. Two eminent psychiatrists were going to say that the kid was perfectly sane; Thelma's task was to counter that evidence, in conjunction with a psychiatrist she'd never worked with before.

Unfortunately, she agreed with the state. So did her team-mate, the psychiatrist.

Thelma pushed the folder away and stared at the filing-cabinets that lined the opposite wall. Pity Geoff Diamond was on vacation; her colleague had far more experience of defence work than she did, he might have come up with an idea or two . . .

Those filing-cabinets . . . they reminded her of jack-in-the-boxes. Who ever knew when some teenage villain was going to spring out, brandishing knife or gun? The line of thought led her straight to P.B. Butcher. She'd lay any money that somewhere, in someone's consulting-rooms, there was a filing-cabinet with Butcher in it. A folder, like Richard Roe's, with its anguished history of childhood abuse, deprivation and pain.

The office phone rang, bringing Thelma to her senses. Richard Roe was going to have to wait.

'They're here,' said the receptionist breathlessly. 'At least, the front part of the limo is, the back part's still coming around the block.'

Thelma grinned and went out into the corridor, ready to receive Richo Delacroix.

Thelma had devised a plan. She'd asked Aurelia to authorize Richo's attending group therapy. Aurelia, as anticipated, had indignantly refused, demanding Thelma give her word not to throw Richo in with other patients. Thelma's reply had been evasive.

Thelma knew Aurelia would send people to make sure her wishes were obeyed, but hadn't bargained on such grisly ones.

'Richo,' she said, holding out her hand. 'Hi. And these gentle-men are . . . ?'

'Manny and Frank. Say hello, guys.'

Four black-tinted lenses briefly swept Thelma for alien signs. She must have been okay, because they let her live. Thelma turned and led the way half a dozen paces down the passage, to a door marked Playroom.

'Now Richo, I want you to go in there for five minutes while your friends and I discuss the timetable.'

She was aware of unease, but whenever Thelma entered rocket-ship mode events tended to pass in a blur: before anyone quite knew it, Richo had entered the playroom, an attractive oriental girl sitting there reading a magazine had glanced up and smiled, 'Hi!', and Thelma was on her way back to her office, each hand firmly clasping a bulging, besuited bicep.

'My diary's in a tizz,' she said, as she closed the door of her office behind them. 'I was just going to have coffee.' She pointed out the flask. 'Join me?'

None of this was supposed to be happening. Manny and Frank looked at each other, while Thelma prattled on and served coffee. After five minutes it had been decided that the goons should return an hour and a quarter from now but be ready to wait, although Richo might be out early if the call came through and Thelma had to rush down to court, and was that clear because it would be no trouble to run through it again . . . ?

Thelma showed them out of her office and went back down the corridor to the practice's playroom, where young children received therapy. Her fingers were already on the handle when the door opened of its own accord and the oriental girl came out, Richo at her shoulder.

'Makiko, I'm truly sorry,' Thelma said, 'I wouldn't have had this happen for the world, but the court . . . ' She finished the sentence with a shrug and a smile.

'Of course, don't worry about it. Next week?'

'I'll call you.'

The girl treated Richo to a secretive smile, turned and walked up the corridor to where Richo's minders were still hanging around, talking in low voices. As the girl approached they fell silent. She was enough to silence the Wailing Wall: slim, but with an ass that flowed all the way down to the basement; svelte crimson dress belted at the waist, high heels, luscious tresses of thick black hair cascading to the small of her back. She daintily inserted herself between the orang-utans and was gone, although her presence somehow lingered.

'Let's get to work,' Thelma said briskly, escorting Richo into her office.

'It seems to me,' she said as she took her seat behind the desk, 'that a lot of your problems fall under the heading of cognition. You began life dyslexic, yes?'

He nodded. 'Not too serious.'

'But a cognitive defect nonetheless. More important, your social cognition isn't all that it should be. You have a depressingly negative sense of society in general and your role within it. Does that pluck a chord?'

'Sort of. I guess I don't care much about other people, is what you're saying.'

'Correct. You don't have to love your fellow men, but I want to bring you to a position where you can rub along with them. Is that a goal worth pursuing?'

'Yes.'

'Good. Now, I want you to take the Rorschach test.'

'Ink blots?'

'You look unhappy.'

'Isn't that all about . . . well, sex?'

'Partly. Let's face it, that's an area that needs work.'

Richo stared at Thelma. He had narrow, penetrating eyes. To her great annoyance, she blinked first.

'Diane did those tests already,' Richo declared.

'Rorschach? Are you sure?'

'I'm sure.' He paused. 'Dr Cheung was a very understanding woman.'

Looking at him, she saw he intended a double-meaning. What *had* gone on between those two . . . ?

'Well,' she said, 'I want you to take the test again.'

It took Richo a long time to go through all the shapes, but Thelma wasted scarcely a thought on his answers. She'd assess them later, cold, then ask her colleague, Geoff Diamond, to cross-analyse them. What troubled her was the absence of any record of a previous Rorschach test. It should have been in his file. Why wasn't it . . . ?

Every so often he would look up and subject her to a level, hostile stare. Thelma wondered uneasily what thoughts were distilling in that frothy vat of a brain. Nothing good. Nothing beneficial to *her*.

'Two old men,' Richo murmured. 'Holding canes.'

That was the last set. Thelma made a note on her pad. 'Remind me: you attend school during the week, right? I mean, you sleep over?'

'Yes.'

'But at weekends, you come home.'

He nodded.

'Ever go down to LA, or take off somewhere at the weekend?'

He hesitated, obviously reluctant to answer. 'Sometimes.'

'Ever play hooky?'

'Why?'

'I'm concerned by any break in your schooling.'

Richo frowned. Then he said, 'Look, if I tell you something, can you keep it to yourself? Can you not tell Dad?'

'You're my client, you're entitled to confidentiality. Didn't Diane tell you that?'

'Yes. But you're not Diane.'

'Tell me anything you want to.'

'Sometimes I . . . I can't stand it any more. I take off, go my own way for a while. At Sacré Coeur, they're just great about it. They don't always even tell my parents.'

'I see. When was the last time this happened?'

'I went down to Mexico City on January 25, with a couple of the guys from school. That's my birthday. The others went home pretty quick.' He chewed his lips. 'Me, I stayed a couple of weeks.'

'Ouch. You spent your birthday away from home, then?'

'Oh, yeah, right, you want me to stay home with the cake and the candles?' Richo grunted contemptuously. 'You should come up to the ranch sometime, and take a look. You should.'

'What did your folks say?'

'Mom knew where I was. Father, no. And *please* don't tell him – he'd flay me and slay me.'

'Richo, I've guaranteed you your confidentiality, but we're going to have to do serious work on this. Not wanting to spend your birthday at home is something a lot of teens might go along with, but school truancy is the worst thing for you at present. Are you going to cooperate with me?'

'I guess.'

'Well then, we'll meet again next week. And see you come, all right?'

He nodded and rose. At the door he turned. 'Hey. Mother asked me to give you this.'

Thelma looked up to see him holding out an envelope. There was something familiar about it. Ah . . . another of Aurelia's letters.

'She's been writing,' Richo observed. 'She loves it.' His lips widened in a slow, suggestive smile. 'Me, I prefer doing.'

Thelma ushered her client out, to find his stooges wandering about in the corridor like disconsolate lost souls. Catching sight of Richo their faces brightened; Thelma wondered how much longer they'd have given it before bursting in to break both her arms.

'Until next week,' she called after them.

Thelma went back inside her office and sat down before her computer. She was halfway through writing up her notes of the session when she heard a discreet tap at her door, and Makiko peeked around it.

'How did I do?'

'Just fine. What did he say?'

'He asked me for a date.'

'And you said yes?'

'Mm-hm.' Makiko's face broke into a grin. 'He said he was smitten with me. Nobody's ever said that before.'

'Deary, that one is smitten with every girl he meets.'

'Oh. Feel like letting me in on the secret now?'

'No, I don't think so. Just don't get too excited about the date, okay? It won't happen.'

Makiko's face showed disappointment. 'Why not?'

'Would I ever let one of my psychology students date a patient? Now fetch my notes on Teddy Brexton, he's due any minute.'

*   *   *

That evening, Thelma took work home. Her family were used to seeing papers spread out over the kitchen table, and they never pried; but Thelma still waited for the house to bed itself down before opening Aurelia's latest missive.

The same clear, round handwriting, with its big, well-formed letters.

Erasmus, the family's rotund marmalade cat, stalked across to settle on Richo's file. He folded his paws beneath his chest and gazed benignly at Thelma. He had a runny nose. Thelma began to read, every so often conscious of the drip of cat catarrh onto Aurelia's life-history.

Madame, what happened to trigger my anxiety was this. Naim went away, and for once he was careless. In the old days it would never have happened, but Naim isn't the man he was. He left a brochure in the secret drawer of his desk: a secret I long ago discovered. This brochure advertised the sale of our ranch, Pinos Altos, and was accompanied by a letter from a realtor. I understood that Naim intended to sell, but, to put the matter beyond doubt, I phoned the agent and, masquerading as Naim's secretary, went through the terms. Naim had dealt on the basis that he would be emigrating permanently to the Philippines, with his children. No mention of a wife. No mention of a chief of staff called Shimon Waldman. Indeed, when I mentioned Shimon's name the agent became evasive. Eventually he admitted that Naim had warned him against accepting instructions from anybody except himself, but that he was to be particularly vigilant against one Shimon Waldman, who might seek to intervene in the sale.

I'm sorry. Sometimes it's hard for me to remember that you don't know. How much you don't know. This happened in February, I should have said.

We began to put two and two together, Shimon and I. We, all of us, were resident in the States under limited visas. No green cards for us! Our time was fast running out. What we needed were the facts. Shimon and I combed Naim's networks in search of clues. Nobody was talking, however hard we pushed. In the end, one person did crack: an old friend of Shimon's who went back to his time in the Israeli Defence Force. By then it was only a matter of obtaining confirmation of our worst fears, and this friend supplied it. Naim had let it be known that he was retiring. He wished to place one final contract. Two deaths, to look like accidents. One man. One woman.

My first thought was of Richo, my son. A word here, Madame. My own life I have always regarded as cheap. Human life is cheap. There are too many people in the world. No one would care if most of them were wiped out tomorrow. I should not care if I were to die today. But Richo was different. I'd fucked him into existence through an intense desire, not for the father whose duty it was merely to supply sperm, but for the destruction of that father. He was mine, however, and I loved him, even though I realized by then how imperfect he was. He was my child, Madame. My flesh, my blood. I couldn't leave him at Naim's mercy.

You understand what would have happened if I'd simply left Naim? (Last time, you seemed to think that was such an easy way out!) Because he'd never treated me with less than respect in front of his friends or his servants, I knew I'd have been allowed to call for the car, to travel to the airport, to purchase a ticket. Richo is seventeen, he'd have had to stay if Naim insisted – and he would. But afterwards, Madame, afterwards I could never have slept a night without fear. For the rest of my life I'd have been on the run. And it was then that I realized the hideous nature of the trap into which I'd let myself fall.

You see, in the eyes of the law I am Naim's accomplice. The only reason why I know so much about him is that for the past twenty or so years I've connived in everything he's done. Search the record: you'll find my fingerprints on every page. I can bring him down, yes, but only at the cost of my own freedom. I'd rather die than face a long prison sentence.

Somehow I had to find a way of placing Richo beyond Naim's reach – that was, and it remains, my only goal. At first, Diane Cheung had protected us. She'd laid down the law to Naim, and he'd accepted her judgement. Until, that is, she abandoned us . . . but fortunately left you to take her place.

I sought, and obtained, Naim's permission for Richo to consult you in succession to Dr Cheung. Marion Lomar, his school principal, supported me. Whatever is for Richo's benefit is authorized, Naim loves the boy, and so grudgingly he agreed. <u>But you are our last hope!</u>

You cannot imagine the life I've led. Don't try. But imagine, if you will, that moment in Paris, so many years ago now, when my course was set . . .

Thelma shuffled through the papers once, twice, a third time. It was all such a mystery! So many references to things that made no sense, but with all of which Aurelia assumed she'd be familiar. She began to leaf through more carefully, counting off the puzzles.

Naim told the agent he was going to the Philippines with his *children*, plural. Yet he had only one child, Richo.

Shimon had been in the Israeli Defence Force? Good grief!

Naim was putting out a contract on the lives of Aurelia and Shimon. *Gulp!*

Aurelia had 'fucked Richo into existence' so as to destroy Naim. Apart from the horror of that odious formulation, *why*, for God's sake?!

What *was* that 'moment in Paris' Aurelia referred to?

Accomplice . . . prison? *Why?*

Before very long, Thelma was giggling. She couldn't help it. Aurelia's account of herself, with its roots in Algeria and Paris, had begun by beguiling her and ended by making her hoot with derisory laughter.

The woman was loopy. No wonder Richo had problems!

Thelma was still laughing when there came a knock at the front door, and Rufus, the Vestreys' American cocker spaniel, went berserk. The honey-coloured dog barked so loud he seemed to bounce up and down on his short, feathered legs, and Thelma's laughter became a frown: she was hardly expecting anyone to come to the house at eleven o'clock at night.

'Daniel!' she cried, happy to see him. 'What brings you out here?'

Erasmus shot through the door, much to the dog's fury.

'Down, Rufy-baby, down, boy.'

'Need. For sympathy, maybe tea, a shot of love in the arm. Hi, doggy, what's your name?'

'Oh, that's Rufus. Rufe. Push him down, do. No tea, unlimited love; how about ice-cold Chardonnay?'

'I guess that will have to do. Listen, am I disturbing the family?'

'Uh-uh. Mom's taking an early night, Kirsty's out on the town. And I've been . . . well, see for yourself.'

He came into the kitchen with her and sat down at one end of the table, looking flaked. Thelma handed him Aurelia's latest outpouring and went to fetch a flagon of white wine from the fridge. 'Crap day?' she asked.

'Yup.' He looked up from the letter. 'This stuff is amazing!'

'Far out, huh?'

He finished the last page and gave the letter back to her, shaking his head in disbelief. 'Wanting a child so as to destroy its father . . . What does Richo say about his father?'

'Nothing too bad.'

'Well, his mother needs a shrink.'

'And you need a drink. Listen, I don't know if I'm stepping out of line, asking this, but is there any chance you could run a Fed check against Delacroix?'

'Sure. I agree, it needs to be done. First thing tomorrow.'

'Thanks. Listen, forget the Delacroixs, I'm really pleased you felt able to come by. I needed taking out of myself this evening.'

'Thanks. I should have phoned first, but . . . I want some advice.'

Thelma sat down and took a sip of wine. 'Shoot.'

But for a while he said nothing, and Rufus came to put his head in Daniel's lap, allowing him to fondle the roots of his ears. Rufus didn't allow just anyone to do that. He was a spunky spaniel, and he knew who he liked – knew who Thelma liked, too.

'The latest corpse . . . ' Daniel began.

'Same perp?'

'I think so. Unless it's like a virus and everyone's going down with it: "Hey, Ma, guess what, Johnny next door's a serial killer and I never catch anything and stay away from school, waaaa . . . "'

'Drink your wine, Daniel.'

They laughed, and drank.

'Forensic cleared Xeres, like I thought they would,' Dan said. 'Nothing to hold him on.'

'So that leaves you with what?'

'Not much. Reason I came out here, actually, was to run something past you. It's off the wall, though. I believe this P.B. Butcher is going to strike again.'

'His note, the one you described, did suggest that. Incidentally, what's this thing with fingers and thumbs?'

'I don't know. One thumb he takes, one he leaves. Three times now. No pattern on the fingers. Ah . . . Thelma.'

'Yup?'

'Do you remember me telling you I had an idea. It was that evening you – '

'The Butcher's note said something about Fountainside; you said that gave you an idea.'

'That's right.' Dan looked around him, anywhere but at Thelma, seemingly reluctant to come to the point. 'We're going to put policewomen on the streets of Fountainside,' he said at last.

'As bait?'

'As bait.'

'It's a bad idea, and you'll regret it.'

'Why do you say that? Apart from the obvious fact you're a woman and the notion outrages you?'

'Dan, think.' Thelma took a risk: she clasped his hands between hers and chafed them gently. 'These women have names. Perhaps husbands, babies, parents. If anything were to happen, what words would you use to those men, those children?'

What will you do if I kiss your hands, Dan?

'It's better to go on the streets with an experienced, tough professional, ready for trouble, than to hope the computer will net us our man once he's cut a swathe through enough victims to provide the data.' The words came out all confident, but Dan rather spoiled it by adding, 'Don't you think so?'

Thelma didn't mean them to quarrel. Daniel needed her support, trust and love. 'You want to nail this guy,' she said. 'Don't you?'

'More than sex. More than love. More than Hilary wants Bill to run for a second term.'

If that is what you want, then you must have it.

'All right. If you insist on putting these girls on the streets, they'll need support and counselling. I can take care of that. By going out with them I'll show – '

'Hey, wait a minute! No way are you going anywhere with them.'

'And why not?' she bridled. 'I've been cleared for Special Force work.'

'Oh, come *on*!'

'Aren't I pretty enough to be on your damn team, or some-thing?' Thelma wailed.

'You know how pretty you are.'

As he said that he stopped laughing, his eyes closed on hers, and she divined that for the first time he was seeing her as a woman, a possible mate. Her blood turned to champagne in her veins, she felt dizzy. But then his eyes unfocused and he said, 'Too pretty to risk spoiling.'

He cares about you. He'd only let you go on the streets if he didn't care about you. Don't blow this. Stay . . . silent.

Daniel stood up and reached for his jacket. 'I've disturbed you long enough,' he murmured.

How true!

'Tell you what,' he went on; 'I'll have you counsel the girls next day. If they want. Okay?'

'Let me think about it. I'll call you.'

'Thelma – '

'I'll *call* you.'

Dan looked at her face and realized his time was up. 'Thanks for the drink,' he said. 'I really owe you for that. And I certainly didn't mean to belittle your Special Force achievement.'

'You didn't. And it's me that owes you, for coming.'

At the front door, Erasmus was waiting to be let in. He intro-duced himself between Thelma and Daniel, slithering around their legs like a furry, amber serpent.

'Where have *you* been?' Thelma demanded, as the cat smooched inside to look for food, under the outraged but thoroughly intimidated nose of Rufus.

'Working on that ninth life, by the look of him.' Daniel sighed. 'See you,' he murmured over his shoulder as he walked down the porch steps. 'I'll think about what you said. But, Thelma – no way are you going on the streets with the girls. Believe it.'

*   *   *

It was eleven o'clock in the morning. Richo should have been at school, but Thelma was coming to interview him so he'd stayed home.

He loaded WordPerfect into his Dell 486 computer and retrieved a file entitled 'Fucks'. He went to the end of the document and considered the last paragraph.

I could see how much she fancied me. She went into the toilet. I followed. The toilet was empty. She waited until I came in, then smiled a lovely big smile and went into the last little room. By the time I got there she had her skirt up around her waist. She was wearing leather panties, with a hole where her hole was. Her hair down there was blonde, like her head.

As a story it had real potential, but he didn't know where to take it. What came next? Should he take out his knife and cut up those hide panties? Or should he jerk off over her shoes while he bit her nipples until they bled?

If he could make a really good story out of it, he'd put it on the Internet. Each time he'd done that, the screen had lit up. People wanted sex, but sex meant AIDS and death, so it was better to do your screwing in your head and in your hand. People wanted to read about sex *and pain*. An orgasm had to hurt – if not you, then at least one other participant.

I walked up to her. I closed the door behind me first. I cupped my hand and laid it over her pussy so that my middle finger could slip up. She grinned at me. Then I started to pull out her hairs, one by one, and when she started to scream I

Richo jumped up and began to prowl around.

The bed took up a lot of space, but the room was big and it had two large windows overlooking the airstrip, behind his *casita*. Above the bed hung a huge laminated photograph of the cockpit of a Boeing 747–400. There were three filing-cabinets, mostly full of pornographic literature and videos, which he kept locked until the evening, when he lay in bed and masturbated while the video-player unwound an endless ribbon of sex onto the ceiling above his head. Just about everything else in here related to scuba-diving or flying. He kept his tanks by the bed, for security's sake, and his regulator he kept *under* the bed. Somebody who saw it (no one came into this room, but why take chances?) might be tempted to put it in his mouth, giving rise to risk of AIDS, one of Richo's obsessions. Drinking in bars had become a nightmare, because bartenders never soaked the glasses in Milton.

A searing pain erupted deep inside his right ear, and Richo swore. He'd gone diving in the *Pinos Altos* lake yesterday and come up too fast, and his ears had been playing hell ever since. Plus he was getting a cold. Catarrh wheezed and hissed through the cavities of his skull. He put a few more ear-drops in and stood with his head on one side for several minutes, before rinsing the mess away. The pain hadn't gone, though. He'd have to stay out of the water. *Shit!*

Slowly the pain subsided. Richo threw himself down on the bed and looked at his Patek Philippe watch, enjoying the way the morning light played across its diamonds. He could stare at this watch for hours. It had been a present from his doting father on his seventeenth birthday. There was something hypnotic about all those stones, all that gold.

Thelma Vestrey was coming to see him.

Naim had hit the roof over him wanting to date that Japanese cow Makiko. Daddy-Darling – always the fucking, fucking, *fucking* same . . .

Where was Thelma?

She was late.

He would have to punish her.

*   *   *

US Express delivered Thelma to Kern County Airport, where she was met by a taciturn Filipino who introduced himself as Gerry, her pilot for the onward leg. Gerry chain-smoked Winstons throughout the flight, driving Thelma wild. Like many ex-smokers she had become the kind of fanatical convert to healthy living that, in a religious context, must have powered the Spanish Inquisition. Gerry either didn't notice her indignation, or didn't care.

The elderly Cessna 414 flew east for half an hour before banking around a large, domed rock and giving Thelma her first view of *Pinos Altos*.

It was a magnificent spread. They'd been flying over hostile terrain: river gorges, granite outcrops, snow-filled cols, and now suddenly here was prosperity and spring. The ranch lay nestled in the shelter of a mountain, with a sweep of meadowland separating it from a lake of olive green water. From the cockpit Thelma could see hundreds of well-fed cattle roaming across slopes of lush grass. There were horses, too, corralled near the house, which was a two-storey stone and wood building of recent construction. Several four-wheel-drive vehicles were drawn up beside the house, and Thelma could see sandy tracks leading off into groves of pine and sequoia, where other, smaller houses peeped tantalizingly through the foliage.

Gerry executed a soft landing. 'Isn't there a road to the ranch?' Thelma asked, as they taxied.

'There's a road up from Kernville, but nobody ploughs it in winter, so it don't open till about now.'

Gerry helped her board a Jeep Cherokee parked next to the hangar. As they drove off Thelma caught sight of a fence, running alongside the airstrip. It was about fifteen feet high, steel mesh, with outward-facing barbed wire strung along the top. Every few hundred yards was a pole taller than the rest, with something perched on it. At first Thelma mistook these black objects for birds' nests. Then she realized: they were TV cameras.

Gerry crossed the runway at the end nearest the ranch, turning away from the fence. Two men were walking along it. One of them held a German Shepherd on a leash. Both had things slung over their shoulders, and somehow they didn't look like walking-sticks. Thelma continued her journey in a thoughtful frame of mind.

Until now she'd been congratulating herself on the success of her plan – that ploy with Makiko. Everything she'd learned about Naim Delacroix from Richo suggested that he wouldn't allow his son to be distracted by the company of strange women. Therefore, once he learned from his goons that her office might not be a 'clean' environment there was a good chance of him insisting on future sessions taking place at home. And so it had come to pass. Now, however, seeing those armed guards, Thelma felt glad that she'd told a colleague at St Joe's where she was going and how long she planned to be away.

The Jeep climbed a curving road to the front of the house. She noticed a swimming-pool on a lower terrace, and a Jacuzzi, although at this altitude the May air was still too cold for outdoor sports. Then the Cherokee was pulling up outside the house, a white-coated steward was coming forward, and Thelma realized with a start that Shimon Waldman also stood at the top of the steps, hand outstretched in welcome.

'So,' he said as she joined him, 'what do you think?'

The panorama spread out below was captivating. Beyond the lake towered the mountain around which their Cessna had flown moments before; Shimon told her it was called Chieftain Dome.

'How big is this place?'

'Two thousand plus acres. Only this inner portion – ' he sketched a circle with his hand – 'is cultivated. All around, as far as you can see, is a ring of forest, rock and ravine. It's a fortress. It was designed that way.'

Thelma tore her eyes away from the glorious prospect. 'Why?'

'The man who carved this out from the wilderness was a hermit. Over there, see . . . '

He pointed to the left. Thelma looked across a stretch of scrub to where soft hills began to rear up towards a sky flaked with puffy white clouds. So much empty space! A friend of hers had a series of water-colours painted in lowland Scotland, and many of them were like this – the loch, the moor – but what did Shimon mean her to see?

'That hut's where he lived.'

Thelma strove to catch a glimpse of it, but in vain. 'It's beautiful,' she breathed. 'You're all so lucky, living here.'

'You think so, do you?'

Not Shimon's voice . . . Thelma turned around to find herself confronted by a new presence.

A man of about her own height, perhaps an inch shorter, had come soundlessly to stand at her shoulder. He was of medium build, a little stocky, and her immediate impression was of mustards and browns. His face was the same dark colour as Gerry's, a Filipino complexion, and he wore tan pants over old-fashioned English brogues, polished the colour of an oak pew, with a V-necked yellow sweater and nondescript woollen tie. His head reminded her of an Egyptian pyramid with its pinnacle sawn off: fleshy neck, tapering skull, short black hair. Every bristle of his thin moustache had been trimmed to the same length – it might almost have been false, designed for him by a theatrical dresser.

He examined her through two dead eyes, two gaps in his skull where most people kept their humanity.

'How do you do?' he said softly, holding out his right hand. 'Naim Delacroix.'

He was sliding his hand into hers before Thelma could react, and she wanted to recoil from its sybaritic softness, its promise of perfumed gardens and easy living, but he was her host, she needed to assess him, and besides, he would not let her go. She felt as the lamb feels when the python coils around it: too late . . .

Beware, baby, beware. Those cryptic words noted by Diane Cheung in Richo's file came back to haunt Thelma. Too late, too late . . .

When Delacroix finally released her hand and stepped back a pace, still without smiling, she saw that he walked with the aid of a thick cane topped by a silver knob the size of a baseball. He held his right arm across his chest, indicating the front door.

'Thank you,' Thelma said brightly.

She took her first step inside the house. The steward, who had been hovering in the background, closed the big studded door with a 'boom!' that echoed. There was no sunlight here in the hall. Naim led the way across a marble expanse the size of the floor-plan of her own house, around a gross fountain on which half a dozen naked stone women writhed like eels, and through double-doors into what must be his study.

Here, at least, there was light, and some sense of normality: no fountains, no marble, just a large kneehole desk, telephones, a fax machine, several paintings, a fireplace, thick carpet, and sensible if well-padded chairs. The room was about thirty feet square, overlooking the pool-terrace, with a distant view of mountains beyond.

Money everywhere she looked, Thelma reflected as she took her seat; nothing ostentatious, but it was there, like air-freshener or white noise.

Her eyes were drawn to a magnificent wooden stand in one

corner of the vast window, on which was arrayed a tapestry. Naim noticed.

'My wife's handiwork,' he said. 'It took her four years. Look, if you want.'

As Thelma rose she couldn't be sure whether he felt pride in Aurelia's achievement, or if it bored him, or if he merely wanted a chance to look at her legs. His voice tended to put stress in the wrong places; that, coupled with a faintly oriental accent, made him seem all the more foreign.

The tapestry portrayed a palatial wooden house set against a tropical landscape. It was an extraordinary creation: more like a brilliant colour photograph than a work of art. This effect lay in the detail: Aurelia must have used an incredibly fine needle. Goodness knows how her eyesight could stand it.

Thelma approached and bent closer. Every minute stitch was the same size, completely flat. Four years seemed too short a time to produce such a masterpiece. As she returned to her seat she wondered about the sort of mind that could devote itself, day in day out, hour after hour, to the manifestation of such detail.

'It's beautiful,' she observed.

'The beach at Talipanan.'

'Where?'

'Talipanan is a beach on the northern tip of Oriental Mindoro, in the Philippines. My home place.'

'The house, it's yours?'

'It's mine. It took two years to build and cost me two million eight hundred thousand American dollars.'

'Do you go there often?'

'Whenever I can. Not as frequently as I'd wish.'

'And Aurelia did a tapestry of it.'

'Yes. The needle is her only pastime. Apart from flowers.'

Silence fell. Time hung suspended in this room. It was as if whoever entered it became stuck at that precise moment of history. It put Thelma in mind of a spider's web.

'Mr Delacroix,' she said, determined to get things moving, 'I want to ask you a few questions about your son. First, home environment. I can't help noticing that this is a somewhat out-of-the-way spot for a young – '

Naim had been sitting with his hands resting on the blotter. Now he slowly raised his left forearm, palm towards her. Thelma faltered, stopped.

'Dr Vestrey,' he said, 'how young are you?'

Thelma gaped. 'I'm sorry?'

'When a Filipino asks a person's age, he puts it that way to be polite: how young are you?'

'I'm twenty-eight. Although I don't – '

'We need to consider your place.'

She stared at him, speechless.

'Few people set foot inside *Pinos Altos*.' Naim drew a little breath and expelled it from deep inside his chest: a sigh of resignation. 'Perhaps you think that is wrong. And perhaps you have a point. But this is my house. And you are very young.' He turned his upraised forearm, bending the hand until its fingers pointed towards himself. 'And we are discussing *my* son, my only son, whom I love to . . . to distraction. Who fills me with care and concern, and because of that, *only* because of that, you've been allowed to visit. You're my guest. As such, you'll respect the rules of my household.'

He paused, but Thelma knew he hadn't finished – she was already used to his habit of constructing his sentences in disjointed phrases. His eyes blinked a couple of times. He lowered his arm. He said, 'Your predecessor, Dr Cheung, understood the rules very well. I expect you to understand them. And you'll observe the utmost confidentiality with regard to my affairs.'

'Of course. Look, Mr Delacroix, young or no, I'm not accustomed to having my professional discretion questioned.' Guilty memories of what she'd already shared with Daniel flitted through her mind; she pushed on hurriedly. 'There are certain standards of parenting that I require and I've some ground rules of my own.'

But it was as if she hadn't spoken. 'People do not talk about my affairs,' Naim said. 'Whether they are . . . professional, or not. They come, if they must, and do what they have to. They go away. And then . . . ' He stood up. He waddled around the desk, leaning on his cane, and for the first time Thelma noticed how pronounced his limp was. He came up to her chair. He inclined his head, slowly, until he could look into her eyes. ' . . . then they forget.'

*   *   *

Richo took one look at Thelma's face and said, 'You've been talking with my father.'

She stood on the step of his *casita*, with Gerry in the background at the wheel of a Jeep, but Richo had no eyes for him. He reached out a trembling hand and drew Thelma inside, closing the front door behind her. 'Come and sit down, I know how he is, come . . . '

To her surprise he bypassed the living-room that she could see through a door off the hallway and pulled her towards the stairs.

'Hey, now wait a minute!'

Richo turned and, with an impatient frown, shook his head. He mimed somebody putting on headphones and adjusting dials, then pointed to the living-room. Thelma, shaken, allowed herself to be escorted upstairs to the threshold of Richo's bedroom.

'Your father listens in on your conversations?' she asked incredulously.

'You bet he does.' Richo indicated that Thelma should take his desk-chair. 'Come in.'

'No, thanks.'

She glared at Richo, insulted that he should think she'd fall for such a cheap trick. From the way his face fell she knew he too was remembering their last but one session together, when he'd kissed her and been struck for his insolence.

'I'm so sorry,' he said in a low voice. 'What I did, that was, y'know, gross, I . . . I really am sorry.'

He looked at the floor. Then she became aware of him peering up at her through his long, girlish eye-lashes, and he was so like a puppy that had been beaten for wetting the floor that Thelma half forgave him.

'Please,' he said humbly. 'Come in. Sit.'

Thelma did so, after a pause. Richo sat cross-legged on the floor in front of her. 'The bugs are in the phones downstairs,' he said, eager to change the subject. 'But I bought a device and had this room swept, and it's clean.'

Thelma puffed out a sigh. 'What a setup!'

'Please say that again.' Richo was staring at her, his face twisted into an anxious expression. 'I went diving yesterday, my ears are bad.'

'I said: "What a setup," that's all. I've never come across a family like yours. It's hardly usual to live like this, is it?'

Richo shrugged. 'What's usual?'

Good question, she mused. How should this boy know about 'usual' when his mother gave every appearance of being mad, and his father could find film-work as a psychopath anytime?

'So,' she said, 'this is where you live. Nice room.'

'Thank you. Here, let me show you . . . '

He jumped up and took her hand, as naturally as a toddler might. He began to lead her around. She stopped by the book-case.

'You have a lot of books . . . diving, these are all about diving?'

'Yes.' But the smile had gone, he seemed nervous. He dropped her hand. 'Come on, let me show you my gear . . . '

She lagged behind him long enough to pick up a flight textbook: *Instrument Rating Manual*, published by Jeppesen Sanderson. She flicked it open.

'Put that down!' Thelma looked up, shocked, as Richo dashed the book from her hands. He slammed it shut. For a few seconds he stood in front of her, distraught; then he recovered. 'I'm sorry,' he muttered. 'Only . . . only I don't like it when people touch my things, I . . . '

Thelma wanted to ask why he'd gone to the trouble of having his basic flying manual bound up in the cover of an Instrument Rating textbook, but she hesitated to push him too far. Anyway, she was pretty sure she knew. *Vanity.*

If no one except Aurelia ever came here, why bother to be vain?

'How long have you had your pilot's certificate?' she asked.

'Four months.'

'How many hours is that?'

'Oh . . . a hundred, I guess. I'd have to look in . . . '

In my logbook, she completed his sentence in her mind; *and I won't show it to you.*

'I saw horses. Do you ride?'

'Nah! I don't like.' Richo shook his head dismissively. 'Horses bite, they kick.'

'There are horses in the Philippines.'

He looked at Thelma as if she'd gone mad. 'What?'

Damn! Always this problem of not knowing how much Aurelia had told Richo . . .

'I thought perhaps you might all go to live there one day?' she improvised hastily.

'You're kidding, right?' Richo wagged his finger at her and uttered his stagy giggle, *Ha! Ha! Ha! Ha! Ha!* 'What would we want to do a thing like that for?'

Thelma smiled a placatory smile. 'You'll be living here for the foreseeable future, then?'

'You bet.' Richo shrugged irritably. 'Jeezus . . . Talipanan. I'd rather die.'

'But your residence permit expires very soon. Didn't you know that?'

He hurried over to his desk and rummaged in a drawer. By the time she joined him he was staring at his passport, open at the American visa, with a puzzled expression on his face. 'But . . . this is just weeks away?'

'Yes.'

Near to the visa was a blue stamp, indicating that Richo had entered Mexico on January 25, his birthday. Next to it was a red exit stamp, dated a fortnight later.

'I don't . . . I must talk with my father,' he said, before putting the passport back in its drawer. 'I think he . . . I . . . '

But then, inexplicably and on the instant, his mood changed. His vacant eyes flashed with life. 'Hey, look!' he cried, pointing through the window. 'They're getting the boat out. Do you water-ski? *I* do. Come join me.'

He danced away, amazing her with his litheness, making for the closets that lined one wall. He started tossing clothes about. 'Here,' he cried, holding aloft a pair of psychedelic Bermuda shorts, 'they suit me, no?'

He ripped his shirt off, folding his muscular arms across his waist and lifting the hem, so letting Thelma see his concave stomach and hard pectorals. 'Ricardo!' she shouted. 'We're not going on the lake!'

He unloosed the cord that held up his pants. They floated down to the floor. His legs were two sturdy, tanned pillars of muscle and sinew, and he wore only a tanga beneath.

Thelma strode towards the bedroom door.

'Dr Vestrey! Dr Vestrey!'

Safely through the door, she stopped and turned. Richo was holding the Bermudas in front of him, for all the world like a virgin caught unawares. 'You didn't think . . . ?' His face was pale, surely he couldn't be faking embarrassment, *surely* . . .

Richo backed away from her until he could go no further. 'I would not have insulted your modesty,' he said in a low voice. 'You're making a mistake if you think that. Please. Close the door.'

Thelma went downstairs and waited outside, wondering what she ought to do. Gerry and the Jeep had disappeared. There was a plane from Bakersfield to Paradise Bay at three p.m., but since her arrival nobody had talked about getting her to the airport.

The door of the *casita* opened and Richo came out. He'd put his shirt back on over the Bermudas, and had folded his arms tightly across his chest, as if afraid the wind might cause it to flap and, horror of horrors! reveal flesh.

'I'll drive you back to the house,' he muttered, and disappeared around the side of the *casita*. A moment later he came back at the wheel of one of the ubiquitous Jeeps. Thelma got into the passenger seat without looking at him, and they drove off through the pines.

'I was hoping we'd get some serious work done today,' she said. 'As it is, you've wasted my time. Please tell your mother, I need to speak with her if there's to be the faintest chance of this therapy continuing, all right?'

'Yes.'

For a while they drove on in silence. Then Richo said, 'Do you live in Paradise Bay?'

'Nearby.'

'There were some murders there.'

'Yes.'

'Young men. In Court Ridge Cemetery.'

Thelma couldn't resist glancing at him. When he'd mentioned murders her mind had automatically turned to the most recent victims: Kastin, Brenton and Patty Ann King. Why was he interested in the *old* murders?

Her mind went back to the handover by Diane Cheung, when certain files referred to in other files couldn't be found. Diane had explained vaguely that the missing dockets related to the Court Ridge murders and had been impounded by the court . . .

'How do you know about those?' she asked.

'I remember hearing something about them on TV.'

'When?'

Richo merely shrugged. 'Please don't mention to my father what happened just now. Look, he's waiting . . . '

They had nearly reached the top of the drive. Naim stood there, resting on his cane. Gerry came up to change places with Richo in the driver's seat, while his employer hobbled to Thelma's side of the Jeep.

'Well, you've seen us.' Naim allowed a little of his contempt to show. 'And boring you found us, no doubt. Future sessions with my son will take place here.'

'That'll work out expensive for you.'

Naim shrugged, and this time the contempt was all there, up front. But then a thought struck Thelma, and she quickly added: 'The treatment's going to extend over quite a few months. I take it Richo'll be available until . . . oh, the end of the year?'

'As long as is needed.'

Well, that was clear enough! So much for emigration.

'That's always assuming I decide to continue,' Thelma said. 'I've barely had a chance to assess Ricardo's home circumstances. I hope to spend more time with you later, Mr Delacroix. Whether this therapy continues or not rests solely with your decision on how far you're prepared to cooperate with me and my methods. Good afternoon.'

Naim nodded at Gerry, without deigning to answer, and as the Cherokee accelerated Thelma mentally consigned the Delacroix household to hell: Naim, Aurelia, their wayward, sexy offspring, guards, German Shepherds, wire fences, the lot.

She was, she realized, much less interested in Richo as a patient than as the bizarre by-product of a weird marriage. And it was becoming increasingly clear that the key to the whole mystery lay with Aurelia Delacroix.

*   *   *

Daniel sat alone in a room on the fifth floor of Paradise Bay's police HQ on Fourth Avenue. In front of him was his Toshiba laptop, to one side the TV, and opposite, beyond his desk, the camera that would transmit pictures of him back to Quantico, where the FBI housed its Behavioral Science Unit.

He adjusted the sound until he could hear Supervisory Special Agent Rodney Dier of the Investigative Support Wing counting down.

'Can you hear me, Dan?'

'Yes, how about you?'

'Reading you fine. Say, we must get together next month – I saw you're due here for biennial.'

Daniel forced his lips into a grin. 'Surely.' *Why did Dier smile that way? Kind of smug. What did he know? What's he read on my file . . . ?*

Dan understood the basic problem: he'd broken into the charmed circle from outside. After taking his psychology doctorate from Annapolis he'd practised in Houston. There he'd swiftly won a reputation as a brilliant operator to have on your side if you stuck a knife into your unfaithful husband, or killed a child for the fun of it, but it had all proved too easy, and in 1988 he'd joined the FBI, poacher turned gamekeeper.

He should have come up the hard way. No one ever forgave you for being on the fast-track.

Dier asked, 'Anything new your end?'

'Ah . . . Well, Symes has finally geared himself up to accepting we do have another serial killer here.'

'Yawn.'

'Yeah, right, but at least I get resources I otherwise wouldn't have. This is one mean PD! They're trawling their files, have upwards of sixty suspects to interview, usual crap. I'm meeting with Symes in fifteen minutes; anything new?'

Dier leaned forward into camera. 'We'll be faxing you the report on the notes and name-card this morning. Main points: the paper originated within the continental United States, the cardstock didn't. The paper can be bought by the stack in every stationers above the size of a bagel-stall. You'll see a whole lot of stuff about texture, wood-pulp percentage, pH, but that's about the size of it so far. No fingerprints. Then there's the graphologist's report: one note was written by a right-handed person, probably under the influence of drink or drugs and either near-illiterate or, more probably, pretending to be. The other was written by a different person. One new possibility: the second note was written by a woman.'

Daniel's head jerked up. 'Are you sure?'

'Well, no. Apparently it's very hard to predict whether a given sample of handwriting was composed by a man or a woman, or how old the writer was. You can have a mature twelve-year-old who writes the same way as his forty-five-year-old father . . . '

'And presumably a man with feminine characteristics would write like a woman?'

'Correct. But there's a consensus here that one of the notes *was* written by a female. I quote: "The greater accentuation of the impulses of release, coupled with the full, round composition, and warmth of ductal tone, strongly suggest a female hand."'

'But not definitely?'

'No. You'll get the full report in a few minutes. Only other thing is the victims' schooling; is anything happening about that?'

Daniel consulted his Toshiba. 'We know two of the dead women attended the same local high school, but the third didn't. Hell, it's been a long time since those babes went anywhere near a school.'

'Maybe so, but PROFILER says to start making some connections.'

Daniel sighed. 'Okay. Got anything on this Arthur character?'

'No. Nor do we expect to. I mean, how many males are called Arthur? We don't even know if it's a last name or a first.'

'Hm. Symes's people don't know of any likely Arthurs.' Daniel hesitated. He had to broach his pet scheme sometime, but he feared rejection, in a case where nothing other than total success could help his career. 'Are you happy for me to run with my stalking horses?' he managed to say at last.

'Yes, we are.' Another voice had spoken down the line from Quantico, a woman's. This was Catherine Rancourt, the Unit Chief, everybody's head honcha. 'We've insufficient data as yet for VICAP to produce a totally adequate profile.'

'Except that he's tall and he's black, right?'

'Tall, yes, but as to black: we're not certain. At first the database indications were that way, but there are so many unique features to this case that everything's in the melting-pot.'

Daniel knew when to yield. VICAP, the Violent Criminal Apprehension Program, was the ultimate in serial crime databanks; if both it and PROFILER, the Bureau's artificial-intelligence-based computerized analysis program, said there wasn't enough information, then there wasn't.

'So we need another victim,' Rancourt continued, 'and preferably she should be drawn from a squad of trained and experienced female peace officers. We've had a discussion with Chief Symes, and he's agreed, but he's come up with a condition we think is reasonable.'

'Condition? What condition?'

'Psychological counselling must be available at all times when the girls go into Fountainside.'

'Well, okay: who've we got down in LA?'

'Sorry, Dan, but we've made a decision on this.' Rancourt smiled: on her thin face the effect was somehow macabre. 'There's an outstanding candidate been drawn to our attention already.'

'Who?'

Rancourt told him.

*   *   *

Thelma found Daniel sitting at the table farthest from the door of PJ's dining-room, a novel propped up against a half-empty bottle of red wine and a melancholy expression on his face. She hesitated in the doorway; then – Oh well, what the hell? – strode towards him.

It was ten o'clock and the dining-room was empty. Her footsteps click-clacked for what seemed like miles before he looked up. His face remained blank at first, but then he smiled; and Thelma realized with relief that he wasn't going to kill her.

'I'm sorry,' both of them said simultaneously.

'No, no, it was my fault,' they sang in unison.

Then they laughed, and Thelma felt she might live after all.

Earlier that day they'd fought the most spectacular public row either of them could remember. She was down at police HQ for a seminar and they'd run into each other – maybe crashed would have been a better word – by the fourth-floor water-cooler.

'How dare you go behind my back?' he'd spluttered. 'How dare you go to Quantico without asking me? You want to cut my balls off, is that it?'

And Thelma, instead of playing it cool and humble and all the rest of that sycophantic woman shit that normally came so naturally to her when in Daniel's presence, had bellowed, 'You got to have some balls first, before I can cut 'em off!' At which point some other denizens of police HQ had started to take an interest, and the quarrelsome pair had been forced to move their act into a store-room, where they hissed at each other like venomous snakes, until at last Daniel had stormed out to attend his meeting with Chief Symes, leaving Thelma furious and grief-stricken with only a filing-cabinet for support.

She'd come out to the motel this evening to make peace; he knew that, and he wanted it. So now he stood up, and held a chair for her, and called for PJ to bring another glass.

'I don't know how we could have done that,' he said in a subdued tone. 'Two responsible adults.'

'I want to explain,' Thelma said. 'I knew from what you'd said you'd never allow me onto the streets. I also knew I could make a contribution that the girls would need. So I took a deep breath and went to Peter Symes, and if I'd thought a bit longer I probably wouldn't have. So I'm sorry. Truly.'

'No, Peter explained it to me this morning, after we . . . you know. He said you weren't out of line, and now I've heard the full story I have to agree.'

He reached out to clasp her hand. Aha, thought Thelma; so that's what it feels like to be electrocuted, all of a sudden I'm in favour of capital punishment. But then Daniel moved his hand away and said, 'I always realized you had the credentials. Heck, you're on the Special Force here. I should have given you a shot at it when you suggested it.' He was smiling right into her eyes now, making her dizzy. 'You're one in a million, Thelma. Guess I cared about you more than I knew, and that's why I blew my top.'

She leaned forward, because if ever there was a cue for a first kiss that was it, but as usual he had to go and spoil things by looking away as he poured more wine.

'How are you, anyway?' he said.

'Good. Good.'

She kept her eyes on his hand, but it showed no sign of coming back her way, and it was too far off to grab.

'Have you managed to ditch that Delacroix crowd?'

'Not yet,' Thelma replied. 'I met the father, though. Fascinating.'

'You're curious, aren't you?'

'*Very.*' But Dan didn't relate it to himself, as she'd hoped he would.

'Careful, now. Curiosity . . . well, you know what it did to the cat.'

'Look, you think it's common, finding case-histories that sing? I mean, Daniel – how many women do you know who've been sold into slavery at the age of ten? How many boys have – '

'Okay, okay.' Dan laughed, and extended his hands palms outward – a conductor taming an over-exuberant orchestra.

'And, really,' Thelma hurried on, 'well, sometimes you make Richo out to be a cross between Adolf Hitler and Attila the Hun. You'll be saying he's P.B. Butcher next.'

'Is that so way out?'

'As it happens, it is: he was in Mexico when Kastin was murdered. I've even seen the passport stamps.' Thelma giggled. 'That's *one* thing you can't hang on my boy.'

'Well, just remember . . . you have a friend who cares what happens to you. Yes?'

Suddenly Thelma heard herself say, 'Yes. So can I take you to dinner this Saturday? Please?'

She turned to him at the same moment he was swivelling to face her. For a while they sat in silence, staring into each other's eyes, and she could see he was going to say yes. It was written in the laughter-lines beside his eyes, in his smile, in the way his shoulders tilted towards her so much more than was necessary for mere polite conversation.

'To be frank . . . '

She waited. Waited and waited.

'I'm a little . . . '

'Yes? Tell me.'

'There's . . . ' Dan choked it out at last. 'There was somebody.'

Thelma stared at him as if he'd suddenly broken into fluent but double Dutch. Somebody. Another woman. Of course, she'd always guessed, so why pretend to be surprised? This was one attractive man. Dan, Dan, Action Man.

Daniel reached out to take her hand again. For Thelma life stopped while she waited for him to formulate whatever was troubling him. *Tell me you want to cheat on her*, she thought; *tell me, oh God! Tell me! I'll do anything, I'm not proud. Motel rooms, pretending to be a survey for Time Magazine when SHE picks up the phone, never showing my face in public. Jesus, I'll even waive my right to attend your funeral, just tell me you want to cheat on her, Dan. Tell me. And then we can go to bed, right now, this minute, as soon as I can drag you around the corner to your room.*

'It didn't actually . . . work out too well, if you want the truth,' Dan said haltingly.

He was looking directly at her. His eyes, she noticed, were deep dark grey, with black flecks radiating out from the pupils. A young man's eyes, lacking red veins or imperfection of any kind. His stomach would be concave when he lay on the bed, and smooth-white, no hair, and his cock-hair would be pale sand in colour, and he would taste ever so slightly of salt and cinnamon . . .

'I'm . . . ' His mouth dissolved into something between a grunt and a grin: the most endearing sound she'd ever heard. 'I'm bemused.'

'I'm not.'

Thelma threw caution to the winds.

'I've wanted you from the moment I first clapped eyes on you,' she said, the words falling over themselves in their need to be uttered. 'Wanted you very basically, physically, without pride or hang-ups. I've lain on my bed at night and ached for you to come and do whatever you damn well please, only please don't say please, just do it.'

She swallowed. Tears were close, and something was happening to her throat: this great big lump that threatened to spoil everything, because she was only going to get one shot at this and if she screwed up . . .

'I've got no pride, you've taken all my pride. I've never spoken to a man like this before, I never could again. I don't care if you've got someone else. I don't want to know her name, or anything about her, or if she's a good lay. I don't mind her, honestly. You can keep her, you can even throw me away later, if you want, but have me first, Dan. Do that. At least have me. Then decide.'

His face clouded over – not a lot, not in an offensive kind of way; just enough to tell her she'd failed – and he backed off slightly, half turning to reach for his glass in a manner that spelled embarrassment. He took a sip, then another. Suddenly all his attention was on his glass, with none left over for her. His hand shook a little, but he could control it.

Thelma got up, collected her purse and ran to the restroom. She locked herself inside a cubicle and cried into a succession of paper handkerchiefs while doing mental acrobatics. The usual stuff: he isn't worth it, you're making a fool of yourself, are you *really* so cheap? There's plenty more fish in the sea, do you want him to think you're trash, what would your mother say, what would your best friend say, what would Kirsty say, and oh *shit*, but who gave a damn? Because fuck them, fuck them, fuck them, they weren't in love with Daniel Krozgrow, and she was, and he wasn't interested in her, not even as a second-stringer. So fuck it, and fuck him too . . . except that tonight, or tomorrow night, some other woman would be doing precisely that and Thelma couldn't bear the thought, it sent her into another fit of the blues, more tissues, oh shit, shit, *shit!*

She came back looking wan, with dark circles around red eyes, but her voice was under control and her shaking limbs could be made to obey her brain, after a fashion, and as long as she didn't ingest anything she wouldn't throw up, which suddenly seemed absurdly important. He was sitting with his glass between his hands, staring into it as if it held the key to the Turin Shroud and only he could read what it said. She wanted to smooth away his frown, but no, that was for other hands to do.

She'd lied earlier: truth was, she wanted to know everything about her rival. What colour hair she had, how she dressed, what job she did, how old she was, how many boyfriends she'd had, was she married, did oysters upset her . . . ? He'd tried to pretend it hadn't worked out – oh sure, isn't that what they all said? – but screw that, because no matter what he said after a half-dozen glasses of red, tonight, soon, other hands would be smoothing that brow: long fingers or short, nail-polish or plain, what colour skin did she have, was she black, did she like to ride on top . . . ?

Suddenly, it dawned. A hunch, yes, but impossible that it should be wrong.

Thelma was back in the Pierrot, watching Dan's face as he'd talked of Diane Cheung.

She knew what colour her rival was. Yellow. Yellow peril . . .

Oh, God. Oh, God. Oh . . . God.

No, don't say anything. You've said quite enough. Leave, go home, and soak your pillow.

She hovered by her chair, she even managed to shoot Daniel a beaming smile.

'Well,' she said. 'At least I got it off my chest. Forget it ever happened, yep? *Please!* And now I have to go. Don't bother coming out.'

Something extraordinary was happening.

She suddenly realized, God knew how or why, that this was her moment. He'd stood up, and he was looking at her, really *looking*, without that awful opaque fuzziness his eyes so often took on.

There was a script, and for once Daniel had read it.

Maybe she should flip her lid more often.

Then they were strolling through reception, out into the warm night; and Thelma was putting an arm around Daniel's waist, half expecting him to throw her off, or turn translucent and vanish in a puff of smoke, and she was allowing her head to loll against his shoulder.

He didn't throw, turn, vanish, or even protest. *It wasn't a dream!*

They should have made a right for the parking-lot. Instead she allowed him to guide her gently left, up the cobbled path that led to the rooms.

He found his key and opened the door. He stepped aside to let her pass. They stood nuzzling each other in the vestibule for a few seconds, and why she didn't fall down Thelma never knew. Daniel fumbled to close the door; they kissed, properly, for the first time. Thelma's hands went up to cup and caress his face.

Daniel took her hands between his own and drew her towards the bed. She could hardly walk. She closed her eyes, willing herself to believe that all her dreams had come true in a moment. I'll open them again, she breathed to herself, and be back in bed at home . . .

She opened her eyes, just as Daniel switched on the lights.

A man was lying on the bed. He held a gun. Its silencer swung between them in a lazy, controlled arc.

'Good evening,' Shimon Waldman said.

For a moment nobody spoke. Then Waldman got up. He was wearing black jeans and a black polo-neck; put a balaclava over his head and he'd be a terrorist from anyone's worst nightmares. 'Sit down,' he said. 'Together, on the bed.'

'Who the hell is this?' Daniel asked quietly.

'It's Waldman,' Thelma muttered. 'Naim's sidekick.'

'What's he doing here?'

'I'm not an infant,' Waldman interjected. 'If you speak to me I'll understand. I know a few big words.'

Thelma sat on the edge of the bed. She assumed Daniel would do the same. But he continued to stare at Waldman, who stood no more than five feet away from him. Thelma plucked Daniel's sleeve. 'Sit,' she murmured.

He began to move. She felt his muscles contract and loosen, so that was all right, he would sit down, then they could talk. But instead of sitting Daniel dived forward, spinning around through a semicircle so that his back cannoned into Waldman. Daniel's hands closed around the gun and he raised them high before thrusting down and back, bending forward as he did so. Waldman grunted, but he didn't drop the gun. He raised his left leg, curled it around and stamped on Daniel's instep. Daniel's face screwed up in agony. He loosened his grip on the gun. Waldman's left foot hooked Daniel's leg. One push was enough to send him sprawling.

Thelma ran over to him. His head had contacted with the sharp edge of a chair as he went down; the gash was bleeding. She helped him sit in the chair and made him hold his handkerchief to his forehead while she went to the bathroom for a face-cloth and hot water.

Waldman watched her shenanigans with a bored smile. He placed a cigarette between his lips. With a brusque movement of his right hand he jerked his gun upwards, and Thelma cried out: now this madman was going to kill himself! But all that came from the silencer was a flame. The gun was a cigarette-lighter, a fancy toy.

Waldman smoked for a few moments, letting the tension ease off, until he judged his audience receptive.

'Naim didn't take to you, Dr Vestrey. Before you got your hooks deeper into his son he wanted me to run a background check. What do I find? You keep company with this asshole here. An FBI field profiler, no less. Naim doesn't like the FBI. Suddenly I need to find out about you, *all* about you.'

'And you do that by breaking into motel rooms?' Daniel sneered.

'And by breaking people's thumbs, yes. Which is what I'll do to you if you speak again, okay?'

A tiny bell rang inside Thelma's mind. What was it about the word 'thumbs' . . . ?

'As a matter of fact,' Waldman continued, 'if I'd come on Naim's business, you wouldn't have heard, seen, smelled me.'

'Aurelia,' Thelma said. 'She sent you.'

Waldman's face softened. 'Now she *did* take to you,' he said. 'And when I tell her about him – ' he jerked his gun-lighter at Daniel – 'she's going to be afraid.'

'Because he's a cop?'

'Because of Waco.'

Thelma winced. The torching of Koresh's Branch Davidian cult was always going to rankle with the FBI, but never more so than with those special agents whose advice had been sought, proffered and ignored – Daniel (she knew) among them.

'Let me tell you a few things about *Pinos Altos*.' Waldman eased forward to sit beside the TV table. He placed his lighter on it, and went on: 'It is, in many ways, like the Waco compound. There's enough food for six months, the same goes for gas and domestic fuel. Three generators. Hand-picked staff of fifty, mostly men. Some of them double as servants, but all of them are ex-services and it's my business to keep them up to the mark. Each man's equipped with at least a handgun. There's an arsenal containing VZ61 Skorpion machine-pistols, Uzis, two light machine-guns, even a 130-calibre line gun for bringing down helicopters. I could go on, but you get the picture.'

'Who's he expecting?' Thelma asked. 'Apart from Daniel Krozgrow and his dog?'

Waldman disdained to answer. 'Know what I think? – You're cooking up something with the FBI, and instead of doing things our way you intend to launch an attack on *Pinos Altos*. Don't. I've not come this far with Aurelia just to watch a holocaust.'

The room was silent. Daniel dabbed cautiously at his wound. Thelma wondered what Waldman hoped to gain from this extraordinary performance. Ask him, why not?

'What do you want from us?'

'First, your promise not to try anything along the lines I've mentioned.'

'Because you think people will die?'

'Because I know Aurelia would die, Richo would die.'

'You care about them so much? Why not just take off, lose yourself before the shit hits the fan?'

'Because Richo's like the son I never had.'

Thelma stared at him. The answer had come out smoothly, without histrionics: a simple statement of fact. *He meant it!*

'You have my word,' she said, 'that we won't try anything like that.'

'Good. Then all you have to do is find a way to keep Aurelia and Richo here, in the States.'

'You seem to think it's so easy.'

'Just tell me what you need.'

Thelma sighed. 'I've already told Aurelia. Let me spell it out again. I need to visit his school. More important, I've got to engineer my way inside that house again, maybe half a dozen times. I need to witness Richo's relationship with his parents. I need support, back-up, above all – time. Now how are you going to get me all of that, hm?'

A troubled, almost defeatist expression had crept over Waldman's face during Thelma's tirade. The line had broken, the initiative was hers. *Keep it.*

'You know, this really wasn't such a smart move of yours tonight, was it?' She stood up slowly, daring him to challenge her. 'Two witnesses to a break-in, Mr Waldman . . . Okay, this is the deal, so you listen carefully. One. We won't call the cops, not tonight. We'll keep your fake firearm and we'll swear affidavits of what happened: step out of line and see what happens to *you*. Two. If you want my help, you'd better start thinking of ways to get me into *Pinos Altos* for discussions with Naim and Aurelia – not just Richo – on a regular basis. I'll give you twenty-four hours. After that, if you haven't come up with a game-plan, I'll forget I ever had a client called Delacroix.'

Thelma walked to the door. She opened it. Waldman assessed her for a long moment. He stood up, and Thelma tensed. But no, he was leaving.

As he skulked past her he pointed to his gun-lighter on the table. 'I'd like that back one day.'

'You should quit. The Surgeon General has determined that.'

He went out. She closed the door and leaned her back against it.

Daniel was lying stretched out on the bed, one leg crossed over the other, tossing Waldman's gun-lighter up in the air, catching it, tossing it up again. Suddenly he caught the toy in mid parabola and pointed it at Thelma with a lopsided smile.

'Pow,' he said.

'You shouldn't point guns at people.'

'Come here.'

She went over to give him a kiss, but they were both trembling so much that they had to stop almost as soon as they'd begun.

'Do you want to call the police?' he asked.

His voice told her he wasn't keen, and that surprised her. 'Don't we have to?'

'Oh, phew . . . When I think of all the paper-work, and the effect it could have on your practice, and . . .'

He tailed off. 'You've convinced me,' Thelma said. 'Thanks.'

'Plus not everybody has to know you were here with me.'

His words reminded Thelma of why they were in the motel-room in the first place. She was feeling better now, much better. 'I'll take a shower,' she whispered. 'Don't start without me.'

Her bladder was almost squeaking in protest, if she kept it waiting much longer it would burst. She trotted into the bath-room and closed the door. She peed for what seemed like ages, and then took a long, long shower. Truth to tell, she wanted to put off the moment. She was about to go to bed with the man of her dreams, and there could only be one first time, so why rush?

Let him wait. Let him get really, truly *desperate*.

The memory of Waldman's intrusion was fading fast, driven out by love and desire. Thelma soaped her legs, and hummed, and wished this night could last for ever.

At last she was ready. She went back into the bedroom to find Daniel still lying on the bed. A rivulet of blood had forced a path down from the face-cloth; that and the trickle of saliva along his chin made him seem strangely childlike and vulnerable. His eyes were closed, his breathing even.

Daniel had fallen asleep.

'You bastard,' she said – but softly, so as not to wake him.

He looked so sweetly pathetic, lying there. Waldman's gun-lighter was on the sheet beside him. Thelma bent down and gently prised it free of his fingers, so he wouldn't hurt himself if he rolled on it during the night. She went to put it on the dressing-table. She was about to lay it down when suddenly she couldn't resist the temptation: she pointed the toy at Dan and whispered 'Pow!' and pulled the trigger.

The gun-lighter leapt in her hand. She heard a muffled thump, as when an arrow hits the target. A bitter stink filled the room. The pillow next to Daniel's exploded into a storm of feathers that drifted down like so many tiny pendulums, left-right, right-left . . .

Daniel awoke. His wide-eyed stare matched her own. Thelma's hand was shaking worse than if she'd suffered an epileptic fit. She dropped the gun. Daniel rolled off the bed. For a moment he stood there, clutching his hands to his head. Then he staggered towards her and they met in the middle of the room, and they hung on as if each meant to squash the life out of the other.

'It was a gun,' she heard herself say, and felt stupid, because she couldn't stop herself repeating endlessly, 'it was a gun, it really was a gun . . .'

'Calm down. It's okay, it's okay.'

'We have to call the police now.'

He stroked her hair for a long while, without saying anything. Then he murmured, 'Tell you what. Will you promise to strike Ricardo off your client list?'

'Oh, yes! God, yes!'

'Then, Thelma – ' he held her tenderly at arm's length, gazing into her eyes – 'You can call the cops if you want. Me – I'm going to bed.'

It took her all of point-five of a second to decide.

*   *   *

Richo lay on his bed in the darkened room, staring at the screen a few feet above his head, where Peter Symes eternally answered Angela Souvrain's question.

Sam Brenton was murdered here, just behind where I'm standing, in the small hours of this morning. I can't tell you more until I've had the forensic report, but it was apparent to the officers who were first on the scene that she'd suffered mutilations . . .

Richo pressed a button on the remote-controller. The video-tape rewound. *Sam Brenton was murdered here, just behind where I'm standing . . .*

His eyes were drooping, but he didn't care. He rewound the tape, and played it, and rewound it, and played it, as if trying to get the words by heart, although in fact he'd memorized them long before.

He pressed the Fast Forward button. Figures jiggled about on screen like characters from a Chaplin silent. Another head came into focus.

Well, the first thing I would say is that I'm not convinced we're dealing with a series of deaths here. As you know, it doesn't become a series until three or more related deaths have occurred. Secondly, and categorically, this has nothing to do with the Gascoign case of two years ago.

'Daniel Krozgrow,' Richo murmured. His right hand lazily sought the ashtray, missed, tried again. At the third attempt his fingers closed around the joint, and brought it to his lips. Finest Moroccan. New stock, just in. Hadn't had a hit like this since . . . since . . .

Richo rewound the tape. *Well, the first thing I would say is that . . .* And again. And. Again.

Richo pressed Fast Forward. This time, no human faces: just scrawl on a sheet of paper. The reporter was reading, out of shot. *I have got you jumping, I will see you do more, you will catch me if you rise from your bed early in the morning and go in search of the sign of P.B. Butcher esquire.*

Rewind.

And again.

And . . .

. . . again.

Richo dozed. The video played on to the end, which came two and a half hours later. The 'clunk' of the tape stalling and then automatically rewinding was enough to rouse him. His head felt remarkably clear. That was the excellent legacy of hash: getting drunk but without the hangover. He looked at his watch. Three a.m.

She was coming today. Dr Thelma Vestrey. Let her not be late again.

He got up off the bed and padded across to the bathroom. He

took a leak. He examined his tongue in the shower's full-length mirror, scraped a brush across its grey-brown root, ran a comb through his hair. His hand descended to his genitals and his penis quickened, like a dog woken from sleep, ready for exercise.

Staring at himself in the mirror, Richo began to stroke the shaft up and down, up and down . . . His right hand went to his right nipple; after a pause he squeezed hard. His teeth gritted in pain.

No. *Later*.

He wrapped a towel around his waist and strode back into the bedroom. What he needed now was a power injection. *Shabu*.

He rummaged in the secret desk-drawer for his supply of 'ice'. First he smoothed a square of foil onto the desk, then shook a few of the white crystals over it. He heated the foil carefully over a small oil-burner, the kind of thing that keeps coffee hot. When smoke was rising from the crystals, and they had changed colour, Richo took a short drinking-straw and inhaled the smoke.

The hit was instantaneous. A stream of liquid power, joy, energy and lust combined entered his bloodstream. He jumped up from the desk and began to waltz around the room, practising his disco steps. This went on for an hour, during which time he never once stopped or slowed.

The drug *shabu* originated in China, and was available in every other bar in Manila for one thousand pesos a gram: enough for between five and ten hits, depending on the user's capacity. It was a stimulant, highly addictive and ultimately deadly. It fried the brain. You can fry a brain only so many times before it dies. Richo knew all this, but the rules, of course and as usual, did not apply to him. Within a day or two he would fall into a stupor from which no one could rouse him, his eyes would turn red, his senses crumble away to nothing. But still, the rules did not apply to him. Only to weaklings.

At last Richo danced himself to a standstill. He was back in the bathroom, standing in front of the mirror again. He stared at himself for a long time. What a stud he was. What a star . . .

Thelma Vestrey. They were going to play together, and be happy. One of them was going to be happy.

Time for a reward.

Richo got into the shower. He turned on the tap. As soon as the first frost-cold drops of water landed on his iron rod of a cock, he came.

*   *   *

The hut on the hillside was scarcely visible from the main terrace at *Pinos Altos*. Hobie's Hut, it was called, named for the man who'd built it and then lived there for nigh on twenty years: a sturdy construction, in surprisingly good condition for its age, with water available from a nearby spring and generous shade provided by a grove of oak and pine.

It was in this grove that, two years before, Annette had almost been bitten by a Mojave rattlesnake and come running back to the ranch, white faced and terrified. After that nobody went there. Nobody, that is, except Jacqui and Annette – who knew that the deadly Mojave had been a fiction, one that had served its purpose of keeping Richo away.

It was gone three o'clock in the morning. A few yards away from Hobie's place, by the spring, a shadow in human shape, somewhat lighter than the surrounding darkness, stood and watched. It held a skein of thread that it turned and twisted and wrapped around its ceaselessly moving fingers.

In the darkness of the hut, all that could be heard was the sound of sobbing.

A match flared and a storm-lantern burst into life, sheltered from outside by oil-cloth hung at the windows. The main room's interior was almost bare, except for a few shaky wooden chairs and a table, plus an oak chest that once had contained Hobie's belongings. Jacqui lay on a sleeping bag while Annette crouched over her, offering comfort.

'He killed my bunny,' Jacqui sobbed. 'It was him, he *boasted* about it!'

Annette softly stroked her sister's hair. 'He's a bastard,' she said.

Outside, the sinister shadow moved closer, twining the thread through fingers that were never still.

'He's been looking at me,' Annette went on, half to her

sister, half to herself. 'I know what he wants. I can see it in his eyes. He knows I've got Mace, though. He's afraid of being blind.'

'Annie, let's go soon!' Jacqui turned into her sister's embrace and hugged her tight. 'I can't stand it any longer, I really can't!'

'Don't worry, we're going. Look . . . '

Annette jumped up and, after a pause to recover herself, Jacqui followed. Annette threw open Hobie's old oak chest. 'I put our passports there yesterday, when I was out on Finny,' she said.

'Oh, Annie!' Jacqui gazed down into the chest. Like all the best oak chests, this one was full of treasure: two backpacks, sleeping bags, water bottles, candy bars, clothes, even money. Two black leather pouches lay tucked at the bottom of the neat piles, and each of them contained upwards of a thousand dollars, hoarded from allowances and gifts these past three years.

Annette and Jacqui were going to run away.

'How did you get the passports?' Jacqui breathed; and the shadow outside pressed its head closer to the oil-cloth window-shade – *Yes, how had she got them?*

'Dad took them out of the safe when I was there one time, and he asked me to put them back. I kept my body between him and the safe, so he couldn't see I kept them. Lucky I was wearing my rainbow shirt, you know, the one with the big pockets?'

'You were brave.'

'I kept wondering what I'd have said to Dad if he'd caught me.'

'What would you have said?'

'Your son is a monster,' Annette promptly hissed, 'who tried to rape his own sister.'

Outside, the shadow quivered slightly.

'He wouldn't have believed you.'

'No one would believe half what goes on here. We're going, just as soon as Dad takes off on his next trip.'

'And then?'

'Oh, come on: you know what then, we've gone over it often enough.'

Hobie's Hut was not bugged, as the main house was, but instinct born of hard experience made Annette lean forward to whisper in her sister's ear, causing the shadow outside to grind its teeth in rage; the thread moved faster and faster now, winding and turning and knotting itself around the shadow's fingers, until in a sudden paroxysm of rage the shadow snapped it.

*   *   *

The day after that awful scene with Waldman in the motel room, Thelma and Daniel had had a long talk. Both of them knew they ought to involve the police, file a complaint; but the thought of all that would follow made them wary. In the end they'd decided, reluctantly, to stand by their original plan: Thelma would cut loose from the Delacroix family, and try to forget what had happened. Daniel, meanwhile, would dig deep into Naim Delacroix's past.

So that same day Thelma had written to the Delacroixs to say she would not treat Richo any longer. As professional etiquette required, she'd sought a meeting at which to explain her decision. To her surprise, neither parent had rung up to browbeat her into changing her mind. Instead she'd received a polite letter from Naim, inviting her to *Pinos Altos*.

Thelma didn't want to go near the place, not after all that Waldman had put her through, but her duty was clear and anyway she felt curious. She told a number of colleagues where she was going and when she'd be back. If Dan hadn't heard from her by four o'clock he was to assume the worst and alert the police. Thus insured, she set off.

Thelma arrived to find that Naim had done her the honour of coming down to the landing-strip. He escorted her to the Jeep, apologizing for his slow gait; this morning he was all smiles and good manners.

'I'm afraid you came on a bad day, that last trip of yours,' he said as they drove up to the house. 'My leg gives me trouble sometimes. Aurelia will tell you, then I become a sourpuss. I apologize. If that's what caused you to write your letter, I hope to persuade you to change your mind.'

He turned his melancholy face towards her, seeking a reaction. Thelma nodded acknowledgement of the apology and asked, 'How did you come to injure your leg?'

'A riding accident. The horse fell on top of me. I was only forty when it happened, but it finished me and riding.' He sighed. 'I enjoyed polo, as a young man.'

Thelma felt a twinge of sympathy. This Naim, so different from the one she'd met last time, had something about him of the gallant gentleman, an impression that was enhanced when, despite his infirmity, he insisted on helping her down from the Jeep.

As they were crossing the marble entrance-hall, Richo hailed Thelma from the top of the stairway.

'You're looking great, Doctor,' he said as he ran down the steps two at a time. 'Blue's your colour.'

'Thank you.'

'You'll stay to lunch? Don't worry, I don't do the cooking around here. Let's go for a walk.'

'But Dr Vestrey's letter . . . ' Naim protested.

'We can talk about that at lunch, with mother.'

Thelma shrugged, and bade farewell to Naim before following Richo out onto the main terrace. The boy ran around with his arms extended, playing at being an aeroplane. It struck Thelma as absurd that a seventeen-year-old should behave that way.

'Have your parents told you this is our last meeting?' she enquired.

Richo acted as if he hadn't heard, still roaring up and down the terrace, uttering horrible growls. Suddenly he stopped and turned to face her. 'Hi!' he said. And then – *'Ha! Ha! Ha! Ha! Ha!'*

Thelma was close enough to see that the whites of his eyes were veined with red, he was sweating profusely, and then it clicked.

'What are you on?' she asked tersely.

'Hi!' he said. 'Hi!' He tilted his head to one side and raised his eyebrows, flirting outrageously. Without warning, his mood changed. He slowly came across the terrace and she saw tears trickling down his cheeks.

'Why are you sending me away?' he asked.

Before she could stop him, he'd gently placed his arms around her and laid his head on her breast, where he sobbed quietly. 'Why?' he pleaded. His voice dropped to a whimper. 'Why?'

Thelma opened her mouth to tell him why.

A shot reverberated around the valley, bouncing off Chieftain Dome before flowing towards the house in a diminishing wave of sound that seemed to go on and on. Richo raised his head and looked into Thelma's eyes. 'Why?' he repeated.

That was when they heard the screams.

Thelma spun around and saw a Jeep moving fast across the landscape, making for the hills. A girl was riding her horse full-tilt in the same direction.

Thelma found herself caught up and overwhelmed in a human tide. Richo was dragging her to the terrace steps, where his father was already clambering into another Jeep. Staff were running about, infected with the start of panic. Thelma was in the Jeep, the Jeep was moving fast, bouncing about on a sandy washboard track before cutting across country.

She could see Hobie's Hut now, peeping out from between some trees. A crowd had already collected there. Richo grabbed her arm and shrieked incomprehensibly. Thelma's hand was clenching the safety-handle so tightly it hurt.

The Jeep ground to a halt outside the hut. Two girls were in the doorway, having hysterics. Richo left his father to hobble as best he could, thrusting the girls aside. Thelma followed. She took one look over the boy's shoulder and turned away, retching.

When she'd finished throwing up she made a slow return to the hut. Now an ominous silence filled the air. People stood about in twos and threes, speechless. Thelma forced herself to go inside.

The body of Aurelia Delacroix lay on the floor; Thelma recognized the stunning green dress from Paco Rabane she'd been wearing the day she'd brought Shimon to St Joe's. Across her chest lay a shotgun. Her head looked like a coconut that had been sliced lengthways, scooped out, and filled with butcher's meat. The only thing to make it recognizable as a human face was one ludicrously out-of-place eye, cyan streaked with gold, that gazed accusing at Thelma from near where you'd normally expect to find a mouth.

Richo came to life. He was standing three feet away from Thelma. He turned and punched her in the stomach. Thelma doubled up with a howl.

'See what your letter did?' the boy shrieked. 'You bitch, you fucking bitch, *I hate you!*'

He wheeled away and threw himself into Shimon Waldman's arms. Shimon, still in a state of shock, smoothed Richo's hair with mechanical movements. The boy seemed to relax, his body slumping against the older man's. But then in a fit of passion Richo pushed him away, pummelling Shimon with his fists, squealing that he wanted to kill him.

Shimon slapped the demented teenager across the face. Richo froze in shock. Shimon bent down to the carnage at his feet. He rose holding a piece of paper. Naim hobbled to read it over Shimon's shoulder. His expression turned grey, he sank to the floor.

'Digitalis,' Shimon snapped. 'Quickly!'

Not quite knowing why, Thelma held out her hand, and Shimon gave her the paper: a suicide note. She read it quickly. Aurelia's familiar handwriting . . .

The message was short and succinct. Memories of her earlier life had haunted her of late, she could no longer bear to go on living. Richo was lost to her, more and more wrapped up in his father's affairs – affairs from which she, Aurelia, was now excluded. Naim planned to leave her. Annette and Jacqui were scheming to run away from home. And the last straw: Thelma Vestrey, her one remaining hope, had abandoned her. A shotgun would bring release, and peace.

Odd, Thelma thought as she handed the note back to Shimon; odd because statistics showed that suicides didn't usually spell out their chosen method. Why refer to a shotgun? And the writing . . . it was the same as in the long account of her life, yet subtly different in a dozen hard-to-identify ways.

Who were Annette and Jacqui?

The note was wrong, wrong, wrong.

Thelma raised her eyes to Shimon. He composed himself quickly, but not quite quickly enough to prevent her seeing the look on his face: satisfaction. A second later, grief had taken its place: but the satisfaction had been there.

With sudden, sickening conviction Thelma knew she was witness to the aftermath of murder.

PART TWO

THE TEMPLE ROCK FUNERAL HOME and Chapel of Peace had done well by Aurelia Delacroix. Everything was of the understated best. They couldn't leave the coffin open, of course, not with facial damage of that magnitude, but the abundance of sprays, the wreathes and floral crosses, the velvet dignity of the place somehow conveyed the impression that all was as it should be and that coffins were *meant* to be closed.

Thelma chose a seat midway between the bier and the entrance doors. A few minutes later, Daniel slipped in beside her. 'Interesting,' he muttered, with a glee that Thelma felt to be out of place, though that didn't stop her asking, 'What did you get?'

'The certificate says Accidental Death. Identification was done by Shimon Waldman, and there isn't the slightest doubt – ' he nodded at the coffin – 'there lie the mortal remains of Aurelia Delacroix. What bugs me is this: if the coroner saw that note she wrote, no way could he have decided the death was accidental.'

'So nobody showed it to him.'

'I guess. Another interesting thing: the whole business was handled out of a deputy sheriff's office up in the boonies, one man and his horse Trigger. No reason for that, with Kernville nearby . . . Have you *seen* that boy's car?'

'Richo?'

'I guess it was him. He drove up as I was coming in. Black customized Porsche, I mean, *God* . . . '

'It goes with the image. Pilot, scuba-diver, stud.'

Daniel was about to reply when the doors behind them opened and the Delacroix family filed in.

Thelma watched the sad little procession wend its way up towards the coffin. Naim and Richo came first – 'That's Mr Porsche all right,' Daniel confided in a hoarse whisper. Naim looked dreadful: grey of face and grey of soul. He leaned heavily on his son's arm. It seemed like Richo hadn't slept for a week. His oh-so-manifest solicitousness towards his father struck a false note in Thelma's mind.

They were followed by two teenage girls, wearing identical black outfits. Thelma thought they were twins, until as they drew nearer differences of hairstyle and expression revealed her mistake. Of course – they were the girls she'd seen at Hobie's Hut. Who were they? Perhaps the mysterious Jacqueline and Annette mentioned in the suicide note? Nieces? If so, their aunt's death seemed to have affected them profoundly.

The service was short. Shimon read a moving account of the dead woman's qualities that bore little resemblance to anything Thelma knew. Much was made of her love for Naim and her devotion as a mother, at which Richo gazed stonily ahead. Thelma felt glad when it was over.

Outside, she stood with Daniel in silence while the family and Shimon paid their last respects.

'I feel I should say something,' Thelma murmured as the mourners came out into the sunshine.

'Leave it.'

She was glad to, because the thought of going anywhere near Shimon was repellent, but at that moment Naim caught sight of Daniel and Thelma, and he raised an imperious hand. Richo snapped a few words, prompting his father to shake his head. Naim started to make his way towards Thelma and Daniel. The two teenage girls followed.

'Dr Vestrey,' Naim said, 'you've not met my daughters, Annette and Jacqueline.'

Thelma's rigid stare continued to the point of rudeness. Somewhere in the background she heard Richo's awful laugh: *Ha! Ha! Ha! Ha! Ha!* Daniel jerked his head around to find the source.

'She didn't tell you she had daughters,' Naim said. It was scarcely a question.

'No.'

Thelma felt so stupid. At any time in her professional relationship with Richo a word from her would have sufficed to bring out the truth. 'You don't have any brothers or sisters, right?' – that's all it would have taken. But his file contained no reference to siblings, no one had so much as hinted at their existence . . .

The girls shook hands. Jacqui had a soft touch and tragic smile that Thelma found hard to associate with a Delacroix. But then she looked into her eyes and saw that in certain moods, in certain lights, she could be every bit her mother's daughter also.

She felt something forced into her palm with the pressure of heart-rending appeal: paper. Thelma, startled, accepted it. Perhaps she should have protested, or at least questioned . . . but the incident was over in a second, and almost without realizing she'd sneaked it into her purse.

Naim seemed not to have noticed. He dismissed both girls with a look and turned back to Thelma. 'I want us to talk.'

He glanced at Daniel, who took the hint.

'Well, Thelma,' he said, 'see you later, then?'

'Yes. Oh, thanks for coming.'

Comfortable pine chairs and benches were scattered through the well-kept grounds, and it was to one such bench that Naim now led Thelma. They sat together in the shade of a cupressus grove.

'Ricardo doesn't want me to do this. But my daughters say if I don't talk with you, they will.'

His tone was flat, abrupt. Aurelia's death had not softened Naim.

'I know the story Aurelia must have told you,' he went on. 'The sister who died, yes? Working in Paris as a prostitute?'

'She mentioned something along those lines.'

'The sister's death . . . it was an accident?'

'She never said anything about it, just left me to assume she'd had a twin sister who died.'

Was there, Thelma wondered, a hint of relief in Naim's eyes as she gave that answer?

'Well now, Dr Vestrey, this is the truth. Aurelia never had a sister, so of necessity the sister never died, she never worked in Paris as a child hooker. Aurelia was the child of a French army officer stationed in Algiers and the daughter of a local merchant. Her parents brought her to Paris in her early teens, and they all lived happily in the 16th arrondissement. I met her while she was still living at home, so I know.'

Thelma reeled on the edge for a moment; then she took a deep breath and plunged in. 'Why did she reinvent herself so thoroughly?'

'Reinvent!' Naim's voice turned scornful. 'The first signs of mental instability arose soon after we were married. She was diagnosed as suffering from schizophrenia . . . hebephrenic, would that be right?'

'Hebephrenic, yes.'

'She developed this delusion that she'd had a sister who'd died young. In those early days the sister went through a variety of names, and the death took many forms, but in the end she fastened upon a twin, Nada, who'd accidentally been shot. Psychiatrists could do nothing for her.'

Naim reached into the pocket of his jacket and brought out a bundle of letters, which he handed to Thelma. 'I wanted you to see these, because there's no reason why you should take my word for all this.'

Thelma skimmed two or three of the letters. They were from some of the most eminent specialists in the field of schizophrenia, with letterheads ranging from London to Vienna to New York to Munich. They bore out Naim's version in every respect.

A passage caught Thelma's eye: 'What troubles me is the way she saps her energies, fretting about the child. She is obsessed with the notion that he, too, must develop schizophrenia, and although Ricardo is only five years old she's already demanding that he be treated . . .'

'May I keep these for a while?' Thelma asked.

'If you want. To me, they are merely depressing.'

Thelma put the letters in her purse. 'What I can't understand is why you never told me this before. Why didn't you come with Ricardo at his first session?'

'Because of the pattern.'

'I don't understand.'

'You weren't the first person Aurelia consulted on behalf of Ricardo. You were the eleventh.'

Thelma gulped down another deep breath.

'I learned how to manage Aurelia. I discovered that when she developed a fixation with a therapist, as she did with Cheung, buying her book, cutting out newspaper clippings, there was no stopping her. The only solution was to stay in the background until the first passion had worn off, and then step in with more, how shall I put it? With more *relevant* information.'

He smiled bleakly. 'I didn't want Aurelia to consult Cheung, or you,' he went on. 'But I agreed, as I always did: to buy peace. I'd have preferred my son to see a man, with a strong personality. A psychiatrist, not a psychologist, because he *is* mad.'

Thelma looked at him glumly. 'I think so.'

'But no, it had to be Cheung; and then, when you inherited her practice, it had to be you. Doctor, I don't want you to go on treating my son.'

'It's perfectly mutual. I'm not qualified to handle mental illness.'

'The same goes for my daughters.'

'What?'

'They've invented this dumb idea that they need therapy. They don't.'

'But . . . excuse me, but what about your daughters? How could Aurelia not mention them? And Richo never talked about them either.'

'Aurelia denied their very existence. Richo . . . he went along with whatever his mother demanded of him. I'm sending the girls to Europe, where they can make sensible friends and receive the discipline they need.'

Thelma was angry. 'What they need is *love*! Can't you see that?'

'They know I love them.'

'But then what happened to make everyone *deny* them, for goodness' sake?'

Naim looked at his watch: a slow, offensive gesture. 'After Ricardo was born,' he said reluctantly, 'Aurelia became desperate to have a daughter. She succeeded; Jacqueline. That wasn't enough, though. She struggled to conceive another child, in vain. So she cajoled me into adopting a girl, the same age as Jacqui. Which is how Annette came to live with us. Aurelia chose her because she had green eyes, like Jacqui.'

'Okay, okay, but what went wrong?'

'She came to believe they didn't exist. Never spoke to them. She told me, often, that they were dead. That's why they were planning to run away, no doubt.'

'That part was true, then? That part of her suicide note, I mean.'

'There was a stash of things in the hut. Yes, the girls were going to run away.'

'Because of Aurelia?'

'I imagine so. Wouldn't you think so?'

Thelma had taken all she could stand. 'Yes I darn well would!' she flared. 'And unless you do something about it, this problem's going to come around and around until one day somebody does something about it. Mr Delacroix, can't you see? In word and in deed, your children are crying out for help – crying to *you*. Their father, dammit!'

Naim stood up. 'I'd prefer to be alone for a while,' he said stiffly.

'No, I won't let you do that – turn your back on me and walk away. You have to start acting up to your parental responsibilities.'

For a moment longer he continued to stare at her through his dark, brooding eyes. Then he turned and walked off. Thelma watched as he rejoined his family and led them away. Only Richo looked back, scowling.

She'd already driven out of the main gate and turned left, heading for Paradise Bay North, when she remembered the paper Jacqui had stuffed into her hand. She pulled into the side and retrieved it from her purse. She unfolded the paper.

'Dr Vestrey, please help us.' (She read.) 'This is a sick household, our brother is sick, our Dad doesn't care. We're in DANGER! Do something! We have to find a way to meet. I'll phone you. Be ready. Please! Jacqueline (and Annette).'

'Whew!' Thelma read the note twice more. *'Whew!'*

What would she do if Jacqui phoned? She'd have to think about that, long and hard.

She put the note back in her purse and stared through the windshield.

She'd finished with the Delacroix family, or so she'd thought until now. But here were mysterious, hitherto-undisclosed daughters, pleading for help.

Aurelia had been mad, her story childish invention.

Except that Naim's was shot full of holes too.

Why hadn't he got divorced? Why had he put up with Aurelia all those years? Fear of what other people might think? Putting up with it for the sake of the children? Scores of possible reasons, none of which sat easily with what she knew of Naim Delacroix.

But Aurelia wasn't around to contradict Naim.

Thelma started her car and found gear. She'd go into the office and write letters to the psychiatrists whose letters Naim had given her. And since she was due to see Daniel that evening she'd find out how far he'd got with that Fed check against Delacroix. Richo might no longer be her patient, but hell, she was curious.

But at the hospital she found something waiting for her that drove all other thoughts out of her mind.

'When did this arrive?' she demanded of Makiko.

'The FedEx package? This morning.'

Thelma slowly lowered herself into her chair, staring fixedly at the package as if afraid it might bite her. She examined the label, looking for the name of the sender. 'Nobody, Inc.' Sense of humour, huh?

She opened it gingerly. It didn't look big enough for a bomb, though you read about these things. But she already knew what the package contained.

Same paper. Same round handwriting, clear, big.

Thelma dismissed Makiko, took her phone off the hook, and plunged in.

Madame, I do not know if I can finish this. Things crowd in on me. Depression, despair . . .

I must make an effort. Even if I don't complete the course, I can perhaps hand on my torch to you.

After the event, I remember being taken back to rue Burq in the car, then nothing more for days. I slept, mostly. No food. I think a doctor came to see me. He gave me a shot. Then I was sitting in the back of a limousine, being driven across Paris, through crowds of protesters. This would have been 1968. Paris seethed with strife. I wasn't frightened. I hoped someone would drag me out and stone me on the cobbles. But we arrived in the sixteenth without incident.

Wait a minute, wait a minute! Thelma skimmed through the wodge of papers. What 'event' was Aurelia talking about? Why did she want to die? What was missing? For nowhere in the package could she find any reference to what had immediately preceded this description.

Thelma shrugged, irritated, and read on.

For the next five years I lived in the barracks. That was the only name I had for it. Rue Faisanderie, close to Avenue Foch. The barracks was five storeys high, forbidding, set around a series of dark courtyards. There were many apartments there. Ours was huge.

The car stopped in one of the courtyards and the driver came around to open the door. He had to carry me. We entered and went up a flight of shallow stone steps to the lift. Then we were in a gloomy passage, knocking on huge blue doors. They opened. And there he was. My salvation. Shimon.

He looked different in those days. Stout, with a moustache that had grown luxuriant. He examined me as if I were a parcel he wasn't quite sure they were expecting. Then he motioned the driver inside and indicated that he was to lay me down on a chaise-longue in the hallway. That done, the driver left me alone with him.

I asked no questions. I simply wasn't interested. Whatever happened to me, happened. A Filipina brought tea. Shimon knelt down by the chaise-longue and helped me drink a cup. He drank one too, first, as if to prove it wasn't drugged. I didn't take note of that at the time, but later I recalled it as the first real building-block in our relationship.

He raised me to my feet, then, and walked me through the apartment. He opened his mouth only once: to show me the suite of rooms where I wasn't to go unless invited, Naim's suite. Everywhere else was open to me. It was very warm, that was my initial impression, and I liked that, because the house in rue Burq had been cold. The windows were all high, as in a typical Parisian apartment of the better class, but many of them had been closed over with shutters. The furniture . . . Naim had no taste then, he has none now. It was all dreadful. The sofas were too soft, the upright chairs too upright, the tables too low, the beds too narrow. Everything reeked of money. He had a Vermeer on one wall, a Titian on another. Shimon said it was a Vermeer. Later, when I became expert in many areas, I checked: the Titian was solid gold, the 'Vermeer' attributed to Frans van Mieris. Both paintings were frightful, like every other antique with which he'd stuffed the place, but they somehow belonged in the barracks. The best things were the rugs: Naim did know about them. But mostly the apartment was parquet-floored. My footsteps echoed through the empty rooms, day by day, night by night. Tap-tap-tap.

Perhaps sometimes the present owners of that sumptuous, ugly apartment awake in the middle of the night, half-conscious of the tap of a young girl's feet along the parquet . . .

For the first time in my life, I was subjected to a proper routine. Shimon showed me my bedroom – clean, comfortable – and a closet full of clothes. The clothes fitted me, but I detested every garment save one: a lavender-coloured dress with a thin black cloth belt. I wore that for our first dinner together. Shimon and I dined alone in a big room, at a table that could easily have seated twenty guests. He began by introducing the servants: Filipinos, husband and wife, Emilio and Grace. (It was Grace who'd brought me that cup of tea, my first day there.) Although they weren't much older than me, they never ventured to cross the invisible line between us. Not for me happy hours spent playing in the kitchen while Grace scrubbed potatoes and Emilio shined shoes. Rather, discreteness. Discretion. Shimon told me to be polite to them. Tantrums would be punished.

Dinner was served. And it was magnificent. Madame, would you understand if I said it was the first real meal of my life? There was a light pasta dish, containing salmon, followed by a daube de boeuf, and cheese, and fresh fruit, including mango, and coffee. I sat down not wanting to eat, but the scent of the daube whetted my appetite. Shimon speared a ravioli and popped it into my mouth. As it dissolved across my tongue, for a second I forgot my plight, my misery, and at once felt guilty – my sister . . .

I burst into tears. This was the nearest my sister ever came to being mourned. I cried, and then I stuffed myself full of stew and frites and mango. Strange: I wasn't sick . . .

After dinner we retired to the salon, the worst room in the house, furnished like a palace frozen in time. Shimon smoked a cigar and drank cognac. Between sips and drags, he laid out my situation for me to examine.

The owner of the apartment was Naim Delacroix . . . 'whom you have met'. Such dryness! Such delicacy! Naim had decided to befriend me, to educate me and to find me a suitable position in the world. He accepted that responsibility. The only conditions were that I must live in this apartment, not go out except in Shimon's company, and study diligently, with tutors, as far as the baccalaureate. I might choose any reasonable discipline, in the realm of arts or science.

I was to enjoy a good standard of living. Clothes and requisites would always be available, as would books. 'But you must learn not to be greedy,' Naim warned me.

He'd spoken earlier of conditions, and next he dealt with the unspoken restrictions, the necessary incidentals. It would be a long time, certainly years, before I was free to take my place in society. I could not attend school, and I wasn't at liberty to make friends, as other children did. My life would be a solitary one. I understood, of course: Naim couldn't risk my prattling out his secrets. 'You will feel like a prisoner,' Shimon said. 'Sometimes.' And as he said that I thought, 'No, always.'

Finally, he informed me that Naim would hardly ever be present in the house. He was an international businessman, with many calls on his time. But occasionally he'd want to see me, and I must prepare myself for that. Shimon knew it would be hard for me to face his master again. He didn't guess at my desire, already forming like a newly fertilized embryo, to achieve true intimacy with Naim.

I could dwell for many pages on the first year of my captivity, but time is limited, my own death so close, and so you must imagine it as best you can, chère Madame. The numbness wore off, honed away by the dictates of an iron routine. I rose at seven, ate a breakfast of croissants and hot chocolate, and set to work with my

tutors, of whom there were two. They were good teachers; I do not
know what kind of men they were, or how much they knew. After
a light lunch, Shimon would take me out. We dissected Paris. As he
thawed, so we delved deeper into the greatest metropolis of Europe.
Shops, palaces, museums, cinemas, theatres, the opera . . . nothing
was closed to me. I used to take his hand, as if he were some dear
old uncle, and we would walk hand in hand through a celestial
Garden of Delights, called Paris.

What was going through my mind? That's what you want to
know, isn't it? How did I cope with what had happened to me?
What emotion did I feel when I heard Naim's name?

Wait.

I applied myself, that first year, and in every subsequent one.
Not content with my morning's tuition, I read extensively, com-
piling a reading-list with the help of my tutors and Shimon. For
a while I more or less camped in the Louvre: Shimon couldn't
take it and delegated my care to his driver. As we walked
through the galleries he would furtively read the sports news
and hope I wouldn't notice. As if I cared! But it strikes me, as I
grow older, how powerful are the young. When I was in Paris
last year I revisited the Musée d'Orsay, going in search of my
favourite paintings. Five views of the façade of Rouen cathedral,
by Monet. When I was fifteen I used to stand before them for
hours, gazing into the canvases, and they seemed great art to me
because they confirmed my fondest hope: things cannot change,
and yet they do. But when I went last year it was enough
labour to haul myself up to the second floor and find the right
gallery. I sat and looked at those wonderful paintings until my
heartbeat steadied, and I tried to recall that intense little girl,
but she had departed without leaving a forwarding address.
Gone completely, gone forever.

I learned about food and wine. Shimon loved eating out. He
taught me how to unearth quality without paying the earth.
France has so many superb wines that never find their way onto a
list outside of their region. Once a decade I will cast my eye down a
carte des vins in some out-of-the-way spot and spy Château
Maucaillou (of which you have never heard) and I will think,
How did you get here, you are from Médoc? Why is my love so far

119

*from home? And I'll drink a toast to Shimon, in gratitude for his
having introduced me to such a sweet companion.*

*By the time Shimon murmured, 'Naim will be here tomorrow,'
I'd acquired a patina of education, poise, wisdom. Now terror shattered it. I threw myself down on the bed and pulled the covers over
my head. I shook, I cried, I sobbed out my sister's name again and
again. To no avail. Naim was coming.*

*He spent Christmas in Paris, with Shimon and me. I was fifteen.
That first time, just being in his presence was like having fish-
hooks drawn across flesh from which all the skin had been flayed.
To look at him was agony, to feel the touch of his lips against my
cheek . . . oh, how I shuddered in my very depths! But he took no
liberties, that first visit. He never tried to kiss my mouth, or go to
bed with me. He displayed interest in my newly acquired accom-
plishments. He used to sit and watch me work, gazing at me from
under lowered eyelids, and every so often I would raise my head
and smile. He took me to the cinema, without Shimon, and afterwards we went to Brasserie Lipp, where I chose the wine. He never
talked of Nada, or the event.*

Thelma pounded her fists on the desk. What event? She wished
Aurelia would come to life for long enough for her to administer
a couple of resounding slaps to the silly woman's face. Why had
she written of her own death being 'so close'?

Thelma squelched the notion of sending Makiko out to
buy a pack of Camels, squared her shoulders, and turned the
page.

*In January Naim left, only to return in early March. During his
absence, my relationship with Shimon entered a new phase. One
day I caught him on the phone, arguing. He was annoyed when he
saw me, and went off by himself to drink, but later he came back,
wanting to talk. I discovered that he had a mistress, and that constantly having to chaperone me was sapping the relationship.
Before I arrived, his job was a kind of chef du bureau, marshalling
Naim's European interests, attending the occasional board
meeting, that kind of thing, and it left him plenty of time to play.
Now he was a child-minder, the laughing-stock of his friends.*

We made a pact immediately. I think Naim must have said something, authorized it perhaps. Anyway, I gave my parole not to attempt to escape or to tell anyone my secret if Shimon would allow me sometimes to go out alone.

Can you imagine what it was like suddenly to be free? Able to roam the streets at will, window-shop for as long as I wanted, stand and stare at the river beside the Quai d'Orsay until it took my eyes away, past the old palace, down to the sea?

Did I try to escape? Madame, madame, does the caged bird sing?! I had money, education, opportunity and, above all, I had the lust for revenge to keep me in my place. During those spring months revenge came to be my life's obsession. I dedicated myself to it completely. It filled my waking hours and inspired my dreams. I hated Naim. I have never stopped hating him.

There's a gap in your comprehension, isn't there? Why did I hate him?

I had – have – a reason. I must tell you. But I can't write it down yet.

Accept my hatred, for the moment. Wait.

How could such bitterness mature into marriage and the mothering of this monster's child? I'm not mad – not yet, not quite. But marriage became my aim very early on, because it's the perfect base from which to rain destruction upon a man, especially if you have the will to wait.

I also had Naim's guilt on my side. He never tried to have me sexually and I thanked the Devil (your devil, my god) for that, because I could not have resisted his greater strength and it would have meant losing my hold over him. Once he knew me carnally, the spell would be broken and in his eyes I'd become just another woman, fit to be discarded.

I fascinated him. His eyes burned every time they lighted on me, and I took good care to keep them afire. I'd acquired some dress sense and a knowledge of perfume. By dint of constant watching along the quais and in the cafés I'd learned which women were truly erotic and which just painted whores. To Naim, I represented the ultimate in womanhood, and I was unobtainable.

Then two things happened in quick succession, altering my destiny. One was small but significant, the other cataclysmic.

One evening, Naim took me out to dine. I knew he had something important on his mind because we went to Bofinger, his favourite upstairs table, behind the twist in the stairway. He had a thing about Bofinger; I never could see it. Over our coups of champagne he seemed preoccupied. Little by little he approached the topic. He was afraid Shimon had turned traitor.

I ate my oysters demurely, saying little. I could see what was coming and all my attention was fixed on finding the right way forward. When it came – the proposal that I should spy on Shimon, especially when he went to visit his mistress – I was ready. I agreed zealously, even hinting that I, too, already harboured suspicions. What was I to look for? Answer: dubious contacts. Whom was I to regard as 'dubious'? Why, anyone!

It was so feeble I wanted to laugh in Naim's face. Did he seriously expect me to protest Shimon's loyalty as a sop to his jealousy? For by then he was jealous, anyone could see it in his eyes, the way he hovered so that even the waiter was not allowed to ease my chair into the table when I sat down.

As soon as Naim went out next day I told Shimon what had happened. We had a good laugh about it; then he grew serious, and after a while succeeded in making me understand that this was not the jape it seemed. Shimon told me to 'discover' some fault of his and report to Naim. He made me go through with it exactly as if it were real: made me follow him at a distance when he walked to his girl's place on the Quai, made me hang around outside in the freezing cold for two hours, got me to follow him down a side street into a smoky café and watch while he drank with a villainous-looking man sporting what I swear was a false moustache!

But Shimon had been more thorough than I realized. When I described the false-moustache man to Naim he recognized him as an enemy. I can still remember how Naim's face turned a strange hue, the colour of smog.

Shimon disappeared for three days after that. I was left to wander alone through the apartment, aligning my feet with the parquet tiles and avoiding the joins, eating solitary meals, listening to the ticking of the clocks. Then he returned, with one arm in a sling and half his face bandaged. Only one eye was visible, with a bruise the tint of cooked beetroot: but through that one poor eye he winked at me.

It was strange: everything went back to normal immediately. Shimon had erred, taken his punishment like a man and been reinstated. But Naim began to treat me differently. For the first time we went to Le Fouquet's, where everybody seemed to know him, and suddenly we were eating at all the best restaurants. He took me to smart, glittery parties, where I became an instant success with his louche crowd. Everyone assumed I was his mistress, when in fact I was not, and this strange mix of truth, fiction, wishful thinking, eroticism made us an electric couple. Later he told me that at those parties he often wondered, as I had wondered, what would happen if he laid a hand upon my rump and squeezed. He felt sure I'd have slapped his face. I wasn't so sure, although I pretended to agree.

At one of those parties, when we'd been sniffing cocaine, he confided that he hadn't believed I would ever betray Shimon, and we sampled our first kiss. He stank of garlic and corruption. But he still wouldn't touch me, not in that way.

The second thing that happened, the cataclysme, occurred shortly after my twenty-first birthday. Naim had given me a diamond ring and taken me to Manila for a week. The night of our return to Paris, the police came and arrested him on a charge of murder.

They battered down the door and took him away in chains; when I tried to cling to him, one gendarme put his palm over my face and flattened me against the wall, bang! so that my teeth rattled and I slid down to the floor, stunned. His women deserted him; the servants faded into the night, taking a lot of things with them; there were no friends to turn to and no funds to pay lawyers. Shimon spent twenty-four hours establishing that all of Naim's property had either been stolen by his associates or frozen by the French state.

We sat in my bedroom, speechless, while night closed down around us. Tomorrow the bailiffs would come, these were our last few hours in what I had come to regard as home. Did I despair? I did not. I resolved to sort out this mess. Naim, overcome with gratitude, would marry me. Then I could get down to the real business of revenge: bearing him a son.

Thelma gathered up the pages, slid them between her hands a couple of times to make sure they were aligned, and flung them against the door.

What upset her, what really got to her, was that there was no escaping this terrible harpy even in death. Her hands stretched out towards Thelma from the grave, beckoning with gruesome, ghostly power.

Thelma got up and reluctantly gathered this latest extract from Aurelia's life history together. Better put it with the rest, she supposed.

The Fed check that Daniel proposed to run on Delacroix now seemed even more important. That he was a swine Thelma did not doubt; but this recital raised far more questions than it answered.

Who'd mailed the package? 'Nobody, Inc' . . . she could chase for a month and never find an answer. *Why* had they sent it?

When had this part of the story been written?

Thelma sighed. The worst of it was that the source of these frustratingly absorbing anecdotes had now dried up. Permanently.

*　　*　　*

'You going to finish that curry or not?'

When Thelma made no reply, Rachel cleared away her plate and came back a moment later with scoops of chocolate-chip ice-cream. While Kirsty tucked in, Thelma toyed with her spoon, dividing listless attention between TV and bowl. Rachel watched her. As soon as Kirsty had finished, Rachel said, 'Up to your room, now. Homework.'

'No seconds?' squawked an indignant Kirsty.

'You're putting on weight.'

'Gee, thanks.' But she went without further protest, and Rachel had an idea that there was maybe a letter she wanted to write, or a call to make, to a certain Randy Baker who hadn't shown up in a while. Whatever; at least she'd gone, and now Thelma was alone in the kitchen with her mother.

Rachel plucked the spoon from Thelma's fingers and treated

herself to a mouthful of Häagen-Dazs. Then she eased a smidgen of ice-cream onto the end of the spoon and lightly flicked Thelma's nose with it.

'Oof! What'd you do that for?'

'I'm a jealous woman in need of attention.'

Thelma rustled up a smile. 'Guess I've been a mite quiet, huh?'

'Want to talk about it?'

'Yes. And no.' Thelma sighed, pushed back her chair and went to switch off the TV. While she still had her back to her Rachel said, 'It's about tonight, isn't it? Tonight's assignment.'

Thelma poured two mugs of coffee before coming to sit opposite her mother. Erasmus saw his opportunity and jumped onto the table to attack the remains of the ice-cream. 'My job,' Thelma said, gently pushing the cat aside, 'is sometimes dangerous.'

Rachel felt her chest tighten. Calm down, she told herself; get the hound on the leash, honey. 'Right,' she said.

'And I like that.'

Rachel nodded.

'Only sometimes . . . when I'm working the streets, holding the guys' hands, it's more dangerous than others.' Thelma tried out a dismissive little laugh, got it badly wrong. 'Like tonight.'

'Is this all to do with Mr Crazy-Name-Zany-Guy?'

Now it was Thelma's turn to nod.

'You volunteered?'

'Yup.' After a pause, Thelma looked at her watch. 'Got to go.'

Rachel reached out to grasp her daughter's wrist. 'Take care, hon.'

'I will.' Thelma laid a hand over Rachel's. 'Thanks.'

She patted Rufus and went off as she had done a hundred times before, wearing a grey skirt and plain white shirt, and, as had happened a hundred times before, Rachel stood on the porch to wave goodbye and wonder what was involved in this secret police assignment. Wonder if next time she saw Thelma her daughter would be laid out on a slab for identification. What she would wear at the funeral, and how Kirsty would take it. How to drown the demons and heal the pain that had no end.

Rachel Vestrey went back inside her house and closed the door

125

behind her, resisting the desire to slam it on the Whole Goddamn Thing.

*   *   *

By ten o'clock the fourth-floor corner conference room was full to overflowing, so that when the girls arrived they had to force their way through one almighty crush. At first only fellas by the door got to look, but as Daniel's 'stalking-horses' penetrated the room a ragged cheer expanded in volume until by the time they were assembled on the platform the room was a riot.

Anita Prince was wearing a short gold lamé dress with calf-length white boots, and carried a glittery silver purse over one shoulder. She was black, which somehow made the effect doubly striking, especially when you took in the white lipstick. Jo Penny's long blonde tresses fell over and around her shoulders in thick curls, dragging the eye below to her enormous breasts and skin-tight stretch pants, right on down to her black leather high-heeled shoes. Janice Sepeda sported tight white jeans that looked as though they were biologically part of her, and a sequined silk blouse open far enough to let the observer know that yes, they might be big, but they were *real*. She was wearing a wig of short black hair, with a kiss curl over one eye, and had on most make-up of the three.

The assembled gentlemen of the Paradise Bay Third Precinct, seeing three very alluring and expensive ladies of the night before them, gave tongue.

Lt Sonny Allerton came in the room, tie knotted somewhere around his breastbone, stomach preceding him like the bottom-bow of an oil-tanker, hair receded past the halfway mark. The cheers, cat-calls and wolf-whistles tapered off. Allerton waved a folder at them, 'Shaaaad UP,' he bellowed.

He stood in front of a flip-chart and began his spiel. 'Same as last time, guys,' he said, 'but since half of you can't remember name of maternal grandparent after lunch, here we go again. This – ' he used his folder to point to the first chart – 'is the Fountainside Quarter, shaaad UP! I know you know that! I know you do! Just listen, okay?'

126

He waited for silence, got it quickly.

'Unmarked cars alpha through foxy here, here . . . here . . . every red cross a car. One man driving, one in back lying down – and I don't want to see any of you sitting up, okay, not like last time.' He jerked his folder accusingly at the known offenders. 'Two-man patrols following the same route at the same pace as before, no deviations, no slip-ups. Jacob, Mr Krozgrow rides with you tonight in echo-car. And like last time, we got Dr Vestrey on our team, so a word from her. Thelma . . . '

Thelma came forward. 'I'm here for all of you,' she said, looking around the room, 'but principally for these three ladies. Anyone, anytime, feels night coming down on him, or her, I'll be available. But please remember – Anita, Jo and Janice have got first claim, because the Butcher's good as told us he's prowling Fountainside and that's where they're going to be, so that's where *I've* got to be, too.

'So that you all know, I'll be rendezvousing with each of them once every hour. We've got the venues worked out to look as natural as possible, so if you see them talking with the occupant of an unmarked car, don't panic until you're sure it isn't me, in bravo-car with Chip. Questions?'

There were none. Lt Allerton banged his clipboard on the desk. 'Move it.'

Daniel had time for a moment alone with Thelma before they went to station.

'Thelma,' he said, 'I know you're fully trained. I know you've had lots of experience. Still, can I remind you of something?'

'Go ahead.'

'Don't ever be afraid to be afraid.'

She looked at him questioningly. 'I'll be in the car, with Chip.'

'I know. Most of the time. But when you're on the street, knowing when to scream is what sorts out the all-time greats.'

'From who?'

'The dead.'

'I'll remember. Oh, Dan . . . that Fed check on Delacroix . . . ?'

'Tomorrow, hopefully.'

'Because something really weird happened after you left this morning. I had a long talk with him, and he accused Aurelia of having been a schizo, and heaven knows what else. And suddenly the man has *daughters*, for goodness' sake!'

'Okay, I'll chase it. Talk to you tomorrow. Good luck.'

The cars left HQ at three-minute intervals, cruising to their stations via roundabout routes. The last two contained Anita and Jo. Janice Sepeda slipped out through a side door and walked down to Fountainside's main square, where she sat down at a pavement café and ordered a white wine. After she'd been sitting there for ten minutes, altering her make-up and combing her hair with the aid of a mirror, a glance at her watch revealed that Anita and Jo would be just about winding up similar routines at Bar Tivoli and Rosie's Diner. Time to hit the street.

She idled along Rink Alley, eyeballing the shop windows, with special attention to fashion boutiques. Fifty metres or so ahead of her, two plainclothesmen strolled in the same direction, joshing the girls they passed. A hundred metres behind, another plainclothesman brought up the rear. Each of them, including Janice, carried a gun, and two of the men had gas canisters taped to the insides of their forearms. The rearguard, more smartly dressed than his colleagues, carried what looked like a cellular phone, but was in fact a transceiver set to whisper. Patrol cars cruised to rendezvous with the stalking-horse at each intersection, or sometimes, when traffic was thick, every other intersection.

There was a lot of taxpayers' money on the streets of Fountainside that night, and Thelma, a taxpayer herself, didn't begrudge a cent of it.

She rode around in the front seat of bravo-car, with Chip Masefield as her driver. Chip was a bulky guy with not a lot of conversation, a combination that made some people mistake him for stupid, but Thelma liked him. Better, she felt she could rely on him.

The first rendezvous went well. Chip pulled in alongside Jo Penny, who bent down to talk with him through the window: a hooker negotiating with a trick, if anyone was interested.

'You okay?' Thelma asked.

'Sure thing. It's a little cool out here, that's all.'

'Take a coffee-break on the half-hour. Patsy Perone's should be crowded enough. I'll be at a table for two, look out for me.'

'No need. Thanks, though.'

Jo raised herself from the window, crowed, 'Fuck you, Joe,' and stalked off. A moment later, Chip eased bravo-car into traffic and was swallowed by it.

Daniel Krozgrow and Jacob Rabinowicz took turns at driving echo-car and lying on its back seat, monitoring the radios. Daniel would have liked to stay closer to Thelma, but the rules didn't allow for that. He worried about her, not sure why: she was with Chip, she'd done advanced self-defence at a special course designed by police academy, and she was fully weapon-wise. But to Daniel she remained waif-like, vulnerable. Janice, Anita and Jo, well, he was concerned for them; but Thelma Vestrey he loved.

At two ten in the morning his radio came to life. 'Seattle three, all stations,' the voice murmured. Daniel, who was on radio-watch, pulled the transceiver close to his ear and waited. His heart was beating faster than usual, his mouth seemed dry. Albany was Anita, Joplin meant Jo. Seattle was Janice Sepeda's call-sign.

'Corner of "A" and Sommerville. Mark on Seattle now, ten yards behind and closing. Tightening. Out.'

Daniel re-set the transceiver to whisper and considered what he'd heard. A mark meant a suspicious character; and he'd targeted Janice. The plainclothesmen were tightening, closing in.

'Jacob,' Daniel said, 'did you get that?'

'I got it. Sommerville in three minutes.'

As the car accelerated away Daniel pulled a map from the elasticated pocket of the front seat and found the location. His chest muscles tightened. Not good.

He called up bravo-car. Chip answered.

'Are you near to that?' Daniel asked.

'Five blocks.'

'Can you get there now?'

'Negative. Thelma's taking five with Albany.'

'She's not in the car?'

'Negative.'

'*Shit!* Well, can you see her?'

A pause. 'Negative.'

Daniel flicked the transceiver onto the seat beside him. 'Jacob,' he rasped, 'get a move on!'

'A' Street was a wide avenue that ran east-west down to the ocean, bisecting Paradise Bay's business district, with banks, insurance companies and mutual funds on either side. Where it bordered Fountainside on its way to the sea, however, it edged a maze of streets that were ripe for development but meanwhile mouldered away. Big, three-storey warehouses, a few of which had been turned into artists' *ateliers*, some weird-and-wonderful New Age stores, basement theatres big enough to hold a baseball team as long as they all breathed in at the same time: that was Sommerville Street. But for every thriving enterprise there were two long blocks of boarded-up windows, and 'To Rent' signs, and spray-paint graphics. Two blocks of lonely walking for a woman by herself.

Anita Prince had had a quiet night, that's what she told Thelma as she smoked a cigarette in the doorway of a tiny bar that was closing up. A few rowdies, two panhandlers, one teenage drug addict who'd spun her this wonderful story about needing money to have his pet cat put down. She was feeling good and Thelma needn't worry about her.

They parted, with Anita heading west. Thelma had to walk a way to meet up with Chip, and bravo-car.

As she turned out of 'A' Street she saw the canyon stretch ahead of her into black and her heart sank.

'Last couple of hours,' she told herself breezily. 'Then it's piping-hot coffee for you, girl, and a doughnut from Uncle Harry's and home to bed.'

She stepped out boldly, humming a tune. The canyon diminished as she faced it down. Ten steps, twenty steps, thirty; all well, all serene. Her watch told her she was half a minute early to cross with Chip . . .

She picked up on the shadow.

She knew she had a shadow without seeing it, because that was part of the training, and perception sharpened with experience. Now the first and most important thing to remember about any shadow was that it didn't exist as a person until you turned and faced it, so you had a little time to work out what to do.

Thelma walked on, deliberately slowing her pace a tad. Somewhere ahead of her, in the real, static shadows, was Chip; she was armed, safe, with nothing to fear.

*

Wen the bich turn into Sumervil I know I have got you again, you are stupid, you are dumb. I know you cars are far away, I do not have a radio but I can hear you in my head. Do you want to know how it was done? I will tell you.

*

Memories of the forensic photographs swam into Thelma's mind. How much strength did it take to cut off a thumb? To take out a womb?

How much did it hurt?

How long did you take to die, in agony, struggling vainly against an attacker more powerful than God?

'Take Mom to the beach this weekend, and Kirsty,' she said, out loud this time, but not too loud. 'Take a six-pack, get sunburned, ouch.'

Her pace had unconsciously quickened. She brought it back and made herself count: one-and, two-and . . .

Chip, where are you?

Time to look back.

Not yet.

Where are you, Chip?

Do it!

*

She turn her head and can see me, not my face. I walk slow this is the best part. If you are too far away when I do it it is not joy to me. My knife is sharp. It is in my bag. I have pass you many times already that night, you do not even look my bag. I can hurt her when I want, you are far away, I open my bag.

*

Five-and, six-and, turn-and, your-and, head . . .

He was about thirty feet behind her, Thelma judged; tall, powerfully built with only his pale pants standing out from the shadows. He was holding a briefcase. When she turned he opened it and reached inside, looking for something, but he strolled easily, without tension: not a man about to attack.

131

Thelma faced the front again and marched on. Ten-and, eleven-and . . .

Something strange about the briefcase. It spoke. A radio inside, perhaps? Voices, men's voices . . . then her follower closed the case and the voices died.

She inserted her right hand into the waistband of her skirt. The .38's grip was warm, comforting.

Still no sign of bravo. Where was Chip? Had he picked up on this guy? Was his radio working? Helluva time to lose a power-pack, Chip.

How old was her shadow?

She could hear his footsteps now, echoing hers: one-and-one, two-and-two . . . That meant he was coming closer. But she must not speed up.

Thelma slowed her pace until she was barely moving. She pulled out the .38 and held it close to her chest.

*

Wen bich slow down I know you are close. I hear you in my head.
All stations, all stations, I am your station, darlings I am where
you get off, this bich is lucky.

*

The other pair of footsteps had vanished. For one throat-constricting moment Thelma feared this was it, he was upon her. Never be afraid to scream, that was the advice Daniel gave, *it is never wrong to scream.*

Fuck that.

'Excuse me.'

She hadn't been expecting him to speak, not from in front of her. *She was looking over her shoulder but the shadow was now in front, blocking her path.*

'I'm lost. Can you help?'

As Thelma slowly turned her head to face him a car cruised down the street towards them, and she tried frantically to convince herself she'd recognized unmarked vehicle bravo.

'I'm sorry,' she mumbled. 'What?'

'I'm a bit lost.' *This guy had no briefcase!* 'I'm English, I was out drinking with some chaps and I thought I knew my way back to my hotel and I must have taken a wrong turning. It's the

Marina Hilton; you don't by any chance know where it is?'

There was just enough light to reveal a frank, manly face, a black moustache and serious, twinkling eyes. About forty, male, Caucasian, five-ten, one-fifty pounds. Innocent.

Another car was coming up, behind her this time, its engine scarcely a purr against the night silence.

'Make a left down there,' she said, pointing with her gun. How the man stared! 'It'll bring you out at the ocean a block south of the Hilton.'

He thanked her and walked away, into the arms of Sonny Allerton holding his badge at eye height; 'Would you mind,' he said, 'answering a few questions, over against the wall, please.'

Thelma's hand was shaking so badly she almost dropped the gun. 'No,' she said hoarsely, 'he's okay.'

He *was* okay, but only after Sonny had put him through the mill: where he'd been, who had accompanied him, what they'd had to drink, times, places, names; and by then Daniel had called the Hilton, which confirmed they did indeed have registered one Simon Albert George Fisher-Scott who had an Amex card, and what better guarantee of respectability could you have than that? By which time the street was so full of unmarked vehicles and blues and flashing roof-lights you might have thought it was Mardi Gras.

A lot of this passed Thelma by. First she rested her back against the wall. Then she slid down it. Next thing she knew her head was between her knees and Daniel was administering oxygen from the black flask they kept in the trunk of unmarked vehicles along with the Bandaid and the tear gas.

'You all right?' he murmured.

Thelma's world steadied. She looked up into those sparkling eyes, registered that kind smile, said, 'Oh, yes, *yes*!' And was sick all over his chinos.

That was when they got the All Stations saying Anita Prince was dead.

*

My darlings I am fond of you, I can have relations with you if you want. What kind of sex you like I can do it all I am man and woman? You are so bad at what you do I am so good. You can catch me if you want I will do it for you anything you ask. If you get up early in the morning you can catch me in Fountenside wen I am careless I am all fingers and thumbs, darling.

Do you know why I like the thumbs? You should think about it it will help you. I am all fingers and thumbs, I am P.B. Butcher. You have seen me. I am in the street where you are every time. You know me.

As soon as I know you are coming all around i go into the house and out again the back. I walk fast but you cannot see me, I am P.B. Butcher. I can smell the other bich. I wait for her in a doorway. First the 2 men then the bich, I wait for the men to go, then slahs her throat open but I do not have time to take anything I am back in the house and gone I am P.B. Butcher why dont you cach me.

*   *   *

Thelma Vestrey slept late next day. She awoke knowing there was a memory she didn't want to face and for a moment succeeded in keeping it down. Then Anita Prince's murder upped and bit her.

She decided to go in to work at St Joe's, keeping her appointments even though she felt exhausted and not very well. She found time to write to Aurelia's various psychiatrists, something she'd meant to do the day before but forgotten in the excitement of receiving the dead woman's last testament.

Around lunchtime, Makiko brought in the second mail, and Thelma opened the top letter to find it was from Shimon Waldman.

A curious missive to receive from such a man: every phrase spoke fear. He needed to talk, urgently and away from prying eyes. Face to face, and alone, he promised enough revelations to put Naim behind bars for a dozen lifetimes and get the children out of his hands for ever.

He knew who P.B. Butcher was.

Thelma re-read that sentence half a dozen times. If Shimon knew the identity of the killer it could *only* be because it was somebody close to him . . .

Where had Richo been last night?

As soon as she articulated the thought she realized she'd been harbouring it, deep down, for days. A gut reaction, nothing more; a ludicrous hunch. But one that, if given shape, form and breath, resolutely refused to die.

Nonsense!

Thelma stared across the room, over Geoff Diamond, hunched at his computer, to her filing-cabinets. For God's sake, she could think of . . . four, no *five* teenage patients who could easily have been P.B. Butcher. Why pick on Richo, for goodness' sake?

Why? Oh, come on . . . !

If it hadn't been for the Mexico stamp in his passport she'd have suspected him long ago. He wasn't just another disturbed teen freaked out on sex 'n' drugs, he was mad. Dangerous-mad. So where'd he been last night?

Well, one way to find out.

Thelma reached for the phone. She dialled Sacré Coeur, Richo's school, explained who she was and asked for the principal.

A moment later she heard a female voice: warm, vibrant. Thelma's kind of voice. 'Dr Vestrey? Marion Lomar. Thank God you called.'

Lomar's relief was matched by Thelma's own: Naim obviously hadn't got around to telling Richo's school principal that Thelma had been fired. But then Lomar's words triggered an alarm bell inside Thelma's head. 'Has anything happened?' she said quickly.

'We had a terrible night, I . . . Richo went into one of his dream-states, have you encountered those yet?'

'Dream states?'

'He's awake but not awake, if you know what I mean. He accused me last night of wanting to kill him.'

'He was with you, last night, then? All night?'

'Why, of course; where else would he be? He huddled up against the wall, he was shivering.' Marion Lomar sighed. 'I knew he had a problem when I accepted him, but . . . '

'Yet you took him in?'

'Mr and Mrs Delacroix have invested heavily in me and my ideas. Invested financially. There's an element of *quid pro quo* that at times I don't find easy to live with. After spending from midnight till four in the morning with a boy who thinks I want to kill

135

him, that's one such time. And his mother's death, such a terrible thing . . . it devastated him. It set him back months, years. Dr Vestrey, next time you come out to the Delacroix place please call in here; we're only ten miles away from *Pinos Altos*.'

'There's a problem with that. Mr Delacroix has terminated my retainer. I no longer treat Richo.'

'No! But that's terrible! That's *unbelievable!* Richo's so fond of you, he looks up to you, he . . . I'll have to speak to Mr Delacroix about this.'

'Well, please don't say I called. Richo may no longer be my patient, but that doesn't stop me wanting to find out if he's all right.'

'Of course. Look, leave this with me for a day or two. Please will you do that? May we go to first names? I'm more at ease with Marion than with Miss Lomar.'

'Thelma. And do keep a close eye on Richo. I know he skips school sometimes.'

'He told you about that?'

'Yes.'

'Oh, dear. Something else for us to talk about, then. Well, thank you, Thelma, and thanks for the call.'

Thelma put down the phone feeling vaguely disappointed. Richo had been up at Sacré Coeur last night, then; had she seriously expected otherwise?

She redirected her attention to Shimon's letter. The last paragraph was very explicit, but she nevertheless read it through several times.

'Come alone. I won't talk to anyone but you. If the cops get brought into this, you'll never see me again. Don't try to have me arrested. I won't talk to any judge. I'll hand what I know over to you; after that, I'm gone.'

He'd enclosed a sketch-map of the *Pinos Altos* estate. The ranch itself sat almost plumb in the middle of an ovoid boundary. Its main gate, connecting to a road, was in the southeast corner. To the southwest, where the egg-shape jutted out irregularly into national forest, was a gate in the fence. Near it, just inside the boundary, Shimon had marked a small cottage. In his letter he stated he knew how to open the gate without being detected.

He'd meet her at the gate at one o'clock in the morning, two days hence. If she agreed, she was to phone the ranch, pretend she'd made a mistake and say sorry in Spanish: '*Disculpe*'. He would be monitoring all incoming calls.

He did not offer her a chance to decline.

Thelma folded up the letter, put it back in the envelope and dialled *Pinos Altos*. Her rendition of '*Disculpe*' made her feel proud, although Geoff Diamond gave her a pretty strange look.

*   *   *

She met Daniel for a drink at Mamaluke's that evening, after work. He looked tired, and older than she'd ever seen him.

'It was my idea to use the girls,' he said quietly. 'It won approval from every level, here in the Paradise Bay Police Department, in Quantico too. Eight female officers volunteered; we chose three. God, I thought I was being so brilliant!'

He stretched out a hand to take hers. 'Thank God you're safe,' he murmured. 'Thank God, thank Christ.'

There was no elasticity to his skin, it felt dry and somehow unhealthy. He was going to live with the tragedy of Anita Prince's death for a long time.

'Making any progress?' she asked, after a silence.

'Mm? Oh . . . yes. If it's not too heavy a cliché, Anita didn't die in vain. We had another message from the Butcher this lunchtime. It's incredible; he tells us how he did it. Handwritten. Same paper, same thumbprint, and a mass of clues. It's on its way to Quantico now. I wonder if this one was written by a woman.'

'A woman?'

'One of the earlier notes was written by a woman, they think. Or it could have been.'

'But that's unheard of.'

'Not totally. And don't confuse two issues: whoever does the killing may not be the same person as the letter-writer. Or writers, correction, because there's definitely two of them. You're certain that the person you glimpsed was male. I think he's male and I think he's itinerant. He comes into town, does what he has to do, and moves on for a while.'

'What makes you say that?'

'He must have had a quart of blood on him after last night. The town's jumping with fear, people are looking over their shoulders at their own kin. If he lived here, someone would have called us by now.'

'Unless he's being protected.'

'Statistically speaking, that almost only happens in Hollywood, and only in cases of one-location slayings.'

He ordered another whisky sour and replenished her wine glass.

'Tell me about your day,' he said. 'Start with the comics.'

She showed him Shimon's note. Daniel read it and sighed.

'Why can't this guy come into town for a *café latte* like any normal person?'

'Because he's terrified.'

Thelma treated Daniel to a blow-by-blow account of her conversation with Naim, after the funeral.

'Everything about that family stinks,' Dan said when she'd finished. 'You really going to meet Waldman?'

'I've said I will. Although . . . '

'Yes?'

'I'm scared.'

'I'm not surprised. Thelma, this is a dumb idea. He claims to know who this killer is, he wants to see you alone . . . can't you see, it could so easily be a trap?'

'Yes, I see that.'

'Waldman might be Butcher.'

'It's occurred to me.'

'Or it might be Richo – which would be my bet.'

'It might, except that he was having a fit of the heebie-jeebies last night when Anita was . . . you know.'

She told Dan about the phone call she'd made to Marion Lomar.

'Hm . . . '

'Dan, it wasn't Richo! He's got alibis for two of these murders – he was in Mexico for the first and at Sacré Coeur last night. And it would be just too much of a coincidence if *your* killer turned out to be *my* patient. Life doesn't work that way.'

'I still think you're crazy to meet with Waldman. I should get a restraining order.'

But she could see how hungry he was to get inside Shimon's mind. That single reference to the Butcher was enough to override any objection, no matter how rational.

'Entering the lions' den,' Thelma murmured, 'is traditionally a job for Daniels. Why not come? Please come. I can't face it alone.'

'I might just do that. Plus four blues, two cars and an assortment of side-arms.'

'And you think Shimon would show? Read the last paragraph again. Thank you, sir, and goodnight.'

'We could do a proper, professional stake-out.'

'He'd be wise to that. There was something in one of Aurelia's letters . . . he did time with the Israeli Defence Force, he's a pro.'

Daniel gazed at her. 'You really believe this guy knows something?' he said at last.

'Yes. And even if he doesn't, what's to lose? Come with me. Pack a gun, I will too. If Waldman turns out to be Butcher, he won't have a chance against the two of us. All you've got to do is stay out of sight, because he knows you, remember.'

'I must confess, I'm curious.' He looked at her, a disconcertingly straight gaze. 'You really want to go, don't you.'

'Yes. If it nails the Butcher, I'll go anywhere, risk anything.' *All for you, my love; for your career, our future* – that's what she meant to say, but it wouldn't have been tactically sound, so without thinking she concluded: 'For Anita.'

His face twitched, he looked away.

'Sorry,' she muttered.

'No. No. I'll come. Let me book us into a motel in Bakersfield, Best Western give the Feds a special rate. We can drive on from there.'

Wow, back to motel rooms again! 'Could you manage to take a break? We could, like, mini-vacation?'

'God knows, I could use some time off; and I'm due plenty. Let me make a couple of calls . . .'

Thelma whipped off a salute. 'Anything you say, chief.'

*   *   *

139

Daniel adjusted the sound and found himself looking at Rodney Dier, whose face filled the screen.

'Morning, Rod.'

'Hi, Dan. We were all extremely shocked and sorry to hear about your loss.'

'Yeah, well . . . it's had a funny kind of inverse effect here. Anita was a popular guy. Symes wanted to terminate the operation but the other girls wouldn't hear of it. It's personal now.'

'Revenge time, huh? Okay, what have you got?'

'Turns out the Butcher's first two victims had something in common – apart from being murdered in Fountainside, that is. Yolanda Kastin and Sam Brenton were both sent out to foster homes when still very young. The same foster home, in fact, run by a husband-and-wife team called Senior.' Daniel scrolled the file up his Toshiba-screen. 'Before she got married, Mrs Senior's maiden name was Roach. Now. The *third* victim, Patty Ann King, was an only child and her father moved around a lot. Was a time when they boarded with a family called Roach. It's not such a common name, and I'm working on it. I've got a sheet here with the details; can we scan it through?'

'Sure. Give me a minute.'

The two men moved to their respective computer terminals and set up the scanning facility. A moment later, Rodney Dier was looking at an exact copy of Daniel's fact-sheet.

'How'd you find out about King?' Dier asked. 'I can see the foster records would be there, but . . . '

'There's a brilliant detective here called Andy ter Haar. Young, hungry. He went after King's folks. The mother's dead, killed in a brawl somewhere in Wyoming. Father's living in a trailer outside of Santa Barbara. Not in any great shape, apparently, but ter Haar fed him intravenous Jack Daniel until he had the background. Incidentally, if ter Haar ever files a job application with you guys, hire him, hire him.'

'Okay. Follow up Roach/Senior, see what you get. I'll run it through the mill here. Anything else?'

'That's it from me.'

'Right. Now, the cardstock Butcher's using comes from Hong Kong. It's on sale only in the Far East, but it's on sale there everywhere. The chances of our tracking down that particular batch are nil.'

'Traces?'

'Nothing helpful on the card. But we now have three notes from Butcher. You've seen the latest graphologist's report, by the way? And the language-analysis?'

'Yup.'

On the basis of strokes, style and content they were now saying that the notes had probably been composed by two different people: one whose first language was not English, and who was right-handed; another who might turn out to be female.

'The dust on the two sheets of paper matches. The second thumbprint had been deliberately smeared, like the first, though we learned a lot from the blood, which one day hopefully can be matched too. Statistical bias says that it came from an Asiatic, plus it contains traces of chemical.'

Daniel frowned. 'So he's not black?'

'Almost certainly not, despite modus operandi and physical indications. This guy reads us pretty good.'

'What's that chemical you mentioned – drugs?'

'Could be, we're waiting on the lab. Knowing our luck it'll turn out to be nicotine.'

'What's PROFILER got to say about fingers and thumbs?'

'Some phallic stuff, if you're feeling insomniac. New York State's turned up three homicides within the past year classified as drug-murder here; Triad stuff. There it was the pinky. LA has so many murders involving excision of fingers that we've given up counting – all drugs-related, nothing classified as serial or spree.'

'Fingers and thumbs,' Daniel murmured. 'In this case, I'm all fingers and thumbs.'

Rodney Dier laughed. 'Talk to you tomorrow, Dan,' he said, reaching for the Off switch.

* * *

Annette awoke with a start. Her bedroom was dark, the clock said three thirty-two. Had there been a noise? Yes! Next door . . .

She pulled on a pair of panties and a robe, because this wasn't a house where girls went about skimpily clad, not with a sick beast of a brother on the prowl, and padded along the passage to Jacqui's room. Her sister was sitting up in bed, weeping. Annette snuggled down beside her.

'Bad dream again?'

Jacqui nodded. 'I can't stand it any more,' she sobbed.

Annette switched off the bedside light and for a while the two girls lay in each other's arms. Gentle rain pattered against the window-pane. They snuggled closer. Annette felt guilty, because Jacqui's tears made her irritated and that wasn't a very sisterly reaction. She'd always had to be the strong one.

'I see Mom's body,' Jacqui muttered. 'Every night.'

'Don't!'

'All that blood, and . . . and . . . oh, sis, why did she hate us so? What was wrong with us, what did we *do*?'

'Nothing. Snap out of it!' Annette lowered her voice to a whisper, so that the guards in the basement wouldn't be able to hear no matter how high they turned up their microphones. She'd been the one to find out about the surveillance, the year before, when she'd confessed to her sister that she was madly in love with a groom, and next day the boy had been fired. 'C'mon! Listen, this Dr Vestrey, maybe she can help?'

'But she's *his*!'

'You called her?'

'Not yet. No chance. And anyway, I'm scared. What if she tells Dad?'

Annette had no answer to that. But – 'I still think we can use Vestrey to help us get away.'

'How?'

'Once we've managed to contact her properly, she'll maybe get a place-of-safety order.'

'You'd tell her about *him*? You'd really do that?'

'Dear heart, we should have told the world years ago: our brother is a sex pervert who shoves his hand in our pants any chance he gets.'

'Father'll never believe you.'

'I'm not going to tell Father,' Annette hissed. 'That's the whole point, you goose!'

'Little Miss Turtle,' Jacqui tittered. 'Little Miss L.M.T.'

'Shut up.' Annette flushed; she hated her nickname.

'How much are we going to tell Vestrey?'

'All of it. Why we're so afraid. What goes on in this place at night.'

Jacqui giggled again. 'You mean, you and Pedro?'

Annette stuffed a hand over her sister's mouth. 'That's over,' she grated. 'I told you!'

'Didn't stop you kissing him this afternoon after trotting, I saw you.'

Annette punched her, but gently. 'Listen,' she said. 'They took all our stuff out of Hobie's Hut; I checked last evening on the way back from exercising Tally. But it won't take us more than a week to put together a survival kit.'

'We could still run away?'

'Sure we could. We don't need our passports. Hundreds of people cross the Mexico border every night. None of them have got passports.'

'Hundreds get caught.'

'Going the other way, *into* the States.'

'But if we got caught . . . '

'Then we'd be in police custody. And if we'd already got Vestrey on our side, she'd help, see?'

'Mm-hm.'

'So tomorrow, we phone and be nice to her, yes? Charming. Sweet little girls with tears in our voices, needing help.'

'Okay.'

'And start getting the stuff together, like we did before. Only leave your violin behind this time.'

'Must I?'

'Yes,' Annette hissed.

'I will if you'll leave your Guns 'n' Roses tapes.'

'Shit, you drive a hard bargain. Deal.'

They slapped palms.

'But be careful,' Annette warned. 'You know what Richo'll do if he gets even a hint of this? Since they found all that stuff in Hobie's Hut, he's been watching us like a rattlesnake.'

Jacqui was trembling now. 'He'll kill us,' she whispered.

'Only if we let him,' Annette replied.

*   *   *

Thelma had just finished packing her overnight bag when the doorbell rang. She raced downstairs, already late, to find a FedEx courier on the doorstep.

'Dr Thelma Vestrey . . . sign here, please.'

Oh, no, she thought, *oh, no!* This couldn't be happening. Her mother must have ordered something from Sears. Please let it be that. *Please*.

She signed in a daze. The courier left. Thelma summoned up the nerve to examine the package's label, not that she needed to. 'Nobody, Inc.' Consigned at Santa Barbara Main, the previous evening, 5:0 p.m.

Thelma's legs were shaking. She carried the package into the kitchen and laid it on the table, and for a moment just stared at it. She sat down. She drew it towards her. But she couldn't bring herself to open it.

Pull yourself together, Thelma. It's perfectly clear what happened here. Aurelia wrote down her life story before she died and now somebody else is feeding it to you in bleeding chunks. Consider the alternative. The alternative is that a dead woman has written this stuff and you know that simply isn't possible.

Who is sending me this? Why?

She opened the packet. Sure enough, it contained a dozen or more sheets of Aurelia's distinctive paper, covered with her equally distinctive handwriting. Thelma skimmed through the first few pages. It seemed to be a continuation of the last instalment . . .

If she was to get to the Bakersfield Best Western in time to meet Dan she had to leave now, this instant. They had three precious days lined up together, every minute counted . . .

Looked like she was going to be late.

*

Madame, there is an English poem which proceeds along these lines: 'If you can keep your head when all about are losing theirs . . . ' Such was our situation in the apartment the night of Naim's arrest. For Shimon, it was the end. For me, however, it was <u>not</u> the end. I knew that what we needed, what we absolutely had to have, was intelligence. Information.

Next day, we moved in with Shimon's girl, and I went to visit Naim in prison. At first, things looked bleak indeed. A Syrian drugs dealer of some prominence had been murdered in Paris, an underworld spy had pointed the finger at Naim. There were witnesses, apparently. At first, that was all we knew. Then, as the days passed, the story became clearer.

The dead man had been shot in the head, at an apartment he rented in Neuilly. Neighbours reported hearing shots at midnight and some time after that, but the latest time the murder could have been committed was twelve fifteen. None of the fabulous eye-witnesses had caught more than a fleeting glimpse of the gunman as he fled. The best evidence the police had against Naim was the statement of this anonymous informer; that, and the facts which their investigation of Naim's business empire threw up. For he was a villain, as nobody had ever doubted; it was just that now we had proof. He dealt in drugs, he dealt in arms, he dealt in human flesh. But what I refused to lose sight of was that the case against Naim depended on guilt by association, coupled with the word of an informer with a police record as long as Le Train Bleu.

I had some savings, by this time: presents from Naim, money accumulated from my allowance. Shimon chipped in, once he saw how determined I was. We hired the most expensive lawyers we could afford. I went to Naim in prison, and I said, looking him straight in the eye, 'How fortunate, my dear, that we were together in bed, making love, that night when they say it happened.' And from that visit, all else derived.

It took time, of course, and many visits to Naim, before everyone concerned had his or her role off pat. But there came a day when I rode down to the Préfecture on Quai de March Neuf in the company of Maître Sallon, penetrating those high and dreadful stone walls with no little trepidation, and I went before the Juge d'Instruction. In my romantic way I'd harboured some thought that he might be a former client of mine and so subject to influence; mercifully he was not, or no doubt I would have ended up in prison too.

I told my story. He listened, attentively, before demanding, 'Why do you lie for this scum?'

Madame, I'd gone prepared for everything – everything except confrontation with cold truth. I'd made Shimon go over the details of Naim's body again and again, until I could be cross-examined about his moles and his scars and never be faulted; I had tracked down his women, learning from them whether he was circumcised (he was), what his preferred techniques were, his chosen positions . . . On matters of detail, I was word perfect. What I'd over-looked was the broad picture. But the Juge did not overlook anything. When he issued that forthright challenge, for a moment the room swayed around me; I thought I might faint. Because, you see, I could not remember why I was doing this. Naim stood accused of murder, he might go to the guillotine or at least to prison for the rest of his life; the insult to the French state would thus be expunged, France would be avenged.

But then the room steadied, and I remembered: I would not be avenged. With composure and with élan, I repeated my story, and challenged them to produce a witness, a voice, one single shred of evidence to contradict my version. They could not. Naim was set free.

Convinced of my loyalty, overcome by the defection of his friends, he married me, as I had all along intended. I soon gave birth to the child I craved. Ricardo, Naim wanted to call him that, so we did; but to me he was Rashid, until he became Richo. At playschool everyone knew him as Richo, because his father was wealthy, and I liked that. Unfortunately he grew up dyslexic, he was a problem child, disruptive and unruly at whatever school he attended. Our lifestyle didn't help. We moved from country to country, culture to culture. Richo never had a chance to put down roots. The doctors healed his dyslexia to the point where now he suffers occasional difficulty spelling a familiar word, that is all. But the deeper wounds, the emotional deprivations, they can never be healed.

Madame, what have I done?

I wanted a child to use as a weapon in my war against Naim. I had a son and fell in love with him – am I not a woman? Am I

not a mother? Nobody exempted me from the laws of mankind.
And my love deepened when I discovered that I would never be
able to bear more children.

What effect did this have on my relations with the man who was
now my husband?

Slowly and painfully, Naim rebuilt his empire, while I watched.
I supported him with outpourings of love, with my fortitude, my
strength. He began to take me into his confidence, to consult me as
well as instruct me. By my twenty-fifth birthday, I had the details
of his life at my fingertips: I knew the name of every banker, share-
dealer, lawyer and hitman (there were several of those!) in each
continent. He mislaid the phone number of his partner in Madrid;
I had it in my purse or, more often, my head. We were moving to
the New York apartment, pouf! – it was stocked with food before
Naim had finished the sentence. A good place to take the new syn-
dicate for dinner – ask Aurelia. Air-taxi to Medellín – see Aurelia.
Can we trust him? – where's Aurelia? 'Aurelia! I need you!' . . .
the sweetest words I ever heard.

We dealt in arms and drugs and, curiously, race-horses. Don't
ask me why. It wasn't as if my husband had a passion for horse-
flesh. Increasingly we moved our operation into South America.
Colombia, no: we avoided the problems there. Peru was our milch-
cow, providing more cocaine in a year than all of Asia put together.
In those days the army ran Peru and the army was hungry for
guns. We had them. 'You want it, we have it.'

Ah, it's enough of a snapshot for you. Isn't it? Or do you want
to know what happened of an evening, after the dregs of the X.O.
had been drained, the last gangster, mafioso, triad, had been sent
home in the stretched Mercedes, after Shimon had been dispatched
to make phone calls, once the lights were turned down low . . .?

We were a couple, Madame, a married couple. We talked, we
laughed. We made love several times a week. I was an inventive
slut. Naim had plenty of stamina. He knew how to make it fun; I
knew how to fake an orgasm. How many marriages do you know
of, just like that?

Not one.

I hated him from the moment my eyes opened in the morning
until last thing at night; in my dreams I hated him. His presence in

the same room made my flesh creep. How did I bear the weight of his body on mine, the gruntings in my ear, his breath-stink in my nostrils? I bore those things as so many women do: with fortitude. But all the while I bided my time and waited for the revenge that would be mine. I waited and waited, and I brought up Richo with a love that at times could be suffocating. Yes, I know that, I admit it. He was all I had to lavish love on. And Naim adored him!

For many years Naim was faithful to me. The memory of Nada's death bound him fast to my side. Whenever he laid hands on me there was something reverent about it, as if I were a sacred relic that his hands were unworthy to soil. Making love to me was Naim's sole act of worship. But suddenly he became ecumenical, and there were other women. He was secretive, like cheating husbands the world over, but never secretive enough. There are certain patterns of behaviour that you change at your peril. When a man comes home after a business trip he'll always unwind in the same way. Naim departed from habit; I knew at once, and my heart lifted up. A new source of guilt! And this meant, please God! that I wouldn't have to endure his stinking body, the colour of shit, next to mine with quite such odious regularity.

I tolerated his infidelities. I could tolerate anything, as long as it led to my revenge. You see, Madame, I was putting together a dossier of Naim's activities that I would one day use to destroy him – not by going to the police, oh no. By going to his associates: the men he defrauded on a daily basis, laughing because he thought they'd never know. My previous idea – breeding a child for sacrifice – no longer had any appeal. I loved my son. Never 'our' son. Richo was, is, mine.

Why did I wait? Ah, easy to ask that now, with hindsight! There were several reasons why I didn't just stick a knife into that bloated belly. There were too many people around, for a start; I was watched, we all were. And then . . . I came to enjoy the lifestyle. I was a wealthy woman, but it would all come tumbling down with Naim, and somehow I never seemed ready for that.

I'm deceiving myself, and you. The real reason why I waited was that I could never find a means of revenge devastating enough to satisfy my obsession. Killing Naim, ruining him in business . . .

what a waste of effort! I bided my time. I waited, as I am <u>still</u> waiting.

Shimon helped me. Not at first, or all at once. His is an interesting story. He was the child of poor European immigrants to Israel. He deserted from the Israeli Defence Force when he was twenty-one and made his way to Marseilles. There, Naim saved him from a life of petty crime, and Shimon saved Naim's life, literally: there was an ambush, Shimon out-shot ten men, grabbed Naim, fought a way through against terrible odds. Naim used to tell the story over and over. Shimon never told it. I mention this so that you may understand some of the hard decisions Shimon was called upon to make. He owed Naim everything, and Naim owed him, too. There was something between those two. They should have been lovers, but neither was suited to the role.

There was another way in which they could have each other, though. They could share the same woman.

I'd found Shimon attractive almost from the start. I was indifferent to the thought of sex with anyone, but if he'd asked me, before Naim showed up, I'd have said yes. Now I resolved to say no, no, no. Because by the time I celebrated my thirtieth birthday I was sure that Shimon wanted me as much as he wanted food, air, water. He'd fallen under my spell, he was mine. All I had to do was ensure he never had me.

We arrive in the year 1991. I was approaching forty, still beautiful, still a slut on those rare occasions when my husband selected me for recreation. I knew everything there was to know about him, down to his real name, for he was not born Delacroix. I'd done it all without incriminating Shimon, or not too much. I would be engaged in fixing something for Naim and casually I'd ask Shimon for some detail, and he'd give it to me without thinking, and I'd add another little piece to my jigsaw of the mind. At some point he had transferred his loyalty to me, without noticing. So when in 1991 he came to me and said, 'Naim is planning to live in the Greenhorn Mountains of California, he has bought a ranch,' it never occurred to me to doubt him, even though none of this made sense to either of us.

What were these Greenhorn Mountains? Where were they? It took us a quarter of an hour to locate them on the map. Shimon

149

*found an old edition of Fodor; we learned about white-water
rafting on the River Kern, trekking, meadows and pastures at ten
thousand feet . . . Madame, it was a <u>wilderness</u>! Part desert, part
farmland, part forest and all remote from anything I would regard
as civilization. Had Naim gone mad?*

*We moved to Pinos Altos. No explanations. No discussions. Naim
issued orders and the circus left town. We buried ourselves alive.
Suddenly we became a large household: there were people living
with us I'd never seen before, and when I say people, I mean
women, Naim's women. He'd imported a harem of young white
girls. Among them was a set of twins, not much older than Nada
was the day she died. I quizzed Naim about these strangers; his
only answer was a shrug. For the first time we quarrelled. Or
rather: I quarrelled, he refused to put up a fight. He walked away.
I bought a gun and kept it under my pillow.*

*Naim is writing a book, or at least, so he claims: a political his-
tory of the Philippines in the twentieth century. Either he's absent
on a trip to his home country, 'research', he calls it, or he sits
locked in his study. I think he's mad. He must be mad.*

*There is a ranch house, which is where Naim lives with me, and
Shimon has his quarters. Richo was given his own casita, as the
Spanish call it, in the grounds. I was tempted to flee, but that
would have meant leaving Richo at the mercy of his father.*

Thelma stuffed the papers into the side-pocket of her bag and
rushed out to the Bronco. So much information to digest, and no
time . . .

She must get this to Daniel, fast – thank God she'd be seeing
him within hours. Delacroix: not Naim's real name. Drugs, race-
horses, a murder investigation in Paris: the FBI *must* have a file
on him somewhere, under some name. Two twins, 'imported' by
Naim . . . *Great God, those were her own children she was talking about,
one of them conceived in her own womb! Yet she'd written that, after
Richo, she couldn't have more children!*

Assume, just assume for a moment, that any of this was true.
Naim must have killed the sister, Nada or whatever her name
was, and that had driven Aurelia over the edge. Was Richo a
replacement for Nada, then?

When had these most recent pages been written? Some time ago, she sensed. Were there any more to come? There *must* be more! She pounded the wheel in frustration: surely Aurelia couldn't have died without setting down the trauma that crippled her?

Daniel was going to have to trace Nobody, Inc., and Thelma didn't care what it cost the taxpayer.

As she drove up Highway 1 she desperately tried to recall the literature on parents who denied their children, or who used them in some way. She must consult Professor Gomez when she returned, then spend a week in the library.

But first and most important, she must speak to Daniel.

*　　*　　*

Jacqui entered the stable so quietly that Annette didn't hear her.

'Sis, what's wrong?' Jacqui went to kneel beside her. 'Why are you crying?'

'I'm not.'

'Oh, sis . . . '

The two girls clutched each other. By now Jacqui was crying too. 'It's Mother, isn't it?' she whispered.

Annette's body shivered an assent.

'Sweetheart . . . we have to come to terms with it someday. She didn't love us. That wasn't our fault – how many times have you told me that? We have to build our own lives now.'

'Yes.' Annette dabbed her eyes. 'I know.'

'Don't cry. You only make me cry, too. Hey, listen. This'll maybe cheer you up. I snuck into Mademoiselle's room early this morning; you know that portable phone of hers?'

'But when she gets the monthly account she'll know,' Annette sniffed.

'So who cares? We'll be over the border and far away, and Bennet College for Young Ladies can go quarry shit.'

'Oh. Yeah. So . . . so what happened?'

'Well, I got through to Vestrey first try.'

Annette's face brightened. 'Is she going to help us?'

Jacqui knelt by the side of the big hutch. She poked a wedge of carrot through the cage at Perry, her white mother-rabbit, and frowned. 'Not sure. She won't tell on us though; she did promise me that.'

'You trust her?'

'Oh, yes. You mean, you don't?'

Annette shrugged. 'She's a poseuse,' she said, putting away her hankie.

'Well, at least she doesn't use the word poseuse.'

Their smiles were wan.

'Vestrey says the trouble is, ethics.'

'What's that?'

'She can't even *talk* to us, without parental consent. Can't – or won't, it comes to the same thing.'

'What else did she say?'

'Nothing much. She said we were always at liberty to involve the police, and we should, if we got frightened.'

'Guess that's it, then.'

'It was worth a try.'

For a while the two girls studied the rabbit in silence.

'I heard them again last night,' Annette said in a shaky voice. 'The footsteps.'

Jacqui nodded. 'About three o'clock.'

They gazed at each other. 'It's not *him*,' Jacqui announced with finality.

'No.'

'I'd think it was Shimon, only he's in New York.'

Jacqui got up and went to fetch a pail of feed. The ponies were restless; on her way back she paused outside several stalls, making soothing noises. 'What's with you?' she muttered.

She put the pail on the floor by the biggest rabbit-hutch and started shredding a lettuce she'd brought from the kitchen. Perry, too, was restless. She ran to and fro, ignoring the green shreds that Jacqui poked through the mesh. The carrot-wedge lay on the floor of the hutch, with only a single set of teeth-marks moulding one end.

'What's up, girl?' Jacqui muttered.

'*Shit!*' Annette suddenly leapt to her feet and started hopping around on one foot.

152

'What is it?'

'Something stung me, yikes! Gimme the flashlight.'

It was three o'clock in the afternoon, but little light penetrated this far into the stable. Jacqui scrabbled for the light and turned it on. 'God,' she breathed, shining the beam on Annette's foot. 'It's already swelling up, and it's so *red*. Look! There!'

She took off one shoe and swatted down, hard. 'Ugh,' she said in disgust. 'All black and squishy . . . '

'Jacqui.' Annette had stopped dancing around and was staring fixedly at a point next to her sister's feet. The other girl turned to look. When she'd swatted the insect, the flashlight, still switched on, had fallen into the pail of rabbit-feed. Jacqui saw what had caught Annette's eye, and for a moment couldn't believe it.

'Be careful.' Annette laid a warning hand on Jacqui's shoulder. 'Don't touch it, you know what'll happen if you touch it.'

Just underneath the lettuce the girls could see a cluster of shiny, dark green leaves. Because they'd been taught to recognize it from an early age, they knew it was poison oak. The oil from the leaves clung to the skin from the moment of contact. At first you didn't even notice; then, about four hours later, the excruciating pain began. And it was so easy to fall foul of poison oak: if your jacket bruised the leaves the oil transferred to the cloth and stayed toxic for up to a year afterwards.

Somebody had put poison oak into the rabbit's food.

'Get the potassium permanganate,' Jacqui said. 'I'll throw this out.'

'Why waste it?' Annette said bitterly. 'It's time Creepo ate more greens.'

'Richo didn't do this.'

'What?'

'I gave them some food this morning, and this stuff wasn't there then. Creepo's been at Sacré Coeur all day, so it can't have been him.'

'But then . . . who?'

The sisters stared at each other. 'I don't know,' Jacqui muttered. 'I don't know.'

* * *

At first Thelma planned to drop her bag off at the motel and wait for Daniel there, but as she bowled along Route 65 another idea caught her fancy. She pulled into a gas station and consulted her map. Now where was Sacré Coeur . . . ? Ah-*ha*. Not far. She'd visit Marion Lomar, *then* check into the motel.

The road from Bakersfield lay first through rolling green plains before starting to climb into the Greenhorns, where it became steep and twisty. There was something Swiss about the landscape, Thelma decided: rolling hills amid which nestled strong wooden houses with barns nearby, and sheep roaming the fields. But the road was tricky; she got lost a couple of times, and without the help of a friendly Ranger she'd never have found Richo's school.

Sacré Coeur turned out to be a grand house in immaculately kept grounds. Thelma's route took her past some tennis-courts and a swimming-pool with a disused air. The house, in contrast, was brilliant white and pristine. Thelma pulled up on a gravel semi-circle, and sat for a moment admiring the ornamental rose-bushes that extended from the front of the house down to a maze formed out of low hedges, with a sundial at its heart. She could hear birdsong, and felt a twinge of envy for students privileged to study in such surroundings.

But when she entered the house through its wide open front door, another impression struck her: this was *too* quiet for a place of learning. She stood in a spacious hallway adorned with portraits of conservative hue, while sun streamed in through four high, oval windows and she could hear her own heart beating.

Cautiously she ventured down a corridor of patterned black and white marble, past the bust of some venerable former alumnus, and so to a door signed 'Marion Lomar – Principal'. Amid such awesome silence Thelma felt like a miscreant come to take her punishment. She knocked.

'Come.'

Thelma entered an airy, book-lined study, in the centre of which stood a large oak desk. Marion Lomar was already rising to her feet. She wore a muted floral print dress, formal yet somehow unintimidating, that showed off to perfection the healthy figure of a woman in her mid-thirties.

'Hello,' she said, extending her hand. 'You're Thelma Vestrey; I claim my free gift.'

Thelma laughed; Marion's open face and feel-good smile were infectious. Everything about her, from the crown of her neatly bunned, ash-blonde hair, to her sparkling pumps, spoke of poise. She had the same effect on Thelma as a glass of cool spring water taken in the heat of midday.

'How did you know who I am?'

'Richo showed me your photograph.'

'My *what*? I never knew he had a photo of me.' *How in hell's name had he come by that?*

'It's very fetching, I can assure you. Richo carries it with him wherever he goes. He shows you off, and now that I've met you, I can see why. Sit down, do.'

Instead of retreating behind her desk Marion led Thelma to the bow window at the far end of the room, and there they sat facing each other across a low table inlaid with bevelled glass.

'I was about to have tea,' Marion said. 'Will you join me?'

As she spoke, the door opened and a white-aproned maid brought in a silver tray with tea-things. 'Margie, please fetch one more cup.'

Thelma saw that the woman was a Filipina.

'Right away, miss.'

The tea was Earl Grey: fragrant, cooling, served in a cup of fluted Royal Doulton china. For a while the two women sipped in companionable silence, each taking the measure of the other.

Marion's face was full of character and discernment, her clear gaze polite but searching. Thelma guessed a wicked sense of humour might lurk there, although she was too demure, too much the schoolmarm, to let it show on first meeting. One thing, and one thing only, struck her as out of place, odd. Marion Lomar favoured pale mauve lipstick.

Apart from that isolated peculiarity, the room, so obviously a place of work, was in perfect accord with Sacré Coeur's principal. The shelves were filled with works of English literature, encyclopaedias, year books. Nearest to Thelma was *Winning Scholarships: Student's Guide to Entrance Awards at Ontario*

155

Universities and Colleges, suggestive of a woman who took life's mission seriously.

A sideways glance revealed Marion smiling at her with moist, parted lips.

'Tell me about this place,' Thelma said quickly. 'I've never heard of it, and it seems so peaceful. Ah . . . I've just realized what it is: no one's playing sports.'

'We place heavy emphasis on academic studies here. The students are free to play tennis and swim after six, but the days are for work, and it's an eight-hour day. Do you play tennis?'

'Yes.'

Marion smiled lazily. 'Perhaps we could fix up something.'

'Why not? Tell me, what do you aim to achieve here?'

Marion continued to regard her visitor through languid eyes of deep hazel, her mind obviously not on the question. Just as Thelma was about to repeat it, however, she said, 'To bring some difficult members of society back into its fold. It works. To a degree.'

'Will it work for Ricardo Delacroix?'

'I used to think so, yes. But he took his mother's death very hard, and now he can be a disruptive influence on the other students.'

'Disruptive . . . and not always here. He tells me you know he sometimes takes off.'

'Yes. The first time it happened, I alerted his father. Oh my, but there was hell to pay! Since then, I've used my discretion.'

'He went to Mexico this year, on his birthday?'

'That was a particularly stressful time for him. Because I knew where he was going, and because he kept in touch by phone, I didn't say anything to his parents. I took a chance. But I had to really pressurize him to come home.'

'He respects you, then.'

'We have a rapport, yes.'

'I shouldn't say this . . . hell, I oughtn't to be here at all, but . . . he's taking drugs, isn't he?'

'I fear so, though he knows he'll be expelled instantly if he's caught. And in fairness, since you took him under your wing, he's improved. You've become an important role model; I sense

156

his drug-dependency has lessened. I wish, oh how I wish, Mr Delacroix would agree to have you back!'

'You've asked him?'

'In a roundabout way. He's dead against it.'

Thelma decided to venture a shot or two. 'Is that because he's emigrating?'

Marion paused with her cup halfway to her lips. 'Emigrating?' She put the cup down in its saucer. 'Mr Delacroix?'

'I thought he might be.'

'Not to my knowledge, no. No, he's insisting that Richo consult a male next time around.'

'Do you think that's a good idea?'

Marion shrugged.

'Is Richo suffering from addiction, or something more serious? Schizophrenia, perhaps? I'd certainly advise that a psychiatrist look him over.'

Marion took a sip of tea. 'I think,' she said, gazing into Thelma's eyes, 'that this isn't the time.'

'Why not?'

'Because we're just getting him back onto an even keel after his mother's death and I'm reluctant to authorize anything that might disrupt his routines. Your sessions, of course, would be excepted.'

'Excuse me, but isn't it perhaps for Mr Delacroix to authorize, as you put it?'

'He's accustomed to act in accordance with my suggestions where his son's concerned.'

'But not with your suggestion that I should be reassigned to Richo's case?'

'No.'

Thelma felt as though she'd belted into an invisible brick wall. One moment she was sitting here, chatting amiably to a woman she liked and respected; the next she found herself encountering implacable opposition. No question about it: Marion Lomar didn't intend Richo to see a board-certified psychiatrist.

'Now,' Marion said, rising, 'would you care to look around?'

'If it's no trouble. Perhaps it's best if Richo doesn't see me here.'

'Of course.'

Thelma was about to follow Marion out of the room when she noticed a huge Bible, alone on a shelf of the bookcase nearest the door. 'What's your policy on religious teaching?' she queried.

'We don't have one.' Marion followed Thelma's eyes; and for the first time seemed in less than perfect equilibrium. 'I . . . was strictly brought up.'

Thelma smiled politely at her, but Marion hadn't finished.

'I believe in Hell, don't you?'

Her words came out in a rush, startling Thelma. Before she could think of a tactful negation, Marion went on, 'We burn, when we die, unless . . . '

She seemed to become aware of Thelma's intent interest in what she was saying, and gnawed her lip. 'I believe in a personal Devil, a personal hell,' she asserted. 'I'm rather old-fashioned. Shall we go?'

Thelma hadn't encountered such fervour in a long time, and it provoked a shiver in her stomach. But as the tour progressed she soon forgot all about Marion's religious convictions, because the school itself turned out to be so odd.

Marion walked close by her side, floating along in a cloud of perfume that Thelma had encountered before but couldn't identify, except she knew it was for men, not women. The classrooms were arranged on the ground floor; they passed door after door, but hardly ever did Thelma catch the murmur of voices. Marion showed her the science laboratories with particular pride. They contained every imaginable item necessary for study and analysis. And they were empty.

Thelma found herself wondering if the entire school was empty.

At last they emerged onto a semi-circular flight of shallow steps at the back of the house, overlooking another manicured lawn. About fifty yards away was a graceful and very old white oak. Beneath its spreading branches sat a group of young men and women, listening to a teacher as he walked to and fro, gesticulating.

'Politics,' Marion murmured. 'American nineteenth century. Sports should be kept in their place, but I've no objection to fresh air.'

As she spoke, she placed a hand on the small of Thelma's back, and turned to smile into her guest's eyes. 'Don't you agree?' she said.

'Mm-hm.'

Thelma moved forward to rest both hands on the low balustraded wall in front of her, disengaging from Marion and her stodgy perfume. Among the students she noticed Richo – Damn! She had a feeling he'd seen her, but was determined not to show it.

The two women went back inside the house, where Thelma said goodbye to Marion Lomar. She drove on to Bakersfield, her mind stuck on a spiral of doubts and fears. The one bright spot was the prospect of seeing Daniel again this evening. The thought of them getting to grips with the latest instalment of Aurelia's story was almost as enticing as that of getting to grips with Dan himself. Three whole days together . . .

Even that prospect was dashed, however, when she arrived at Best Western Inn on Pierce Road. A message awaited her, saying that Dan was tied up and couldn't make it. There was a number for her to call; Thelma headed for the bank of phones.

'Where are you?' she asked when Pacific Bell connected them.

'San Luis Obispo. Great to hear your voice.'

'You can say that again. And again. And again.'

'Look, I'm with the sheriff, on a multiple-rape case, so tonight's off.'

'So when can you get up here?'

'I don't know. Thelma, I'm sorry. Another time.'

'Oh, *Dan* . . .'

'Listen, honey, in a way it's not so bad. This meeting with Shimon, it's become a terrible idea. I've got some material on Delacroix. He mixes with strange people. Drugs and arms dealers in centre frame, though there's no evidence linking him to any deals.'

'*Yes!* Dan, it fits!' Hastily Thelma poured out the gist of Aurelia's most recent chapter. 'I have to show you this, when can we meet? Can I fax it to you?'

'Yeah, why not? Here's the number . . .'

Thelma wrote it down.

'Listen,' Dan said, 'what happened today? I was expecting you to have checked in around four, when they told me you hadn't shown I was worried.'

'Oh, bless you. Actually, I went to Sacré Coeur, you know, Richo's school?'

'Why, in God's name?'

'After Anita was killed, I thought I'd check where Richo had been that night, so I phoned the school. He was there the previous night, so he's out of it. The principal invited me to visit, so I did. And it's such a strange place. Too quiet . . . Dan, could you come out here tomorrow?'

'Uh, tomorrow I've been rescheduled to San Francisco to meet with the Racial Equality people. Another reason why I couldn't make Bakersfield.'

'They cancelled your vacation? Oh, *Dan* . . . '

'Yeah. I know. Sorry.'

A thought struck Thelma. 'That means you won't be going down to Fountainside with the girls tomorrow night.'

'No. I've already contacted Symes. They don't need me with them every time.'

'But I've cancelled, too. I lied about it, I said I had a really important appointment I couldn't break. Oh, this is turning into such a shitty day.'

'But now you can go with the girls, if you want.'

'I guess.'

'And if you do go tomorrow night, you take care.'

'Yes, *sir*.'

'You going to tell me what underwear you've got on or shall I call a 900 on line two?'

'Line two. See ya, Big Guy. Love you . . . '

Thelma hung up and turned away, swallowing bitter disappointment. Outside on the lot she could see her Bronco. Tank up, hit the road, home in time for supper. Fax Aurelia's letter to Daniel. Call Peter Symes, say she could make tomorrow's assignment after all. Take Rufe for a long, stimulating walk . . .

She moved toward the glass doors, jangling coins, her face thoughtful.

'Excuse me, Dr Vestrey . . . '

She turned to face the reception-clerk.

'Will you be requiring the room?'

She opened her mouth to say no, before realizing that this was a very good question.

She knew what she ought to do. Dan was right: best to stay away from *Pinos Altos*, certainly best not to go there alone. Waldman had connections with some dangerous people, and might himself be dangerous.

But it wasn't quite as simple as that. Inviting Dan along had seemed a good idea at the time, but ever since she'd been suffering from doubts. Deep down inside she knew, she just *knew*, that Waldman would detect she hadn't come to the meeting alone. He'd vanish into the night, and that would be that.

And really, she did have to talk to Shimon – on his own terms if those were the only terms available – because she'd do anything for Daniel. Anything at all that had to be done to make his career for him. Armed with Shimon's information, she was going to find out who P.B. Butcher really was, and let her beloved Dan take all the credit. Whereas if the police breezed in with a warrant, Shimon wouldn't talk, the case would collapse, and Daniel with it . . .

She'd brought along her personal hand-gun: a Lorcin L–380 that she knew how to use as well as she knew how to apply lipgloss.

What could she lose?

'I'll take the room,' she said crisply. '*Non*-smoking.'

*　　*　　*

Jacqui lay in a deep sleep, dead to the world.

She passed from stupor to wakefulness in the blink of an eye and lay quite still in her bed, trying to identify what felt strange. She'd woken in the night before, especially after nightmares, but this was different. Not frightening, just different.

She turned her head in an attempt to read her bedside clock. No numerals gleamed back at her. Power-cut? By turning her head still more she could see only black where the window should have been grey.

What was wrong? Had she gone blind in her sleep? Then she did feel frightened. She sat up in bed, groping for the light-switch. She couldn't find it. Her hand closed around empty space, although Jacqui knew exactly where the switch was.

Somebody was standing between her and the window, blotting out the residual light.

It was *him*. Had to be.

Jacqui did not scream, which later she would recall with some pride. With all the speed she could muster she rolled over and thrust her hand under the pillow. The room might be dark, the lamp might have vanished, but the precious can of Mace that Annette had bought her was there. Not pausing, she continued her roll until she came around on her back again. She held out the can at arm's length and . . .

Someone grabbed her wrist.

Her other hand was free. In a trice Jacqui had swapped the can. She waved it around frantically so that her assailant wouldn't be able to get a grip on it. Her forefinger sought the button. No joy.

A heavy body was bearing down on hers. She couldn't feel the breath of another person, nor was she conscious of a smell: only the sensation of being forced onto the bed by an irresistible weight that stressed her chest, making it harder and harder to breathe.

Jacqui looked for eyes gleaming in the dark. There were none. *Why weren't there any eyes to aim the Mace at?*

Her finger found the button. In the same instant, her attacker let go of her other hand. Jacqui screamed and half managed to sit up . . . only to meet a fist coming down. It narrowly missed her chin. Jacqui howled again and tried to roll to the right, but the hands were around her throat now and she was being remorselessly flattened onto the bed. Her head began to swim, her heart thumped like a Sten gun, she could feel her strength slipping away from her as if a vampire clung to her throat.

Jacqui's finger pressed the button in a last, reflex action.

There was a muffled scream. The hands around her throat relaxed their grip. Something crashed into her desk and a chair went flying. Through a cloud of red mist, Jacqui saw the edge of her bedroom door illuminated in the dim night-light of the passage. A figure staggered out through it and Jacqui yelled again, for here was the worst of nightmares come to haunt her: a flowing black figure without head or hands or arms . . .

'What is it?'

Annette came running into the bedroom. She flicked on the main light. Jacqui sat up, rubbing her throat and fighting back tears. Her room was a mess: furniture upturned, her electronic alarm clock on the floor, the bedside lamp tossed into one corner.

'Sis,' she yelled. *'Stop!'*

Annette, who had been coming towards the bed, froze. Jacqui, her eyes wide with shock, pointed to the floor by her sister's feet. A hypodermic lay there, three-fourths filled with ice-blue liquid. Annette bent down.

'Don't touch it,' Jacqui hissed.

They heard footsteps in the passage. Naim entered the bedroom. 'What's all this noise?' he demanded.

Jacqui was about to explain what had happened. Annette forestalled her.

'A bad dream, Dad. That's all.'

Jacqui gazed at Annette. Annette returned her look. Both girls were aware of the syringe lying on the floor. Somehow Naim failed to see it. He stared at his daughters a moment longer, turned on his heel and left.

Annette went to close the door after him. She kept her hand on the handle for a long time, staring at the floor. 'Nice,' she said with what might have been a sob in her voice, 'nice to know who your friends are, yeah?'

Jacqui patted the bed; Annette came across to snuggle down beside her.

'Listen, sis,' she said. 'We skip tonight, okay?'

'What, you mean . . . *now*?'

'Give it half an hour – it's twelve thirty – then let's get the hell out.'

'But . . . our things?'

'What isn't already at Hobie's, we can take. I'll get a bottle of water from the ice-box, it'll be enough.'

Jacqui shivered; but – 'Okay,' she muttered. 'I can't spend another night with *him* around.'

'It wasn't Richo who attacked you.'

'Of course it was!'

'I got a glimpse as I came out of my room. There was this black thing at the end of the corridor, turning the corner, wearing a chador.'

'A what? . . . Oh, those things Muslim women wear?'

'Right. No eyes: which maybe explains why your can of Mace didn't knock her out.'

'*Her?*'

Annette nodded. 'From the way she moved, I'm sure of it. Small frame; short, hobbling steps . . . you nearly got wasted by a woman, sweetie. Get your things.'

* * *

With the help of Shimon's map Thelma was able to find her way to the gate in the perimeter fence quite easily. The road petered out half a mile from the estate boundary, in a small clearing that had evidently been used by backpackers in the recent past. Using a flashlight, she found the uphill path he'd described and followed it without exerting herself too much, although the occasional boulder grazed her toe and sometimes a low-hanging pine branch would brush against her face, making her start. She was conscious, too, of the woods being alive all around her: the coo of an owl, the rustle of some animal making its stealthy way through the sagebrush, and sometimes an ominous sound she could not decipher but which made her hurry on, indifferent to the mud rising over her Timberlands.

She had been going for about twenty minutes when she saw the light.

Thelma halted, and half withdrew behind the bole of a pine tree. Her heart beat fast, not only from exertion. Where was the light coming from? Shimon had written that this part of the boundary was patrolled only twice every twenty-four hours, but could she trust him? She wished Daniel was here, after all.

Thelma went forward. This time, though, she walked slowly, and took greater care where she put her feet.

164

The light continued to burn but the nearer she approached the fuzzier it became. Why? Ah: the *Pinos Altos* boundary fence! Its wire mesh hung between her and the light, she saw that clearly now. And yes! – there was the gate, just as Shimon had described it.

The brush grew thickly here, and many pines crowded against the fence, but a path of sorts was visible as she shone the flashlight down. What had Shimon said about this place? – that Aurelia had appropriated a small cottage by the boundary and made it her own, insisting on having her own exit into the forest. But the path was too well worn to be explicable by the comings and goings of just one woman.

Thelma drew her gun. She ventured forward cautiously until she was standing three feet away from the gate: four steel tubes moulded together to form a rectangular frame, filled with panels of stiff mesh. Thelma shone her flashlight over it. The electric wires had been bunched and run along the top of the outer frame, excluding the gate itself from the gadgetry of defence. There was a hasp for a padlock, but this was empty.

Thelma turned the catch that held the gate shut. It yielded; the gate swung open with a muted squeak. She stepped through it and listened. No distant sirens, no automatic searchlights powering out of the night, no armed guards materializing like ghosts through the trees. *She was in!*

Here the path became more obvious: someone had planted white-painted stones at regular intervals. These markers snaked up a slope towards a cottage with a red-tiled roof and adobe walls that tapered slightly inwards. The light, she now saw, came filtering through one of the downstairs windows.

Thelma had come about halfway to the cottage when she was overwhelmed with a feeling, a *knowledge*, that she wasn't alone. She turned back, swinging her flashlight from side to side. No one was visible, nothing moved. The light revealed only trees, bushes, brush, a few wild roses, a swathe of mown grass. *Yet somebody was there!*

It must have been five minutes or more before she could nerve herself to go on. As she neared the cottage she kept stopping to scan the darkness, but the result was always the same: nothing, no one.

Thelma reached the front door: panelled pine, with a brass knocker and a heavy handle. It was ajar. She pushed on it gently; it gave. Her back prickled. The darkness behind her contained something, somebody, more than one person. He, they, could see her, even though she could not see them.

Thelma gave the night one last piercing look. She passed through the front door.

Carnage.

Every single item in the room was smashed, defiled, stained or torn. It had been a pleasant room once, Mexican in style, with brightly coloured curtains and rugs of mysterious pattern, and an open fireplace, and carvings on each wall. Everything had been ripped down and left in a heap in the middle of the floor. A pile of papers still smouldered on the hearth. Directly in front of Thelma, blood trailed by divers tributaries and streams to an inner doorway.

Like a woman under hypnosis she bypassed the bloodstains and continued through the open door.

She was in a well-appointed, modern kitchen, full of gadgets and esoteric utensils such as butter-curlers and champagne bottle-stoppers. Most of these were scattered about the red-and-black tiled floor. Shimon Waldman lay sprawled with his shattered head towards Thelma's feet. Beside his left arm was a solid-looking brass Buddha, coated with blood. Thelma was no detective, but it seemed pretty clear to her that somebody had used the heavy figurine to batter Shimon to death.

She turned, made a stumbling run for the front door, and was violently sick.

She was tempted to mop up the mess, but then the rules re-established themselves inside her head and she remembered: don't touch anything, call the police, first state your where-abouts . . .

But the police were here already, in the persons of two sheriff's officers. They stood in the main doorway, hands on hips, watching her with stony interest. Thelma stared from one to the other. They were young, tough-looking, mean. Their tan uniforms fitted them tightly, showing off their muscles. Nothing about their stance suggested they perceived themselves as coming to the rescue of a helpless maiden.

'Well, well,' one of them said, stepping over the threshold. 'What do we have here?'

He advanced on her quickly and snatched the gun from her hand.

'I . . . I came in and . . . my name is Thelma Vestrey, I'm a psychologist. Consultant Psychologist to the Paradise Bay Police Department.' Thelma surprised herself with the mildness, the sheer *rationality* of her response.

'I'm charging you with the wilful murder of a male unknown on or before the twentieth day of May. You have the right to remain silent.'

She waited for him to complete the Miranda script laid down for peace officers arresting on a charge of felony, but he didn't; and this gave her hope, because it meant her arrest was unlawful and everything that now followed would be equally unlawful.

The sheriff's officer took out his cuffs and, with slick expertise, pinioned Thelma. She gazed down at her manacled hands and she told herself what millions of others have told themselves at the beginning of the end: this is not happening.

'March, m'am,' said the officer.

They led her down the path, through the gate, back the way she'd come. Her head was in a whirl. Innocent people had rights; it would all get sorted out. Her vanity case was back at the motel. What would happen to her car? Shimon was dead, murdered.

One of the sheriff's men, the one who'd not spoken, seemed somehow familiar. She had seen him before. Recently. When? Where?

The children – Annette, Jacqui, maybe even, God knows, Richo – were in the most terrible danger. She must get help, call the police, she was under arrest and the sheriff had done that.

She knew this man next to her. *How?*

Daniel, where are you, my lovely, lovely Daniel? Her stomach was heaving, but she must not throw up again. She was going to be all right. She was.

They put her in an unmarked Ford Crown Victoria, parked next to her own car, and it struck Thelma that this was a plush vehicle for out-of-town law officers to drive. The silent sheriff's man walked around to the Bronco and knocked twice on its roof. There must have been somebody inside it, because the engine fired, it drove away. Wait a minute, who would have a key to her car? A moment later the Ford followed the Bronco down the track, and the woods fell silent.

For five minutes, nothing happened. Then Annette and Jacqui emerged from behind the stand of pines beside the cottage, where they'd been hiding ever since they'd caught sight of Thelma coming up the path alone; Jacqui turned to Annette and asked, 'What was all *that* about?'

Annette stared at the lighted cottage, now closed and quiet. It might contain some answers. Then again, it might not.

'That's her business,' she said sourly, 'none of ours. Hit the road, sis.'

*　　*　　*

Thelma sat in the back of the Ford with the silent man, while the other one drove.

'I wish to make a phone call,' she said, after they'd been driving for a while. 'I have that right.'

The driver turned to her, his face a blurred map of line and shadow. 'M'am,' he said quietly, 'you don't *need* a phone call.'

Thelma thought. If she didn't need to call anyone, that could only be because these weren't real sheriff's men.

Who were they?

Why did one of them look so familiar?

Where were they taking her?

Why? Why? *Why?*

She had no idea of their location. The road was a narrow one, snaking its way around hills and through gorges, and climbing, always climbing. There was no other traffic. Occasionally in the gleam of their own car's lights Thelma would glimpse road signs, none of them hopeful: ROAD NOT MAINTAINED AT NIGHT, BEWARE FALLEN ROCK; SNOW NOT REMOVED ABOVE JOHNSONDALE; DANGER, DO NOT SWIM: 163 LIVES LOST IN KERN RIVER SINCE 1968.

They had not passed evidence of human habitation for more

168

than half an hour when Thelma caught sight of a barn beside the road. Soon after that they skirted a broken-down shanty, close by the remains of a stone structure that might once have been a house. On the other side of the road, the granite hillside rose sheer into darkness. The Ford ground to a halt outside a building in better condition than the rest. The taciturn sheriff's man pulled her out and she glimpsed a few old signs and boarded-up windows, remnants of what once must have been a village. Then they were going up some shallow wooden steps, across a veranda and into the building.

The driver followed. He unhooked a storm lantern from its nail on the veranda-pillar and lit it before coming inside and closing the door. Thelma examined the faces of her captors: no longer pale impressions, but hard-edged visages carved by lantern-light from the surrounding darkness, like burnished moons. And her sense of having seen the silent officer before intensified: she would have it, any moment now she would have it . . .

The room was about twenty-five feet square. There was an old wooden desk, and a chair to match. A filing cabinet stood in one corner. Next to it lay several cardboard boxes, labelled A–K, L–R, and so forth. Even by the light of the storm lantern Thelma could see that dust lay an inch thick over everything, including the notice-board headed *Tulare County Sheriff: Hornville*, with its faded *Lists of Arraignment*, and *Traffic Violations (Procedures) Amendments*, and the encouraging poster, *Don't Drink And Drive: We Can Wait*, sponsored by *Andry, Coverill and Jones, Morticians Who Care*.

But for one detail, this would have been just an abandoned sheriff's sub-office in an abandoned, one-horse town: an office that hadn't been properly cleared and would never function again, a dirty piece of antique Americana. Part of the shabby room, however, had been adapted: two walls of bars had been erected at right angles, squaring off one corner to make a cell. The bars were embedded in the concrete floor and they disappeared up through the ceiling. There was a steel-bar gate with an impressive-looking lock, and a small window protected by a grille set high up in one of the cell's walls. The corner housed two blue plastic buckets and a scoop; there was just enough light to let Thelma see that one bucket contained water while the other was empty. A thin mattress lay on the cell's floor, aligned with one wall.

'I've had enough of this,' she heard herself snap. 'You take me into town and charge me with whatever you damn well want to, but this farce is ended, right? Take me out of here, *and do it now.*'

The two men exchanged a look and a shrug. The silent one came forward to unlock her cuffs. Thelma felt her heart lift up, because that meant they were acknowledging their mistake, another moment and she'd walk free . . .

The silent officer thrust her into the cell and banged the barred gate shut. For a moment his face was close to hers, and her mind gave a skittish little jump, letting her know she was within seconds of identifying him; but then the moment of inspiration faded, leaving her none the wiser. He turned the key and, without another word, quit the room. His colleague set the storm lamp on the floor and followed. She heard the sound of a car driving away. She was alone.

Thelma's first words to herself were: I must not panic. Her next: *God help me, what am I going to do?*

Keep calm. Don't cry; that was particularly important. Tears wasted breath, energy and emotion. Tears drained you. But a great wall of water was building up behind the dam of her eyes and the strain of keeping it there had become painful.

Do not emote. *Think.*

Information, that was the first thing. Gather as much information as you can, then use it to save yourself. First – where are you?

She was in a cell fifteen by fifteen feet. The floor was concrete. The walls were of stone blocks, whitewashed a long time ago. The ceiling . . . she couldn't see the ceiling. The bars . . . one inch thick, rigid steel, no give in them when she shook them. The gate . . . it rattled and clanged under the pressure of her hands but the lock was solid and she knew she hadn't the slightest chance of breaking out that way.

She counted the bars: nine inches between them, seventeen one way, eighteen the other. Why the difference? Come on, what did that matter? At the midpoint between floor and ceiling the bars passed through a thick metal stringer. The ceiling was about ten feet above the floor. By placing one foot on the stringer Thelma could hoist herself up to feel where bar met ceiling. There was a raised circle of plaster around each bar, but above that she could detect some firmer structure holding the bars in place. No hope there, either.

She worked her way up and down each bar and was just wondering what to do next when she heard the engine. Imagination? No, a car was coming. Definitely.

Good news or bad?

She clasped the bars of the gate, put her head on one side, closed her eyes and listened. Whoever it was drove a powerful vehicle: the roar of the engine told her that. Daniel? For the briefest of seconds she allowed herself to hope . . . but if Daniel spared her a thought tonight it would only be to imagine her tucked up in her bed at home, and it might be days before he got around to worrying about her. Was it the sheriff's men coming back? Perhaps the Tulare County sheriff himself had come to set things right in person, make amends, offer hot coffee laced with cognac . . .

In her heart she knew that what she could hear was the beat of devils' pinions, not angels' wings, and a shudder passed through her frame.

The car came on fast. Its lights swept past the windows of her prison and died simultaneously with the engine. A door slammed. Thelma heard footsteps. How many? One person. He – or she – was coming onto the veranda. The footsteps stopped. Thelma heard a cigarette-lighter click, and after that came a moment of profound silence.

She counted her heartbeats. She'd reached one hundred and ten when the door opened and Ricardo Delacroix stepped into the room.

'Hi, darling,' he said chirpily. 'Chimp in a cage, huh? Fancy a peanut?' He laughed, *Ha! Ha! Ha! Ha! Ha!* in his high-pitched falsetto, as he approached. Thelma shrank back, but he was faster: his hands closed around hers before she could jerk them away and he brought his face in to touch the bars, squashing his cheeks against them, making his mouth ready for a kiss.

Thelma looked away, fighting the nausea that goes with

physical disgust. Then, quickly, she looked up and spat into his left eye.

It was a futile gesture, and a dangerous one, but it had the desired effect: he released her hands. He stepped back and he said, 'Hey. You. Chimp, I'm talking to you.'

He sounded amused, rather than angry, but there was a dangerous edge to his voice. Thelma backed away until the corner of the cell blocked her. The lantern was behind him, so all she could see was his silhouette against the dim yellow light.

Richo moved away from the bars and squatted down facing her. He lit a cigarette. Its red tip moved from between his knees to his lips, and then back again while he exhaled in a long, sibilant hiss.

Thelma began to wish he would speak. Once she knew the worst, she could try to face it with dignity.

'You remember Mom's story,' he said at last. 'Paris?' He threw back his head and yodelled: 'I love Paris in the springtime, I love Paris in the fall.' Then he was Bogart: 'We'll always have Paris, shweetheart.'

Answer him. Don't be a punchbag; act, don't react. 'I remember. Enough to destroy anyone, don't you think?'

'Anyone . . . except Mother. My mother. Mommy dearest. She became a slave, and she adapted. And the big question, class, is this: will Thelma be able to adapt?'

'Why don't we pose some realistic questions instead? Such as: what are the likely consequences for a teenage boy who behaves in this way? What can be said in mitigation at his trial?'

While she was speaking, Richo's shoulders began to shake. Now he could contain himself no longer and burst out laughing: not his horrible falsetto trill, but an almost human sound. 'I'll see you tomorrow,' he said when he'd done. 'Meanwhile, here's something to think about. Home assignment, right? This is the way it goes. You can take your chance with the local deputy sheriff, who's in our pockets, by the way – he fixed the inquest on Mom's death – and stand trial for Shimon's murder, knowing you were found at the scene of the crime, with the murder weapon by your side. Or you can come live with me, chained to my bed. You won't be the first, Thelma. And you surely won't be the last. But it's going to be a heap of laughs, I guarantee that.'

He rose and made his leisurely way to the door. 'I'm giving you a real choice,' he said, as he opened it. 'You see, nobody can hang a motive on you for icing Shimon. You might get away with it. You just might.'

He seemed on the point of passing through the door, but then he changed his mind. He closed it again. He came back towards the cell, and she saw he had a key in his hands. Her body tensed. Adrenalin coursed through her, bending every muscle, every nerve, out of shape. Pain gripped her lower back. She shrank into the corner, turning her face away as he unlocked the gate and penetrated the space that until a moment ago had been hers alone, an invader against whom she had no defence.

He approached, silently as a cat, until they were almost touching. Should she strike him? No: do not under any circumstances tempt fate. *You weak, shrivelling idiot!* Yes, but that's okay, control it, do not descend to his level. *Snotball!* Leave it, leave it, *leave it* . . .

Slowly he reached out a hand and stroked her right forearm. His touch was gentle. He was trembling.

'My sisters,' he whispered, 'want you. But you're mine, darling . . .'

His fingers travelled lightly up her arm to the shoulder, across the tops of her breasts, down the other arm. His breath in her face was indescribably sweet: perfumed, incensed. His fingers closed, ever so softly, around hers and, after a pause that was timeless, he squeezed them. 'Mine,' he repeated, the word coming out as a sigh, tentative, almost as if he, even he, couldn't quite make himself believe.

Thelma jerked her hand away. She was sobbing. Her skin felt as though it had grown thorns and been turned inside out: she could not move, couldn't keep still. *Do it!* her conscious mind screamed at Richo. *Do it, get it over with, let me die!* But . . . one final giggle, *Ha! Ha! Ha! Ha! Ha!* and he was gone. The engine of his Porsche fired, he revved it; she heard as if next to her, as if a dozen miles away, the screech of tortured rubber, and it was over.

Until tomorrow.

Thelma sank down to the concrete floor, sobbing uncontrollably. She reached out a hand to support herself and it made contact with something dry, something soft. By the light of the lantern, she saw it was a thick, legal-sized envelope, and that her name had been written across the front of it in shaky capitals.

Richo must have dropped it. She hadn't seen or heard him do it.

Dropped it deliberately or by accident?

Deliberately.

Open that, warned the inner voice of self-preservation, *and you'll regret it. He wants you to read it. Don't!*

She opened the envelope.

'Madame, this is what you've been yearning to know. Isn't it? About what Naim did to me. And to Nada . . .'

The storm lantern flickered, burned brighter for a moment, and then, its supply of oil exhausted, went out.

*　　*　　*

The Happy Valley coffee shop had seen better days. Its restrooms were unspeakably squalid and were swamped by three inches of water whenever a wet wind blew from the southwest. The sign on the door – a big NO, followed in smaller letters by 'shoes, shirt, service' – was furry with age, its cellophane protector mostly gone; and anyway, it was a long time since it had provided an accurate indication of prevailing standards. The counters had not been cleaned in a while, but then neither had the cups, plates, cutlery or waitresses. The advantage of this place to Jacqui and Annette was that it was far enough off the beaten track to risk stopping at.

Annette messed around with a dish of Pigs in Blankets while her sister sipped moodily on a Sprite. They'd chosen the booth farthest from the windows, where shadows congealed to cover up some of the dirt, and there they brooded on how far the hunt might be up.

Annette had thought of a clever way of covering their tracks. She'd found a blank page in her address book and, using ballpen, written a fictitious name and address before tearing out half the page in such a way that only the last part of the address was left. The impression of what she'd written could clearly be seen on the sheet of paper underneath. Her hope was that Naim would send the police haring after them towards Oregon, in the wrong direction. It was smart – too smart, perhaps? No matter how many times they went around, the problem always came back to the same starting-point: they were on the run, the police would be looking for them, the only factor on their side was time and time was spreading itself thin.

They'd allowed themselves fifteen minutes, no more, for a pit-stop. The minutes had nearly run out when Jacqui uttered a soft hiss and reached for her sister's wrist. 'Don't turn,' she murmured.

'What is it?'

'Cops.'

Annette felt Jacqui's hand cold on her skin. For a second she fought off the desire to look over her shoulder; but instinct proved too strong.

Four highway patrolmen had come in and were ordering. Fortunately they'd chosen a table on the far side of the coffee shop. Once they'd ordered they began to take an interest in the few other diners, though not in a professional way: just as people do when they're on a break, and bored, and in search of something more interesting than their own lives.

Annette had the sense not to move a muscle. Jacqui slowly released her wrist and sat back, keeping her eyes on her half-empty bottle of Sprite. 'Act normal,' she advised softly. 'Don't stop talking.'

Annette gazed back at Jacqui, but her mind had gone blank. 'So . . . so where are we, then?' she asked.

'Search me. *And don't keep looking around.*'

They were, in fact, some twenty miles north of the US-Mexico line, a way off Route 54. It was five fifteen in the afternoon and they'd travelled fast; God, as Annette remarked, favoured the beautiful and the young. The worst part had been at the beginning, when they'd walked six miles on the road leading south into Kernville, at the head of Lake Isabella, without finding a ride. Then a farmer picked them up and drove them the last four miles

175

into town, mercifully asking no questions; and while Jacqui sat in the little park, Annette went the rounds. In Country Gourmet and Cheryl's Diner, the three bookshops, barbershop and Bank of America she drew a blank. But there was a lady buying pants in Whisky Flat Tattle Tale Fashions, and she planned to drive into Bakersfield later that morning, and why, she'd be only too *glad* to give a ride to two high school students at the end of their field trip to the South Fork National Wildlife Area. So by ten o'clock, there they were, bouncing their way through a desolate landscape of moor beneath a cloudy sky, with yellows and sickly greens playing over the hills whenever splodges of sunlight managed to thrust through the canopy above.

From Bakersfield, it was easier. They caught a bus that drove first along the desolate, dead straight highway that leads through the San Joaquin valley to the Grapevine. Distant mountains reared right and left, black shapes haloed with white cloud and a hem of bright light; then they were through the pass and descending again, past Six Flags Magic Mountain, and so into Los Angeles, where they caught another bus heading south for San Diego. There they'd left the beaten track and struck out towards the east, riding a country bus that had eventually dropped them at the Happy Valley eatery, this dubious oasis in a desert of one-storey concrete dwellings and petty businesses.

'We just keep heading south,' Jacqui murmured. 'Keep the sun on our right, watch the stars.'

'Pity about the compass Dad confiscated.'

'And the flashlight.'

There was a long silence, while the two girls stared across the table at each other. From somewhere over by the door came a muted buzz of conversation, punctuated by the occasional burst of laughter. Was it Jacqui's imagination, or did the word 'girls' occur with unnatural frequency . . . ?

'What do you think Dad's doing now?' Jacqui asked. Her voice cracked in mid-sentence.

'Raising Cain. Sis . . . we have to make a move, and I've got to pee. *Got* to.'

Almost as if cued, the four men got up, reaching for their wallets, chewing on picks, joshing the waitresses.

'What are they doing?' Annette breathed.

'Standing . . . going . . . oh, shit.'

'What?'

'They're looking around. One of them's looking right at us.'

Jacqui took a long, bored swig on her Sprite. Casually she reached out for one of Annette's sausages and popped it in her mouth. She began to chew on it. Every so often her eyes flickered towards the door. Annette held her breath and closed her eyes, listening for footsteps. Her heart beat so fast she felt ill.

Suddenly Jacqui spat a mouth of sausage onto her plate, making Annette recoil. 'They've gone,' Jacqui said. 'Good golly, how can you eat this?'

They waited until the men had climbed into their cars before calling for the check. Annette went to the toilet. Jacqui casually lifted the newspaper one of the patrolmen had left and took it outside, where she sat on a wooden chair and scanned it while traffic roared past through the pink, sticky evening.

She checked the front page, scanning each dateline, but there was nothing about two missing teenage girls.

The highway patrolmen were still sitting in their cars. What were they doing? *Why hadn't they gone?*

If Annette came out of the washroom now, the patrolmen would see them together: two girls, early teens, alone . . .

Don't get up, she told herself; don't do anything to draw attention. You're just a schoolkid on her way home, stopping off for a shake. Forget about how the clothes you're wearing are too smart for this neighbourhood. Forget about how your sister is going to come out and sink you both. Turn the page, Jacqui. Read.

At once an item caught her eye – 'Kernville' – and her heart fluttered, but it was only a story about how some hoodlums had jumped a couple of deputy sheriffs, tied them up and stolen their uniforms . . .

Jacqui paused. Last night, she and Annette had seen Thelma Vestrey being led away by two sheriff's men. It had been troubling her on and off all day, though because she'd had other things to worry about she'd never really sought to analyse her unease. Reading this news item, her fears sharpened into focus. What had Vestrey been doing, up there in the forest so late at night? Why had the sheriff come to take her away?

Annette was taking such a long time! Jacqui darted another look towards the patrol cars. One of them had driven off. The other stayed where it was. She could see the driver using his radio. *That doesn't have to be about you – ignore it.*

There was a payphone on the wall behind Jacqui. She stared at it. Calls to the police were free . . .

What was Annette doing in there? *Why didn't the other car drive away?*

A girl on the run would hardly be likely to use a phone in public. In fact, making a phone call, like any other kid calling her boyfriend, could be a good way of allaying suspicion.

Jacqui got up and folded the newspaper away in her backpack. She hesitated a few moments more. Then she went over to the phone, lifted the receiver, and dialled 911.

'Um,' she said, when the sergeant asked her business. Um.

'Hello? Hello, caller, are you there?'

'I want to inquire about Dr Thelma Vestrey. St Joseph's Hospital, Paradise Bay. I want to know if she's all right.'

'Please state your name, full address and phone number. Hello? Caller, I repeat, I need to know your – '

A hand appeared briefly in front of Jacqui's face. It descended on the hook. The connection was severed.

'For God's *sake*!' Annette hissed.

'You hurt my hand!'

'Those cops'll do worse than that if they catch us. *Move!*'

*   *   *

At about the same time, the quality of the light in Thelma's cell began to change. Until four o'clock, or thereabouts, it had been shot through with clarity, illuminating every sordid detail of the dilapidated room. Now it was losing its oomph. Like a child's party balloon deflating, the light sagged and softened, and shadows appeared where none had figured before.

Thelma, wiping sweat from her forehead, focused on the

sheriff's desk. Moments ago, she'd been able to see through the knee-hole to the other side. Now no longer.

She sank down to the floor and rested her back against the wall. The battle still raged, but she was losing. Her watch told her it was five twenty-eight. Inside her soul, it felt like midnight.

Her eyes strayed to the envelope, containing Aurelia's secret. She'd read the latest instalment as soon as it was light, and several times since then. Her brain couldn't seem to get a fix on what she'd read. It only made partial sense.

Aurelia was still holding back.

Thelma heaved a wretched sigh. *Dummy*, she addressed herself, *why did you have to choose October 19 last at eleven thirty a.m. to quit smoking? Not even an in-case-of-emergency-tear-cellophane pack in your purse, not so much as a butt-end in a cuff. You dumb broad. You shmuck.*

Nobody had come to her prison all day. Nothing had happened to distract her from increasingly stressful thoughts.

Again and again she went over her prospects, always rating them as nil. Her one hope was that Daniel would realize something had gone wrong, and come to rescue her. But he was worked off his feet, it might easily be a couple of days before he got around to calling her, and even then the sound of her answering machine was unlikely to send him rushing off in panic.

She'd told Rachel and Kirsty she was going on a trip with a friend, they might take two days over it, they might take three. Because she'd persuaded Dan to come on that mini-vacation with her, in the Greenhorns, she'd taken time off work and wasn't due back at St Joe's until after the weekend. Her staff might put out an alert if she didn't show up then, but since they had no idea of her whereabouts they wouldn't be able to help the police much. Besides, all that was next week, and Richo was coming back tonight.

At around midday she'd descended into a painful sleep, dreading that she might have to go along with Richo, and woken to a perception of sheer helplessness. Much of the afternoon had been spent fighting it.

Now she opened her fist and smacked herself across the right cheek, hard. She cursed herself for being so stupid. So damn *weak*, for Christ's sake! *Work, damn you!*

She forced herself to stand up. Her leg-joints protested and she leaned against the wall for support. She had work to do. *So you quit smoking: Great! Work won't make you breathless, then!*

Thelma took off her grandma's eternity ring, held the big diamond face outward, and resumed where she'd left off when the light began to change.

There was one window in her cell. It was barred, but as dawn developed into day, she'd noticed something. The window-frame consisted of one-inch-square wooden slats, set in whitewashed brick. For the most part the wall was solid. But the mortar between the bricks was flaking away in several places where it edged the slats, weakened by long, damp winters.

Thelma had fallen into the trap of excitement. She'd at once begun to hack at the powdery mortar with her fingernails. Result: broken nails. Then she'd conceived the idea of using her grandmother's ring: one large diamond flanked by lesser gems, set in a gold band. *Oh, Gran, I'm so sorry you had to die, but if it weren't for the ring you left me . . .* She'd used this to pick away at the mortar around the window-frame. If she could only dislodge enough, maybe she'd be able to punch out the whole frame, bars and all?

Every time she stated her objective to herself she despaired, because saying it out loud showed it up for the craziness it was. But she went on anyway. She had to go on. If she stopped, she started to think. That meant madness, despair, death.

And, yes, she'd made one important discovery: why the silent sheriff's man had looked familiar. He was one of the students she'd seen lolling underneath a tree in the garden of Sacré Coeur Academy. Richo's college. Information that might one day prove useful to the police . . . if it didn't die with her.

Whenever she seemed to be getting somewhere, gouging out crumbs and powder to the depth of half an inch, three-quarters, one whole inch, she ran up against solid mortar that wouldn't give. She wiped away her tears, readjusted the ring, and tried another place.

She'd given up looking at her watch, because it lied to her. How could time pass so quickly? What was wrong with her watch? A jewelled Nurt de Cartier, her father's graduation gift, it had never let her down before; she must have it fixed, when she *(say it!)* when she got out.

Sticky, acidic white powder coated her shoes, her hands, her jeans. Her whole body glistened with sweat. Her throat hurt, it cost her pain to swallow. Her head ached. Her eyeballs, tight with tears, felt like balls of hot coal. She was dead on her feet, the light had begun to die, she was dying . . .

Thelma, exhausted, threw herself down and once more reached for the envelope.

Madame, this is what you've been yearning to know. Isn't it? About what Naim did to me. And to Nada . . .

How does one deal with tragedy? The death of a parent, the loss of a close friend; these things lay us low, even in middle-age. Three years and a week after we came to Paris, Nada died. I could have saved her. It was my fault that she died.

Basma came in all excited one day. She said, 'This rich playboy, young and good-looking, has come to town and he wants twin girls.' They had to be twins, birth-certificates were a prerequisite. As she said that, I could feel Nada go wild beside me, though nobody else would have detected so much as a twitch. We had no papers, you see, no means of identity, and here was the possibility of acquiring them. It didn't matter if they were forged, although probably (this is I who speaks, the modern, knowledgeable 'I', not that thirteen-year-old little girl) Dr Kobrussi had handed over our identity cards when he sold us. What mattered was that the client required to see birth certificates, and Nada and I must somehow find a way to get our hands on them.

We took endless trouble over our make-up that evening. The other girls knew we were on to a hit, but there wasn't much jealousy in that house. They came and lent us things: a lace bra for Nada, I remember, some Chanel perfume for me. We did that for each other whenever Prince Charming was reputed to be hovering in the wings. Transference, isn't that what you'd call it, Doctor? We put all our hopes and dreams on to the lucky one. In three years we'd never seen a 'lucky one' actually make it out of the sewer to wealth and freedom, but who ever abandoned hope?

Just before Basma took us down she made us each swallow a

tablet, saying they were vitamins and we would need them, because the client was a tiger in bed. We didn't argue.

The car came. Nada and I had a send-off from the girls, those who weren't yet on the streets or ratcheting up the meter in the bedrooms: hopes ran high for us. We left. The car crossed Pigalle, I remember, and went on down the hill. And after that I can't recall. My head felt light and strange, as if I'd been drinking for a long time and wasn't in control of myself.

We had to walk the last bit. We staggered down this narrow alley, still feeling light-headed. At the end, our driver produced a key and unlocked a door, which opened to show us a flight of stairs, leading down. The door was on a spring, it closed behind us with a snap. We descended alone: there was no one to welcome us and the driver stayed outside.

At the bottom of the stairs we could see dim light. Nada and I turned the corner, giggling nervously, and there it was: the zinc.

Do you know what is a zinc, Madame? I'm not sure if you're familiar with Paris. It is a kind of bar, once very popular but now, I understand, in decline. Zincs take their name from the metal which forms the bar counter, but they are a lifestyle, a philosophy, a sub-culture. It was there that a Parisian workman went to drink his cup of coffee, well laced with brandy, before setting off for the factory or the building-site. It was there that drunken fights began with cheap rouge and ended with knives, there that the students plotted the overthrow of France, there that lovers met and kissed and quarrelled and made up. They were the streetwise streetlife of Europe's greatest capital in a capsule. Nada and I loved them, for they were great equalizers. (You can believe the French when they place egalité before fraternité.) We saw this zinc, and we relaxed.

It was dark, smoky, with nicotine-brown walls, lacking none of the usual accoutrements: a coffee-machine, bottles, glasses, a sink, tables, ashtrays stuffed to overflowing. Yes, one thing it lacked: customers. There were only two men in the place. They sat at a table in the corner farthest from the stairs, smoking Gitanes, with a bottle of Ricard between them.

One of the men beckoned us. The bar was lit only by table-lamps; as we approached we saw that both were young, both foreign-looking. Playboy types – slack chins, vacant eyes. Their skins were brown, like ours, yet their eyes were different. We'd not met Filipinos before.

The man who had beckoned said he was called Naim. I found out later that he had many aliases but he preferred this one because of the way it sounded: so anonymous, you see, Naim-name. The other man never spoke the whole time we were there.

There was a gun on the table, between the lamp and the bottle. Nada and I stared at it while we answered Naim's questions. He was interested in our backgrounds, he said. We handed over the papers we'd been given, and the two men studied them carefully by the light of the lamp. While they did this, Nada and I looked sometimes at the gun, sometimes at each other. The atmosphere was starting to feel oddly oppressive. As if the walls were imperceptibly moving in on us . . . Already this escapade was turning sour. I caught Nada's eyes flickering towards the stairs and knew she was frightened, more frightened than I, and this was unusual, because normally one could not slip a sheet of paper between us. But I was not scared, merely interested in watching where Naim put our birth certificates, once he'd finished reading them. I hoped that later, after he'd screwed us, we'd have an opportunity to steal them.

I was falling asleep, I realized, and I wondered what had been in the tablets Basma had fed us. Not that I cared; I was past caring by then.

Naim caught me looking at him. He winked. Then he went to the bar and came back holding a bottle of champagne and two glasses. Nada and I giggled some more at that. He popped the cork and poured.

'You aren't going to join us?' I asked. He shook his head and indicated his shot glass, filled to the brim with Ricard. We drank. The alcohol was the finishing touch to whatever Basma had made us swallow. We sat there, swaying slightly, feeling no pain. I was completely detached, up by the ceiling somewhere, looking down on these two delightful little girls in their party dresses, so sweet. Nada's eyes were closing. Mine were, too.

I entered this happy dream, inspired by champagne and drugs and the hope of things to come. In my dream Naim had begun to

tease my twin. For a while I hung around, somewhere up by the
ceiling, vaguely interested. Then he handed her the gun.

I came out of my dream at once; but could not do anything about
it. Do you understand, Madame? I was no longer dreaming, but
nor was I in any state to intervene. I began to struggle towards my
sister, my head a belfry of alarm bells. The harder I fought, the
further she retreated!

Nada was playing with the gun, while Naim encouraged her.
The other man sat there looking on, his face cleansed of all
expression.

Nada spun the revolver's magazine. She was putting the gun to
her forehead.

I awoke, fully, and launched myself across the table at her.
There was an explosion, my sister disappeared in a cloud of smoke.
It cleared, slowly. There, on the other side of the table, was my
sister Nada. What was left of her. Her body stayed upright in the
chair. Of her head, little remained.

Then, as I watched, her torso slowly subsided below the table.

I shrieked. Of course. But the thing is, Madame, that I went on
shrieking, without pause for breath, like an express train thun-
dering through the night, throttle open, whistle open . . . Somebody
slapped me; no effect. They shook me, they were swearing at each
other, at me, the air was full of panic; still I shrieked. Then one of
them had the sense to pinch my nose while the other stuffed a
handkerchief into my mouth. The handkerchief stank of Eau
Savage. To this day I cannot smell it without wanting to vomit.

After the event, the death I could have prevented, a strange thing
happened. I became Naim's slave.

*   *   *

Something about tonight felt different. Janice Sepeda couldn't
say why; just that in a mysterious, undefined way, it was *her*
night. Something was going to happen and she was destined to
be part of it.

She made up in the women's room on the fourth floor of police
HQ, alongside Sue Rather and Gelica Chyne. She combed out her

long blonde hair, she hitched up her bra, noting with satisfaction the way her breasts jutted out arrogantly towards the mirror. She applied a little green mascara and stepped back. Fabulous. *Come on, boy: I'z a ready for you.*

Last thing she did was pin a tiny red ribbon shaped into an 'A' on the inside of her blouse. 'A' stood for Anita who'd died, but not in vain. The girls all wore these ribbons, in commemoration. Not that they needed reminding what had happened to Anita Prince.

Peter Symes wanted to call off the stalking-horse operation, saying it was too dangerous. The girls had told him to get real. They were *angry*.

Janice didn't say anything to the other guys, either before Lt Sonny Allerton's briefing or after it. But this was her night, and she went onto the street with a sense of pending drama that never lessened.

She did everything as scheduled. Down Ramp Alley, doing the shop windows. Pause for cappuccino at Bar Tivoli, check watch, synchronize with Sue and Gelica . . .

No Thelma Vestrey tonight, and that was good: who needed a know-all shrink to mess things up? She missed the reassuring presence of Daniel Krozgrow, though. Shit, what could he find to do in San Francisco that was more important than this?

Two friendly shadows in front, one behind. Walk, walk, walk. Remember to indent for new shoes, new *feet*.

Ten thirty, eleven, eleven thirty, twelve. Checkpoints checked, to the half-minute. Down streets quiet and streets boisterous, Janice Sepeda passed on her precisely timed way.

Several times she thought *he* was watching her, and the third time she knew he was.

She became aware of being observed as she stood for a while by the marina wall, eyeing the boats. The sensation was strong enough to be undeniable: as when sophisticated avionics detect the radar beam that detects *them*. She forced herself to count to five before turning. She rested her back against the wall and hitched her elbows onto it, idly looking to right and left. It was twelve thirty, and the crowds were thinning out. One or two guys stared as they passed, but that was the whole idea: the skin-tight white jeans and heavy make-up were designed to magnetize. Nobody stopped to talk to her. There was an air of home-going, of winding down and sorting out who was going to sleep where, and with whom. Groups emerged from night-clubs and bars, stood around, and split into sub-groups before finally dissolving into the night. It was a time for lonely men to make their moves, but nobody moved in on Janice. What's wrong with me? she thought. Why doesn't that guy approach me, the guy I can't see, what's making him shy?

Are you there, Mr Butcher? Can you see me? Do you like what you see?

Twelve forty-five. Time to go.

She strolled away from the wall, heading across Marina Square for the dark maze of streets around 'A' Street that eventually turned into Fountainside, and whatever it was inside her that knew these things decreed that she was no longer being followed.

She next sensed *him* three quarters of an hour later, outside Rosie's Diner.

She'd recognized one of the waiters taking a smoking-break and stopped to chat, glad of the chance to rest and make contact with something human. Suddenly she wanted a cigarette. She didn't usually smoke, just when she'd had too much to drink; tonight she was stone-cold, but still she had to smoke. The first couple of drags tasted vile. Then the nicotine hit and it wasn't so bad. The two of them stood there with the bright lights of Rosie's behind them, and six or seven other patrons of the all-night eatery schlepping around the doors, and Janice felt safe. Safe like she didn't want to move.

Because out there, beyond the fringes of Rosie's garish red and yellow lighting, *he* stood, and he was looking at her, nobody but her.

So it seemed perfectly rational and natural that she should decide this was the moment for taking a leak. Of course, it was a cop-out: while peeing she'd be inside, and safe, *and so what?*

Janice pushed through the chrome-and-glass doors. She swung past the horseshoe counter into the passage where the His 'n' Hers rooms lived. As she reached the corner of the passage, right at the back of the diner, she looked over her shoulder and nodded once. Troy, her rearguard, was peering in the window, alert to her nod. He'd signal Tony and Peter, the vanguard. They would stay outside, maybe unwind a tad, because for the moment their stalking-horse, 'Seattle', was safe, and they could use a break from tension, too.

The passage was twenty-five feet long. On the right was a blank wall. On the left, two doors: first the men's room, then, almost at the end, the ladies'. The far end of the passage consisted of a fire-door: a big, heavy slab of steel with a horizontal push-bar halfway down it and a red-and-white warning: THIS DOOR IS ALARMED. The passage was lighted by two equidistant ceiling bulbs. A couple of guys were coming out of the john as she passed His: young, friendly, well-dressed. They were discussing how someone had had two hits Thursday, including a run-scoring double on the ninth: she was to remember that later with perfect clarity, even when everything else had become a blur.

As Janice reached Hers, the two guys went out into the diner, and it became quiet again. She pushed on the toilet door, only to find herself in darkness. Hell! But Janice knew the layout of Rosie's; her hand automatically went to the light-switch.

A vice-like grip closed around her wrist in the same instant as the door swung shut, and a stinking hand sealed itself across her mouth.

She kicked out straight in front of her, able to see nothing, but he was ready for that and her foot traversed empty air. He laughed: a high-pitched giggle, the most evil sound she'd ever heard. He stank of perfume – cloying, nauseous. The hand across her mouth was smooth, with nothing masculine about it. Later she remembered that, too: a woman had got her. Not a man. A woman. Just a passing fancy . . .

Things happened with the speed of light.

She knew that P.B. Butcher would slice her up, using a surgical scalpel, that a blade was travelling towards her, only she couldn't see it. One hand was trapped, but the other stayed free. She made a fist and swung it through an arc at face-height. It contacted with bone. The giggle turned to a squeal of rage.

She managed to open her mouth a fraction: enough to get her teeth into the heel of the hand that gagged her. It jumped away, but her triumph was short-lived, because next second a fist landed against her jaw, twisting her head around to land with a crack against the tiled wall.

'You bitch,' she heard a voice say. 'You are dead, darling, you are my death tonight, I want to hear you scream, darling.'

The voice came from there, and *there*, and nowhere. Through a haze of pain, Janice heard it, and registered its timbre, and knew she would never forget its overweening ugliness. Here was someone who meant to do great evil. Death stood in the room, she could hear the beating of his wings.

But she could see nothing.

'Scream, darling,' said the voice; and again she had this eerie sense of being in the presence of a woman, a female masquerading as male. Then the fist thudded against her stomach and she felt herself sliding down the wall, clutching her middle, her assailant neglected while pain absorbed her entire attention.

I must not fall, she told herself. *Stand. Fight!*

He had let go of her. Wheezing in agony, she levered herself back upright and swayed against the wall. Where was he? From which direction would the thrust come? *Had he got his knife out?*

Visions of her little brother, John-Boy, flashed through Janice's mind. He'd grow up well. Just don't let him do anything silly. Don't let him join the police, Dad, *don't*.

'Where are you?' a voice screamed. Jesus, that had been her! And another voice answered from her left, maybe three feet away, maybe ten, maybe inches away . . . 'I'm here, darling, over here. Ready?'

She stopped breathing. He must have done likewise, for she could hear nothing, not even the squeak of a shoe – it was coming back to her, as she'd entered the restroom a shoe had squeaked, *she must remember that* – not a giggle, not a whisper. Janice stretched backwards, groping for the door-handle. Nothing moved. No one spoke.

How long before Troy twigged something was wrong? How long had she been in here – a minute? An hour?

Somebody else must come in, eventually. The diner was a quarter-full, there had been some women among the clientele, hell, this was where the whores came between tricks . . . *why didn't anyone want to piss or shit?*

A click. Funny, familiar. Like . . . like . . . ?

A briefcase clasp, snapping open.

He was taking out the knives.

The next thing she'd hear would be the sound of her own life-blood gushing forth to splash on the floor, how would it feel, would it last long, *how long did it take to die?*

With all her heart and soul and strength Janice strained to listen, while her hand never ceased in its search for the door-handle.

He could see her. The realization sapped her will. He'd been in here a long time, letting the night-watch rods of his retinas acclimatize. He could see her, but she still could not catch so much as a moving shape that might be him.

A noise. Close. Cloth, air disturbed . . .

She flung herself off the wall, diving right. Something hissed past her side, just below the breasts, to land against the door with a reverberating 'thunk!' *Knife!*

She whirled into a pirouette, around and around, lashing out with her free leg every chance she got. On the third circuit, she made contact and was rewarded with a grunt of pain. She charged towards the sound. Another squeal . . . she was winning!

Janice tripped. She struggled to retrieve herself, but her left leg twisted under her, she was conscious of hot pins being driven into her ankle as it sprained, and then she was lying on the ground, face down.

'Janice! Are you all right?'

As if down a time-tunnel, light-years away, she heard Troy's voice. He must be in the passage. Too late, too late. He was in the passage but Butcher was *here, now.* The knife would be coming down. Janice tried not to groan. In vain. No chance he'd miss: she was making enough noise for him to find her with his eyes shut.

Light.

The door was opening. A figure fled through it: for a second Janice saw a face. Young, feminine, dark, not Caucasian, not completely anyway. She'd know that face again. She'd know it on the day of judgement, let the last trump sound. Next instant came the crash of the fire-door opening, slamming, the bell ringing in an endless, uneven trill.

Another door banged shut, and next second Troy was kneeling by her side. She knew what he'd done: he'd checked the passage, found it empty and, with commendable if ridiculous thoroughness, ploughed through the first door he encountered, not stopping to read 'His' beforehand, not registering she wouldn't be there but in the women's room next to it.

'Did you see him?' she croaked.

'Who? Are you okay, shit, *speak to me!*'

'I'm okay.' Her ankle hurt like hell, her heart was about to explode and her jaw felt broken. None of which mattered. She was alive.

Troy hadn't seen anyone, she realized; he must have still been casing the men's room while Butcher made his escape. She was the witness. She was the *only* witness.

She'd recognize P.B. Butcher's face again: know it out of a hundred, a thousand, a million. But she was the only one who would. And as pain brought down a merciful veil of unconsciousness, her last thought was that Butcher knew that too.

*   *   *

Shafts of moonlight slanted down into Thelma's cell. She sat at the bottom of one of them with her knees drawn up to her chin and her hands clasped tightly around her calves. She stared at the door, listening.

It was five minutes before midnight.

She'd given up attacking the wall with her grandmother's ring when the daylight died. The area around the window resembled a First World War battlefield: raked, criss-crossed, gouged. All to no avail, for she discovered, late in the afternoon, that the bars had been countersunk so deeply into the brickwork that even if she'd managed to dislodge the wooden frame she would have brought herself no nearer freedom.

She'd drunk nearly half the water. It occurred to her to wash, clean herself up a bit; but then the voice of caution had intervened, reminding her that Richo might not come back when he said he would. Even if he did, perhaps he wouldn't want to give her more water.

What if he'd met with an automobile accident and was lying dead in some morgue – no longer a threat to society, but taking with him to his grave the secret of Dr Thelma Vestrey's whereabouts?

Suppose he'd simply decided not to come back?

She had brought herself to urinate, twice, in the empty bucket; her bowels she'd cemented shut. There were limits. But she suffered from cramps of increasing severity.

She remembered a newspaper article offering advice to women faced with the threat of rape. A hair-comb drawn across the attacker's nostrils could cause enough pain to stop even the most determined. And one of the best methods of defence was to defecate at the moment when you could no longer fight him off. So Thelma ignored the stomach cramps, and she kept her bowels closed, and she prayed that Richo would come back soon, so that they could finish this.

It was an odd kind of prayer; she acknowledged that. Truthful, though. The old cliché, 'the suspense was killing me', crept into her mind, making her, against all odds, laugh out loud. Yes, better to die with eyes ablaze and fists flailing than to sit here, with your legs drawn up under your chin, waiting for the worst.

She could hurt Richo before he finished her; maybe she could hurt him a lot.

Her mind ranged over what she'd read of Aurelia's life history that day. To have lost a sister in such circumstances . . . but was it true? *Could any of it be true?*

The denial of her own, 'twin' daughters . . . using a son to hurt Naim, perhaps by killing him . . . ? No, Aurelia adored Richo.

Aurelia was holding something back. Still she had not given Thelma the vital key.

Somewhere far away, the other side of mountains and pine ridges and waterfalls and rivers, a car cruised along a road. Thelma raised her head. So far away . . . She closed her eyes, forging every nerve into an instrument of hearing. An engine.

After a while she could no longer hear it. She opened her eyes, stood up and took a few steps around her cell before once again concentrating on the world outside. She held both palms to her temples, and strove to listen. Nothing.

Not Richo, after all.

* * *

When Janice had been fixed up by the medics, and debriefed, and had talked with Peter Symes, and been commended, and criticised, and gone back to review her statement, and had a second session with Symes plus Dr Freixa from Forensic, and been formally reprimanded by Sonny Allerton for breaching procedures, and informally praised by him for being one hot-shit cop, and failed to pick out anybody from an ID parade; after all this had gone down the pipe, and Janice Sepeda no longer knew if she was a good and useful member of the force, or a liability, or indeed if she was any longer *on* the force, Daniel Krozgrow, who'd jetted in from San Francisco at lunchtime, took her across the road to Uncle Harry's and bought her the biggest Caesar salad she'd ever seen. Plus a vanilla malt, with extra on the side in the mixer-flask.

'You,' he said with a smile, 'are a very silly young woman. Know that?'

'It's been mentioned once or twice.'

'You shouldn't have gone into Rosie's – '

'What was I supposed to do, leak on the street?'

'If necessary, yes; though cops don't pee, or did they omit that from your training?'

'Well, shit.'

'That's out, too. Having once gone into Rosie's you shouldn't have used the john; having once entered the john, you should have observed the light was kaput and reversed out of there like a stunt-driver rehearsing *The French Connection*. You want another malt?'

'So why aren't I fired?' Janice asked sulkily. 'No. Thanks.'

'Because you saw the Butcher and you say you'll know him again – '

'Or her.'

'We'll talk about that, but you're not going to be fired because even now our artists are putting together a Photofit ready for the six o'clock news. Thanks to you. What you have to do is take time off. Go to the beach. Oh, did Thelma counsel you last night?'

'Thelma didn't show.'

Daniel's eyes narrowed. 'That's not like her. Know why not?'

Janice shook her head.

'Hm . . . Okay. You go chill out; then come back and tell me if the Butcher's a man or a woman. Can do?'

'Can. You think it's a male, don't you?'

'But I wasn't in the bathroom with you last night. And at least some of the Butcher's literary work is thought to have been created by a woman. Janice, don't go about this the wrong way. Relax. Let it come to you.'

'Okay.'

'Coffee?'

'Sure. Mind if I smoke?'

'Go ahead.'

Janice flung open her purse. All she'd meant to do was pull out a pack of Marlboro Lites, but after last night her hands weren't quite in control of their destiny and the contents of the purse went flying. For an instant it was touch and go whether she'd laugh or cry, or maybe combine the two in a good, old-fashioned bout of hysterics. Laughter won out.

A vial of liquid rolled across the counter in Daniel's direction. Idly he picked it up and began to roll it between his fingers. 'Ear-drops,' Janice heard him mutter.

'Mm-hm. For after scuba-diving. You know, you get water in your ears, it's bad to leave it there.'

'Oh, you're a diver, I didn't know . . . '

Although Janice was still stuffing things back inside her purse, she sensed that Daniel had suddenly become ultra-alert. 'What is it?' she asked.

'Hydrogen peroxide.'

She took the vial from him and squinted at the back, where the pharmacist's label listed active ingredients. 'Oh, yeah,' she said.

There was a pause.

'Hydrogen peroxide . . . ' Daniel mused. 'It was on the card-stock he used.'

Then he shrugged and turned to Janice with a smile. 'Guess that adds just another use for HP to my list. Listen, have you seen the artwork on the Butcher?'

'Yeah, the guy showed it to me at the end, after I'd given him the description and he'd done his drawing. It's pretty good. Too masculine, though; I told him that.'

'Wait there.'

Dan slid off his stool and disappeared through the door to the street. Janice stuffed everything back in her purse and ordered a Coors Lite. She'd been given the rest of the day off, and she needed a drink. Plus several cigarettes. She was three-fourths through the first beer and contemplating a second, when Daniel came back carrying a plastic portfolio.

He spread out the artist's impression on the counter. 'Janice,' Daniel said, 'I've seen this guy before. Definitely a guy, male. And get this: he's a scuba-diver, I know that. But don't ask me how I know, or where I've seen him, because I just haven't got a clue.' He tapped his forehead. 'It's locked in here.'

He stared at the drawing a moment longer, trying to get a fix. 'Is there anything else you remember about the attacker?' he said slowly. 'Anything that can't find its way onto this.' He tapped the paper.

'Um.' Janice thought. 'I've told you about the way Butcher smelled?'

'Yup. Doesn't help.'

'And the laugh.'

'A kind of giggle. High pitched.'

'Right.'

'Can you imitate that for me?'

'Oh, God!'

'Come on. You can do it.'

Janice looked around the diner. 'People will laugh.'

'No they won't.'

Janice closed her eyes and thought. She tilted her head back and . . . *Ha! Ha! Ha! Ha! Ha!*

There was a moment of silence while heads turned to see who

had gone bananas. Daniel broke it. He said: 'Ricardo Delacroix.'
Then – *'Shit!'*

He leapt off his stool and was halfway to the exit before Janice
realized he'd gone. 'Take a break,' he hollered to her from the
door. 'You've earned it!'

Dan raced back to his office, and before his butt hit the chair he
was punching numbers into the phone. No reply from Thelma's
home. He tried another number.

'Best Western, Bakersfield? My name's Daniel Krozgrow, I'm an
FBI field co-ordinator. I'm calling from Paradise Bay police head-
quarters and I urgently need some information concerning one of
your guests. If you wish to verify me, please get the number from
Information and call back now.' There was a pause. Daniel put
down the phone. For a minute and a half he stared at it, drumming
his fingers on the desk. He picked up on the first ring.

'Hello . . . yes, thank you. I'm trying to trace Dr Thelma
Vestrey, she and I had reservations with you two nights ago . . .
she *did*? She checked in and . . . yes, but when did she check out?
She *never* checked out? . . . I see. Look, can you see if you can
find her? I mean, is she by the pool, or . . . thank you. Yes, call
me back.'

He replaced the phone.

He'd meant to call Thelma from San Francisco, but he'd been
tied up and it was after midnight when he became free. He knew
she lived with her mother and kid sister, and he hadn't wanted to
disturb the household. Then this morning he'd called St Joe's
from the airport, but as far as they were concerned Thelma was
still on her mini-vacation. There's nothing more you could have
done, he told himself. Pity he couldn't make himself believe it.

What did he have here?

One of Thelma's patients was Ricardo Delacroix: seventeen,
disturbed, nobody quite knew how disturbed. He was a scuba
diver, Thelma'd told him that. Dan had seen him at his mother's
funeral, which was why the Photofit pic looked familiar. Then
there was the laugh. And it was the laugh that clinched it.

Pull him in.

Where was Thelma? She wasn't at home, she wasn't at St Joe's;
perhaps she was still in Bakersfield?

But then the motel manager called again, and no, she wasn't there, although her bag was.

The original plan had been for both of them to visit *Pinos Altos* secretly, two nights ago, to meet Shimon Waldman.

Had she gone to the rendezvous? Could she seriously have been that *stupid*?

That's exactly what she would have done. Not because she was stupid, but because she was too brave.

Richo had got her.

Pull him in.

Dan stood up and began to prowl around his office. Calm down, he told himself, *think!* Be rational.

He came to a halt, looking down at his desk. After a while, his eyes focused. A yellow message-slip was lying half concealed by papers in the in-tray. He reached for it, read it, then snatched up the phone and got the duty sergeant.

'Ted, there's a message on my desk that someone put in an AUA on Thelma Vestrey. What is this? When did it come in, for Christ's sake?'

'I'll get the clip . . . Ah . . . yesterday evening the San Diego County Sheriff got a 911. A girl, didn't give a name, said she wanted to know about Thelma Vestrey of St Joseph's, Paradise Bay and was she okay? Then she got cut off. San Diego checked with the hospital, found out that Thelma was with Special Force and ran the AUA just in case.'

'Nothing since?'

'Not a thing.'

'Thanks.'

Daniel put down the phone. *Arrest Richo, do it now, now, now . . .*

He picked up the phone again, this time connecting with the operator. 'Hello, get me Legal, will you?'

'Busy. Will you hold?'

'Yes.'

But after a few seconds he put down the phone. He was overlooking something. Something very important.

He began to pace the room again. *What was the missing link?*

Then he remembered. Richo had an alibi for two of the murders, Yolanda Kastin and Anita Prince. He'd been in Mexico when

Kastin was killed, and according to Lomar's version as related to Thelma, he was at school the night of Prince's murder. Thelma had even seen the Mexican passport stamp, she'd told him that the night they'd made up their quarrel, the night Waldman came to the motel . . . the night they'd first slept together, no, don't think about that . . .

Daniel pulled the phone towards him and dialled an internal number. 'Hi, Andy? Dan. I need some fast, under-the-table footwork, okay? I want you to contact Mexico and find out if a certain Ricardo Delacroix entered or was in the country any time this year. Off the top of my head, you want to talk with the Bureau of Immigration's Travel Control Services, and you'll find 'em at the international airport. They're fine people, I've worked with them before. Get hold of a guy called Jun Flavier, remember me to him, say it's urgent.'

'Okay.'

'And Andy – who's good in Legal?'

'You should try to talk with Ben Knight.'

'Thanks.'

Daniel consulted his internal phone directory, and a moment later was talking to Knight, who invited him to his office on the third floor.

'I've got a problem,' Dan confessed as he entered Knight's room. 'I'm damned if I arrest someone and I'm damned if I don't.'

Knight, an Amerasian in his early thirties, shot Dan a bright smile. 'Why not sit down and tell me about it?'

It took Dan half an hour to dot all the i's and cross all the t's. Knight was an attentive listener. He took no notes, but from the occasional shrewd question he shot across the table Dan realized he didn't need to.

At the end of it, there was a long silence, while Ben stared out the window.

'You say you're damned if you don't arrest this guy, Richo,' he said eventually. 'But . . . damned if you do?'

'If I'm right, and he's holding Thelma Vestrey, there's no reason why he should ever disclose her whereabouts.'

'Hmm. Yes. No DA could afford to bargain clemency for an

animal like the Butcher, not even if it meant saving Dr Vestrey's life. I see that. Look, do you have a photograph of Richo?'

'No.'

'So there's nothing you can show to Janice Sepeda for ID?'

'No. Only the Photofit. And then there's that weird laugh of his.'

'That's not ideal. To be frank, I doubt if you have enough for an *arrest* warrant at the moment. What you can do is pull Richo in for questioning and you can put him on the line for Janice to pick out.'

'Same problem – Thelma disappears for good.'

'Search warrant, then. You're much more likely to get one of those.'

'But which premises do I search?'

'His father's spread.'

'And if she's not there?'

'Well, look, we have to take it as it comes. If she's not there we think again, but she might be there.'

'And I have enough for that?'

Ben pursed his lips and took another long look out the window. 'Yes.'

'So when can I get it – the warrant, I mean?'

'Just as soon as we can round up a judge. I'll need you and Janice.' Ben glanced sideways at his tray, which was overflowing. 'I was wondering how to kill time.'

'Thanks, owe you.'

The warrant came out of Judge John R. Roberts's chambers a little after four. A quick phone call to the Tulare County Sheriff, who would have to execute the warrant, and Daniel was on his way up-country.

There was a flight from Paradise Bay to Bakersfield at five: he caught it by a hair. From Bakersfield he took an air-taxi to Kern Valley Airport, a single strip of tarmac nestling in mountains by the side of Lake Isabella, and in Kernville he managed to find a 4X4 Isuzu Trooper 3.1 for rent. The garage-owner gave him directions to *Pinos Altos*. The road was steep and twisty, but the weather stayed fine and it was too late in the year for even residual snow.

It was dusk when he finally neared the estate. He'd arranged to meet the Tulare Sheriff's party half a mile down the road and was driving slowly, keeping a look-out for other vehicles. Suddenly he saw headlights racing towards him. Daniel squeezed the Isuzu into the side, losing paint against stone, and a low-slung sports car roared past with a blare of its horn and reckless disregard for traffic.

A Porsche. Black.

Daniel was already turning the car around.

It had to be Richo. He'd seen the boy's car at Aurelia's funeral, and how many people drove black Porsches on the *Pinos Altos* road?

He sped off in pursuit. For a while he kept up, and even managed to close the gap a little, until he realized that Richo would see his lights in his rear-view mirror and slowed down.

Why was he doing this? He should be rendezvousing with the Sheriff, preparing to enter *Pinos Altos* . . . No. Richo knew where Thelma was. He had to!

Call the Sheriff on the car-phone. Damn! – No phone in the car, and he'd left his portable in the office.

Drive to *Pinos Altos*, collect the Sheriff . . . don't be a fool, that way you'll lose Richo.

No help for it. *Drive on!*

The Porsche's headlights were bright enough to be seen carving out its route even if the car itself was no longer visible. For ten nerve-racking minutes Dan trailed those beams, allowing the space between the vehicles to open up, only to find at the end of it that the lights had vanished. He pulled over to the side and swore.

Something made him look up. High above him, travelling at a tangent, were another pair of headlights, climbing fast. There'd only been one turn-off, he'd seen no other traffic . . .

Daniel reversed around and tore down the road. Sure enough, there was a scarcely visible junction, with a side-road that immediately went onto high gradient. After about a mile of twisting and turning the surface degenerated to packed earth, and here the broad tyre-marks of the Porsche showed up in his lights like railroad tracks.

A vicious corner reared up unexpectedly. Dan's car half floated into space; he wrestled with the steering-wheel and stormed on.

*   *   *

The fire truck and Detective Andy ter Haar arrived neck and neck. Andy's radio told him that the police Emergency Services squad was still more than a mile away. He jumped out of his car and gave the street a quick once-over, before crossing the sidewalk to greet Mrs Richmond.

It was a poor neighbourhood, hungrily clinging to its pathetic share of the wilderness that separated Paradise Bay's middle-class enclaves from Highway 1. Another street to the west and Cleeve would have become Clarence Hill, with trees growing out of the sidewalk and dogs on leashes to water them, but Philadelphia Street was definitely part of down-at-heel Cleeve. Andy knew all this because he'd come here before, as part of the ongoing inquiry into the death of Patty Ann King. Tonight he'd been on his way home, relieved by the graveyard shift, when he'd caught the 10–13 on the radio and, recognizing the address, gone for it.

Mrs Richmond was standing outside her apartment house wearing curlers and a quilted bathrobe. At first she didn't recollect him, then she managed a half-smile and said, 'It's you!'

'Hi, how are you?'

'I've got a bomb in my third floor back.'

Andy liked Mrs Richmond, not least because she stayed calm. She told him about the bomb in much the same way as she might have volunteered that the second floor front was a man of the cloth, or the attic was gay – with a mixture of puzzlement and quiet concern. She was about fifty, and had been in the rented property business all her life – each and every grey hair a tenant, or so she'd told Andy when he'd ransacked the place after Patty Ann King's death. Patty, the third of P.B. Butcher's victims, had been rooming with Mrs Richmond when she died.

'Tell me about it. *After* we get your tenants out.'

Mrs Richmond and Andy went inside. As they worked their way through and up the building, she explained.

'Carla found it . . . Carla's the new girl, took poor Patty's room on the third . . . couldn't sleep . . . light sleeper, so she said . . . Oh, Mr Simpson – ' (this to a tenant) – 'I'm so sorry, but the police say we have to evacuate . . . nothing to worry about, it's just that we have a bomb . . .'

By the time they reached the third floor there was pandemonium in the street. By now another two fire trucks had reached the scene and fire-fighters were busy laying out their hoses, while blues cordoned off the sidewalk and began to knock on doors. Up on the third storey, however, it was still relatively peaceful and Andy was glad of that, because he wanted to learn more about this unlikely piece of ordnance before the Emergency Services arrived and like as not blew them all up.

Mrs Richmond knocked on a door at the back of the house. It opened to reveal a slim girl of about twenty-five, who might have been pretty but for the multi-coloured smears of make-up disfiguring her face and the cigarette that dangled from her lower lip.

'Carla, dear, this nice man is Detective ter Haar, and I really don't think you should be smoking that thing, not with a bomb in your wall.'

Carla ignored Mrs Richmond. She said to Andy, 'You with Vice?'

'No, m'am.'

'Come in.'

Carla stood aside; Andy entered.

A scarf had been thrown over the single bedside-lamp, casting the room into shadow. He was aware of strong scents competing for attention, and bottles everywhere, some small enough to contain perfume, some big enough to house gin. The bed was made with pink, flounced sheets on top of which lay a selection of soft toys. The bed had been pulled out from the wall. Andy could see where a wooden panel had been removed to disclose a cavity and he cursed himself for not having found it when he'd searched the room that first time.

'It's in there,' Carla said, her voice a creaky mixture of streetwise streetwalker and frightened kid. 'Ticking,' she added.

Footsteps came rumbling up the stairs. Andy knelt down and

looked into the cavity. He saw a big cigar-box, tied around with blue ribbon knotted into a bow.

Three guys burst into the room. 'Lieutenant Todd, ES,' the lead man panted. 'Where is it?'

Andy stood up and pointed. 'It's ticking,' he said.

But he was wrong: the ticking had stopped.

*　　*　　*

Thelma did not think it possible she might sleep. She'd endured two full days and a night in her cell, and during that time she'd dozed occasionally, but never fully lost consciousness. A cloud crossed the sun, an animal skittered near the outside wall: she was instantly alert. Hunger raked her stomach. Yet somehow she did sleep. She awoke to find the cell in darkness again, with moonlight flooding in through both windows, and a figure standing in the middle of the floor.

She scrambled up onto her knees. She was panting, but she couldn't help that. This was what terror meant. Every year some people died of fright, and this was how.

The figure did not move. For a long time it stood there, looking down through the bars, without word or gesture. Thelma's mind steadied a little. Her body calmed itself to the point where she could think.

Richo.

Slowly he raised his hands. He took off his shirt, letting it fall to the floor. He removed his right cowboy-boot, still not taking his eyes off Thelma. He placed his right sock inside the boot and kicked it aside. Then he did the same for the left boot.

His jeans were held up by a thick leather belt with a metal clasp. This jangled as he undid it. First the right leg came out, then the left. With a smooth flick of the left ankle he sent the jeans curving away, almost up to the ceiling. Underneath he was wearing a skimpy tanga of brilliant white. He inserted both thumbs into its waist-band, and seemed about to lower it, when a thought struck him and he turned sideways on, placing himself between Thelma and the big window, so that his body appeared to her in silhouette.

He slipped off the tanga. His cock sprang out and upwards, a long, solid black stump against the ivory moonlight. His butt was rounded and full, his legs packed with muscle . . . Thelma looked at him and she shivered. He was so strong, but she had to resist him, *had to*.

She was exhausted, she was weak from hunger. But she would fight.

She retreated to the far corner of the cell, where the buckets were. Drench him with urine, that was the first thing. Then poke out his eyes. Or twist off his balls, if that seemed easier, at close quarters.

If he survived that, and forced her to have oral sex with him, she'd bite off his penis. How much blood would flow? Would she choke? Drown?

Would she do it? *Could* she?

Yes.

But while her mind was dissecting possibility after possibility, Richo had not been idle. He'd found something, and now was fitting it to his right hand. Thelma floated off her comforting magic carpet and fell smack up against reality.

'Can you see it, darling?' he asked, in that silvery lilt of his.

He was still standing sideways to the window, letting her view his inflated penis, but now there was something else to watch: a row of metal points along his fingers, like miniature witches' hats. His hand undulated and a moonbeam snagged the tips, making them dance and glitter. Because Thelma was dizzy from lack of food and sleep, the illusion took hold. She couldn't tear her eyes away from the wicked steel points.

'Don't fight me, because, shit, I'm in love again. And if you fight me, darling, I'll have to mark you D-minus.' He held up his hand. 'With this.'

*   *   *

Daniel careered around a corner and in his headlights caught sight of a dilapidated sign: 'HORNVILLE. POP. 654.' He jammed on the brakes. He didn't know of any Hornville . . .

The Isuzu pulled into the lee of an old barn. Daniel's eyes quartered the road-map, but in vain.

Go on.

As he'd entered Hornville the road had become paved again, so there were no more tyre-tracks to follow. Daniel crawled through the shanty-town, keeping a look-out for the black Porsche. He passed several broken-down houses, a store, what might have been another store, or offices.

There was no sign of another vehicle, no trace of human habitation. Daniel drove on.

*　　*　　*

Richo was inserting a key into the lock of Thelma's cell when they heard the sound of an engine.

He might have been transformed into stone: a statue of a naked youth, his head bent down to the lock, one hand on the bars, the other about to turn the key. Thelma's first instinct was to cry out. She crushed it. Nobody would hear, it could only enrage Richo. He was high, not just with sexual arousal. He'd taken something before coming here.

The sound of the engine grew louder. Lights from outside, moving lights, described an arc across the ceiling. The engine slowed, as did the arc of light. Thelma held her breath, and prayed, but the car didn't stop.

Thelma could not believe it. Against the odds, a car, outside help, had come to this benighted burg at precisely the right moment . . . and gone away again.

Richo thought it hugely funny: *Ha! Ha! Ha! Ha! Ha!* The key clanged in the lock, the door swung open.

*　　*　　*

Daniel continued out of town, along the paved road, until eventually he found himself in open country again, climbing to nowhere. He drove on for a mile, two, three. There were no turn-offs, no more houses, no people, no livestock.

The road gave way again to moist, tamped earth. That was

when Daniel noticed the absence of something else: tyre-tracks.

He stopped the car. *Lost him, Goddamnit!*

The Porsche had driven into Hornville. Either it was still there, or Richo had left by another route.

Daniel slammed the car into reverse.

It wasn't easy to turn around on such a narrow road, with a void on one side and a vertical granite wall on the other, but he managed it. The return journey seemed to take less time. He cut the engine while still a way out of town, worried that Richo might hear it.

He parked by a ruined house. The moon was full, but the sky had clouded over: when he switched off the headlights, darkness closed down totally.

He got out. Check the buildings . . .

* * *

Richo stood three feet away from Thelma. He'd locked the door of the cell behind him and left the key in the lock. She eyed it, calculating distances. Not now, but if she got a chance, however slight . . .

'Strip, darling,' he commanded.

She didn't move.

Richo sighed. Then he giggled softly, as if this were all part of the game and she was doing exactly as he wanted. He raised his right hand to the collar of her shirt and, with extraordinary gentleness, laid one of those wicked metal points against her neck. When he moved it downwards it felt like a paper cut: a sting, an irritation, nothing more. Then she was aware of a drop of liquid gathering, trickling, falling down her skin in erratic jumps, and she looked down to see the trail of blood he had drawn.

Thelma's hands went to the buttons of her shirt.

* * *

Daniel proceeded slowly. He entered every ruined building he passed, not leaving until he'd made sure it really was deserted, and without light this took time. He strove for silence, tip-toeing everywhere.

Once some animal uttered a screech and pattered away, leaving him agitated, but apart from that he heard no sound. It wasn't a peaceful night, however; he sensed that. Enveloping evil oozed from the shadows, the ruination all around, the smell of antique decay and rotten wood.

He'd finished with the general store and was standing in the square, undecided as to his next move, when the moon emerged from behind a cloud, and twenty feet away he saw something he'd missed earlier: a bulky shape tucked close beside the wall of the store so as to be invisible from the road . . .

The moon shone down, igniting a glint of glass and the brighter reflection of chrome.

Richo's car.

*   *   *

Thelma was naked now, like Richo. He stood close enough for her to feel his body-heat. He ran the metal point covering the knuckle of his little finger down her left breast. A stream of warm blood followed his hand. When he reached the nipple he paused and then, with quick, surgical precision, jabbed it. The pain was excruciating. Thelma's face strung itself into a rictus of agony, but she did not cry out.

Her heart was beating to a strange, slow rhythm. Her skin tingled. She and Richo stood on either side of an invisible curtain. Beyond that screen was where Thelma kept her animal self: hate, the desire to inflict pain. She'd kept the beast there, chained, for so long, and now Richo was about to twitch the curtain aside.

Like a person who strives to recall a dream on waking, Thelma tried to remember her ploys and stratagems. She'd prepared ways of dealing with Richo, ways of thwarting him. Why wouldn't they come to her aid?

His breath smelled sweet; his lips were full, and coated with moisture. He was lowering his head to one side, bringing it closer. She thought he was going to kiss her, but he didn't. As long as he refrained, the curtain would remain in place. As long as he avoided a semblance of tenderness, she could control the animal.

He reached for her wrists. He raised and spread her arms, pressing her back against the wall. Her buttocks flattened themselves against the cold, damp bricks. Slowly, oh so slowly, he lowered his mouth to her neck. She was conscious of his breath, still coming in gasps of excitement. Would he kiss her? Bite her?

Ever since childhood she'd made plans: for next year, next month, the next quarter of an hour. Now she rode the cutting edge of life. There *was* no next second, there *was* no time.

With the first brutality he'd displayed, the initial gust of the coming storm, he kicked her legs apart.

Thelma screamed her heart out.

*   *   *

Daniel approached Richo's Porsche. It looked empty. He bent down to look inside. On the back seat sat a holdall, the sort of thing jocks carry to the gym, but made of leather.

A voice . . . no, *laughter*.

Dan shot upright, looking this way and that. *Someone had laughed*. But where?

He surveyed what he could see of the square. He'd already explored all the ruins, so where had that laugh come from?

Dan's flesh erupted into goose-bumps. The laugh . . . there'd been something inhuman about it. Exaggerated. Cruel. Suddenly he wished he wasn't alone. Crazy it might be, but the darkness had started to get to him. *Pull yourself together!*

He was in the right place, he knew it. That had been Richo he'd heard. *So where was he?*

Thelma's scream told him.

Daniel pivoted around, straining to see what lay beyond the black visor of night.

The scream came again. He began to run, turning his head this way and that in search of the tremulous wave of sound rippling towards him through the darkness.

He crossed the square diagonally, praying not to trip over anything. But as he rounded the corner the scream diminished, then died.

Daniel skidded to a halt. With every ounce of concentration he possessed he scanned the darkness for a repetition of that ghastly noise; but all he could hear was his own heart beating.

He found himself wanting her to scream again, and the horror of that made his guts squirm.

The wail started up again. *Behind you!*

Daniel belted off back the way he'd come. He'd already searched everywhere, here he was in the square again, with nowhere to go, no road worth following . . .

Over *there*!

He set off again, heading towards what he took to be the source of the screams. They were growing louder, he'd guessed right! But the noise was fading into a gurgle of despair. 'Don't lose it,' he prayed, 'hold on, Thelma, I'm coming, *hold on.*'

He rounded a corner. Straight ahead of him was a one-storey wooden building.

Daniel homed in on the scream, knowing it was Thelma he could hear, knowing this was the place and her time had run out . . .

*   *   *

Richo was slackening. His body deflated, like an outsized beach toy with a slow puncture. He released Thelma's wrists. She punched the side of his head . . . Richo reeled, squeaking out his terrible falsetto giggle. She kicked up between his legs but he jumped aside, still laughing. Somehow he was through the barred gate, locking it again; in the time it took Thelma to slump to the floor he was buttoning up his Levis, a man possessed, at the core of some monstrous energy field. He threw on his shirt, he put on his boots, and still that horrible giggle echoed inside her head, *Ha! Ha! Ha! Ha! Ha!*

He finished dressing. Thelma began to retch. She hadn't eaten for a long time, but her stomach was full of bile and she wanted to vomit up Richo. She wanted to swallow a stomach-pump and rid herself of him as if he'd never walked the face of the earth. Her entire world had shrunk to a pool of foul-smelling liquid on the floor and excruciating pains that extended to every part of her fibre. She scarcely heard the door bang open.

What aroused her was the sound of glass shattering. She raised her head. The window had gone. Where before had been a frame, and glass, now was only a hole, with shards outlined against the fitful moon. She heard running footsteps and a voice she knew. A voice she loved. 'Daniel,' she cried. 'I'm here, oh God . . . '

The sound of running footsteps died away. Thelma struggled up to rest her back against the wall. Her stomach felt as though it had been washed and wrung and hung out to dry. Her head was going around and around; she couldn't see her own hand when she held it up. Outside, sounding far away, a car engine fired, revved and disappeared into the distance.

Someone struck a match. Thelma turned towards the spark. As she did so the lantern-wick caught, and she saw a man in the middle of the room, struggling to get up.

Daniel.

Richo had left the key in the barred gate. Seconds later, Daniel was kneeling on the floor beside her, and Thelma knew she had come through. She was safe.

He'd been hurt. Blood dripped from his forehead, but Daniel didn't care. He gently wiped her face with his handkerchief. She shivered, managed to get a grip on herself. She hugged him close and for a few minutes rocked in his arms, like a baby. She was safe, safe.

'Daniel,' she whispered, her voice scarcely more than a bull-frog's croak, 'thank God you came. Thank God.'

'Jesus, you're . . . I love you, Thelma.'

'Love you . . . Are you okay? Did he hurt you?'

'Not much. Neither of us could see a thing.'

Thelma made a great effort. There was something she had to do, something no one else could help her with, and it must be done quickly.

'I need . . . this is girls' stuff. Go outside, please.'

He stared at her. 'You've been through a terrifying experience, you're – '

'Just . . . go. Leave me a handkerchief. A clean handkerchief.'

Unwillingly he did as he was told. As he went through the

209

outer door he cast a glance over his shoulder and caught a glimpse of something white, his handkerchief. Thelma saw him standing there; 'Daniel,' she said, and this time her voice was sharp; 'please.'

Five minutes later they were climbing into the Isuzu Trooper.

'He got away,' Daniel said sourly. 'Doesn't matter; that car's easy to trace.'

'It doesn't matter,' Thelma agreed from the back seat. 'We've got him now. I took a sample. Internally.'

Daniel's heart missed a beat. He started the engine and drove off, but he was on auto-pilot. The sense of what Thelma had said struck him in the solar plexus. She'd been raped. Thelma Vestrey, the woman he loved; she'd been raped by a mad boy who was probably also a killer. He'd shot his seed inside her. Thelma had collected it. Using his handkerchief.

The road ahead blurred. Daniel blinked. After a while the blur lessened, without ever quite going away. But the rage inside him did not blur.

A dozen miles down the road he came to a gas-station. It was shut; Daniel roused the owner and commandeered his phone. By the time they reached Bakersfield the hunt for Richo would be under way.

Afterwards, Daniel had little recollection of their journey. Once or twice he thought a car might be following them, and he made an effort to concentrate on his mirror, but his was a one-track mind that night. Thelma had been raped by a killer. He was going to have to live with that. How? How long would it take to obliterate these memories? And by the time he remembered he was supposed to be monitoring the mirror for tails, the headlights he'd seen behind would always have disappeared.

Two hours after they'd left Hornville, Daniel pulled into Best Western Inn's parking-lot, and there, for the first time in many an hour, he saw a ray of light. Two deputies were standing in the doorway to reception; slightly ahead of them . . .

'Janice,' he breathed, as he let himself down from the driver's seat. 'Janice Sepeda, as I live!'

'Hi.'

'What brings you here . . . no, that can wait; help Thelma.'

The little party walked into the motel's all-night Junction Restaurant and found a table. In the small hours of the morning, business was thin: they had a corner of the room to themselves.

'I was in the squad-room on stand-by when your message came through,' Janice said, 'and they wanted somebody to go up, so I volunteered. Thelma, honey, what *happened* to you?'

'Oh . . . lots. Janice, do you have a cigarette?'

'I surely do. Here . . . '

Thelma accepted the Marlboro Lite with shaking fingers. When Janice proffered a Zippo, Thelma grasped her wrist with both hands to steady the flame.

'Jesus,' she said, leaning back in her chair, 'that is good, that is so good . . . ' She laughed, not a pretty sound. 'Used to be so good.'

'Keep the pack, honey.'

'Thanks. Here. Here. Gimme your lighter.'

'Honey, shouldn't you – '

'Gimme the fucking lighter.'

Janice handed over her lighter. Thelma stood up, a little wonkily. She held the lighter out in front of her, then swung her arm like a pendulum. On the backward stroke, the Zippo cracked open, on the forward swing the hem of her jeans caught the wheel and a flame sprang out.

'Neat, huh? Isn't that neat? Pack a day, I used to smoke. Look, see here . . . '

Thelma dropped down into a chair. She picked up the complimentary booklet of matches left in the ashtray, folded over one match with the fingers of her right hand and, in a seamless movement, flicked its head against the rough paper to ignite it.

'Pow!' she said. 'Thelma the Magnificent!'

'Stop it.' Daniel reached out to grab her hand. *'Stop it!'*

Thelma stared at him, as if she didn't know who he was. With quick, violent movements she shoved the matches into her purse, along with Janice's pack of Marlboro Lites. Then, suddenly, she collapsed into her chair like a stuffed soft toy.

'Honey . . . ' Janice put a soothing arm around Thelma's shoulders. 'Why don't we just rest awhile, hm? The two of us, yes?'

She flashed a silent message at Dan through narrowed eyes. He nodded and took off with the deputies. He wanted to check on progress, anyway.

They didn't have much to tell him, though. A major manhunt was under way for Ricardo Delacroix. He wasn't at *Pinos Altos*, nor was his car. His description had been wired to the four corners of the state, but Richo had disappeared without trace.

* * *

The street was amazingly silent, Andy reflected. Must have been more than a hundred people gathered at either end of Philly, beyond the police cordons, yet not one of them spoke.

He sat in his car with a note-pad on his knee and Carla Maddox next to him. Subconsciously they were waiting for the 'boom!' that would shower glass over them and rock the car, signalling the end of Mrs Richmond's, but they kept talking anyway. A discreet radio call had confirmed what Andy suspected: despite her tender years, Carla already had several two-thirty raps under her belt. Mrs Richmond was soft on hookers. She'd told Andy, straight up, when he was investigating Patty Ann King's death: they have to have places to lay their heads just like the rest of us decent folk. Andy had agreed, dismissing as unworthy his speculations about Mrs Richmond's antecedents before entering the property business and commencing her collection of grey hairs. But Patty Ann King had been a hooker, and Carla was a hooker, and this was her story . . .

She never slept well, because her hearing was exceptionally sharp and ever since she'd moved in with Mrs R, she'd been plagued by this darned *ticking* noise from behind the bed. But she couldn't find anything, until after a while it drove her crazy and she started poking around with a screwdriver and what should pop out but this panel . . . ?

Behind which, Andy prompted gently, you saw the box.

Damn right I did.

And you called Mrs Richmond.

Not exactly.

Well, exactly, then . . . ?

Oh, *exactly*, blah! blah! Well, all right: I didn't see what the fuck it had to do with her. Or with anyone.

Except you.

Meaning?

Oh, come on. You thought there might be something valuable inside.

Meaning?

Look.

No, you fucking well look!

And it could have gone on like that all night, only Andy didn't have the time or the stomach, so he compromised on, You thought you'd take care of it for the real owner in case she came back for it, right?

Right.

He was starting to quiz her on whether anyone had come around to ask about the cigar-box when the object itself made an appearance: a man came through Mrs Richmond's front door holding it out in front of him like one of those velvet cushions that precede royalty, and laid it on the front porch.

'Stay there.'

Andy got out of the car, leaving Carla in the passenger seat, and raced up to the house.

Lieutenant Todd arrived at the same instant. 'Well?' he said to the man who'd brought out the box.

'It's clean. Some letters, and an antique watch. We'd need to check it out back at base, but I have a feeling it's French, and old.'

'How come it continued to tick so long?'

'How long is long?'

Andy explained the Patty Ann King connection. 'She's been dead almost a month,' he concluded.

'If it comes from one of the big old European houses it could go on a darn sight longer than that,' the bomb disposal expert observed.

'Okay if I take the letters?'

Lt Todd shrugged. 'Give me a signature, okay?'

Five minutes later Andy was sitting in his car, studying the letters under the dash-light.

'Ever see these before?' he asked Carla.

She stared at the stack of thick, creamy-white paper, covered with gold letters composed in a fine italic hand. 'Yuck,' she said.

'Is that a no?'

'You bet it is. I mean, Jesus . . . that is sick-o.'

Andy smiled. 'Back to bed,' he suggested.

'You and me both?'

'Not tonight, honey.'

She surveyed him, much as a potential buyer surveys a painting or a statue. 'Do I detect a note of interest?'

'Could be. Got a card?'

'No. But you can find me at Mamaluke's most evenings.' She laid a tentative hand on his thigh. Andy didn't move it. 'You're kinda cute, know that?'

She was a good-looking kid, under that make-up; young, too. Andy ter Haar was a very fine cop, but he had this little weakness . . .

'See you around,' he said with a smile. 'Maybe.'

The police were dispersing the crowd. Andy sat there long after the last curious bystander had gone, reading through the stash of letters. Then he picked up his radio and called HQ.

'Hi, is Dick around? . . . Dick? Andy. Listen. I got something. I'm coming in and I want you to organize someone from Legal to meet me. Ben Knight for choice.'

'At this time?'

'I've got a pile of letters from Marion Lomar of Sacré Coeur Academy to Patty Ann King. Love letters. I want a no-knock warrant on Sacré Coeur Academy and I want it yesterday.'

'Because you found some *love* letters?'

'The Lomar woman had been screwing Patty since she was a teenager. She set up a meeting in Fountainside at roughly the time Patty was murdered: I've got the letter right here in my hand. So you just get some lawyer out of bed, or out of the bar, and tell him he's got good and useful work to do. For a change.'

*   *   *

The deputies wanted Thelma to make a statement, but Daniel said no, she wasn't in a fit state, and in the end they had to accept

214

that. He booked a couple of rooms, one for himself, one for her, then went to find how she was getting on.

As he walked through the restaurant between rows of empty tables, he saw that Thelma looked pale but in charge of herself. She was tucking into a tuna melt, with a salad on the side and a milk-shake to wash it all down. Janice, seeing Daniel, excused herself and headed for the restrooms.

Dan sat down. 'How are you?' he asked Thelma, wondering what she'd do if he tried to take her hand.

'Okay, I guess.' Her smile was brittle: a socialite remembering her manners. How long, he wondered, before he could break through that? Would she consent to see a therapist? Should *he* see one, too? He was in charge of Thelma Vestrey's rehabilitation, her readmission to the world of the living, and he hadn't the slightest notion of how to behave.

'Do you remember,' she said, 'how I got angry with you when you suggested Richo might be P.B. Butcher? How I said life didn't work that way?'

He nodded.

'Stupid, wasn't I?'

'No. Just wrong. As things turned out.' Dan hesitated. 'Is Janice . . . '

'She's been great. Just great.' Pause. 'I asked her to . . . deal with your handkerchief.'

'Uh-huh, uh-huh.'

Silence.

What was she thinking about? About the sex, maybe? What had it been like for her? He knew he should be asking whether it had hurt, physically and mentally, knew he ought to offer comfort . . . but his mind kept turning down a dirty road in pursuit of more basic information: had it been *good*? Had it been *wonderful*? Did Richo know how to use it, was he a skilled artisan when it came to cocksmanship, was he an *artist* . . . ?

'We need to get you to a hospital,' Dan said. 'For examination.'

'No.'

'But you were . . . damaged.'

'Not in a way they can suture.'

Daniel didn't know how he was going to say it, but he managed, somehow. 'Darling . . . is there any way . . . could it be that you are pregnant?'

'I'm on the pill.' She spiked him with a direct look. 'A week after I first met you, I went on the pill.'

'Uh-huh, I see.' He struggled on. 'Look, this doesn't get any easier, but . . . the sheriff needs your evidence. A statement.'

'They've already got the only evidence that counts. Or they soon will. It's in Janice's purse, right now.'

Daniel glanced at his watch. Janice had been away for ten minutes or more. She had to do . . . something with his handkerchief. Maybe she'd needed to pee as well. All the same, what could be keeping her?

It would be easy to put Richo away for kidnapping and raping Thelma, but Daniel was determined to nail him for the Butcher murders as well. Since discovering what the boy had done to Thelma, he was particularly keen on that. Without Janice Sepeda and her ability to identify the Butcher's voice, however, The People had no case worthy of the name, unless you counted Matthew McManus and his hearing the killer say 'Arthur' the night of Brenton's murder, but McManus might not be able to ID Richo's voice, and anyway he wasn't the kind of witness you exactly longed to go into court with.

Janice had been gone a long time.

'Thelma,' he said, 'I hate to ask you this, but . . . well, do you think you could go check on Janice?'

Thelma rose and left. Daniel followed her with his eyes until she'd left the restaurant, then signalled the waitress for coffee. She brought him a cup. He was just adding Sweet 'n' Low when he saw Thelma hurrying back.

'What is it?' he said, jumping up.

'She's gone. No one in the restroom. But there's blood. *Come.*'

The ladies' was down a short passage. Daniel skidded through the door. There, on the tiles before the row of wash-basins, lay a small red spot. He knelt down and touched it with his forefinger. Wet.

'Holy shit,' he muttered. For an instant he stayed frozen. Then he demonstrated how he'd come by his nickname of Dan, Dan, Action Man.

Within a flicker of time he'd briefed the Bakersfield Police Department, organized a search and lined up the motel staff for interview. No one had seen anything, but that was hardly surprising: between one a.m. and six the place worked half-shift and movement was discouraged so as to ensure peace and quiet for the guests. Unless a motel employee had a specific task to perform, such as delivering room-service, he stayed put. The ladies' restroom was on the ground floor, next to a fire exit that hadn't been locked. To snatch Janice would have taken courage, but only a lucky break could have prevented it.

Daniel stood on the threshold of the fire exit, staring out into the night. Richo must have tracked them here, recognized Janice as somebody who could identify him and decided it was worth the risk. How long ago had he struck? Minutes, surely? Janice had gone to the restroom. Assume he'd been waiting, that he took her on the way in. That would have given him, what, twenty minutes at most before the alarm was raised? Allow another fifteen minutes while the police were called, the staff assembled. Gone. Long, long gone.

On the other side of the road, next to a Burger King, was a white, three-storey building. 'ROADRUNNER MOTEL', said the sign; 'VACANCY.' To judge from the paucity of cars on its forecourt, business was bad. Daniel counted a blue Ford, a pick-up, two Toyotas, a Cadillac and a maroon Plymouth Sundance. Maybe one of the guests had seen something. It couldn't hurt to check.

First he had to find a way of making Thelma go to hospital.

* * *

Janice lay on the floor and stared at the tiles. She still could not believe what was happening to her. This wasn't real. This was everyone's worst nightmare.

He'd come up behind her, soundlessly, as she was pushing on the door to the Ladies' room, and delivered one hard blow to the back of her head before smothering her mouth with a pad that had been dunked in some foul-smelling liquid. She'd struggled. Her head swam, she was falling, falling . . .

She'd awoken in this nondescript motel bathroom, unaware of

how much time had passed. She'd vomited, passed out again. When she came to, it was to discover that somebody had cleaned up her sick. She was sitting propped up against the toilet, with her legs stretched out in front of her, bound at the ankles, and her hands tied behind the toilet: an excruciatingly uncomfortable position that had already put her arms to sleep.

Someone had stuffed a nasty object into her mouth and taped it shut. She could breathe, but only just. The thing in her mouth was a tampon, she realized. It made her want to vomit again, but somehow she kept control. The back of her head felt like it had been drilled by a student dentist on his first day out of med. school. It lay propped against the toilet stand, and whenever she moved the wound shifted against the porcelain, opening up again.

She had not seen her captor, but she'd heard him: enough to know that he was mad.

Janice could see a slice of the adjoining bedroom: modest furnishings, the corner of a TV, part of the window. Through the glass was just visible part of a sign: 'ADRUNNER MOTE'. She had no idea where she was, except that it might be called Roadrunner Motel. Janice couldn't think of any other way to start off 'adrunner'.

There was somebody in the bedroom. He paced up and down, talking to himself. He threw himself on the bed. He lit matches, burning some substance that stank. Once he'd come to look in on her, or at least Janice thought he had, but there were times when she slipped into unconsciousness and maybe the memory dated back to one of those times. His eyes were fiery red. Could a real person have eyes like that, or did they only exist in dreams?

He was doing something in the next room. Sounded like sharpening a knife. Janice quelled the nausea in her stomach by a fearsome act of will, and began to plan the following day. Eight o'clock: get up. For breakfast, coffee, pineapple juice, one egg, boiled. No, she fancied scrambled for a change . . . and a painkiller.

She'd got as far as vegetarian risotto for lunch when Richo lurched through the bathroom door. Janice took her first proper look at him, saw the face she'd been most dreading to see. He was the man in Rosie's that night. The Butcher.

He was carrying a large, screw-top jar half full of colourless liquid. This he put down inside the bath. Janice watched him remove the cap and place it on the side of the tub.

He went out.

A moment later he was back, this time carrying a large book. *Scuba Diving Manual*. Richo swayed in the doorway, muttering to himself, while he tried to find a particular page in the book. But either he was drunk or on drugs, because his motor system seemed incapable of carrying out his brain's commands. The book fell on the tiles next to Janice. She twisted her neck and caught sight of a chapter-heading: 'Amputation'.

If she was sick, the tampon would kill her. *Hold on.*

What was this boy doing with a book on surgery bound up in the jacket of a scuba-diving manual?

Janice knew.

Her insides crawled around in a circle before settling down into their accustomed places. She wanted to faint. Why shouldn't she just fade away . . . ?

Richo retrieved the book. He propped it up on the cistern, somewhere above Janice's head, and ran out of the bathroom. She could hear him in the bedroom. It sounded as if he were upending a bag and shaking its contents onto the bed. Then he'd got hold of some object that made a clinking noise.

He came back carrying two knives. One was short and stubby with a rounded metal handle and a removable blade. A scalpel. The other was long, and thick, and serrated, and it had a big hole in its handle so that you could insert all your fingers and use it like a saw.

Janice did faint, then, and stayed under for a while; but Richo took her face in one hand and shook it to and fro until she had to come out from under her stone and face the cruelty in him.

'I'm sorry,' he said, in a voice that rambled hither and thither up the scale. A voice she recognized, from that night of horror in Rosie's Diner. 'It shouldn't be you. Should not be you. I meant it for her, you see.' He looked over her head, as if consulting the book, then looked down. 'Thelma's the one I love,' he crooned suddenly. 'I loo-oo-ve her. I do. But you recognize me, see? You can kill me. Why are you trying to kill me, darling?' He was kneeling in front of her, but now he moved back hastily. 'Why are you trying to kill me, darling? Why are you trying to kill me, darling?'

A pause. Janice was praying, but he didn't know that. He didn't know anything. He just kept staring at her through those livid, blood-red eyes, she'd never seen such eyes, and then he said, 'Why have you come to kill me, darling?' He wriggled away from her, into the corner of the bathroom, holding the knives crossed in front of his face. 'Why have you come to kill me?'

After that he said nothing for a while. He watched her narrowly, and she could gauge how the madness came and went. Then he crawled towards her. He squeezed her cheeks in one palm and shook her head from side to side. 'Why?' he squealed. 'Why have you come to suck my blood, darling? Why have you come to kill me, mm? *Mm?*' He was frowning horribly. 'You are Thelma. You are. I've seen you before. Rosie's. You were outside Rosie's. You *are* Thelma. Why do you want to put me in the asylum?'

Janice tried to shake her head in negation. His grip prevented her. All she could do was look up imploringly through terrified eyes, and pray. She wished she'd gone to church more. She wished she'd listened to her mother more. She wished she'd been nicer to John-Boy. She wished she were back in bed with her boyfriend, Carlito. Because she knew she wasn't going to get out of this, she wished for everything she could think of. A Scotch. The best sex ever. A new car. Someone to love. Carlito, she wished for Carlito.

Her bladder gave way under the strain. A pool of liquid spilled out of her. Richo saw it. He bent down and sniffed it. He licked it. And then, to her disgust and horror, he began to lap it up, like a dog.

'Why, darling?' he said, raising his head. Urine trickled down his chin. 'Why have you come to suck my blood, darling?'

Still on his knees, he shifted around to the side of her head. She felt him fumbling with her hands. He'd cut the rope that bound her to the toilet. Both arms were powerless, sapped of blood. A few seconds later, agonizing pins and needles shot through her upper extremities. He'd brought her left hand around and lain it on her stomach. She couldn't move it. She should hit him, yes she should. *Make yourself!* With a mighty effort she succeeded in lifting her hand half an inch.

Meanwhile, Richo was doing something to her other hand. Tying it to a water-pipe. She must use her free left hand, she must, or he'd tie her up again and the chance would have gone. Janice made another effort. Her arm refused to budge.

Richo backed away. His eyes were watchful now: still red, no longer mad. He gazed between her face and the book on the cistern above, frowning. He laid his implements on the floor. Janice twitched with excitement. If she could only force enough life into her left arm, maybe she could reach the scalpel, and then . . .

But it was Richo who picked up the scalpel. He raised her left hand and held it in front of his eyes, which strayed between it and the book. Janice jerked her arm. It moved. Richo snatched it back into place. A final glance at the textbook propped against the cistern, and he sliced the scalpel downwards.

What followed was unbearable. It takes more than a quick strong push against the joint to sever a woman's thumb, it isn't like carving a roast chicken of a Sunday.

When he'd finished he wiped the sweat from his eyes and he said, 'Do you know, darling, why I had to do that?'

Janice's hand felt as if it had been fried in boiling fat. The pain extended up her arm to the shoulder, and somehow into the heart, into all her vital organs. Her body hurt, every inch of it. When she did not answer Richo shook her chin. 'Hey. Darling. Why? Do you know why? Why?'

He cocked his head and raised his eyebrows as far as they would go, interrogating her like the policeman from a comic opera.

'Do you know why?'

He shook her head again, left-right-left.

'Do you know why? Be-*cause*.' And he laughed: *Ha! Ha! Ha! Ha! Ha!* 'Because,' he went on, 'my mommy used to beat me. When I was six, she beat me. She beat me so bad I had to go to hospital. I got a split in my skull, can you imagine that, darling? And do you know why she beat me, mm? Be-*cause*, darling! *Ha! Ha! Ha!* Be-*cause* . . . I couldn't do up the buttons of my nice new winter coat. And what she said, as she was beating me *senseless*, darling, can you hear me?'

His red eyes had glazed over while he was talking, but now they bored into her again, filled with rage. *'Can you hear me?'* he screamed, and through the smear of pain that coated her vision Janice was glad, because if he screamed long enough somebody would come.

'What she said was, darling . . . "Ricardo, you're all fingers and thumbs." He threw back his head and laughed as if he could never stop, as if all the world had reduced itself to a single joke, and this was it: *Ha! Ha! Ha! Ha! Ha! Ha! Ha! Ha! Ha! Ha!*

'So she beat me,' he went on. 'And beat me. And beat me.' His voice dropped to a monotone, his eyes lost their focus. 'Because I was all fingers and thumbs. And now I need your fingers, darling. All of them. Because, you see, I'm all fingers. And thumbs.'

He picked up the scalpel. 'We have time,' he said. 'The night is young, darling. And I never had a full set before.'

*   *   *

Deputy Sheriff Kurt Masterman was nice as apple pie. About thirty. Married, with a baby. He'd written a book on treks through the Southern Sierra and published it himself. Well, aw, (he admitted to Thelma) with a little help from Dad, I guess. She liked him. He was tanned, and lanky, and he wore a wedding-ring – always a good sign, in Thelma's opinion – and the only time he didn't meet her eye was when talking about his book, and only then because he didn't want her to see his pride.

When he said that Tulare County had no deputies answering the description of her abductors, she believed him. He told her two of his men had been overpowered and stripped of their uniforms, the same night, and that made sense. He also told her how Jacqui and Annette had witnessed her abduction.

'What happened to them?' she asked.

'They ran away. Got as far as Indian Springs. Their daddy had gone down to San Diego to pick them up when we came to serve the search warrant last night. He's back now, though.'

It was just after ten. Thelma had, with great reluctance, submitted to a vaginal examination. There was no sign of Richo, or of Janice Sepeda. Richo's car had been found abandoned not far south of Kernville. His new Cessna 152 was hangared at Bakersfield Town Airport; no one had been near it for more than three days. Between twelve midnight and eight a.m., nine vehicles had been reported stolen within a one-hundred-mile radius of Hornville. As Kurt pointed out, there must have been other thefts, not yet reported or even discovered. Richo wouldn't have found it difficult to locate a set of wheels. Now Thelma had returned to Tulare County with Daniel, and was about to show Kurt Masterman Shimon Waldman's body.

She found the clearing where she'd parked that night, without difficulty. In daylight the path to the boundary fence presented no challenges. Another deputy was waiting for them on the *Pinos Altos* side of the barrier, along with a man he introduced as Mr Delacroix's steward.

Thelma led the way up to the cottage, every so often stopping to explain some detail to Kurt. He was a careful listener, and he knew how to ask questions, too. But at last they reached the front door, and there could be no more putting off the evil day. Naim's steward stepped forward with a bunch of keys and unlocked the house. The deputies entered first. Thelma stood on the step, glad of Daniel's supporting arm. They waited. She tried to prepare herself mentally. Then Kurt came out.

'Dr Vestrey,' he said gently, 'would you mind stepping inside?'

She went in, Daniel at her heels. She stared around the living-room and gasped aloud. *What was this?*

There were no traces of violence. Pretty curtains hung from the windows, the rugs were all neatly aligned with the walls, no bloodstains, no broken pots.

Nobody. No *body*.

She advanced slowly towards the kitchen door. It stood open, allowing her an unimpeded view of the room beyond. Everything sparkled. If a spoon was missing from a rack, Thelma couldn't see it. The floor was clean. It looked like a holiday cottage that had just been made ready for this weekend's incoming guests.

'Would you mind telling us again just what happened that night?'

Thelma stared at Kurt. He still couldn't have been nicer, but she knew what he was really saying: You may be a hot-shot psychologist, but there ain't no law says you can't be crazy as a coot, too.

Thelma repeated her story and left the cottage, very distressed. Kurt was busy questioning the steward. With half an ear, Thelma gleaned that no one had been near the cottage since the night of her abduction, and the only set of keys had been locked in the key-safe. Kurt wasn't buying that easily, but Thelma had heard enough.

'Daniel,' she said, 'please take me home.'

Before they could leave, however, the deputy who'd escorted Naim's steward to the cottage fielded a call on his walkie-talkie. 'Mr Krozgrow,' he shouted. 'Call Andy ter Haar, can you?'

Daniel took Thelma to one of the sheriff's cars and punched in some numbers on the phone. Moments later he was connected with ter Haar, although the line was terrible. Daniel routed the call through the hands-off speaker so that Thelma could hear.

'Andy . . . what gives?'

'Two things. We've now got a major file on Richo's school principal, the Lomar woman. Previously Martha Roach, until she married, and then got divorced a year later. Changed her first name, too, by the looks of it: hard to blame her.'

'Roach? Why does that name sound familiar? Andy, I can barely hear you . . . '

'Marion Lomar spent years on the bottom of the Cal-Ed pool, down in the mud. Any kind of New Age education got her vote. There were plenty of wealthy takers with problem kids. Everyone listed with the Board of Education as a pupil at Sacré Coeur seems to have been in trouble before age thirteen.'

Thelma became aware that ter Haar was unhappy. He was keeping something back.

They'd found Janice.

' . . . Lomar herself . . . well, she was orphaned as a child, spent time with relatives, who were into fostering – '

'That's it! They fostered the murdered girls!'

'Got it. And Marion, Martha, whatever, kept in touch.'

'Whoa! What – ?'

'We found love letters from her to Patty Ann King. Lomar set up a meeting in Fountainside the night Patty was killed.'

There was silence while everybody thought about that. *Lomar and Butcher aren't mutually exclusive*, Thelma mused. A woman . . .

'We've got a pretty good picture of Lomar now,' ter Haar went on. 'She spent time in care, even worked the streets of LA for a while. Traded up with the help of a mark, married him – briefly – got a degree, got respectable. Odd background for a pillar of the educational establishment.'

'Leave a copy of the file in my office, will you?'

'Yes. Oh, and we're going into Sacré Coeur today. Ben's been working overtime on search warrants.'

The connection faltered and died. It took three attempts to re-establish contact.

'Daniel, there's something else.'

Thelma caught Andy's tone, knew its meaning. *They've found Janice; she is dead.*

'What?'

'Half an hour ago, they found Sepeda's body in a Bakersfield motel. I asked Tulare to let me be the one to tell you.'

Daniel said nothing for a while. He gripped the steering-wheel. His knuckles turned white. He continued to stare down at the phone-speaker while his lips worked their way around his teeth a few times. Then he said, 'How did she die?'

The silence crackled for a moment. 'She bled to death. All her fingers had been cut off.'

'Mm-hm. Mm-hm. I see. Find the perp?'

'Not yet. Apparently there's enough prints to start a library, but it'll take time to sort out. Whoever did it – '

'Richo Delacroix did it.'

'Whoever . . . was careless. Using ice, they think, stoned out of his brain. But he did have enough brains left in his skull to steal Janice's purse.'

Daniel didn't seem to understand, but Thelma did. Her sample of Richo's semen had vanished, that's what ter Haar meant, though the poor sap was too tactful to spell it out.

'Daniel,' Andy continued, 'I am very, very sorry.'

'Yeah. Me, too.'

Daniel jabbed his finger down on the button and the background squelch died for good. Thelma laid a hand on his sleeve. No reaction. She wanted to say, 'I'm sorry, too,' but something in the cast of his face prevented her, so she gently released his arm, then folded her hands in her lap and gazed out of the windshield without speaking.

Kurt Masterman came to stand by the Carina and tapped on Thelma's window. 'M'am, can you and Mr Krozgrow come at once to the main house? We have cars the other side of the fence . . . '

Daniel stared at Kurt a moment, then sprang to life. 'What's breaking?'

'They've found traces of what may be blood in Ricardo Delacroix's house. Sheriff Hudspeth heard there was an FBI field profiler on the premises and asked for you specially before they proceed.'

He whisked Daniel and Thelma up to Ricardo's *casita* to find a scene of chaos. Sheriff's officers were milling about with pump-action shot-guns over their shoulders, detectives knelt to examine door-frames while they talked into tape-recorders, a couple of photographers jumped around like agitated cats, filming anything that stayed still long enough not to blur . . . to Thelma, it had an air of activity organized solely to impress.

The man for whose benefit this display was being put on stood outside the cottage. He wore dark glasses, a white Stetson and charcoal grey suit. Sheriff Hudspeth was a man big in girth and personality. When he shook hands with Thelma he made no concessions to her femininity: it hurt.

'Terrible business,' he muttered in a sad bass voice. 'Feel sorry for the father.' He glanced over his shoulder to where Naim stood resting on his stick, alone.

Kurt filled the sheriff in on the result of his visit to the cottage. Hudspeth considered that, then went over to speak to Naim. 'Mr Delacroix,' Thelma heard him say, 'I wonder if you could contact

Mr Waldman, find out when he expects to be back from New York?'

Naim nodded. Sheriff Hudspeth ambled back to Daniel. 'Mr Krozgrow,' he said, 'this here is Jane Parker, assistant county medical examiner . . . '

Daniel nodded to a thin woman with greying hair who stared back at him without interest through thick, rectangular spectacles.

'She's found blood, spilled not that long ago. Place is in a mess. Glad to have you aboard.'

'I'm only a profiler, Sheriff, not a detective.'

'You're FBI, son, which is all I care about.' Hudspeth laughed, his bass voice booming out over the lawns loud enough to make all heads turn. 'Eyes of the world upon me, huh?' He shook his head, still chuckling. 'Eyes of the world upon me . . . '

He turned and lumbered inside the house. Thelma and Daniel followed, with a gaggle of officers bringing up the rear. As Hudspeth had said, the place was a mess, though some of it was attributable to the sheriff's people, Thelma thought privately. They went straight to the kitchen. A half-empty bottle lay on the table in a pool of whisky, with no sign of a glass. On the floor, surrounded by a white chalk circle, was an irregularly shaped stain the colour of rust. Another chalk circle had been drawn at the door to a utility room. Thelma and Daniel advanced. In the utility room were a washing-machine and dryer, a sink, cupboards, a big stand-up refrigerator and a chest freezer. A third chalk circle had been drawn on the tiles in front of the chest.

Hudspeth turned to one of his officers. 'Have Mr Delacroix step inside, will you?'

A moment later, Naim hobbled in to join the group standing around the chest freezer.

The freezer was fitted with a padlock. There was an awkward semi-silence, while people coughed behind their hands and shuffled their feet.

Thelma's throat had gone dry. They were going to prise the freezer open; she felt terrible and didn't want to be here when they did.

Hudspeth seemed to sense what was going through everyone's minds. He turned away from the freezer and gestured at the stand-up fridge. 'Taken a look inside?' he asked.

'No, sir.' The officer who had spoken stepped forward and shot an inquiring look at his boss. Hudspeth nodded. The officer tugged on the door. It swung back to reveal a dozen cans of beer, some one-litre bottles of Coca-Cola, a few plastic storage boxes. The officer pulled open the freezer compartment and Thelma turned her head away. But in the top section all they found was a pack of raspberries, frozen rock-solid, and twenty-four ice-cubes.

The officer closed up the refrigerator. He glanced at his watch and made a note of date and time on a slip of paper, which he stuck on the fridge door. Then there was nothing left to do but examine the chest freezer that stood against one wall. Thelma wondered if she was the only spectator who perceived its resemblance to a coffin.

Queasy memories of stories she'd read came oozing into her mind. Jeffrey Dahmer used to rape, kill and then eat his young male victims: it was the stench of boiling human flesh that helped unmask him. Had he ever wondered what to do with leftovers? she wondered. Had he frozen them for next week . . . ?

Why padlock your freezer? *Oh, come on, it's a sensible precaution! Meat's expensive.*

Meat's expensive, life is cheap.

Hudspeth was speaking. 'Better get that thing open.'

Two officers approached the chest and bent to examine the padlock. They conferred in low voices. One of them looked up. 'Take a long time to pick it, Sheriff. How about a bolt-cutter, that okay?'

'Just get it open, son.'

There was a respite while another officer went off in search of the necessary instrument. Jane Parker wandered across to the outer door and stared through it. Another officer exited for a stroll; Thelma knew how much he was yearning for a smoke because she felt the same. Naim shifted his weight painfully from one foot to another, but did not ask for a chair. Nobody offered him one.

At last the officer came back with a pair of bolt-cutters.

Everyone stood back to give him elbow-room. The padlock put up stout resistance. At the fourth attempt it snapped open and fell to the ground with a clatter that made them all jump.

The atmosphere in the room became electric. When Hudspeth moved his arm, the rustle of cloth shocked Thelma. It sounded like the approach of an executioner: ominous in its silence, not perfectly silent. Jane Parker coughed. The officer who had wielded the bolt-cutters moved backwards, as if satisfied with his achievement but disinclined to volunteer further.

Hudspeth sighed. In the end it was he who walked forward, he who laid a hand on the lid of the chest. He glanced over his shoulder and for a second his eyes met Thelma's. He opened the lid.

It came up with the 'umph!' of a broken vacuum – such a homely sound, one they were all familiar with. Hudspeth stood looking down into the chest, while with his left hand he continued to support the lid. Then he folded it back against the wall and turned to face the company. Only the top few inches of the chest's interior were visible from where Thelma was standing. No human cadaver. No frozen liver, of dubious provenance; no free-standing head. Just empty space.

Hudspeth said, 'Jane. Come over here.'

She went to look into the freezer before speaking quietly to the nearest officer. He went out, to reappear a few seconds later with a leather bag bearing the initials JP. Parker opened it and took out a pair of white gloves. She reached down into the chest freezer and lifted something.

Thelma jerked her gaze to the floor, and felt ridiculous. She looked up quickly to see Parker holding another of those storage-boxes, a big one.

Thelma joined in the general movement towards the freezer. It was empty.

Parker placed the plastic box on the table and gingerly opened it. Inside were three rolls of clear plastic, each containing a foil pellet about the size of a stick of butter. She unwrapped one of them. White crystals spilled out, some of them skidding onto the table's surface. Parker went back to her bag and located a pair of long tweezers. She probed the crystals, held a big one to the light, tasted it, spat it out.

'Ice,' she said crisply. 'Methamphetamine.'

'You're sure?' Hudspeth asked; and for a man with a resonant bass voice he almost sounded relieved.

'No, but I'd bet on it. Soon tell you, once I'm back in the lab.'

The room was breaking up now. People who hadn't moved a muscle stretched, smiled at one another or just took a little walk. The guy who'd gone outside earlier did so again, and this time he lit up a cigarette before he was through the door. Thelma smiled wanly at Daniel, who grinned. Only Hudspeth stayed aloof. He stood by the chest freezer, staring down into it, one hand running to and fro along the top's inner lip.

'Shift it,' he barked suddenly.

The room stilled. Smiles faded. Hudspeth slapped the freezer. 'Shift it to one side,' he said.

Two officers exchanged glances and came forward. Thelma and Daniel, on the point of leaving, stopped while the two men strained to edge the big freezer sideways.

'More,' commanded the sheriff.

Another grunt, another heave. And there was a trap-door, with a thick metal ring countersunk in its centre.

If the room had been quiet before, now it was like deep space. Hudspeth had evidently had enough of ambience, however, for he issued a brisk chain of orders, and within a minute the two officers were climbing down a ladder, their way illuminated by a hand-held flashlight. Hudspeth followed.

Daniel let go of Thelma's hand and went to kneel by the side of the square cavity. Hudspeth's head didn't quite disappear below floor level. He looked down, then glanced up again at Daniel. 'Hell of a stench,' he observed. 'Guess this is what we've been looking for.'

His head dipped. Daniel swung onto the makeshift ladder and swiftly went down. Moments later he reappeared, deathly pale and breathing like a bull. He hauled himself out of the hole, then ran for the door with a handkerchief pressed to his face.

Hudspeth came up next, followed by his two officers, all three the worse for wear.

'Jane,' Hudspeth said, 'I hate to ask you to do this, but . . . '

The woman shrugged, and disappeared down into the floor. She emerged again five minutes later, looking white but calm.

'Three separate cadavers,' she said, as she climbed out of the hole. She wiped her hands against her skirt several times, but that was the only sign of distress she displayed. 'Partially dismembered. Collection of surgical knives and other instruments. Textbooks on surgery and anatomy, bound up to look like novels. A dozen bottles containing severed fingers and thumbs. Better get a photographer down there, Harry.'

Hudspeth nodded. 'See to it,' he said to a deputy. 'Mr Delacroix . . .'

Naim's face turned the colour of old cigar ash.

'I think, sir, that you and I had better have a talk about your son.' Hudspeth smiled around the room, a master of ceremonies winding up the show. 'Thank you, ladies and gentlemen, thank you very much. I want every blade of grass on this estate combed and sifted. Now if you'll excuse us . . .'

*   *   *

Next day Thelma awoke at dawn. She knew a moment of innocence, a time when her mind was still wiped clean of memory: she lay sprawled in this strange, huge bed, a virgin sheet of paper on which the day was free to compose. She stretched her left leg, relishing the feel of cool cotton against her skin. The first hint of things past forced its way through the barrier – for a dreadful second she lay on the floor of the cell, watching Richo undress – and then the protective shield of innocence went smashing down, allowing horror to sweep her into full consciousness.

Her foot made contact with something that wasn't cotton. Something warm, and soft-hard. Another foot . . .

She shot upright and away from the thing in her bed, for a moment convinced that Richo had come to snatch her. Only when she was sitting up, trying to still the power-hammer inside her chest, did her eyes open completely to reveal Daniel Krozgrow asleep by her side.

She stared down at his recumbent body, concealed beneath the sheet. What had happened last night? Memories were lurking behind the remains of that earlier barrier; she could summon them if she chose. Did she choose?

No choice.

They'd gone to eat dinner in Paradise Bay: a quiet Italian place not yet taken over by the cognoscenti. She'd noticed when he ordered a second bottle of wine, and resolved to keep her glass covered. Somehow that resolution had foundered. It was excellent Soave, and it went down like nectar. They'd been so busy talking, because that was their way of covering up what couldn't be faced: Janice's death, Thelma's rape, and the rage. Silence had been outlawed, and one way of bridging silence was to drink.

Daniel had invited her back to PJ's. Suddenly Thelma hadn't fancied going home to face Rachel and Kirsty, so she'd said yes. On the way he'd stopped off to buy a quart of Jim Beam. She'd gone with Daniel to his room.

Flashpoint had been instantaneous. She'd scarcely shut the door when she was in his arms, and let's not mince words, lady, you put yourself there! No crap about you 'finding yourself in his embrace,' or 'seeming to lose control'. You flung yourself at him and he caught you halfway.

What therapy. What unbelievable, indescribable, luscious, slurping, licking, fondling therapy perfect love could be.

They should put it on Medicare.

Looking down at him now, she could rationalize what she'd done. She'd wanted reassurance that sex didn't have to be dirty, or painful, or anything other than fun. She'd needed to express her gratitude, and the love that he at last was ready to accept. Rationalization, hell! She'd wanted him like a bitch wants a sire.

She loved him. Always had.

Thelma shook Daniel's shoulder. He sneezed, yawned, opened one eye. She shook him again and in a voice like thunder demanded to know: 'What the *hell* do you think you're doing here?'

He struggled up, shamefaced, and looking so vulnerable that for a moment Thelma was tempted to relent. What a great chest he had: lean, but tanned and with the ribs concealed by a pleasing amount of firm flesh. 'So this is it?' she stormed. 'You thought you'd take advantage of me when I was down, right?'

'Thelma, I – '

'What possessed you? What made you think you could just *lie* there . . . when I need you so much?'

The last word got smothered; her lips were busy below the sheet. He came almost at once, taking her by surprise, but when she caught her breath, and had finished choking, all she could do was laugh helplessly while he joined in.

'I'm late,' she said.

'But it's only six o'clock!'

'I'm late, you're distracting me. Come around this evening, at home: you need to go down on one knee to my mother. Oh my God, my mother! She'll think I've been murdered, raped and burned. *Again!*'

Thelma was already out of bed, but now she rushed back and kissed his throat, his lips and ears and eyes. 'I love you. Love you, love you, love you. Hunk. Come here . . . one last kiss. One. Two. Two and a half . . . '

Dan cupped her face between his palms. 'I love you, too,' he said simply.

While Thelma was in the shower, the phone rang. When she came out, Dan's face was grim.

'What happened?'

'Andy called. They went up to Sacré Coeur yesterday evening, with a warrant. Lomar wasn't there, nobody knew where she was – they said. So Andy searched the place from top to bottom. Nothing. Not a damned thing.'

Thelma sat down on the bed, towelling her knotted hair. 'What did you – ouch! – expect?'

'I was hoping they'd find Richo there.' He shrugged. 'Papers. Letters. Some explanation for all this *crap*!'

The last word exploded from his mouth like a shell from a cannon. He leapt out of bed and went to stand by the window. Thelma could see from his back how angry he was.

'He's there,' he said, turning back to the room. 'I know it.'

'Who's where?'

'Richo's being harboured at Sacré Coeur. Lomar would have known about the man-hunt from TV and radio, she'd have had plenty of time to hide him and make the place squeaky-clean. She's shielding him.'

'How can you be so sure?'

'Where else could he be? Reason it out. He's not at *Pinos Altos*, we've looked high and low, the place is crawling with cops and is going to stay that way for a week. His face has been on every TV in the state. The guy's got to sleep, eat, live. Someone's harbouring him. Has to be, has to be. And then there are those letters connecting Lomar with Patty Ann King.'

He strode up and down the room, butt-naked, and as Thelma watched her she felt that fountain of pure love rise up again within her. 'Dan,' she said, 'come here, sit down.'

But he wouldn't. He continued to stride around, massaging his brow, until at last he said, 'I'm losing him.'

'Richo?'

Dan nodded. 'He's murdered again and again, but I don't care; he raped the woman I love, raped Thelma Vestrey, and for that I am going to get the guy if it kills me.'

'Hey. Big man. Quieten down. I know you love me, I know you want to get back at him. So do I. But this is business, police business, and –'

'No.' He rounded on her, pointing the finger of accusation. 'No, this is personal. Understand? *Personal!*'

For a moment she feared to respond, so far beyond the power of rational thought had he progressed.

'Dan, this won't help,' she said at last.

'No, but I know what will.' And now he did come to sit on the bed beside her, and take her in his arms. 'I'm going up there and I'm going to take that school apart.'

'*What?* Are you crazy?'

'I was never more sane in my life.'

'But . . . but if you're caught, it'll be the end of your career. Jesus, Dan – of your *life*, maybe!'

'I won't get caught.'

She considered it for a minute or two. Then she said, 'I'm coming with you.'

'You are not.'

'Give you a choice, Dan.' Thelma spoke with quiet authority, putting all she knew into it. 'Take me with you, or I'll report this conversation to Police Chief Symes, and to hell with you!'

'You wouldn't do that.'

She didn't waste words answering him. She rooted through her purse for her address book, picked up the phone, dialled a number, and said, 'Peter? Thelma Vestrey here. I'm sorry to trouble you at home, but – '

There didn't seem to be any point in continuing, because Daniel Krozgrow had ripped the phone from its wall-socket.

*   *   *

Midnight found Thelma and Daniel standing outside Sacré Coeur Academy, having driven all the way up in Dan's car. The gates were tall, steel, and set in a sturdy brick wall. Daniel stepped back, the better to view his surroundings. The wall, covered with ivy and other climbers, curved away to right and left. It was about twelve feet high. Getting in would be possible, if not exactly easy.

'Better get the car out of sight,' he said.

He reversed his Carina down the tree-lined road to a turn-off, where an unmarked track led into the woods, and drove some twenty yards beyond the green screen. He got out. He considered retrieving the hunting-rifle his father had given him on his twenty-first birthday from its permanent lodging-place in the trunk. No, he decided reluctantly: too cumbersome. In fact, he wouldn't even take the FBI-issue .38 he kept in the glove compartment. If he and Thelma did get caught, far better if they weren't armed. That way they might get away with a misdemeanour rap. Might.

Moments later he returned to find Thelma where he'd left her, standing before the main gates.

'Anything move?' he asked.

'Not a thing.'

She bent her knee and cupped her hands together, making a step for Daniel. He launched himself up to the top of the wall and sat astride it for a moment, spying out the land, before spreadeagling himself along the bricks and reaching down for Thelma.

On the other side of the wall, bushes and small trees had been laid out in beds. Daniel let himself drop, without mishap, and a moment later Thelma joined him.

'What next?' she hissed.

'We stay by the wall and do a circuit.'

It took them the best part of an hour to circle the house, taking it real slow, never straying more than a few yards from the shelter of the boundary wall. No lights showed up in the house's façade. Everywhere was quiet as a mortuary.

'Penetrate,' Daniel whispered.

They chose a strip of lawn that led straight up to a downstairs window: no gravel or concrete paths, no risk of making a noise. The window, a big sash-type, was open an inch or so. Daniel felt with his fingers for electric contacts, found none. He lifted the lower half of the window. It gave.

'No rugs, step light,' he whispered.

Seconds later they'd entered. By now their night vision was good enough to show them that they'd landed in a drawing-room. They moved soundlessly across to the door. Not locked. Daniel opened it cautiously, tensed for the first peal of an alarm, his eyes darting every which way in search of the winking red eyes that meant anti-burglar electronic beams. Now they were in a corridor, with black and white square floor-tiles and moulded white archways to break up its monotonous length.

Silent and slow, it took them five minutes to locate the door they wanted: the principal's office. This, however, was locked.

Thelma examined the door: solid-looking, probably oak, not the kind of thing to give to a shoulder-shove. But Dan was busy at the keyhole; and suddenly the door swung open.

'Don't ask,' Dan said pointedly, as they entered.

This room was the other side of the house from the moonlight, deep in shadow. Dared they risk a light? Thelma wondered. Again Dan was equal to the occasion. She heard the muted jangle of keys, and next second a thin beam lanced out to scud across the ceiling.

'Key-ring flashlight,' he whispered. 'Where do you want to start. Oh, my . . .'

Thelma had been making her way towards the sound of his voice; now she heard the noise of breaking china and she froze. *'What?'*

'I stepped on something. A cup, I think.'

Together they knelt down, and Dan directed his flashlight at the floor. Sure enough, shards of broken cup lay at their feet. Close by was a shattered saucer. A sweep of the light-beam revealed a silver sugar-bowl lying on its side, a creamer and a pool of liquid. The creamer, also silver, had been crushed out of shape, as if by someone stamping on it.

Thelma sought to read the runes. 'An accident . . . ?'

'Or a fit of temper.'

They stood up. Dan directed a series of light flashes around the room. The desk drew them like a magnet, only that too was locked.

'Over to you, expert,' Thelma whispered.

But the desk was made of sterner stuff than the door. Dan had been working away at the centre drawer for several minutes when Thelma, who'd been detailed to hold the flashlight, noticed several files scattered across the desk-top. One of them was sopping wet. She re-directed the flashlight, casting Dan into darkness.

'Hey!'

'Shh! Look . . . there's a teapot, here on the desk. Just . . . kind of flung down.'

They stared at the mess. Daniel reached out to the soggy cardboard folder, but Thelma gasped a warning: 'Remember how it's lying, so you can put it back right.'

He nodded, then picked up the folder and opened it.

'Jesus *Christ*!'

Thelma stared over Daniel's shoulder at half a dozen glossy photos, lying face up on the desk-blotter.

'Showtime,' she muttered.

It had been some party, that much was obvious.

The top photo portrayed a group of teenagers snorting cocaine. The boy nearest the camera had looked up at the moment of flash and was grinning, his red eyes somehow just right for the scene unfolding behind him.

237

The next photo showed two girls, naked from the waist up, embracing in a kiss. They seemed to know each other pretty well.

The next photo showed three naked young men. Amid such a tangle of limbs it was hard to work out who was doing what to whom, but one boy was plainly suffering.

The next photo showed a teenage girl being held down by some laughing boys, but she wasn't laughing . . .

'Dan,' Thelma said, 'we're neither of us wearing gloves.'

He took out a handkerchief and began to polish his prints off the glossy pics. 'This school,' he breathed, 'is a front for pornographics.'

'And a few other things too, I'd guess. Maybe it's just one big meat-rack, had you thought of that? These are photos, and you can bet somebody pays well for them. What do you think they'd pay for movies? Or for the real thing? Incidentally, how did the blues miss these yesterday afternoon?'

'Like I say, Lomar knew they'd be coming.'

'Hm. Give me your keys, I'll take a shot at the desk.'

'All right, but be careful. I'm going exploring.'

'Can you manage without the flashlight?'

'Yes.'

Daniel stood in the passage for a while, letting his eyesight sharpen and keeping his ears cocked, then padded to the far end of the corridor, where it opened out into an entry-hall.

He climbed a broad staircase to the first floor. Everything here was as silent as below. He tried several doors. Each gave onto a bed-sitting room. A couple of them had mirrors fixed to the ceiling above the double-bed. He opened one or two drawers, but found nothing that didn't belong in the room of your average student.

Then he came to a room that was different. As soon as he opened the door, he was hit by the smell: pungent, sweet, cloying. Where would the occupant keep his grass? There were only half a dozen possible places and Daniel knew them all. Sure enough, a flower-pot outside the sash-window gave up its treasure: about an ounce, he judged, concealed beneath the roots of a geranium. His fingers delved deeper, making contact with a foil package. He unwrapped it and brought it to his nose. A quick taste confirmed his judgement. Crack.

He slipped out of the room and stood in the corridor, considering what his next move ought to be. Where were all the students? The staff? *Where was Richo?*

He checked every room on the first floor; all were unlocked. There was a smaller staircase leading up. He followed it as it curved around upon itself until he came to the second floor, where the passages were narrower and the furnishings sparse. Two or three store-rooms, filled with suitcases and cleaning materials; a handful of bedrooms; a small room containing a photocopier, Apple Mac and printer; and what was *this* place . . . ?

Daniel entered and looked around. The moonlight showed him an enlarger, plastic baths, bottles of chemical, and a line with pegs strung over a sink. Of course: here they didn't take the kind of pictures you could send to be processed by Kodak, they needed their own dark-room.

Over by the window, where the moonlight was strongest, stood a table. Daniel approached. Several small bottles were littered around: he picked one up and read the label: 'Red 38'. Another said, 'Cyan 12A'. A pad of white paper lay in the middle of the desk, and next to it several ultra-fine brushes in a tub of water. The only other object on the desk was a driver's licence. Daniel held it to the window and could just make out a name, but it meant nothing to him.

The desk was a puzzle. Somewhere in his brain it set off alarm bells, but he couldn't think why.

No sign of Richo. No sign of *anyone*.

He ran downstairs, taking them two at a time, no longer concerned about noise. Hell, this house was dead. Once in the entrance hall he paused, undecided. Something made him go towards the back of the house, following the staircase wall. In the far corner he found a door. He pushed; it opened at once, and for the first time since penetrating the house Daniel saw artificial light.

He pulled the door shut again and flattened himself against the wall. After so long tramping through the house, paying less and less heed to the noise he made, this spelled disaster. Light could mean people. Had they heard him?

A minute passed. Daniel ventured another push on the door. It swung open to reveal a wooden staircase lighted by a single bulb. It was dusty and it smelled dank. From somewhere down below, he could hear the monotonous drone of voices. Something odd about them . . . amplified.

Daniel looked carefully at the stairs. His leather-soled shoes would ring a tocsin on the bare wood. He took off his shoes and placed them against the wall before beginning a cautious descent, shod only in his socks.

There were fifteen steps and he took each one as a separate project, lowering his weight onto the tread and not going on until quite sure the wood wasn't suddenly going to give and make a noise. Going down those stairs took a long time.

They ended in a cellar, a parameterless place extending away into gloom every direction he looked. Ah, no – over there, another light. The floor was made of stone, damp and ice-cold to his feet. Daniel began to move towards the light, praying he wouldn't trip over anything. The sound of voices was louder now: the artificially loud and stilted soundtrack of a home movie, or amateur video.

Ten yards or so away from the light he realized it was coming through a doorway: a smaller cellar lay beyond this one, and that housed the light-source. He moved closer. Five yards. Four . . .

He could see a corner of the inner cellar now. A red glow supplemented the weak light-bulb that hung from its ceiling: could they be burning charcoal? There was this smell . . . and a heap, lying on the floor. A body . . . ?

He was at the inner doorway now, silent as a shade, peering in. A room, fifteen feet by fifteen maybe; on the far wall a screen, a porno movie, set in a bath-house but not just soap-and-water, that was blood on the screen, and Daniel, staring fixedly at it, had a nauseating conviction that this blood was real. *Snuff movie*. His stomach churned and he averted his eyes. They made contact with half a dozen people lying on mattresses, gathered around a brazier. The atmosphere in this tiny space was thick enough to euthanase Manhattan and have enough left over for the Bronx.

Daniel felt his head going around and around. Another minute and he'd fall over. But despite his nausea, he recognized one of the bodies on the floor.

Richo.

A recumbent form shivered and stirred, began to turn towards the doorway. *Get out – now.*

The figure stared straight at Daniel. It began to stand up. It went on and on standing up, slowly uncoiling itself towards the ceiling, rearing, a serpent ready to strike . . .

Daniel took a step backwards. He turned and pitter-patted away towards the stair-light, taking great deep breaths of unpoisoned air. He raced up the stairs and closed the door at the top, searching in vain for a key. Did those voices he could hear belong with the movie, or were they attached to real people, real ghouls?

He put on his shoes and raced along the corridor to the principal's room. Thelma was sitting at Marion Lomar's desk, a pile of letters spread out in front of her.

'Go!' Daniel hissed. 'The vampires are here and I'm fresh out of garlic!'

In the silence that followed they heard the sound of a door closing.

Thelma scooped up the letters and stuffed them into her shirt. She switched off the flashlight, and together they made for the window.

Jammed.

Thelma gestured at the door; Daniel nodded. They were through it in a trice. They heard steps and skated down the corridor, into the room through which they'd entered. The window was still open. As Thelma and Dan rushed through the door the footsteps behind them gathered momentum.

Thelma dived through the window, somersaulting onto the flower-bed below. Daniel followed. By now there was a babble of voices behind them. Daniel grabbed Thelma's hand and ran.

They were halfway across the big stretch of lawn, the wall looming up ahead, when the first shots hit.

Daniel was close enough to hear the 'ping' of a bullet ricocheting off the brickwork. He flung himself to the ground and rolled sideways. Thelma did likewise, crawling away from him to widen the gap between targets. Whoever had the gun was unscientific. Stoned, more likely, as Daniel grimly observed to himself; and a smack-head with a hand-gun could be more dangerous than a marksman with a precision rifle.

The next few seconds confirmed his assessment.

The lawn was peppered with shots: left, right, fore, aft, everywhere but in his body and that seemed like a miracle. Sometimes the bullets came close together, sometimes separated by as much as a ten-second delay.

Daniel raised himself on elbows and knees and advanced at a fast monkey-crawl. The wall was nearer now: twenty feet to go, fifteen . . .

Thelma grunted. Had she been hit? No, she was up and running: a hunched, dwarf-like shape in the gloom, zigzagging across the final stretch of grass . . .

She'd made the wall and was ready to jump.

'No!' he cried. 'They'll see you!'

Thelma dropped to one knee, realizing that on top of the wall she'd be a clear target; in half the time she'd need to help him up, and then for both of them to clamber over safely, they'd be trussed and hung out to dry. Somehow they had to hold onto the cover of the wall, where darkness lay deepest.

Keeping on hands and knees they began a manic crawl along the boundary line. After a minute they came to a tree blocking their path. They manoeuvred around it and sat down to draw breath. There was confusion on the lawn, with voices here, there and everywhere, but no sense of strategy.

'How many?' Thelma whispered.

'About a dozen.'

'Armed.'

'You said it, child. Armed, drugged, dangerous as hell. Richo's there, I saw him.'

'Your mobile!'

'What?'

'The phone! Call the cops!'

For a moment it seemed like the greatest idea since MS-DOS; then Daniel remembered. 'I left it in the car.'

To judge from the voices, the crowd had gathered on the lawn midway between house and boundary. Some kind of discussion was going on.

'What would you do,' Daniel asked softly, 'if you were them?'

Thelma thought. 'I'd put a man on the gate, two more on the lawn, and send the rest around the boundary, moving in opposite directions. I'd flush us out.'

'Great. So let's move now, before they think of it.'

A bullet underlined the wisdom of this view. It came winging in high, almost parting Daniel's hair, to land with a 'smack' against the bole of the tree. In less than a second they were on their knees again, moving fast.

It was a tough route. Numerous flowers and bushes had been planted in these beds. Many of them were thorny or just plain hard; Daniel and Thelma had no way of seeing what they were about to blunder into. Before long their hands and faces were running with blood.

Eventually they came to a shallow angle in the wall. Thelma looked back. Trampling noises in the bushes! Whoever was following them came on fast, oblivious to thorns or other hazards.

'What do we do now?' she hissed.

Daniel had been doing some surveillance. 'Look over there,' he whispered. 'See that tree by the wall, silhouetted against the light? It's got low branches. Assuming they haven't staked it out, that's our exit.'

'But it must be a hundred yards away!'

'Got any better idea? *Shit!*'

He, too, had picked up on the rapidly approaching footsteps. Simultaneously, they heard another man making his way along the wall from the opposite direction. Their pursuers had followed Thelma's advice. She and Dan were caught in a pincer.

Daniel cast a desperate look at the tree: an oak, old and sturdy, but far away. In order to reach it they'd have to leave the cover of the wall, heading straight across the lawn.

'Make for that tree. Duck and weave.'

'Wait! What's that on the lawn?'

Daniel peered into the darkness, and saw what had attracted her attention. 'A hedge,' he whispered.

'Aim for that!'

243

For the past few seconds the air around them had remained silent. Now, suddenly, both pairs of footsteps were upon them. A cry, a shot, the sound of a bullet hitting brick . . . Thelma and Daniel scudded across the grass as if with the Devil on their backs. Daniel vaulted the hedge and landed on his face with a crash, as a bullet hummed through the dense twigs around him. Cautiously he raised his head. He was lying next to Thelma on a patch of grass between two hedges, each about the height of his waist. His brain made the connection: they were in a maze.

Where was the oak tree they'd seen from the shelter of the wall?

Slowly, cautiously, he raised his head above the privet. And was rewarded, instantly, with a bullet. The big tree that was their only exit lay perhaps thirty yards on the other side of the maze. They had to get there, now, before somebody had the bright idea of surrounding the maze. Daniel took Thelma's hand and, keeping on his knees, began to move along the line of the hedge.

Which way to go?

At the first fork, Daniel took the path that he judged would take them towards the centre of the maze. A quick, hazardous glance showed him that there was some tall object marking the middle: a sundial, perhaps. To get to their oak tree, and safety, they'd have to by-pass the sundial, reach the other side of the maze and clear those vital thirty yards, all before the posse caught up with them.

A fusillade of bullets rang out, criss-crossing the airspace immediately above hedge-level.

This wasn't going to work.

Dan risked another quick look. He'd chosen well: they were almost at the centre. But the same glance showed how people were lumbering around the maze in an attempt to head them off.

Suddenly a laugh echoed out across the lawn. *Ha! Ha! Ha! Ha! Ha!*

Daniel's hands clenched, his back tingled. 'Come on,' he grated.

Another turn, another fork, and there, straight ahead, lay the sundial. Daniel was about to crawl past it when a thought struck him, and he reached up. Sure enough, the metal plate was detachable: teenage memories of how to set a sundial came crowding back into his mind. Grasping the heavy metal dial by its gnomon he moved on, but not quickly enough, never quickly enough.

One chance. One chance only.

'Thelma,' he whispered. 'We're going to stand up and vault these hedges and travel like sidewinders till we hit that tree. Can you do it?'

'Sure.' But her voice trembled.

Daniel hesitated, wasting precious seconds. If they were caught, would these people shoot them in cold blood? *Yes!*

Go.

He wrenched Thelma to her feet, hurdled the nearest hedge with her clasped to his side . . . and immediately became entangled with the next hedge, too close to its fellow to be manoeuvred comfortably. Shots rang out, but haphazardly; no hits. Another hedge successfully conquered. And a third. One more, no, *two* more . . .

They cleared the final hedge, and there was the oak tree, straight ahead. But then the darkness wobbled and dissolved: greyness stood there, greyness turning into the white of a shirt. A man, holding something.

A burst of shots danced around Daniel's feet. The guy had an automatic weapon *and this was the end*.

Daniel whirled around in a full circle, holding the sundial's plate horizontal in the curl of his fingers.

The metal plate left his hands spinning like a Frisbee. The man in front of him said 'ouf!'; then he was down on one knee, holding his brow. Daniel's foot knocked against something heavy as he and Thelma flashed by. He ran on another step, stopped, turned back. His clutching fingers made contact with steel, not the sundial, longer than that. A gun! Then he was running again to catch up with Thelma, who had almost reached the tree. A shot sang past Daniel's ear. He wheeled around and, running backwards, fired round after round into the darkness, pitching the barrel low, following a thirty-degree arc right, left, right again, until the darkness fell silent and stayed that way.

He was at the tree. One last burst from the gun before he

dropped it; then he was cupping his hands to heft Thelma up. She was rising past his chest, his face; her foot was on his shoulder and he sagged beneath her weight. Then she got a grip on the lowest branch, her feet were scrabbling for a hold, and Daniel was hauling himself up after her.

Precious seconds flew by while they tried to find a way along and through the branches; at one point Thelma fell, slipping through the foliage, and Daniel's heart came into his mouth, but then he saw that she'd alighted on the wall, she was teetering, she was gone . . . but *over the wall*, into the outside world, safe.

He prepared to jump. Then he heard it, high, shrill – a paeon of defiance: *Ha! Ha! Ha! Ha!*

Dan landed on soft earth and sprinted into the woods with Thelma until they could run no further. The woods were as quiet as the moon. They fell down and lay like corpses. It was several minutes before either of them could speak. Slowly, painfully, they got up and retraced their steps, until they could see the brick wall again. No lights, no sign of pursuit. They followed the wall as far as the driveway. Moments later they came to the turn-off and, with help from Thelma's flashlight, found the Carina.

Daniel backed out and roared off down the road, anxious to put miles between them and the possibility of pursuit. After he'd been driving for about ten minutes he pulled in to the side and reached for his mobile phone.

'Damn!' he said.

'What?'

'This thing's confused by the mountains, I think. Have to drive on . . . '

A few miles down the road they came into open country, where the phone worked. Daniel called up Paradise Bay Police HQ and asked for Andy ter Haar.

'Andy . . . Daniel . . . In deep shit. Listen. I've just done an illegal penetration of Sacré Coeur Academy . . . Yes, I know. I *know* . . . Andy, will you just listen to me? The place is filled with druggies who watch snuff movies and may be making them. It's a front, an illegal operation from start to finish. *And Richo is there, I saw him.* Yes. Yes, I – *what?*'

He listened in silence for a moment before saying, 'Owe you one, buddy,' then retracted the aerial.

He drove off, heading fast for the nearest highway.

'Ter Haar got through to Mexico City,' he said. 'And you know what?'

'Ricardo Delacroix never went near the place?'

'Not this year. However that alibi got set up, it's a fraud. God *damn*!' He banged the steering-wheel. 'Those bottles, in the dark room, the stuff I couldn't figure . . . it was printers' ink. They were *forging* stuff back there.'

'What?'

'There was a dark-room, see? And in it were these bottles marked with colours and shade-numbers, and brushes as fine as a single hair. I saw a driver's licence there, too; they forge things, and that means they can forge a visa-stamp.'

'This school,' said Thelma, 'is turning into quite a remarkable little centre of learning. The sex education classes must be a wow. Aurelia Delacroix was writing to Marion Lomar.' She drew a packet of letters from her breast. 'Careful how you touch them. I'm not so much worried about prints, but they might burn your fingers off.'

The road coiled and turned like a demented snake. Daniel had no chance to read, to take his hands off the wheel for a second. 'Tell me,' he said.

'Aurelia had been writing Lomar for upwards of two years. They were having some affair, you can believe it. I've only got one side here, but it's obvious Lomar was insanely jealous. Aurelia kept writing, trying to reassure her, but Lomar wasn't having that. Towards the end, it got murderous. Lomar convinced herself that Aurelia was getting it away with Shimon Waldman. The last letter was really short, really sweet. Aurelia denied everything and suggested it might be time to quit, and why didn't they talk it over Wednesday?'

'Date?'

'Not clear. Lots of the others aren't dated either. No envelope, so I can't get anything from the postmark. And somebody – Lomar, I guess – has written "lying bitch" across it, in big capitals, like a child's. In gold ink.'

Daniel had to concentrate on keeping the car on the road. 'So Martha's got a vicious streak to her . . . why the fuck did she change her first name, d'you think? Martha. Marion. *Martha.*'

Daniel stood on the brakes and the Carina screamed to a halt. 'She used to be called Martha, so what should I tell *Arthur*!'

He gazed at Thelma. 'Don't you get it? Matthew McManus said Brenton's killer spoke just one sentence: "So what am I to tell Arthur?"'

'And you think it could have been a mistake for – '

'*Martha!* Martha Roach, now Marion Lomar, with a family connection that embraces all three victims.'

'So *she's* the Butcher! That's why some of the notes looked as though they'd been written by a woman.'

'And McManus couldn't be sure if the person he heard the night of Brenton's murder was male or female . . . No, no . . . the killer was saying, "What am I to *tell* Arthur, Martha?" Lomar didn't do the murders. But she knew about them, all right. And King's she set up.'

For a moment Daniel sat there thinking. Then he suddenly rammed into gear and took off, back the way they'd come.

'Dan!'

'We're going to *Pinos Altos*. That cottage where you found Waldman.'

'Why?'

'Because another thing Andy just told me is they'd had a call from Naim Delacroix. Now according to Naim, Waldman was supposed to have gone to New York. But Naim says he hasn't been able to make contact with Waldman, who's seriously overdue. He didn't attend any of his New York appointments, and his monthly Corporate American Express statement came in with no entries.'

'I'm not surprised. Waldman's dead, and I think I can prove it if only I take another look inside that creepy cottage.'

'Worth a try. Hold on.'

They reached the cottage in less than half an hour. The gate in the boundary fence was locked. Daniel was about to use his magic key-ring on it when Thelma said, 'Wait!'

'What's the problem?'

'The electric alarm.'

'Shit, I'd forgotten . . .' He stared up at the wires running along the top of the gate's frame. 'Oh, to hell with it – Delacroix's all shook up, the chances are it isn't even armed. Even if it is, we can be out of here in a second.'

He tried several keys in the lock before finding one that fitted. They made their way up the path and gained entry to the cottage by the same means. Thelma closed the drapes and turned on the lights. She stood in the middle of the main room, now fully illuminated, looking around. At first she thought she'd made a fool of herself, after all. Everything was the same. Everything except . . .

She drew in several breaths. 'What's the smell?' she asked. 'Disinfectant? Why would Naim disinfect this place, if I'm wrong and there never was a body here?'

'Good point.'

Thelma moved across to the nearest window. 'These drapes had been torn down,' she murmured. 'Flung across that sofa . . . there.' She swung around; and that was when she got her first, definite fix on what had happened. Somebody had moved the sofa. And . . . she narrowed her eyes. Somebody had re-upholstered it.

She turned back for another look at the drapes. These were of a pattern identical with that she'd seen the first night, but, as she now saw, they were new. The colours had had no chance to fade in sunlight.

The sofa material looked slightly different. Only slightly, but Thelma was sure. That rug in front of the kitchen door, it had been in another place . . .

She lifted the rug. Something on the floor caught her eye and she stiffened. A big, brown stain. From the look of it, somebody had devoted much elbow-grease to erasing it, but without success. It had to be blood.

'Dan, look.' She pointed. 'They cleaned the floor but it didn't come up even. See the tide-mark?'

He nodded. 'Okay, let's take this place apart.'

Thelma strode into the kitchen, switching on all the lights. For the next five minutes they went through every cupboard, each drawer, ransacking the cavity beneath the sink, opening the dishwasher, even checking its salt dispenser. Here, however, there was nothing unusual, and that didn't surprise her, because whoever had done the cover-up would certainly pay most attention to the kitchen, where the murder had been committed.

In one corner was a door; beyond it, a light-switch and a flight of stairs. Thelma clattered down the steps, fifteen of them. At the bottom was another light-switch. She pressed it.

'Wow!'

Daniel, a few steps behind, craned forward to see what had caused her to freeze. For a moment he could scarcely believe his eyes. Then he too said, 'Wow!'

They were standing in a bar.

It wasn't an ordinary bar of the kind your average householder installs next to the den. It was fully equipped, for one thing: tables, chairs, ashtrays, a chrome coffee-machine, bottles and glasses of every size and type.

For another thing, all the signs, all the posters, were in French.

For a final thing, this bar was squalid. The table-tops were soiled with ash and spilled wine. A broken glass lay on the floor. The cloth draped over the beer-tap stank of old grease.

'It's a *zinc*,' Daniel said, in a voice of reluctant admiration. 'Son of a gun . . .'

'A what?'

'Oh, it's . . . it's a kind of French bar.'

And then Thelma remembered: *Do you know what is a zinc, madame? . . . Zincs take their name from the metal which forms the bar counter, but they are a lifestyle, a philosophy, a sub-culture.*

'But . . . why?' she asked weakly.

'God knows.' Daniel's admiration had given way to unease. 'Time to go.'

As Thelma's foot touched the first stair she couldn't resist a final look back. What sights had this cramped, claustrophobic room seen? What turning-points had been reached, what momentous events had occurred, between those four grubby, nicotine-stained walls that seemed to bear inexorably inwards as they rose to the filthy ceiling above?

Dimly she understood that Aurelia had recreated the place where, according to her, Nada had died. As to why, Thelma had no idea. This cellar wasn't the mystery, it was the *key* to the mystery. But she had no means of cracking the code.

Daniel announced his intention of searching outside.

'You can do the upstairs rooms,' he said.

'Be quick. We don't know if that fence-alarm was armed.'

In a closet beside the front door they found a large flashlight. Standing on the step, Thelma watched its beam illumine Dan's way until he disappeared down the path.

She went back inside and started work on the bedrooms. She'd been at it about half an hour when she heard quiet steps on the stairs. Thelma stood rigid, not daring to move a muscle. 'Dan?' she whispered.

'It's me.'

He came into the bedroom; she took one look at his face and said, 'Tell.'

'Best come see.'

She followed him outside through the kitchen door, along a path carved by the flashlight, across a small paved area and into some brush. Daniel cast about for a while, evidently searching for a landmark.

'There,' he said, pointing down into the light-beam. 'See it?'

'A footprint?'

'Yeah. Made by somebody carrying a heavy object.'

'Because of the deep indentation, you mean? Or did you just guess?'

'Not exactly. Come, I'll show you . . . '

He led the way deeper into the brush. The ground dipped, they passed through a row of cupressus bushes, then found themselves in a gully. Dan pushed along it, every so often stopping to shine the beam down and let Thelma see how the footprints continued away from the cottage. The gully became deeper. At last they arrived at what looked like a dead end: brushwood and dead branches piled into a tangled heap.

Daniel turned to look back the way they'd come. 'What's your estimate?' he asked Thelma. 'I'd say we were about half a mile from the cottage.'

She followed his gaze. The lights she'd left on seemed far away. 'If you say so.'

'No reason why the sheriff should have searched this far yet. Not after they'd seen inside and realized there wasn't a corpse where you said.'

'What? Why would he want to search here?'

For answer, Daniel pulled a couple of branches out from the pile and shone the flashlight down.

A hand, plus the beginnings of a shirtsleeve.

'Oh, God,' Thelma breathed.

'Recognize the watch?'

She forced herself to look again. 'No.'

'Waldman was wearing it that night in the motel.'

She felt guilty at the relief that flooded through her, but for God's sake! – She'd been *right*!

Daniel set about attacking the pile of dead wood and undergrowth. A minute's hard labour, and there could be no mistaking the identity of the corpse. Shimon Waldman had been shot through the right temple with a bullet that had exploded out through the upper left quadrant of his skull, leaving the facial features almost untouched. To judge from his appearance he'd been dead for quite some time.

'So,' Daniel said. 'You were right.'

They began to walk back, maintaining a sombre silence. At last they came to the lawn. They were in the middle of it, the cottage a bare twenty yards away, when Thelma became aware of an angry buzzing sound. An insect, or maybe a swarm of insects?

But now the night spawned monsters.

At their eleven o'clock a pair of eyes floated up into vision, close and rapidly advancing. One red eye, one green, and a third, flashing red eye above and between them. The noise became a vicious roar. The monster saw its prey and swooped for the kill.

Daniel grabbed Thelma's wrist. 'Run!' he shrieked.

As they fled towards the cottage the pilot anticipated them and swooped low, almost brushing the grass with his starboard wingtip, so that the aircraft came between them and their goal. They separated and darted in opposite directions. The plane moved fast, but it needed time to manoeuvre, enough time for them to reach the safety of the house.

Thelma was petrified, yes, but she was going to survive this. Not so difficult: they'd phone for help from the cottage, and anyway after a while the plane would run out of fuel and have to land. Or crash, she didn't give a damn. All they had to do was make the cottage, now just ten yards away.

But as they reached the steps an angry clatter greeted them, and Thelma looked up to see chips of wood flying off the front door. Three shots rang out behind them: two close together, another after an interval: more than one marksman! *What was going on?*

Daniel grabbed her hand again. 'Car!' he gasped.

They zigzagged across the lawn to the path that led to the gate. More shots. A branch snapped and fell into Thelma's path, bare inches away, but she vaulted it and stumbled on without pause. Now the plane was coming up behind them again. It almost clipped the roof of the cottage before heading tightly around to aim its nose at the running couple. Lower, lower . . . the racket of its engine made Thelma's head feel like it was going to explode.

The gate in the fence was shut.

A fusillade of shots hammered against the fence, making it tremble and spark fire. Their attackers had the range. Another dozen bullets gave them the target, too: now it was the turn of the gate to rattle.

Thelma risked a glance over her shoulder. The plane's searchlight was carving a swathe across the grass towards them. She flung herself flat, not knowing what Daniel was doing, not able to care.

Daniel waited until the plane was right overhead, then sprinted for the gate. For about five seconds the riflemen in the woods had no clear line of sight, unless they were to risk hitting the aircraft. By the time the plane was away, Daniel had the gate open and was on the other side. Thelma caught a glint of moving metal. Was that him beckoning to her . . . ?

The firing began again: a steady pump of shots through the fence. Thelma rolled. Over and over she went, ever nearer the fence. But where was the gate? A bullet fell low, sending a spurt of soil over her face, and for a second she froze. *No time to waste, lady: get going!*

She raised her head to find herself looking at the cottage. She wrenched her body around through a semi-circle. The plane was coming back. Its searchlight focused far away, but it was bright enough to let her see the gate. No one had spotted her yet. As the plane approached, however, its beam would be bound to pick her out; and then she'd be easy meat for the marksmen behind her.

Thelma leapt up and ran.

She had the sense to dodge left and right. Once she deliberately fell down, hoping they'd think they'd hit her, and rolled several more yards before getting up and sprinting through the gap to Daniel.

The searchlight had them in its centre now. Daniel pushed Thelma down flat and placed an arm around her shoulders, while the brush became alive with the buzz and splat of rifle-fire. The plane roared overhead, almost parting Thelma's hair, and the light died with its passing. Together they raced down the path to the car.

God, let nothing go wrong! Thelma's prayer was answered. The engine fired first time, Daniel found gear and had the parking brake off, all in a flash. As they roared down the narrow road a final bullet found the fender: 'ping!'

'Shit,' Thelma breathed.

'You said it.' Daniel fought to keep the car going straight, his nerves all over the place. In the dim light of the dash she could see great drops of sweat pouring down his face, and his eyes blinked rapidly.

'Take it easy,' she said. 'Deep breaths . . . '

He obeyed; it calmed him. 'Phone,' he said.

Thelma picked up the car-phone. 'What do I dial?' she asked in panic.

'Operator.'

She punched in the three-digit code. No result. She tried again. This time she heard the tone once, twice, three times, then nothing.

'I can't get through!'

'Interference. Mountains, weather, shit, I don't know. Keep trying!'

Thelma turned to gaze out of the rear window. No lights. 'Slow down,' she said. 'We've lost them.'

But he kept up the pace.

'Slow down, you're going to kill us!'

He braked sharply, then dropped a gear. The road twisted around, ran between banks of pines, and entered a mini-canyon. This was a paved section, but the surface was poor, with only two ancient white lines to indicate where hard gave way to soft. Several times Daniel had to navigate around rocks that lay in their path. Thelma started to feel sick. She remembered this road from before, and knew that many miles separated them from the nearest stretch of proper highway.

They passed through a Sequoia National Forest gate and the road widened. Now the landscape was opening out. There was enough light in the sky to let Thelma see Chieftain Dome rearing up to the left, perhaps ten miles away, perhaps more. A dark sea separated them from the mountain range on that side; to the right, densely wooded slopes layered themselves up to a distant snowline, steely white beneath the moon.

The road descended a steep stretch to a ninety-degree right turn over a creek. As the car swung around, Thelma looked back. Headlights were catching up fast.

'We're being followed.'

'Got it. Must have tracked us from Sacré Coeur. Or that damn fence alarm . . .'

Daniel shifted into second and roared away. The car lurched from side to side, the screech of tyres seemed never out of Thelma's ears. Ahead, the landscape danced up and down, right and left, in a sickening résumé of every car-chase movie she'd ever seen. One particularly violent manoeuvre sent her head crashing against the pillar, and her teeth rattled.

'Where are the guns?' she managed to get out.

Daniel shot a glance in his mirror, looked front again and jammed on his brakes. The car negotiated another ninety-degree turn, then another. Only when he was on a short stretch of straight did he manage to get out, 'Rifle in the trunk. Thirty-eight your glove . . . '

She thrust herself against the seat-belt tensioner and opened her glove-compartment. She took out the .38, putting it on the shelf between them.

She took another glimpse out the back. Hard to judge whether the lights of the chase-car had gained or not. The road twisted so much that their pursuers might be a mile away as the crow flew, but three miles by road.

Daniel sent the car skidding dangerously near the edge. For a mind-numbing moment the Carina shuddered; then, with a shower of gravel, it was back on course.

'Stop!' Thelma commanded. 'Get the rifle!'

'Too risky.'

'Too risky not to.' Thelma peered through the windshield at a view that was doing its best imitation of a cocktail-shaker. 'See that sign: campsite, something?'

Daniel nodded. 'I'll stop; be quick.'

Another hundred yards took them to the campsite intersection. Daniel squealed to a stop, half on the road and half off. Thelma was out and running back before the car finished rolling. She threw open the trunk and saw the rifle straight away. She was about to grab it when a sound distracted her, and she paused.

On the other side of the road, beyond a high earth ridge, lay the valley separating them from *Pinos Altos*. Lights were speeding across the void towards her. One red. One green. One flashing red light between them . . .

'Daniel!' she screamed. 'Out!'

He opened his door. 'For Christ's sake, hurry!'

'I can't fire this thing!'

She was wrestling with the bolt of his rifle.

'What the *fuck* are you – ?'

'The plane! Shoot it out of the sky!'

He looked at where she was pointing. Behind them they simultaneously heard the sound of an automobile engine. Dan jumped out of the driver's seat and ran to take the rifle from her. He operated the bolt rapidly a couple of times, then dived into the trunk. He came out holding a bandolier which he slung across his shoulder. Next moment he was loading the rifle. He only had time to cram three rounds into the magazine before the plane's pilot switched on his searchlight.

Daniel raised the rifle and fired. The plane came on. By now it was less than two hundred yards away, at a height that would bring it almost level with the road. Daniel fired again. This time the searchlight shattered, and Thelma wanted to cheer. She looked up the hill in the same instant as car lights appeared round the corner.

The plane was almost directly above them now. Daniel aimed his rifle and pulled the trigger. The sound of the shot was lost in engine-roar. Thelma had a confused impression of white, tapered wings; landing-gear; a small, single-engined airplane. Then it was climbing rapidly to avoid the trees that on a summer's day would shade the campsite from the sun.

They'd had their chance, and failed. The plane lived to fight another day, although lacking its searchlight perhaps the pilot would have to land . . . ? No. Thelma knew who was at the controls, and Richo wasn't about to give up so easily. Besides, whoever was trailing them in the car came armed and ready to fight.

She swung around. There was the chase-car, descending the hill fast, its lights less than a quarter of a mile away. Even as she looked a shot rang out; something smashed through the Carina's rear windshield, which cracked into white frost.

'Run!' Daniel hollered. Thelma ran.

He was already heading off into the campsite, but she raced to the Carina's nearside and wrenched open the door. She stuffed Daniel's .38 into her waistband. She was about to slam the door and run for it when she saw the keys dangling from the ignition, and snatched them out. Then she was haring into the trees, with the sound of another car braking almost on her heels.

She sped off in the direction she'd seen Daniel take. 'Daniel,' she called hoarsely. 'Where are you?'

No reply. She ran on. Suddenly she was aware of a presence behind her and she swung around in mid-run, almost falling over. What prevented it was a muscular pair of hands that seized her around the waist and clamped her mouth shut.

'Dissolve,' Daniel whispered in her ear.

He led her off to the side, away from the main track she'd been following, only now he was moving slowly, concerned more about noise than pace. Here the floor of the forest was sandy, so their progress was silent. They passed between empty glades, each with its own campfire hearth. Pine needles lay thick in places; elsewhere, tall sequoias drooped their feathery foliage almost to the ground. Then they were passing beyond the semi-organized campsite into thicker forest: a meld of Jeffrey pines, white fir, mountain mahogany and dense brush.

After they'd trekked about half a mile Daniel called a halt. They scrambled up a slope to take cover behind a tree and looked back along the path. For the first time in a while, Thelma became aware of the plane. It continued to describe large circles about five hundred feet overhead. In the intervals between the plane's comings and goings she could hear the sound of voices on the wind, but not so as to get a fix.

'How many people?' she breathed.

'Two, I think.' Daniel looked skywards. 'And Richo. Imagine yourself in his shoes. You're our star witness, and if he can kill you, who's going to send him to jail? He'll do *anything* to get you.'

'Even crash into me?'

'Even that. He's probably got drugs coming out of his ears.'

'So who are the other guys out there?'

'My guess is, Sacré Coeur alumni, also with plenty to lose from a positive ID by Dr Thelma Vestrey.'

'There's some pretty highly motivated people out there tonight, then. What are we going to do?'

Daniel thought. 'Thanks to you, we have our own armoury. I doubt there's anywhere for Richo to land his plane near here.'

'Rocks, ravines, rivers – that's it.'

'So as long as he doesn't decide simply to, er, drop in on us, we can discount him, because he's got no light. The *real* enemy's out there, on foot, with hardware.'

'They'll track us. Sand, remember?'

'We draw 'em deeper in, away from the road, towards the high ground where the plane can't fly without risk of smashing into a cliff.'

'Then what?'

'We take 'em, one by one.'

Leading her by the hand, Daniel slithered off their perch and they resumed their trek. Thelma could see a high ridge ahead, jet black against silver-grey clouds floating in a moonlit sky. It must have been about two miles away, she judged, but already the land was rising. The path petered out. Now their steps took them between boulders and over thick scrub that scratched her legs. It also made a noise.

Simultaneously they heard the crack of a rifle and flung themselves flat. Impossible to judge where the bullet went, but the detonation had come from behind and to their right.

'How close are they?' Thelma whispered to the dirt.

'Five hundred yards. He's got a night-sight, betcha. *Move!*'

They staggered up and ran. Before they'd gone very far they found themselves in a wilderness of huge boulders. But then, without warning, they emerged from this cover to find themselves on the lip of a vast natural saucer. The high, protective ridge now looked a good deal further away than they'd thought. Between them and it stretched a meadow, with neither tree nor rock to mar its concave surface.

'No good,' Daniel muttered. 'They'd pick us off before we got ten yards.' He looked over his shoulder. 'Back to the car. No, wait . . .'

The plane had circled far out over the meadow and was coming towards them. Straight ahead of it was the wall of trees that separated Daniel and Thelma from the road. If Richo intended to buzz them he'd have to climb fast immediately afterwards.

'Wait here,' Daniel commanded.

He slipped away from the shelter of their boulder and ran down into the meadow.

As the first shots zipped past her, Thelma threw herself flat. Daniel did likewise . . . or had he been hit? Cautiously she raised her head. He was lying on his back, the rifle to his shoulder. Unless the plane altered course, it would pass right over him.

The pilot had seen Daniel. The nose of the plane went down, its engine note changed to a whine and, with a sick feeling at the

259

pit of her stomach Thelma realized that Richo planned to dive straight at him.

She stood up and ran down the slope.

She never knew she had so much courage. She just kept running, with bullets singing past her head, her waist, her legs, and she knew it wasn't her night to die: they could have stood her up against the wall in a firing-range at ten yards and still not put a round within a hand's breadth of Thelma Vestrey . . . or so she kept telling herself as she ran, waving her arms above her head, keeping well to Daniel's left.

The moon shone down, flooding the landscape with silver. Richo must have seen her. His right wing-tip dipped dangerously fast, and he pulled up. Then he was heading straight for Thelma, with nothing but meadow grass to provide cover, and a couple of mad marksmen behind her.

Daniel waited until he could see the wheel-fairings above his head before he started firing. He got off three rounds, each just ahead of where he judged the propeller to be. The aircraft couldn't have been flying more than a hundred feet above the ground. The noise of its overtaxed engine obliterated all else, but Daniel knew at least one of those bullets must have hit.

The plane yawed left. Its engine coughed, then powered up to full thrust. The Cessna was climbing now, but to Thelma its flight-path seemed oddly askew. The plane pointed left, but it kept flying ever more to the right; and although its nose had pitched up it didn't seem able to climb.

Thelma had other things to worry about. The grass around her was fluttering to the rhythm of bullets fired from the cover of the boulders. She rolled left and right, still telling herself they couldn't hit her. Somebody pulled a razor-blade sharply down her skull, nicking her ear: nothing to worry about, nothing at all.

Then Daniel answered the enemy, peppering the boulder-line with low-level shots, until at last his was the only rifle firing. He rose to a crouch, searching the meadow for Thelma, saw her, raced towards where she lay. A single bullet missed him by a mile. Daniel threw himself flat beside Thelma and loosed off five rounds. In the silence that followed he reloaded swiftly, but their opponents had had enough for the moment.

260

'Are you okay?' he panted.

'I'm fine.'

'Back to where we came from, then.'

Together they got up and ran. The homeward leg was harder: the path lay uphill and they were running away from the moonlight, into darkness. They heard two more shots. Seconds later they were lying in the shelter of the rock whence they'd started.

'You're just *crazy*,' Dan said. 'Running down the hill like that . . . what happened to your head?'

Gingerly she put a hand to the side of her skull. It came away wet, and stained.

'Jesus . . . ' Daniel took out his handkerchief and dabbed at the wound. 'He damn near took off your ear.'

'Ouch! Leave it . . . '

'But sweetheart . . . '

'What happened to the plane?'

'I guess I severed some vital cable. Richo can't steer. I was aiming at the wings, 'cause that's where aircraft keep the gas, but he was moving too fast.'

'What do we do now?'

'Richo's out of it. The other guys are weak, frightened, but I've only got six rounds left. We have to make it back to the car, else they'll just hunt us deeper into the wild.'

'And once we're at the car?'

'We run for it.'

Thelma could see any number of flaws in that, but however she looked at their situation it stank, so . . . 'Which way?' she asked.

Daniel set off. Thelma wondered if he felt as confident as he looked. She would have put a shade more right into their course, couldn't say why and so kept quiet. Soon they were back in the trees, only this time there was no path. After about twenty minutes they were clearly going downhill when they ought to have been rising. Daniel paused, sniffing the wind. He held up his left hand and pointed.

Somewhere close they could hear the sound of running water. Daniel scrambled up a steep bank. As Thelma came level with him she saw they were at the junction of two creeks, where a waterfall cascaded down a low cliff. They *must* be off course. She moved away from Daniel, far enough to dip her hankie in the crystal-clear stream. Its iciness numbed her wounded ear. She scooped up several mouthfuls and drank with gratitude. She was just about to take another scoop when suddenly Daniel shoved her sideways into the water.

Thelma's head broke the surface. She was gurgling, frozen, half-drowned, nearly blind; but she was conscious enough to see the huge rock fall and land to split the flow where she'd been crouching a second before, to hear the smack and crack of hostile rifle fire, to be aware of Daniel desperately unslinging his own rifle. He knelt and got off a single shot, aiming high above Thelma's head, where the waterfall split the cliff, before launching himself to one side, behind a rock.

Thelma struggled up and floundered towards him. The creeks flowed fast here, it was uphill work, but there were plenty of boulders to give her cover. Daniel leapt out from his hiding-place and hustled her back into the trees.

'That was close,' she breathed. 'Thanks.'

'They're better than I thought. Must have been tracking us, but I never saw them.'

'We got off course. Let's keep going left.'

Now it was Thelma's turn to lead. She struck off through dense stands of pine and fir, letting her instincts guide them. Their feet made a lot of noise in the brush. They moved fast, but things got in their way, and she feared to sprain her ankle. Her relief when they finally struck a path was heartfelt.

They turned right and began to jog. The trees were thinning now. Thelma caught sight of the first dead campfire and knew they were less than a quarter of a mile from the road. She realized that Daniel's analysis of their pursuers was correct: they were willing to wound but afraid to strike. Anybody with any guts would have moved in to finish the job, but they were spineless, and that gave her hope.

She could actually see the Carina, parked by the side of the road some two hundred yards away to her left, when Daniel seized her sleeve and pulled her into the shelter of a sequoia.

'Split,' he breathed. 'You make it to the car – circle around the back, it's safer. Get it facing towards the forest, reverse it across the road onto that ridge, and switch on the headlights. I want the campsite lit up like high noon, got it?'

'Yes. Where will you be?'

'Outflanking them. They'll come down this path, thinking the lights mean we're taking off. I'll be waiting for them. Because the ridge is above the road-level, they'll be aiming high but I'll be lying low. *'Go!'*

She shot off like a hare, heading out in a wide, flat circle that hugged the treeline around the car-park. There was an open stretch of about fifty yards between the last of the pines and the highway. She put the trees to her right and lay face down, assessing the task ahead. The Carina stood sideways on. A quick dash and she'd be in the front seat. *Keep your head down! Drive fast, but remember that on the far side of the ridge is an abyss: do not reverse into it; the ridge is not wide . . .*

She upped on one knee and sprinted for the car. She landed against the passenger door and knelt, listening. The night was still. No! Far away she could just hear that distant, angry hum. Richo was still flying! But Daniel had shot out the cables, hadn't he said so?

Don't worry about that, don't fret, *just do what you have to!*

Keeping her head low, Thelma worked her way around the back of the car and jumped into the driver's seat. She saw her purse lying on the floor where she'd dropped it. Without any conscious command from her brain she picked it up and yanked out Janice's pack of Marlboro Lites. She flicked open the Junction Restaurant's book of matches and next second was drawing down life-enhancing nicotine. *You must be mad to smoke at a time like this!*

Keys . . . no sweat. Into the ignition, gear in neutral, parking brake off, ready . . . *now!*

The engine fired first time. Thelma heard voices shouting, dangerously near. She engaged gear and turned to rest one hand over the passenger seat so that she could see out the rear window, the cigarette still dangling from her lips. The back windscreen had been starred by a bullet, *damn*, how could she have forgotten that? If she reversed she'd risk driving straight over the ridge, with nothing to stop a free-fall all the way to the valley floor.

Thelma hauled on the brake. The car stalled. She opened the door and a bullet hit it. She eased her way out and chucked her cigarette on the ground. Using the open door as cover, she crawled around to the back of the Carina. One good blow with her shoe put paid to the remains of the glass. Now all she had to do was get back in and drive. *Daniel, where are you; why don't you shoot?*

As if in answer to her prayer, Daniel fired the first of his remaining rounds. Thelma seized her chance. She whipped back up the side of the Carina and in through the open door. She slammed it shut and restarted the engine, trying to keep down, dreading every second to see the front windscreen dissolve into deadly shards of glass. Then the car was moving, and she had no choice but to raise her head.

Another bullet clipped the wing mirror. She wrenched the wheel left and right, giving the Carina an S-shaped track through the sandy car-park. The wheels changed note, so she knew she was on paved road. Then – disaster! – the trunk-lid started to ride up. A glance over her shoulder revealed only metal through the hole where the rear windshield once had been. *How to judge the distance?*

Thelma found neutral and yanked on the parking-brake. Another bullet smashed into the radiator-grille. She must get out. The enemy would be advancing on the car, firing as they came. Chances were Daniel would shoot them down before they got far, *if* all went well . . . but suppose a stray bullet found the Carina's gas-tank and barbecued her? *Get out! Run!*

She opened the door and made a dive for the deck, wriggling out painfully as her damaged ear hit the edge of the door. She lay on the ground, breathing heavily, until a bullet whined inches above her head. That galvanized her. She jerked into a crawl, elbows-knees-elbows, until she was around the back of the car. But . . . *Remember the gas-tank! Get away from this bomb! Move!*

She slithered away and was about to stand up when she realized that the buzzing noise of the plane's engine had become markedly louder in the past few seconds.

'Hey, you! Get up. Hands on your head.'

A man was standing ten yards away on the other side of the

car, the passenger side. He had his legs apart, a rock-solid stance, and his rifle was levelled across the Carina at her.

'We have your friend,' he mocked. 'He's here.'

As he spoke, Daniel moved into the Carina's headlights. His hands were behind his back, obviously manacled. A few steps behind him came another man, one rifle in the crook of his arm, Daniel's slung over his shoulder. Thelma took a look at this second man in the car's headlights and recognized the quiet 'deputy sheriff' who'd escorted her to Hornville.

She stood up.

A lot of things went through her brain in about one-tenth of a second.

If she got this wrong, she was going to die.

Daniel was also going to die.

They were going to die anyway, but for some reason their captors weren't ready to dispatch them yet, so she had time. Not much, but some.

Dan's .38 was in the waistband of her jeans, right-hand side. It had got wet in the creek and maybe wouldn't fire.

Assuming the guy with a bead on her didn't shoot the second she moved, she'd still have only one shot.

If she aimed at the man holding Daniel she might hit her lover by mistake.

If she aimed at the other man, Daniel would undoubtedly be shot by the survivor.

The Carina formed a partial screen between her and the man covering her. Could he see her right hand . . . ?

The noise of the plane had become overwhelming.

She eased her right hand away from the side of her body. The man covering her didn't say anything. She tried to open the gas-tank filler-cap, locked . . .

The plane was coming up from the valley floor. Soon it was going to breast the lip of the roadside ridge and be on top of her.

The plane was going to hit her.

Richo meant to slice her up with his propeller.

And that's what went through her mind in one-tenth of a second, before she zipped her hand to her waistband, drew the .38 and blasted a shot into the side of the Carina's gas-tank.

There was a 'clang!' as the slug hit . . . and nothing. No explosion, no fire. Nothing except the splash and drip of gasoline.

The man with the rifle laughed: she could see his mouth move, though the plane's engine drowned out the sound. He brought his weapon to shoulder height, aiming at her.

Thelma dropped the gun. Her hand dangled lifelessly, came to rest with the fingers in the tiny pocket-within-a-pocket beloved of jeans manufacturers.

Her book of matches . . . she must have stuffed them there instinctively after lighting up the last cigarette of her life.

What happened next was born of pure, crazy instinct. Thelma snatched out the book, flicked it open, and gave herself up to the ancient routine. Fold a match over, scratch, throw . . .

The gas-tank went up like plastic explosive, just at the moment Thelma flung herself flat and Richo flew over the airspace where she'd been standing.

Once she hit the ground she crawled forward level with the blazing remains of the car and sussed out the ground. She could see the .38; she grabbed it. Both pursuers had staggered back, stunned. She shot the lone rifleman, aiming for the centre of his torso; he went down with a whistling scream. Daniel seized his opportunity. He kicked out sideways at his captor, catching him on the left knee. Thelma swivelled. One shot missed. The second caught the man in the shoulder, spinning him around. He fell face down and stayed there.

At last Thelma was free to scan the sky. The plane's tail was on fire. It descended with a slow majesty that, amidst all this mayhem, she found astonishing. The landing-gear clipped a pine, slewing the aircraft around and pitching its nose down at a steep angle. Another few feet of descent brought it into a stand of firs, which cushioned it, letting the Cessna down gently until it was almost on the ground.

Thelma crawled over to help Daniel. His wrists had merely been knotted together; it was easy to undo them. The second she freed Daniel's hands, he was running. At first all she could do was stand there in amazement. Then she saw him over by the burning wreckage of the plane and she screamed, 'No!'

She ran after him like a crazed woman, screaming, *'No, I'm not losing you to him, I'm not . . .'*

Daniel reached up through the tangle of branches. He opened the door on the pilot's side. A dark shape fell into his arms, causing him to stagger beneath its weight. Flames lapped at the wings, where the Avgas was. Thelma put her arms around Daniel's waist and wrenched. *'Drop him!'* she spat.

But Daniel hauled the unconscious boy out, managing to get his hands under Richo's armpits, until he could drag him backwards like a swimmer rescuing a drowning man from the sea. He kept on pulling, while Thelma pummelled him, and wept, and screamed obscenities, and then the plane roared up to heaven with a 'whoosh!' of flame and a pall of evil smoke that obscured the moon.

Thelma looked down at the charred thing by her feet. Those beautiful features, blistered and black . . . but Richo wasn't dead. He ought to be dead.

'Thelma . . . ' Daniel was sitting with his back against a tree, his voice tired and shaky. 'Check out their car. See if those creeps had a mobile phone.'

She took a long, last look at Richo, his broken body twitching in pain, and trudged away to the car that had pursued them. Sure enough, there was a phone. She dialled the operator, getting through on the second attempt: reception here, in the open campsite, was better than on the mountain road. She asked for the sheriff's office, explained what had happened. Then she sat in the car and stared through the windshield at Daniel arranging Richo's limbs in an effort to make him comfortable, and she waited for the emergency services to troop up and rescue them all. The survivors. Thelma. Daniel. And – great, good Goddamn – Richo Delacroix.

*   *   *

They put Richo in a room by himself, down the end of the corridor where St Joe's kept patients who were under police guard. Two officers were assigned to watch him. They waited outside with Thelma while the resident on emergency standby ran a damage-assessment. He came out looking grave.

Thelma knew him, a kindly-looking man who resembled everybody's favourite uncle and played the meanest game of tennis. 'Jonas,' she said, taking him aside, 'what's the prognosis?'

'Pretty foul. He's got second degree burns on fifty per cent of his body, internal damage to kidneys and pancreas, fractured ribs, broken arm, smashed ankles, massive trauma intensified by that long, cold wait after the crash, and slow internal bleeding. There's a sliver of metal dangerously near his heart. If he lives, he'll be in a wheelchair for the rest of his life. Hey, Thelma, I heard the story. What had he got against you – were you charging too much, or what?'

Thelma dredged up a wan smile from somewhere. 'We must have a game, Jonas. Soon.'

'Yeah, well, see you down at the club.' He looked at his watch. 'The father's waiting in my office, I'd better put him in the picture.'

Richo underwent two operations during the morning and late afternoon. They removed the metal from his chest, stemmed the life-threatening haemorrhaging, treated the burns and the fractures.

Thelma phoned Rachel at work to say she was okay, and contacted Kirsty's school to leave the same message. She spent most of the day at home, resting. She kept an eye on the TV. Richo's nocturnal escapade was the talk of the airwaves. He led each news item, and there was even a special programme devoted exclusively to a reconstruction of the chase. By lunchtime, no inhabitant of the state could fail to be aware of Richo's existence unless deaf or dead.

At four o'clock the police came to Thelma's house and she made another long statement to complement the one she'd given the previous night. They told her that Shimon's body had been recovered from its hiding-place; Lomar was still missing.

Richo emerged from his second bout of surgery shortly afterwards. They hooked him up to a life-support machine and left him with his father and two guards. At every point, Thelma had a friend on the ward – a nurse, a doctor, a paramedic – and from her home she was able to monitor Richo's progress.

She went out shortly before six, not ready to be reunited with Rachel or Kirsty just yet, and drove around aimlessly for a while. No matter where she went, however, the Bronco seemed to gravitate towards St Joseph's. In the end she gave up and drove to the hospital. She went to her room and lay down on the couch, having first asked a nurse to call her if Richo regained consciousness.

At ten minutes to midnight, Richo came round. He was able to recognize Naim. He ingested a small amount of water.

Ten minutes after midnight, Naim's heart began to palpitate. He felt very ill. On the advice of a doctor he left the hospital, knowing there was no more he could do for his son, and had himself driven home.

Thelma heard about that five minutes later. By twelve thirty she was at Richo's bedside.

The boy drifted in and out of painful sleep. Sometimes he had his eyes open and seemed to recognize her; at others he apparently slept, twisting as if prodded by invisible hot spears. After a while, Thelma got up from her chair and went to speak with the two police officers who dozed at the foot of the bed.

'Guys,' she said, 'take a break. If anything happens, I'll call you.'

The men exchanged glances. 'We really can't do that, Doctor. Thank you kindly, though.'

'Well, up to you. I'm not sleepy. I want to talk with this boy at some point. In private.'

'Oh, yeah, we heard: he was your patient, right?'

There was a big age difference between the men, Thelma noted. The older one, perhaps in his mid-fifties, was wearing a wedding-ring. She addressed herself to him.

'I wish the father hadn't gone home.' Thelma spoke in a low voice: almost talking to herself.

'Mm.'

'I think this kid's going to die. Pre-dawn, probably.'

The older policeman shifted uncomfortably in his chair. There was a lengthy silence. Then he said, 'Maybe one of us should go check with HQ, see if they can contact the father.'

'I wish one of you would. Officer . . . ?'

'Jackson. Pete.'

'Pete, do you have kids of your own?'

'Two, m'am. One boy, one girl.'

'Grown up?'

'Yuh.' Another silence. 'Tell you what, I'll go make that call now.'

'Thank you.'

Jackson rose and left the room. Thelma smiled at the officer who remained. 'I'm sorry,' she murmured, 'but I didn't catch your name?'

'Emilio Ferandi.'

'Seen much of this kind of thing, Emilio?'

The man shook his head.

'Tragic.'

'You were fond of him?'

He obviously hadn't heard about the rape. Thelma, desperate for time alone with Richo, sensing she was close to getting it, breathed in and lied. 'I was, yes.'

Emilio studied his hands, folded in his lap. 'I guess,' he said at last, 'you kind of want to, you know . . . say goodbye. Or something.'

Thelma quickly raised a hand to both eyes and muttered something that might have been 'Yes.'

Emilio studied his hands a moment longer. Then he got up and quietly left the room.

Thelma approached the bed.

'Richo,' she said. 'Can you hear me?'

For a long while Richo's eyes remained closed and he said nothing. Then he stirred slightly. His eyes fluttered open. Thelma looked into them and saw the light of intelligence, albeit burning dimly.

'Why did you kill all those people?'

He heard the question, no doubt about it. He lay staring up at the ceiling. Just as Thelma had given up hope of him answering he said, 'She . . . told me to.'

His voice was a dry croak, but the words came out clearly enough.

'She . . . who?'

'Mother.'

'She . . . *told* you to kill?'

His lips twisted into a contorted smile. 'See . . . what she's got . . . for the twins.'

His eyes closed, the smile faded. Thelma sat on the urge to shriek at him and tried again.

'Richo . . . why did Aurelia want you to murder?'

He said nothing. Thelma cast a glance at the glass panel set in the door. No one outside. She bent close to his face. 'Why?' she repeated.

'Fing . . . thumb.'

'What?'

'Said I was all fingers . . . and . . . '

'What are you saying?'

'I wasn't. Then. Now I am. That's what she wanted . . . '

He floated away, but his eyes didn't quite close: she could just see the whites roll up. Thelma looked again at the pane of glass. The corridor remained empty.

Suddenly Richo's eyes opened wide. 'They thought . . . Gascoign . . . killer,' he whispered. He rolled his head until he was staring at Thelma. 'Ask . . . Johnny.'

'Johnny who? Richo – *who is Johnny*?'

But he was unconscious again. Thelma gazed down at him in a mixture of frustration and rage. He'd raped her, tormented her, he had brought her to the edge of insanity, and now this! *What did he mean?*

She wanted to shake him, but did not dare. He was breathing irregularly now, in a shallow, troubled sleep. Damn, damn, damn.

Thelma stood up. She went to the door and looked both ways along the corridor. Emilio Ferandi was wandering up and down at a distant intersection, evidently playing some kind of complicated game on the linoleum squares. Thelma walked out into the corridor. As she came up to Emilio, Pete Jackson joined them.

'I spoke to Mr Delacroix's housekeeper,' he informed her. 'The father didn't get home yet, but they'll tell him the minute he does.'

'Thank you.'

'Is he okay?' Pete asked.

'He's sleeping.'

'Guess we'd better get back, then. Emilio?'

'Sure.'

The three of them began to walk slowly towards Richo's room. Coming down the corridor towards them was a nurse, fully gowned and masked, her rubber boots making a rhythmic, squeaky sound. Thelma caught a glimpse of her face, or of as much of it as was visible behind the mask. The nurse pushed through into Richo's room. A moment later she came out, turned away from Thelma and the two policemen, and began to run in the opposite direction.

Something about the nurse seemed familiar. Thelma frowned, scrabbling after a memory that constantly eluded her. Boots, gown, mask, cap . . . what could have been familiar about any of that? Or rather, why should anything *so* familiar have attracted her attention?

Perhaps it had been the way the nurse walked; was that it?

The nurse's eyes.

Thelma gazed at the wall. What had her eyes been like? Blue, a remarkable shade of blue, with gold . . .

She tore along the corridor, leaving Pete and Emilio standing. A bell began to ring: harsh, urgent. Over the loudspeakers a voice kept repeating, 'Dr Jonas Campford to Emergency Twelve, Dr Jonas Campford to Emergency Twelve . . . '

Richo's eyes were open, two dull black buttons. They stared straight into Thelma's brain.

She noticed things, then. How the tubes had been wrenched from his arm, the sheets thrown back; how one leg dangled over the side of the bed, as if somebody had tried to drag him up, to hold him, perhaps. To cuddle her baby. To say goodbye, one last time . . .

Two interns forced their way past, carrying resuscitation equipment. Within seconds the room was full of doctors, paramedics. Thelma went out to the corridor and rested her back against the wall. She felt sick.

Aurelia Delacroix had risen from the grave. And it wasn't over yet.

272

PART THREE

NEXT MORNING Thelma slept late. When she awoke her bedside clock told her that it was eight nineteen a.m. on June 15. The date seemed significant; returning consciousness reminded her that this was when Naim and his family were supposed to be flying to the Philippines, never to return. Big deal. Thelma turned on her side.

She lay there for a while, protected from the sunlight by drawn drapes and a cloud of deep depression, listening to homely kitchen sounds wafting up from below and trying to work out what she felt.

She'd been imprisoned and raped, Janice Sepeda had been murdered, thus joining a no longer very exclusive club around here; there'd been a cross-country chase during which she'd killed two men. Aurelia Delacroix, whose mutilated remains Thelma once inspected at close range, had come back from the dead. Aurelia must have been a figment of her imagination – Thelma had been in a state yesterday, for heaven's sake – and not worth worrying about. (In the early hours of the morning she'd told the senior hospital administrator about the nurse she and the cops had seen, but then she'd gone home without discovering the woman's identity. They'd look into it, the administrator had assured her.)

Thelma knew she ought to feel something about all of this, and maybe one day she would, but right now she just needed help in getting through this day and the next. She sat up, reached for the phone and dialled Daniel.

He picked up, bright as a button – really ugly behaviour for eight twenty-five in the morning. 'What time did you get back?' he demanded. 'I tried your number until eleven, then I fell asleep.'

'I got back incredibly late, or unbelievably early, depending how you look at it.' Thelma hesitated, decided she didn't want to bother Daniel with Aurelia Delacroix. She could almost script his tactful suggestion that she'd been under too much strain and perhaps should see a therapist . . . 'I had things to clear up at St Joe's.'

'Lunch,' Daniel commanded. 'Have I got news for *you*!'

His bonhomie was starting to do her good, and although she couldn't face the thought of food she hungered for Dan's presence. 'Clinton resigned?' she teased him.

'Don't mess with sax players, lady, they can turn nasty. No, the master of *Pinos Altos*. Pierrot, twelve o'clock, okay?'

'Okay. Incidentally, and I hate to raise so mundane a subject, I do love you very, very much.'

'Me too, darling.'

Daniel made a kissing noise down the phone – Thelma thought that's what it was, it could have been a belch – and hung up. She showered, dressed, embraced Mom and Kirsty, fended off their questions, drank a cup of coffee so hot it burned her mouth, raced Rufus around the block twice, and shot out the Bronco.

She'd go to the hospital, she decided; work was the answer to most things.

Makiko beamed at her, then tut-tutted and cooed over her bandaged ear. The student wanted to hear about Thelma's adventures. No time, less inclination: Thelma saw the stack of mail awaiting her (not something she'd been in the mood to face the day before) and picked up a paper-knife.

But there was one item that Makiko could not keep to herself any longer.

'There was a call from Jacqueline Delacroix, about an hour ago. Sounding panicky.'

'Tell.'

'Apparently, the girls ran away from home. They got picked up by the police and while they were in custody Jacqui asked about you, said she was worried.'

Thelma had been slitting open letters, but now she paused. 'Worried?'

'They saw you being picked up by the sheriff that night you were kidnapped.'

Thelma gazed at Makiko in astonishment.

'It was Jacqui's call that made the police put out an alert for you. Without it, Daniel might never have gone after you.' (The thought entered Thelma's mind as Makiko articulated it aloud.) 'She wants to talk with you, urgently. Matter of life and death.'

But Thelma was already dialling *Pinos Altos*. The line sounded weird. She checked it with the operator and discovered there was a fault. Surprising . . .

'What time did you say Jacqui called?' she asked Makiko.

'About an hour ago.'

Thelma replaced the receiver with a frown. She must speak to the girls, *must*. The solution would come to her, but meantime there was this stack of mail . . .

Most of the letters could wait. Five could not: replies from the eminent psychiatrists she'd written to requesting information about Aurelia. Four of the five were the anticipated terse one-liners: without your patient's signature (form enclosed), forget it.

The fifth was long, abstruse and written by a man whose first language was evidently English, but whose two lines of qualifications suggested a leaning towards foreign climes. There was a doctorate from Heidelberg and another from Paris; there was an MD, there were masters in Psychiatry and also in Clinical Psychology – an interesting and unusual combination – plus a Certificate in Behavioral Medicine, whatever that might be and Thelma didn't know, granted by the University of South Florida in Tampa. The letter's postmark was Austrian, the address in Vienna.

There was a paragraph of blah about how he really shouldn't be doing this; Thelma skipped half a dozen lines and resumed . . .

Madame Delacroix was referred to me shortly after she'd adopted a daughter called Annette. She was suffering from depression serious enough to make her husband and their medical practitioner question whether she might seek to end her own life. She was my patient for twenty-three months, after which she discharged herself.

I set us two tasks. First, to fire-fight the depression, give her reasons to go on living and put her on the road to enriching her life. Secondly, to proceed as far as possible with conventional Freudian

*analysis with a view to effecting a long-term improvement in her
mental condition and life-attitudes.*

*After about eight months of treatment, during which I saw her
once a week, she began to display marked hostility towards me. On
three occasions it became necessary to terminate the sessions early,
so disruptive did she become. I warned her that I couldn't go on if
she behaved in that manner. For a while after that she was placid;
the analysis made progress. Then the symptoms of ill-will returned.
I am not talking here about normal transference. She wanted to
harm me. She perceived me as a threat that had to be eradicated.*

*Therapy thereafter assumed a roller-coaster quality. I quickly
learned that if I wanted a quiet life I must keep off the subject of
her children: in particular, the two girls. For a while I seriously
toyed with the idea that my professional responsibilities might
require me to involve outside agencies to protect the children's welfare. Before I could reach a conclusion, however, the matter was
taken out of my hands.*

*Mme Delacroix came to my consulting-rooms armed with a knife
and tried to kill me. I managed to escape and raise the alarm. With
the help of my nurse-receptionist I was able to overcome the patient
and administer a sedative. I informed her that I did not intend to
involve the police, but our relationship must cease forthwith. I
summoned M. Delacroix. He listened attentively to my account of
what had happened, said little, and took his wife away. I never
saw either of them again.*

*My dear Dr Vestrey, take care. I believe this woman is psychotic
and dangerous, but she is adept at concealment. Above all, be prepared for trouble if you broach the subject of her daughters. I got
too close to discovering what they meant to her, what they stood for.
She intends certain things to happen to them, in a way I cannot
believe is benign. If you have greater success than I, please be so
good as to inform,*

Your respectful professional colleague,
Ezekiel M. Levin.

Thelma folded up the letter, having read it four times, and stuffed
it back in its envelope. The mists parted to reveal a tantalizing
and tantalizingly brief glimpse of difficult terrain, only to close

again. Who *was* Aurelia Delacroix, really? Who *is* she . . . no, don't be silly, forget that.

According to Dr Levin, she had plans for her daughters. What had Richo said, on his deathbed . . . ? Something about, See what she's got for the twins. At the time it had made no sense. But . . . See what she's *got planned* for the twins . . . ?

Lunchtime. Daniel would know how to contact Annette and Jacqueline: that's what hunky FBI profilers were for. She snatched up her purse and rushed off to find Daniel already sitting at their favoured table overlooking the ocean. She kissed him. She ordered a Perrier and lime. She sat down and said, 'Well?'

'Well, still no sign of Lomar, for one thing – there are warrants out for her arrest, both state and federal – and all of her staff and most of her students have taken off as well. Next, it's a lie that Aurelia was the daughter of well-to-do Parisians.'

'No kidding?'

'We got the dossier in from Paris yesterday and it's that thick.' Daniel held his hands a phone directory's width apart. 'She was born in Algiers and entered France in suspicious circumstances while still a child. There *was* a twin, she *was* called Nada, but she disappeared: no death cert, nothing. Aurelia and Nada both got criminal records early on.'

'Soliciting?'

'Right. Aurelia was put into an orphanage, was going to be deported, but she ran away. Next time they picked her up off the street, same thing happened; then the police lost track of her until she showed up in the company of Naim.

'It turns out Naim had been raised in Manila by a Filipino father, Chinese mother, and an American grandmother left behind at the end of the war. The father was a successful profiteer, dealing with Americans and Taiwanese. Dubious businesses, nothing concrete on file. The mother was strict, but a heavy smoker: she died of lung cancer when he was a teenager. Two brothers, three sisters. They lived in a big house with two Mercedes in the car-port. Fancy lifestyle: parties, dancing at the US embassy, deals with Marcos. Naim was quick to develop a powerful *barkada*, that's the Filipino word for gang, and most of them are still in place under Ramos. Lots of friends at school, networking that's continued to this day, but with tentacles into India and Pakistan.'

Daniel leant across the table and lowered his voice. 'He conforms to a classic pattern. No criminal record, but a long history of consorting with guys in black hats. Now you know that the biggest criminals, the *capi*, are always squeaky-clean, but the one thing they do have is contacts. And Naim's contacts have always been dreadful.'

Thelma subjected him to careful scrutiny. She'd never seen Daniel so unguarded when discussing Naim Delacroix. She could understand why he'd got all personal over Richo, but this was new and she asked him why.

'Because the family's bad right through, and I sense huge kudos for the guy who nails Naim to the floor.'

So, she thought; identifying the Butcher isn't enough. Human beings, so strange: always needing more. Well, give him more.

'Listen,' she said, and told him about her abortive phone call to *Pinos Altos*. 'We have to get in there.'

'Hm. On what grounds, though? That call from Jacqui: could it be construed as a request for official help?'

'She told Makiko it's life or death.'

'Hysterical teenager . . . ?'

'They're leaving *today*! Don't you remember?'

'You mean, their visas ran out?'

'They will, at midnight.'

'Shit. Maybe that's why the phone's out – he had it disconnected. This is starting to come together.'

'Wait a minute, Dan, we're being stupid.'

'Why?'

'Because nobody's going to let Delacroix out of this country until the inquiry's been wrapped up. I mean, Shimon's body was found on his land, for goodness' sake!'

'So he must still be in the US?'

'Yes, but more than that . . . why aren't the police up at *Pinos Altos* with him right now, taking statements or whatever?'

'Maybe they are.'

'And they don't know the phone is out? Oh, come on! Hey, give me a minute.'

Thelma went to the phone. She dialled St Joe's and asked for the morgue. The information she wanted took a bit of digging out, but the wait was worth it.

'You'll never guess,' she said, sliding back into the chair opposite Daniel's. 'The police at the hospital contacted Naim to tell him his son was dying. Naim said he'd come. But – he never showed up! They've got Richo in the deep freeze, because they don't know what else to do with him. *Naim's disappeared.*'

For an agonizing moment Daniel hesitated. Then – 'I'll call the Tulare sheriff's office, you get on the phone, make two reservations for Bakersfield.'

'We could take my car.'

'Flying's quicker. If we're going to do this, let's do it like we mean it.'

They made their phone calls and left the restaurant. A detour to Thelma's house to collect Dan's .38, none the worse for its wetting, and they were on their way to the airport.

'I spoke to Kurt Masterman,' Dan said as they walked across the tarmac to the waiting Dash–7. 'Of course, he didn't know anything about the Delacroixs' visas expiring. He said they hadn't planned on visiting *Pinos Altos* until tomorrow, out of consideration for Naim's loss. They don't reckon he'll be able to help much anyway, because he's got a cast-iron alibi for the time of Waldman's murder: he was in Texas, on business. But Kurt does agree we should check on the girls' welfare.'

'It all seems kind of casual to me.'

Dan shrugged. 'That's a typical local sheriff's office for you.'

Once they arrived in Bakersfield it was no trouble for the town's main air-taxi operator to fly them up to Kern Valley Airport. There they rented a car, in fact the same Isuzu Trooper Dan had hired the night of Thelma's rape.

It was a beautiful evening. The sun went down behind Chieftain Dome, the road was shaded by numerous trees and peaceful, in delicious contrast to the last time they'd visited this neighbourhood. The air was balmy. A light breeze sifted through stands of Jeffrey pines, blowing their feathery branches hither and thither.

They reached the main entrance to *Pinos Altos* at about five o'clock. Half a dozen men from the sheriff's office were bunched this side of the gate, Kurt Masterman in charge. The guardhouse appeared deserted. Nothing stirred, except birds and the occasional bold rabbit. Kurt reached in the window of his Jeep and hooted. No response. But on inspection the main gate turned out to be ajar.

Now that was odd. The sheriff's party perked up to a degree. Everyone got into one of the four vehicles parked outside the gate, and before long they were at the house. Which was empty. Abandoned. A shell.

It took them an hour to fan out and search the various *casitas*, but first impressions turned out to be correct: this was an estate without human occupants.

Another powwow. Things were looking more serious; division of labour seemed called for. Kurt put together a plan for alerting state forces, with priority given to notification of ports of exit, especially airports. Daniel would plug into the Quantico net and start things humming. With the exception of two men left to guard the main house, everybody back to town, pronto.

They were a mile down the road when Thelma said, 'We forgot to check out the cottage where Waldman was killed.'

'Why would anyone be there? Come on, honey, the place was abandoned.'

Another half mile passed beneath the Trooper's wheels. Thelma said, 'I want to check it out.'

'Do you know how long this is going to take?'

'Five minutes.'

'*What!* Are you kidding? By the time I've dialled into Quantico, woken up the duty officer – '

'Five minutes is all it'll take to check out that cottage.'

They wrangled, but Thelma stood firm. Daniel slowed, pulled into the side and waited for the two sheriff's cars travelling behind him to pass before reversing around. Kurt flashed his lights, but Daniel didn't respond and the sheriff's posse roared on down the road into town.

A quarter of an hour later, Daniel parked the Trooper in the semi-clearing where Thelma had left her car the night of Waldman's murder.

Now here was a funny thing. Someone had driven a battered old pick-up into the undergrowth, but not deep enough to prevent its fender from showing. While Daniel made futile efforts to contact the nearest FBI office on his mobile phone, Thelma hiked over to the truck in the hope of finding somebody with useful information. The pick-up, however, was empty. On the back lay half a dozen blue oil drums. Thelma called, 'Is there anybody there?' No reply. She sighed and turned away. As she was setting off back towards the fence, she heard a sound behind her. She stopped. Was that real, or was it her imagination? An animal, perhaps . . .

She turned to survey the pick-up. The sound she'd heard, or thought she'd heard, had resonated in a curious way. If it didn't seem absurd, she might even think it had come from inside one of the oil drums.

Daniel gave up on trying to defeat the mountainous terrain with his mobile phone and came to join her. Thelma explained what had just happened. Daniel hoisted himself on to the back of the truck. Several drums were sealed. The lid of one of them, however, was loose. He removed it.

'Jesus!'

Thelma jumped up beside Daniel and together they stared into the oil drum. It contained a man clad in the uniform of a *Pinos Altos* security guard. He was dead. Someone had shot him in the nape of the neck.

The sound Thelma had heard earlier repeated itself. This time, no doubt: a moan. Jacqui, Annette . . . ? Feverishly she went from drum to drum, and quickly found another one with a loose lid. Thelma pushed it aside to disclose a second guard, not quite dead but dying. She and Daniel tipped the drum on its side. Blood gushed out over the floor of the truck. The early summer sun dipped behind Chieftain Dome; Thelma felt the onset of the big chill.

Daniel knelt beside the man, cradling his head on his thigh. 'Okay, fellah,' he murmured, 'we're going to get you to a doctor. Take it easy, now. What happened?'

The guard's breathing was laboured. He struggled to lift his head. For a moment it looked as though he might speak. Then they heard this terrible rattle in the back of his throat. His head lolled forward. End of story.

Daniel laid him flat on the boards of the pick-up. There was a bunch of keys attached to the dead man's belt. Thelma unclipped them. Together with Daniel she got down from the truck. They went to the gate. It was locked, but one key fitted: soon they were inside the grounds. Neither of them spared a thought for the electronic alarm system.

A light was on inside the cottage.

Thelma and Daniel stopped. They debated their next step, taking up predictable positions. She was all for going in and saying 'Hi!' to whoever they found inside; he counselled caution. A compromise: they would creep up and peer through the window.

What they saw was Marion/Martha Lomar asleep in a chair, an empty bottle of Canadian Club by her side. What they heard was a distant voice, female, crying out.

The door was closed but unlocked. They tiptoed inside, although one look at Lomar showed that she was likely to be out of it for some time. The voice was louder now: 'Help . . . please help us.' Thelma scuttled through into the kitchen and approached the door to the cellar, which was where the sound was coming from. Now she recognized the voice as Annette's.

She glanced back into the main room to see that Daniel had drawn his gun and was covering Lomar. Thelma remembered a detail from her second visit and went through to the utility room, where there was a clothes-line. She threw it to Daniel and waited long enough to see him begin to truss Lomar to her chair before starting down the stairs.

The *zinc* was just as she remembered it, with this exception: Naim sat strapped into a chair, facing the wall, while Jacqui and Annette lay trembling at his feet. They'd been shackled to a pipe by a length of chain.

Naim, hearing steps, tried to twist his head around. Thelma ran to him. He looked at her through anguished eyes and begged to be released. But he'd been handcuffed to the chair, which was secured to the floor by steel bolts and brackets.

'Wait,' she said, 'I'll get help.'

Naim protested. Annette shrieked, *'Please!'* but Thelma needed Daniel.

She got back upstairs to find that the trussing process had woken Lomar, who was struggling to free herself, swearing the while.

'The cellar,' Thelma said. 'Come.'

They went downstairs. 'Do you have keys for the handcuffs?' Thelma asked.

'No. We'll take care of these people in a moment.' Dan pulled a chair up close to Naim's. He sat there with his gun in his lap, and he said, 'I want to hear what's been going on. The whole story, from the beginning.'

'For God's sake, they're in distress!'

'I see that.'

Daniel settled himself a shade more comfortably. There was a gleam in his eye. Looking at him, Thelma realized that here was a person she'd never met: no longer merely an ambitious man, but someone who intended to get to the top no matter what. The perception jolted her. Then she understood that, ambitious or not, he had a point, and she redirected her stare from Daniel to Naim. 'Yes,' she said. 'Tell.'

Haltingly Naim began to speak. After a while his voice cleared, the words came out more quickly.

'From the start, we kids had everything. I left college and drifted around the world. The money was always there. My father never questioned me. When I was twenty, I came to Paris, where I sank lower. *Ennui*, that was the great enemy. I'd tried everything, seen everything. I thought. A friend offered me an experience . . . He described it. At first, I hesitated. But the friend scorned my sensibility, that's what he called it. My . . . sensibility. He laughed. Nobody laughed at me, nobody. He took me to a basement bar in a seedy part of the city.'

Naim broke off and looked around the cellar. 'It was like this,' he said. 'Exactly, even down to the ashtrays and the stains on the tables.'

He shuddered, his head sank low on his chest. Thelma looked around uneasily. The walls seemed to taper in, pressing upon them. Imagination! Perk up, *think*! She forced her attention back to Naim. After a moment, he recovered enough to go on.

'Two young girls were brought in. Aurelia and Nada, those were their names. They'd been drugged. They sat down . . .'

As he spoke, Thelma imagined she heard a noise on the stairs behind her. Nothing loud: a trick of the wind. Spellbound, she continued to stare at Naim, oblivious to all but him.

*

Yes, Madame, he is telling you the truth. At last.

Naim produced a two-franc coin, tossed it and invited me to call. Tête. He lifted his hand, read the coin and winked at me. 'You win,' he said.

Then he explained what he wanted, while the other man gazed at us with a smile of curiosity disfiguring his lips. One of us would walk out of this cellar alive, having killed her twin. Since I'd won the call, I was cast in the roles of survivor and executioner.

We didn't react. <u>Couldn't</u> react, I should say. Tears rolled down our cheeks, but we didn't scream or struggle, or even move. My limbs had had the bones stripped out of them, they were like the flesh you see in a butcher's window, cold and dead. The men rose. Somehow Nada and I, two puppets, were on our feet. Nada had her back to the wall. I was standing in front of her, with some heavy object in my hands. I tried to look down, couldn't. Other hands were lifting mine. I stared into Nada's eyes and read her death there, along with my own. It was fore-ordained, it was destiny.

She began to cry then, real tears, forced out by an emotion that somehow survived and rose above the drug. Reading her mind, I knew she forgave me and she was asking me to do it quickly. But I had no strength, no idea how to fire the gun, no will or ability left.

'Do it!' I heard Naim command, as if from many leagues distant. 'Or you'll both die!'

Madame, I have asked myself over and over since that dreadful day, <u>Why did you not let him kill you both and have done with it? Why did you sacrifice your sister so that you might live?</u> Perhaps he was bluffing, perhaps he would have proved incapable of killing us both? Perhaps so many things . . . Each moment presents us with decisions, we take them from the second we are born to the time of *our deaths. Bootless to protest that I had no choice; I had.*

It is the case, Madame, that, once I believed Naim would kill us both if I refused, I chose to kill my twin sister Nada. With that I have lived; with it I must die.

An infinity of time passed: five seconds, three hours, God knows. There was an explosion of light and sound. When the smoke cleared I saw Nada sliding down the wall, her neck at a strange angle, leaving a blood-red smear on the whitewash. I'd shot her through the eye. The right eye.

Naim's face appeared between me and the body of the sister I had slain. His eyes were animal. In three years, and more, of debauchery and degradation, I'd never seen such eyes. I wanted to faint. But I couldn't.

Then he smiled.

*

Down in the cellar, not a sound disturbed the stillness. Thelma, Jacqui, Annette and Daniel stared at Naim with faces that expressed horror each in its own way.

'I want to be sick,' Jacqui muttered. She began to retch. Annette put an arm around her shoulder.

'Can't you *do* something for a change?' she snapped at Thelma. 'Instead of just looking down your fat ugly nose at us?'

Thelma, flushed, ran to the sink and filled a pitcher with cold water. She gave everyone a glass. Naim took a long drink and began to speak.

'My first idea, when I came to myself next day, was to make amends to Aurelia. As if I could!' Naim's laugh was a pitiful sound. 'I gave her shelter. And I threw myself into decent work, I gave up drink and drugs, I swore never to sink back into the pit. But after a while, I couldn't resist coming to visit her. To see how she would react, to see if – God help me! – she might find it in her soul to offer me forgiveness. And I became drawn to her. She responded to the life I offered. Shimon helped. She began to show me little signs of affection. We became close. We married. And then, only then, she started to reveal what I should have seen from the beginning. She was mad.'

Naim heaved a long sigh, and was silent for a while. When

Daniel eased his leg into a more comfortable position the crack of a joint came as a shock.

'I sent her to the best psychiatrists,' Naim resumed. 'She tried to kill one of them. After that, she improved; it was as if she'd cleansed her system of something. She became even more sophisticated, more charming, more . . . able. She helped me in my businesses. When I suffered my first heart attack, and was lying helpless in a hospital bed, she kept my affairs in order and when I was allowed home she nursed me back to health. I loved her. I depended on her. I thought, in my wretched need to find peace, that she had forgiven me.'

*

Forgive? Forgive! No. My path was set.

It happened the day I learned Naim was coming back to Paris; that shortly I would behold the face of the monster who had made me kill my sister, the monster I'd not seen since that night in the zinc.

My first reaction was one of horror. I threw myself down on my bed and soldered my eyes shut against it, willing it not to be true. And behind my sealed lids arose a vision. It was the Virgin Mary that I saw. Religious art held a pernicious fascination for me and no doubt that was the explanation. I rose and went to ask Shimon if we might go to church. He looked at me closely, but agreed – something that's always surprised me, for why should I, an orphan from Algiers, suddenly wish to visit a Christian church? He was fond of me by then.

I asked to go to Notre Dame; that was the only church I knew. I'd visited La Chapelle, of course, but it was just so much stained glass, so many tourists. Despite the crowds, Notre Dame was fixed in my mind as a place of worship, the home of a dreaded god, God of sacrifice who'd killed his son and might therefore understand me.

Now this was December, the coldest day of the year. I don't know the exact time, but it had already fallen dark, and hoarfrost coated the streets of Paris. Everywhere I looked was bleached white beneath the moon. Ice crystals glittered on gutters, windows, roofs. The car was warm. When the driver opened the door for us and we got out it was like running up against a frozen wall.

The interior of Notre Dame was cold also, but stuffy and oppressive.

Have you ever visited the great cathedral of Paris? It has its moods. On a hot day in August the mass hangs heavy in the perfumed air, the crowds mill to and fro like mighty currents in a vast ocean, cameras flash and whir; there's no magic. The celebrant holds aloft the Host, and one glimpse at his face confirms he knows that it's nothing but a mixture of flour and water. Whereas on a spring morning, all is light and grace and the organ notes are as pure as the little boys' alto voices.

In coldest winter, Notre Dame's different. Then is the time of solstice and sacrifice. It was a pagan edifice I entered that bleak, white night. Candles hewed caves of lesser shadow from the gloom. I had no sense of surrounding walls or of a roof above my head. It was like entering Ali Baba's stronghold: rubies, emeralds, sapphires, pearls, but the moment you looked at them they vanished into a mish-mash of flickering flames and raiments and marble.

There were few people in the cathedral and the place was oddly silent, as if muffled for a funeral. A service was in progress. The choir chanted, the priest intoned, the organ made its occasional entrance. Yet the air was heavy with stale incense, languor and a deep, unsatisfied longing on the part of the people. I sensed a riot in the making, a roughness, a . . . how to say this? A desire to rend the fabric of the church apart and dissect the remains in search of the soon-to-be-born Christ, is the closest I can come. The congregation felt cheated in a way none of them could understand.

Slowly I began to walk down the aisle, the left-hand aisle, Shimon at my heels. I was looking for a statue of the Virgin, having some muddled idea that I might pray to it. But the people distracted me. I read their faces. Each person seemed preoccupied with his or her own demon. In many eyes I fancied I read what I'd seen in Naim's, a year before, and fearfully I would shy away.

It was while turning my head to avoid one such glance that I saw we were opposite the Chapelle St Vincent de Paul. I stopped and read the marble inscription: Leon-Adolphe Amette, Cardinal Archbishop of Paris. The name calmed me, I repeated it under my tongue several times. I knew that _ami_ was French for friend;

Amette did not sound dissimilar. The chapel seemed empty. Ah no, not completely: there was a light on over the confessional box.

I understood little about the Roman Catholic religion, but I knew that you could tell your sins to a priest who had power to absolve you. A sign indicated that French was spoken in this confessional. I turned to Shimon. I said, 'I want to speak to the priest.'

He looked at me for a long time, while the heathen came and went around us. Seeing it through his eyes now, I can understand the pressure on him to say no. He must have realized I wished to discuss Nada, and even in my talking to a priest under the seal of the confession he would have perceived great risk.

Also, he was wondering how much of a public scene I was prepared to make if I didn't get my way, and whether he could handle it. When we were out together he never let me be alone for an instant, except in the toilet, when he would wait outside. Normally I behaved demurely, with obedience. This was different. This was potential disaster.

As a fifteen-year-old girl I understood none of what must be going through his mind. When he nodded I turned and made as if to enter the chapel, but he caught my sleeve and asked, 'Do you know what to say?'

I stared at him. Of course I knew what to say: I'd murdered my sister, I needed to beg forgiveness. But Shimon didn't mean that. 'He won't talk to anyone who is not a Catholic,' he said gently. 'So you must persuade him. You do that by saying, when you go in, "Forgive me, Father, for I have sinned."'

I had studied the French tongue with diligence, and these words caused me no problems. I entered the chapel.

The space is not great – I inspected it again last year – but to me it seemed bigger than the ocean. I felt sure the priest was watching me as I approached. I settled onto the wooden seat and drew the curtain across, concealing me from Shimon, who continued to stand in the aisle. I spoke the incantation. I heard a rustling from the other side of the grille, and a few muttered words, mostly inaudible, but enough to show me that the priest was ready to perform his side of the bargain.

My tongue refused its office.

'Yes, my child?' came the prompt. This time the voice was clear, and from it I conjured up an image of a tall, spinsterish man with glasses and fussy hands. God knows why. I needed to 'see' him, I suppose, before I could trust him with my secrets. But I didn't trust the owner of this reedy voice. What to do? Back out? Impossible! Confess? Equally out of the question.

I was smitten with an idea. I told him a terrible affliction had befallen my dearest friend. (I thought that stratagem the last word in cunning; it is a provocative and painful memory.) This friend, I explained, had fallen into the power of an evil man, along with her sister. Now the man was insisting that my friend kill her sister, or die in her place; the pressure was growing intolerable.

I fell silent, and waited. This would have to be a dummy run, I now realized; a learning experience. Next time I would know how to deal with Monsieur le Curé. For now, I was curious to discover what he would say.

'Your friend . . . is she a Catholic?' he enquired, after a long pause.

'No.'

'You are?'

'I am.'

'You believe in God, in Christ our Saviour, the Holy Virgin, the saints, and the teachings of the Church?'

'Fervently, I do.'

'Fervently you do. Then you can recite for me the sixth commandment.'

That put me in a fix. For a moment I couldn't think what to do. But I understood 'commandment' and my intellect prompted a response: this must be something to do with killing people. 'Not to murder,' I rapped out, and held my breath.

'Not to murder,' he repeated quietly. And then he said nothing more, as if there was no more to say.

'But what can I tell my friend?' I wailed.

'Your friend is not a Catholic, and on that account already her soul is in peril. If she commits murder, she must expect to burn in hell. Tell her that.'

'Is there no hope for her?'

'Our one and only hope is belief in Christ Jesus who died upon the cross for our sins. If we believe in Him, and are received into the bosom of the Church, there is hope for the meanest sinner. Without Christ and the Church – nothing.'

He asked me about my own sins, then, but I'd had enough of sin. I stumbled out of the confessional, back to the aisle, and Shimon. I pushed past him, blinded by tears and turned in the direction of the high altar. I found myself walking down the central aisle towards where the priests were standing. They saw me; one of them frowned. Before the lowest step I stopped. I threw myself down, full length, and closed my eyes to find the Virgin there, waiting for me. I spoke to her. What I said was this. 'Lady, I am beyond redemption and hope in my world or in yours; I dedicate my life, my body and my soul to the settling of accounts. Grant me my revenge on Naim and I will do anything you desire. Refuse me my revenge, and be accurst!'

I stood up with a clear head, I turned, and I swept back the length of that glorious cathedral while people fell back on either side. Shimon caught up with me as I pushed through the heavy door, but he made no attempt to touch me. We got into the car in the rue d'Arcole and drove off. I knew from the way Shimon looked at me that he was afraid.

I said, 'Naim is coming tomorrow. He does so much for me, I want to buy him a Christmas present. What do you think he would like?'

*

Thelma asked Naim: 'When did she start to change?'

'After my convalescence. I spent six months in the Philippines, attending to family affairs. Aurelia didn't want to come. She hated the East.'

Daniel asked, 'Were you ever in prison?'

Naim's eyes hooded themselves for an instant, with a flash of his old haughty fire. 'No.'

'So when was this hospitalization?'

'The summer of 1976.'

Thelma remembered a passage from Aurelia's account: *The second thing that happened, the cataclysme, occurred shortly after my twenty-first birthday*. 1976, or near enough. Another mystery solved.

'Shimon . . . he was the problem.'

They waited, but Naim had dried up. Daniel prompted him: 'Where did Waldman fit in?'

'They became . . . close. When I returned from Manila, it was to find them having conversations to which I had no key. So what? I turned a blind eye. If they were lovers, that could hardly shock me – me, who'd killed Aurelia's sister! And somehow, after that, we drifted apart. In my absence she'd taken over responsibility for the children's education. That suited me. But I worried when I realized that she wouldn't listen to any of my ideas about how they should be brought up.'

Naim gestured at the girls. Jacqui looked away. Annette scowled at him through eyes full of hatred.

'They were made into twins. By Aurelia. Dressed the same. Educated the same. Forced to eat the same foods, share the same hobbies. Until they rebelled, that is. And Richo . . . '

Naim sighed.

'For a long time I didn't realize she was going mad. Let Shimon worry about that, I told myself. He was the only one who could steer her through her depressions, and they became both worse and more frequent. And this year, when I brought in the psychiatrist to have her committed – '

'You did what?' Daniel and Thelma both leaned forward, but it was Thelma who spoke first. 'You were going to put your wife in an *asylum*?'

'And quite possibly my son too, if that was the only way of helping him.'

'But at the funeral, you never told me that!'

'I wanted you out of my life, Dr Vestrey, so I told you the story I kept for everyone.'

'Did Aurelia know what you were planning?'

'She guessed why I asked her to see the psychiatrist. And she knew also that I was going to pension off Shimon.'

'Why do that?'

'I'd had enough. Brooding, always brooding . . . watching me. Cuckolding me, yes: that's what I felt, by then. Let him worry about her! Let him visit her in the straitjacket, sit by the bedside when she took too many pills, let him pay the doctors! And he . . . '

Naim bit his lip and looked away, but Thelma wasn't about to let him off. 'And he *what*?' she thundered. 'Come on, *talk*!'

'He knew too much about the past. *Our* . . . past.'

Thelma was about to press the point when suddenly she saw what Naim was getting at. 'He knew about Nada,' she breathed. 'Didn't he?'

Naim's laugh scarcely broke the oppressive silence. Thelma slowly sat back, trying to crack the code. What was so damned funny about . . .

'He was the friend who suggested it. He was.'

Naim turned to look her in the face. He stopped laughing. He nodded, once. And for a long time after that, there was silence.

'How did you get here?' It was Daniel's question.

'Early this morning the police phoned and left a message with my housekeeper, to await my return from the hospital. They asked me to come back to St Joseph's. While I was reading that message, I had another call. There'd been an accident, that's what the police said. My son. Somebody had to identify . . . the body.'

'But you never went?'

'My first thought was to see the girls. To tell them . . . or to let them sleep? We'd had a bad time of it since they ran away, we weren't speaking. Should I wake the servants? There were only three or four left, most of them had quit after the sheriff ran-sacked the place . . . I was walking down the corridor, in a daze, trying to work out what to do, when I heard a noise behind me. Somebody hit me . . . I woke up here, with the children.'

Thelma asked Annette, 'How did *you* come here?'

'After we ran away, and got caught, Jacqui moved in with me. We slept in the same bed. We were scared. She wanted you to come rescue us, but you weren't at the hospital when she called this morning. Aurelia got us as we were going back to our room. She had a gun.'

'So . . . your mother's *alive*? It's not just my imagination, I *did* see her!'

'Oh, yes, Madame.'

*   *   *

Five heads jerked around to the sound of the voice on the stairs. Aurelia waited until she had their attention. Then – 'It was me that you saw, in the hospital.'

She stood with one hand on the rail. A sozzled-looking Marion Lomar lounged by her side, grinning stupidly. When Aurelia descended one more step, Thelma could see she was holding a gun. Something big that brooked no argument: a Police .44, she guessed.

'Frisk them.' Aurelia pointed at Daniel and Thelma.

'It would be a *pleasure*.'

Lomar came down, falling off the final step and cursing. While Aurelia covered the cellar from her vantage point halfway up the stairs, Lomar patted Daniel in a desultory way, before moving on to Thelma. This time the search was more thorough. Thelma felt this woman, stinking of men's cologne, paw her most intimate crevices and all the while she thought of Daniel. His loving touch. How tenderly he kissed her, and caressed her, and made her feel cherished. The memory did more to prevent her from poking out Lomar's eyes than Aurelia's gun.

At last the ordeal was over. Lomar had found the .38 and this she now handed to Aurelia, who placed it on a higher step before coming downstairs. She positioned herself by the bar, with a commanding field of fire, and she said, 'Sit down, next to your FBI friend. You know I have no conscience, don't you, Dr Vestrey?'

'Yes.'

'And that killing is second nature to me.' It wasn't a question, more a meditation on her own soul.

Thelma sat with her hands folded in her lap and her back straight as if set with a plumb line. Daniel couldn't take his eyes off the Magnum in Aurelia Delacroix's hand.

'Perhaps you were surprised to find me still alive?' she drawled. She reached behind the bar and came up with a pack of Gauloises. 'You were fooled because you wanted to be,' she remarked through a haze of smoke. 'So simple really. Finding a female corpse of about the right age and frame was the hardest part. We had to dye her hair, I remember: that slut we picked up, hitch-hiking. Shimon and I. Then, a false eye, in the middle of

295

the wreckage . . . my eyes are distinctive, don't you find?'

She preened herself, glad to have an audience.

'We had faked dental records all lined up, but we didn't need them. Naim was too ill to identify me, but Shimon could do it, even *you* helped do it. Because, you see, no one who viewed the corpse ever cast doubt on its identity.'

She smoked in silence for a while longer. Then she said, 'You want to know why.'

'I'm curious,' Thelma agreed.

As Thelma spoke she was thinking, That day when we found Aurelia's body in Hobie's Hut, Richo knew what was going to happen beforehand, that's why he behaved so strangely with me. Then she thought, How long will the sheriff of Tulare County take to come back to *Pinos Altos*? Once he's at the house, how long before he thinks of searching this cottage? She had to make herself believe he would come. *He must.*

'What you have to understand, Madame, is that I'd sworn to be revenged on Naim if it took me until the end of eternity. I had taken a *vow*.' Aurelia looked down and smiled, as if at some sweet, secret memory. 'I dedicated myself to destroying him utterly: his name, his family, his fortune, his body, his very soul . . . no aspect of him was to escape my vengeance. So I set out to win his trust, realizing he was just a fool who'd got into bad company, that he was malleable. I could've killed him, perhaps I might even have got away with it, but where was the satisfaction in that?

'I conceived a son. From the moment of his birth, he was strange. I needed help. Marion, take a bow.'

To Thelma, listening for nuance and timbre as if her life depended on it, knowing that it did, it seemed as though Aurelia felt only the most profound contempt for Lomar. Not that she confessed it openly; but the scorn was unmistakably *there*. Lomar didn't recognize it, however. She did as she was told, coming forward into the centre of the cellar to take an inane bow.

'She had a way of looking at children,' Aurelia drawled. 'Exploitable, corruptible, little helpless creatures on which to work out the vilest fantasies. And, oh, what a price they command! My Leparella sized up Richo very quickly: he had potential. What could be worse for any proud father than the discovery that his son was a monster? And dear Dr Diane, she was wonderful too.'

Aurelia laughed a throaty laugh. 'So that took care of Richo. Drugs, sex, alcohol, the most *recherché* psychological care . . . my little boy wanted for nothing.

'After a while, he even began to see things we'd missed. It was his idea for me to write some of the Butcher's notes. And he always signed them with a cut on his right thumb, which only a left-handed person would do. Clever, no? But then – he was a genius. All he lacked was direction. So Marion and I taught him the value of cruelty. Of *excess*.'

Keep her talking, Thelma ordered herself. Distract her. Make her forget what she intends to do. You are a psychologist; prove that those fancy degrees have some worth. *Talk!*

'Your daughters,' she said, with a glance at them as she spoke. 'Where did they fit in? I notice you never entrusted them to Marion . . . '

She was proud of that. So many key-words: 'daughters', 'entrusted', the use of Lomar's first name. Warm the atmosphere, let's have room temperature down here while we're waiting for the sheriff to organize room service. And it worked – Thelma could see from Aurelia's satisfied expression that she'd pressed the right buttons.

'Ah . . . ' Aurelia acknowledged the girls for the first time. 'I had *very* special plans for them.'

She moved away from the bar. She went to stand by Thelma's chair, still able to cover Daniel, and laid a hand on her shoulder. 'You're a professional,' she said conspiratorially. 'Look around. Consider what you see. Does a possibility strike you, perhaps?'

It did. There was to be a re-run of Paris. All that Aurelia needed was a *zinc*, like the one where Nada had been murdered. Naim, of course. And two twin girls . . .

She glanced at Annette and Jacqui. Annette's face had taken on a streetwise, canny expression Thelma remembered from their first meeting. Jacqui's remained untainted. What would they do? How would each child react once she realized she'd been reared for the oven?

'The way you faked your death,' she said quickly, 'was genius. But, again – why?'

Aurelia laughed. 'You professionals, my dear. You *always* miss the important thing.'

'So tell me. Please.'

Aurelia looked for a chair from which she might keep the room covered. She pulled one around until it was to her liking, and sat down.

'I had no choice. Naim was turning against me. He'd forgotten his guilt over Nada: history that had faded like one of my tapestries. He planned to put me in an asylum, get custody of the children, *my* children – can you imagine such a thing? He was going to send the girls to Europe! He told me my son needed hospitalization, needed rescuing from bad influences!'

She laughed again and inhaled a lot of smoke.

'But that was my lucky break, you see. It let me consult *you*, when Diane abandoned us. I had to find a way of keeping them all in the States, while I perfected my revenge. But Naim didn't like you, he wanted Richo to see a male doctor. So I began to think: if I died, there'd be an inquiry, police, problems. Naim would have to stay and deal with them. By dying, I bought time.'

'But not enough time.'

'No.' Aurelia shook her head briskly, acknowledging a good point. 'We thought of a way around that, Shimon and I. We planned to reveal I was still alive that night you went to the cottage, alone. With you on our side, a witness to my existence, Naim would've been caught up in an inquiry that might have run for months. But Shimon had to go and get drunk before you arrived. He kept pestering me to accept that Richo was *his* son. He made me mad. He got violent. I shot him. In self-defence.'

It all began to make sense. Thelma recalled the devotion Shimon had displayed to Richo, and the boy's ambivalence when Aurelia's 'corpse' was discovered, first throwing himself into Shimon's arms, then rejecting him. Other memories crowded into her mind, but she cast them out. *Keep talking!*

'And who was Richo's father?' Thelma asked. 'Really?'

Lomar slumped down in the nearest chair and started to bang the table with her fist, making no noise, always stopping short of hitting the surface with genuine violence. Her face had lost its earlier vacant look. She was staring at Aurelia through eyes that resembled diamonds for hardness and brilliance.

Aurelia raised her eyes to Thelma's and said, 'Who knows?'

Nobody moved. No one breathed.

'You and Shimon were lovers?' Thelma asked softly.

'Always. Always. From Paris . . . it wasn't something we could control, it . . . even that last night, when I . . . kill . . . he took me on the floor.'

She lifted her head until her eyes were gazing at the ceiling. Instinctively, everyone else followed suit. The ceiling became transparent. Thelma knew they could all see the naked bodies writhing above them, could see the love-bites that turned to tear-ings and maulings, the rain of blows, the accusations and counter-accusations, until one naked body leapt up and dived for the nearest weapon . . .

Lomar rose. Thelma expected her to fall, or at least stumble, but she stood there rock-steady. She was staring at Aurelia with a terrible intensity: its heat radiated outwards, leaving none of them unscorched.

'He was Naim's son,' Aurelia announced suddenly. 'He *had* to be.'

Of course. *For Aurelia's revenge to be complete, Richo had to be Naim's son!*

'You knew that.'

Thelma came back into the real world with a jolt, for this last assertion had been addressed to her. Aurelia pointed an accusing finger in her face. *'You knew that!'* she croaked. 'And you would have helped, if only you hadn't gone to that school, with *her* – ' The finger described an arc, coming to rest against Lomar. 'That bitch there, who screwed everything up every chance she got, who wanted to screw you, dear Doctor, and why not? You had two legs, look half-human . . . not that being human ever mat-tered, not to *that*.'

Her finger began to shake. After a while she clenched her hand to her chest. She was fighting back tears. Looking between the two women, one hard and smooth as ice, the other wrestling with emotions Thelma could only guess at, for an instant she sensed the dreadful power that must have kept them going all those years. The furnace door opened a crack, slammed shut again, but Thelma had seen, and it would mark her memory for life.

She shuddered. Until now she'd feared only death, but something worse than physical death was abroad in this stifling, dingy room.

Aurelia made the effort. She controlled her breathing. She stood up and strode to the bar. From behind it she pulled out two sets of handcuffs. With speed and efficiency she forced Thelma to thrust her hands between the wooden bars of her chair-back, and manacled her. A moment later, Daniel had been led to the bar, where he stood with his hands shackled to its rail.

'Witnesses,' Aurelia hissed. 'Thank God, gracious God, that at the end I have witnesses.'

The manic energy went out of her. Allegro dissolved into lentissimo. She drew herself up and straightened her hunched shoulders, becoming a person of stature: one who assists at a ritual, or waits upon a god. She undid Naim's handcuffs with a key that hung on a chain around her throat, and secured his left hand to the arm of his chair, leaving his right hand free. It was numb. Before life returned to it, Aurelia had strapped his forearm to the chair. Naim's hand could move, but the strap limited its range to the narrowest of arcs in front of him.

'Now!' Aurelia cried. 'Choose! Choose as you made us choose, all those years ago.' She pointed at the girls, crouching at her feet. 'Kill one. Which will it be?'

She opened the fingers of Naim's right hand and thrust her gun into it, closing his fingers around the weapon with almost a lover's pressure. She stepped back. Because Naim's hand had been bound so tightly he could only point the gun ahead of him: Aurelia was careful to stay out of range. She said, 'Kill one, and I'll release the rest. My life is over. My life is . . . *accomplished*.'

The room was silent, utterly silent. Jacqui and Annette might have been sitting for their portraits, so still they were. Only their eyes betrayed a terror beyond the scope of words. Naim stared at the wall. Lomar stood upright, hands by her sides, but she did not take her eyes off Aurelia's implacable face.

Thelma found her eyes focusing on Daniel. His expression told her nothing. Did he want Naim to choose, and kill, so that his own life could be saved? Was that the man she loved?

Daniel spoke. 'You know what you have to do.'

His was an extraordinarily commanding voice. Everybody turned to look at him and, with one exception, nobody understood. Naim, however, nodded. While the other occupants of the room continued to stare at Daniel, he twisted the gun. He reversed his grip, so that now the barrel was pointing at his chest, and his thumb was on the trigger. He closed his eyes. His mouth worked soundlessly; perhaps he was praying, or merely counting.

He pulled the trigger. In this small, stuffy room the shot sounded like a grenade.

Voices screamed, furniture went flying. Naim's chair tipped backwards, taking his body with it. Aurelia hurtled forward, battling to get at the girls. Daniel wrenched at his handcuffs, cursing, but succeeded only in wasting energy. Lomar alone stood there unmoved, her eyes following every movement Aurelia made as if tied to her lover by invisible wires.

Stillness at last descended.

Annette held the Magnum in her left hand. Although that hand was fastened to the pipe, the gun was pointing at Aurelia, and Annette had enough play to track her with it if she moved. Her face contorted with hate and effort as she struggled to pull the trigger.

It was too much for her.

Jacqui slid her left hand along the pipe. Her handcuffs clanked against metal, but she managed to close her hand around Annette's. They strove to work together. The hammer rose up, up . . . Aurelia stood rooted to the spot, hypnotized by the sight of death forging an inexorable path towards her.

Thelma mouthed, 'Do it . . . do it . . . *do it!*'

Marion Lomar stepped forward, a brisk, businesslike school principal. She took the Magnum away from the girls as though it were a stick of gum confiscated in class. Annette squealed in frustration. Jacqui sobbed. Aurelia stared at Lomar through wild eyes. For a moment she was speechless. Then she began to laugh.

Lomar joined in. The two women laughed and laughed: it was

the funniest thing they'd ever seen. They couldn't stop. They were still laughing when Lomar swung around and fired at Daniel. She missed. Beyond his head, a bottle exploded into a hundred shards of glass. Liquid cascaded down from the shelf.

Lomar stopped giggling. 'Oh, shit!' she said. '*Ricard*. My favourite. Ricard, Ricard, Ricardo.'

Aurelia chortled. Lomar smiled at her. She turned the gun on Thelma.

'Ricardo,' she murmured. 'My best ever pupil. My *star* pupil. And you killed him. Just before Aurelia got there, that night . . . you killed him.'

While Aurelia went to St Joe's for Richo, Lomar had been at *Pinos Altos*, dealing with Naim; Thelma found it odd that this perception should come to her in the final seconds of her life. But then, why not? You had to think of something.

'No,' she said. 'I would never have killed him. You know that.'

Lomar stood behind Aurelia, who was grinning at Thelma in scornful dismissal. Now Aurelia said, over her shoulder, 'Do it.' And Lomar said, 'Yes.'

She pulled the trigger.

Aurelia's head fell off. A shower of blood fountained over the room. Something hard hit Thelma's face: part of Aurelia's skull. She had no time to make a fuss about that, however, not even when Aurelia's corpse – a real corpse this time, no faking – collapsed across her and rolled onto the floor, leaving a morass of blood and grey matter and tiny splinters of bone in Thelma's lap. Thelma had no time to appreciate any of this, because Lomar held the gun aimed at her and she knew Aurelia's death had been merely the warm-up.

'Why?' she yelled, and this was not part of any plan, it was because the prospect of launching into the dark and not knowing was too much to bear.

'Aurelia always thought *she* had classy fantasies,' Lomar replied in a child-like voice. 'Never thought to ask about mine. Swore she'd never slept with any man except Naim. She swore. That lying, *cheating* bitch . . . '

Her face contorted, signalling she was about to fire.

Behind her, Daniel kicked out with his right foot. A piece of broken glass, part of the bottle of *Ricard*, flew up and hit Lomar in the leg. She yelped. With a snarl she rounded on Daniel, meaning to dispatch him first. Thelma jumped up, taking the chair with her, lowered her head and charged. Lomar went down, but she didn't drop the gun. She lay on the floor, thrashing about in an attempt to sit up.

Thelma turned around through one hundred and eighty degrees. She took an awkward little run backwards. Lomar wriggled out of her way – she thought. But Thelma tripped over Lomar's legs, and lost her balance. The chair went down, down, down, with all of her weight behind it. A chair-leg punctured Lomar's eye and kept going down . . .

*   *   *

After which it was self-help time.

The sheriff didn't come riding out of the sunset, no matter how much Thelma willed him to. Once the smoke had cleared and the hysterics were a thing of the past, she became practical. Either they were going to rescue themselves or they were going to die; simple as that.

Aurelia had been wearing a key around her neck, on a long chain. She'd used it on Naim's handcuffs, and perhaps it would fit all the sets. Thelma made several abortive attempts to grab the key before realizing that she'd have to tip her chair over if she was to have any chance of success. So she crashed over on one side, and wriggled, and made contact with a lot of slimy stuff she didn't want to think about, let alone look at. In the end she had the key between her fingers. Next problem: what to do with it?

She humped herself over to Annette, who was able to help a little, but the chair got in the way and everything was at the wrong angle, in the wrong place. It took Thelma two hours to open the first lock.

At last they came up out of the charnel house, into the cold fresh air of night, and Daniel put his arm around Thelma as a prelude to a kiss. They stood there, leaning into each other, breathing in the soft, natural scents around them. They were alive, and life had never seemed so sweet.

Daniel had to drive ten miles down the road before he found a place where his car-phone would work. While he was summoning the sheriff, Thelma did what she could to comfort the two last surviving members of the Delacroix family, although she could see the forlorn road that lay ahead of them and it was enough to break her heart.

One by one, bit by bit, the girls assembled a picture for her to marvel at. Their upbringing hadn't been so very far removed from your average American family, and yet it was light years away. School, ponies, parties, boys, music: the usual mix. Except that school was exclusive and private; ponies came in strings; the parties were supervised and held only at the houses of friends whom Naim had had vetted by private detectives; the boys were all servants in one guise or another; the music was Mozart or Guns 'n' Roses with nothing in between.

Oh yes, and they'd had a brother who wanted to rape and kill them.

'Why must people have children?' Thelma said wearily, as later she and Dan wandered hand in hand through the woods. 'Why must we bring them into this horrible, horrible world?'

Dawn was near. Pale light had begun to pour through the trees in designer-straight shafts, softening the night, dissolving darkness into palest gold. Dan stopped and drew her to him. He squeezed her tight. 'I have an answer,' he murmured.

A car was coming along the track; no, more than one. The sheriff had arrived at last, the world beckoned.

'So tell.'

'On our wedding-night. But this I guarantee . . . you're going to *love* it.'

He kissed her. And – *Yes*, she thought. *I believe I am . . .*